DON'T DISCONNECT

TIFFANY CAMPBELL

Published by: Write to Inspire, LLC
Published in Columbus, OH

Author: ByTiffanyCampbell.Com – writtenbytiff@gmail.com
Facebook.Com/AuthorTiffanyCampbell

First draft edited by: Tiffany Reynolds – missroseangelos@gmail.com

Second draft edited by: Elyse Applewhite – elyseapplewhite@gmail.com

Cover Design by: Tasha Branham – tasha.n.branham@gmail.com

Book Formatted by: Barbara Rodriguez, Ya Ya Ya Creative – www.yayayacreative.com

ISBN No. 978-0-692-75668-3

PRINTED AND BOUND IN THE UNITED STATES OF AMERICA

To my reader: Before I met you, before you picked up this book to read, I prayed for you. I hope this story blesses you as much as it has blessed me. I wrote this, especially, with you in mind.

To my family, friends and church home: Thank you for your continuous love and support from the moment this book was birthed in my heart. I will continue to strive to make you all proud.

With Love,
Tiff.

Tina,

Thank you so much for your support! You're such a beautiful ball of energy! I hope this book blesses you.

Tiffany Campbell

CHAPTER
-ONE-

"Sour skittles and iced tea. Why am I not surprised?" Mr. Harold chuckled while scanning my items. I snickered, digging into my pocket to pull out three dollars.

"It's always the remedy to a long night Mr. Harold, you know this." I explained as he received the bills from my small fingers.

"You mean an early morning?" he squinted with a playing smirk as I shrugged.

The ability to tell the difference between night and day escaped me.

"It's all about perception."

"One day I hope you don't have to work so hard Kole. A pretty girl like you needs to learn to have some fun while you're still young."

Mentally, my eyes rolled as far as one could imagine.

Pretty? Young? Fun? Those words didn't exist in the world I came from.

"Maybe. One day." I replied lightly tapping the counter; he offered one last warm smile.

"See you around. Get home safe!" he called as I strolled through the convenient store doors, chucking him the peace sign on my way out.

I zipped up my jacket feeling the cool 7 a.m. breeze against my cheeks, throwing the hood over my mess of hair as I made my way home.

I watched my Chuck Taylor clad feet with each tired step. I just finished working a double just so my roommate Gina and I could afford to keep the lights on for the month. I promise, ever since I made the decision to move in with Gina, something was always on the verge of getting cut off. She begged me to stay with her just so I could help with bills but seeing how her boyfriend lived there as well, I didn't understand how between the three of us things couldn't get paid. I paid my portion of the bills on time, every month and even offered more when she would come up short. Things just weren't adding up but my frustration surely did, so I planned to get to the bottom of it before she left for work.

I exhaled, watching the air from my lungs materialize into the cold air before noticing a piece of paper sticking out of our front door. I quickly snatched it, scanning the words in search of what I already knew.

"What the fu-," I stopped, pulling my keys out of my pocket to open the front door.

"Yo!" I yelled, quickly surveying the room. My mood was immediately heightened once my eyes laid on Gina's limp body as she slumbered on the couch – the very place where I slept. To make matters worse, she had a bed. I didn't.

"Yo!" I called again walking up to her and roughly shaking her arm to pull her from her sleep.

She groaned, turning over and stretched, looking at me through slit eyes.

"Damn Kole. What?!" she replied, aggravation present in her tone.

"What's this?!" I asked shoving the pink slip in her face. She looked puzzled before snatching it from my fingers and reading over the words. Her face remained dull before she shrugged in response.

"It's an eviction notice-"

"Yeah I'm aware. Because I can read." I replied smartly. "What I don't get is how is that possible when I gave you the full amount of rent on the first because you didn't have your half!"

She remained quiet, looking me square in the face.

Waving a hand in front of her, "Am I talking to air?! What did you do with the money Gina if you didn't pay rent?!"

Tiffany Campbell

She smacked her lips, standing to her feet now and walking away from me. "None of your business-"

"None of my business?" I cut her off, following her as she marched to the kitchen. "None of my business?!"

Silence.

"Gina. What did you do with 600 dollars if you didn't pay rent?! You need to pay me that money back. Today."

She opened the fridge leaning forward to look over its contents, "I'm not paying you nothing back Kole! Ain't none of this in your name and you were a homeless rat before this anyway. Why the fu-"

Before she could even finish her wise cracking rant I had pushed the refrigerator door so hard into the side of her face she had no choice but to stumble over.

Everything in me had reached the breaking point.

My hands were still shaking from the beating I had given Gina just a day before as I sat in a jail cell surrounded by other female inmates.

Anger resonated through my entire being, and at this point I didn't even care. How dare she say those things and how dare she spend my money with no care in the world, knowing we were about to get evicted? She knew I literally had nowhere else to go and no one to turn to, and she mocked me for it? Mocked me like I wasn't anything. Mocked me like I wasn't anything.

I was growing tired of being treated like I didn't mean anything to anyone.

I didn't have anyone in this city. The only person I did have was in a coffin. She was the only person that ever loved me on this earth, and she left me; leaving me to call on no one else but ... *her.*

"Sommers!" My name being called caused me to look up closely at the guard while he used his key to open the cell.

"You made bail."

My brows met at the center of my forehead. *Seriously?*

"I ain't got all day. Come on." The larger black male called, beckoning me out of the cell.

I hopped to my feet, cradling my right arm with my hand out of nervous habit as I scurried my way past the envious stares of other prisoners and met the guard at the gate.

"You seem surprised." he studied, locking up.

"I am."

I collected my personal belongings from the front desk before I turned to face the waiting room. My eyes landed on *her* as I quickly rolled my eyes.

"Well don't look so happy to see the person that bailed you out." Sharon said, while I finally brought my eyes to meet hers.

Nothing about her had changed, except she had gained a little weight. Her light brown skin still glowed, her shiny hair still swayed just below her jaw line, and her eyes were still as soft and tired as I remembered from the last time we saw each other.

"Come on little girl, I'm not trynna sit in here all day." she said turning on her heels, forcing me to follow her out.

Once we reached outside of the prison doors, I froze.

"I'm not going with you."

She scoffed before turning to face me, "Like hell you're not. What, you think you're going to go back to that girl's house you beat up? Newsflash sweetheart, you're not welcome over there."

I shifted my weight from one foot to the other. "My stuff is over there-"

Tiffany Campbell

"Baby, your stuff was on the front porch when I stopped by before coming to pick you up. You guys are through. You're lucky she decided not to press charges!"

"Well I'm not coming with you!" My voice rose higher than I intended. She was the last person I was going to live with. I swore on my life I would never go back there.

"Kole. You don't have a choice. You don't have anywhere else to go and that's evident. No one is going to have your back in this God forsaken city like I would in Raleigh. Now come on. You're coming home."

I cringed at the word home. I bit the inside of my cheek, looking anywhere but at her.

She sighed, grabbing the bridge of her nose and allowing her head to fall forward, her hair brushing against her full cheeks.

After a moment she lifted her head, heals clicking in my direction. She stopped before me, placing both hands on my shoulders.

"Listen, I know you don't want to come home with me. I know the fighter in you is fighting so hard against this, but aren't you tired of fighting baby? You're out here putting your hands on people now. Getting arrested. Maw Maw isn't here anymore, and I don't think you should stay here either. Please. Just ... give this a chance. And if it doesn't work out, you're free to go. You're grown. You can make your own choices. But you need support right now. Let me help you to a point where you can fully support yourself and you don't have to depend on some crackhead girl for a place to stay." she smirked at the end referring to Gina, causing me to sigh.

As much as I didn't want to admit it, my egg donor was right. She was all I had left in this world with any real stability, and as much as it pained me, I needed her in this moment.

I was homeless, and I refused to be on the street again. I told myself I would never put myself back in that position the moment I started living with Gina.

I made a lot of broken promises.

"What do you say? Hm?" she questioned, searching my eyes with a soulful look. In her expression, I could see the bit of her that cared.

"Whatever."

"Now look, if we're going to be living together, then we need to lay out some rules." Sharon's voice boomed in the quiet car.

The hour and a half ride back had been awkwardly suffocating, besides the CD she played to drown out the silence.

"Rules?" I questioned as she nodded her head, gripping the steering wheel while changing lanes.

"Yes. You haven't lived with me since you were 11, and things have changed. I think the most important thing we need to have is some structure this go-round."

"And communication." I added bitterly as she scoffed at the statement.

"I am communicating. Communicating these rules we're going to have," she sassed, causing me to shake my head in response.

"First rule. You're getting enrolled into school when we get back."

I couldn't hide my dismay on that, "Why? I'd rather work."

She chuckled sarcastically, "Oh honey, trust me. You're gonna do that too! But the most important thing you need is an education. You can get enrolled in the community college not too far from the house. It's a good start until you get some direction about yourself."

I watched as she talked with her hands and drove at the same time. Nothing about her animated character had changed, at all.

"Second rule. You need to be in the house every night by midnight. There's nothing good for you out there after that time, period."

I shrugged. I didn't have any friends, or any activities I planned to be involved in. I wouldn't fight this curfew – at least not now.

"Third rule, you'll be at church every single Sunday"

I laughed out loud causing her to stop mid sentence and cut her eyes at me. I looked ahead avoiding her stare, watching as she exited the expressway.

"What's so funny?"

"I'm not doing that. I'll abide by all of your other rules except that one."

We were exiting the freeway and everything seemed so different now.

"What's so wrong with church?"

I shook my head, "Nothing right about it. That's what's wrong. I don't believe in that whole fairytale that church tries to sell."

"Well too bad you don't have a choice," she replied casually while turning into my old neighborhood towards her home. I felt the hair rise on the back of my neck, as the memory of this place and what it meant to me slowly began to come back.

"You can't make me do that Sharon. You can't make me believe what you believe."

"Well if you're living with me, you're going to church. So there's no need for us to continue having this discussion," she answered shortly while pulling into her driveway.

I looked ahead at the childhood home I grew up in and the anger I felt before starting to come back. I hate that I was in this position and so flat on my ass that I had no choice but to come back here if I didn't want to be on the streets. I hated everything about this house.

"Well get out, don't have all day. I got your room together before I drove out to come get you this morning," she stated, slamming the car door. Why does she insist on being so childish? She stopped, looking directly at me.

"Get my mail since you wanna sit out here!"

I released the breath I didn't realize I was holding and unbuckled my seatbelt, forcing myself to take a step out of the car. I closed the door slowly behind me before looking around my old neighborhood, getting re-familiarized with my surroundings again.

How am I going to cope?

I trudged towards Sharon's mailbox at the end of the driveway and opened it to remove the mail inside. I flipped through some of the bills she had and realized that her last name was different than mine and there was mail addressed to a man named Corey. She was married now?

"Whoa, Nic? Dominic Sommers, for real?" I heard a deep yet raspy voice call from a short distance as I snapped my head up at my first name being used – I haven't heard it in years.

I looked ahead, my eyes landing on him with a bright smile present on his face. The moment we locked eyes, he laughed in disbelief before bringing his feet towards me.

Jesse Palmer.

Everything within me went still.

"Dude, how long has it been?! You're back home now?!" he questioned standing only a few feet away from me as I studied his features.

Everything about him had ... grown. He stood tall now, at least six feet, with a low haircut and his light brown skin had grown darker than what I remembered. His features were strong and his arms filled his shirt, several tattoos scattered across them. His brown eyes still had the same light in them that I always adored and his smile was just as perfect with the dimples to match. He was beautiful. I just couldn't handle the warmth radiating from his being right now.

"It's Kole." I answered shortly.

His brow rose, turning up his nose. "Kole? You go by your middle name now?" he questioned, shoving his hands in his sweatpants pocket.

I fidgeted under his watch, unsure why he was studying me so closely.

"Yeah."

He seemed puzzled by my distant reaction towards him but that didn't change his demeanor.

"Well ... what's up, what are you doing back?"

I sighed, running my hands through my mess of hair, doing anything to avoid his stare. "Just – going through a transition right now. Won't be here long."

He nodded, "Okay I feel it. I was just stopping by to say what's up to my mom. I got my own place now, you should come over sometime, we can catch up on everything," he offered, voice full of hope.

"Look, Jesse." I started as he hung on to my every word. "I'm not that girl that used to live across the street anymore. We don't have to hang out and kick it n' shit. I'm just passing through," I replied. I finally found the courage to look into his face. His bright smile that was once there had faltered.

"Yeah? Well good look with that Nic. I was just reaching out, happy to see that my friend was back. But clearly you got it all figured out so … I hope it works out for you," he shrugged, keeping a smile as he prepared to walk away.

I sighed but my heart wouldn't allow me to feel anything else for the situation. He understood and that was all I needed to know.

He turned his head, catching that I was still watching him walk off.

"Judging by ya aura now, Kole is befitting," he said simply before turning away towards the house, leaving me there alone.

I chuckled bitterly before shaking my head. He'll realize that he made the right choice by walking away.

I wasn't fit to be in anyone's life, especially as a friend. Not anymore.

"Nic, man … we shouldn't do this." Jesse panicked in a hush whisper while I balanced my weight on his clasped hands, peeking over the fence.

"Why, you chicken?" I questioned with a risen brow as his eyes widened.

"Yes!" he admitted dramatically.

"I'm scared! Mr. Johansson doesn't play about his yard! We're going to get caught and he's going to tell on us."

I rolled my eyes before jumping off his hands, landing onto the plush grass beneath us.

"No we're not. Not if we do this quick. I saw our ball and the one from last week too! Plus the gate is open"

Tiffany Campbell

"That means he's home!"

His ten-year-old face was still filled with worry while mine was filled with excitement.

"I don't know-"

I cut him off, "Ugh! Who is the girl between the two of us? Sometimes I forget." I sassed with one hand on my hip.

"I'm not a girl!"

"You sure? Because you're definitely acting like one!"

His face grew red with rage.

We fought like this all the time whenever he got too scared to do something really fun. We had a mean stare down before Jesse pushed me in my shoulder and turned to storm off.

I froze. "Wait, where are you going?"

"To get the ball. Dummy!"

My entire being lit up as I raced to catch up with Jesse while he slowly approached Mr. Johansson's open fence door.

"This is all your fault you know," he hissed, feeling me behind him. "You're always over kicking the ball."

I rolled my eyes as we inched closer, "Shut up Jes."

"I'm just sayin! It's always you getting us into trouble." he said back, peeking around the opening of the door.

"You see the balls?"

"Yeah, we gotta do this quick. I think I see him shuffling around through the windows."

My heart quickened as I gave Jesse one heavy shove through the door before we both fell through to the other side.

"What the heck Nic?!" he screeched as quietly as he could while I took off running towards the kickball.

"Get the baseball Jesse!"

"Aye!" we heard from the window of Mr. Johansson's house.

"Crap!" I giggled, grabbing the ball and watching Jesse snatch the baseball with a huge devious smile on his face.

"Aye! What I tell y'all kids about running through my yard?! Hey!"

Mr. Johansson started walking quickly towards his patio doors as Jesse and I took off, laughing the entire way.

I blinked as one of the fonder memories from my childhood vanished from my mind. Ever since seeing Jesse, I couldn't stop thinking about some of the moments we shared before I left. He seemed to have grown so much since then. I found myself wondering what life had been like for him after I moved – what he had gone through and how he adjusted to the changes life threw at him.

But, it didn't matter now. I pushed him away, just like I did everything else. I was a horrible influence on Jesse back in the day and I knew I would bring nothing but trouble and pain his way now. That's all that seemed to follow me these days.

Tiffany Campbell

"Hey," Sharon called standing in the doorway of my room.

I looked up at her from my bed.

"You plan on leaving these four walls to come down and eat?" she questioned, crossing her arms over her chest, staring right through me.

I shook my head no as she flashed a look of dismay in response.

"Well come on anyhow. Corey wants to meet you," she said, using her hands to call me from the bed.

"Who's Corey?"

She rolled her eyes, "Don't play dumb child, my husband. I told you about him at the funeral."

I certainly don't remember that happening. I was probably too gone out of my mind. The day we buried my grandmother was the same day my soul must've gone with her. It's the only explanation I had for feeling this empty and alone.

"I don't want to meet him."

She sighed, looking me in my eyes and knowing exactly why I didn't care to meet this man.

"Baby, Corey is different. I promise he's good. Just come judge for yourself and if you don't like him, fine.

Since I was stuck here for the time being, I might as well see what he was about. If he was anything like ·

"Ohh Kole, you need to wash this head of yours. Jesus!" Sharon grimaced running her hands through my oily mane.

"And it stinks! After you wash it, I'll flat iron it for you – can't be out here looking like nobody loves you."

If only she could hear the groans running through my head. She was good for pointing out the obvious. I planned on getting myself together when I was good and ready to do so.

We reached the bottom of the steps and I slowly followed Sharon towards the dining room where an older nice looking gentleman sat at the head of table holding an infectious smile.

Wait, Corey is ... white?

"Corey, this is my daughter Kole – Kole, this is Corey my amazing husband!" Sharon cooed looking at her beau as his blue eyes pierced mine.

"Kole! Such a pleasure to finally meet you!" he smiled, standing to his feet and extending his hand towards mine.

I looked at Sharon strangely before looking back to him and returning the gesture. His hands were calloused, yet soft and warm.

"It's because I'm white isn't it? That's what that look is for huh? Baby, I told you this was going to be a problem for us," he teased looking at his wife, causing Sharon to laugh and me to crack the first smile I had in days.

"Have a seat baby girl; I want to know more about you. Sharon has told me so much," he said, pulling out my chair and waiting patiently for me to take a seat.

Once I did, he and Sharon both sat in their seats in front of the dinner that was awaiting all of us to dig into.

"So you were staying in Greensboro for a little while with your grandmother, right?"

I nodded, still in shock of everything happening. All of this was different.

"That's interesting. How you like it out there? I've never been fond of the city myself but I hear it can be a decent place to live."

I shrugged, "It was cool. I got accustomed after being there for so long."

"Right, you moved out there when you were 11 and you're what – 22 now, 23?"

"I'll be 23 in June."

I answered just as Sharon set the fully made plate down in front of him.

He looked to her lovingly, "Looks delicious, thank you baby."

He smiled before poking out his lips for a kiss. She blushed and happily obliging to his silent request.

My eyes were probably bugging at the sight before me.

"H-How did the two of you meet?" I blurted, studying Corey's sandy blond hair and pointed nose. He was truly handsome; I could see why Sharon would fall for him.

"I was her boss," he grinned while Sharon rolled her eyes at the confession.

"Keyword being *was*. We met while I worked for him but we didn't start dating until I was promoted to a different position."

"Love at first sight, right babe?" He winked with a playing smirk.

"For me or for you?" she questioned, the grin never leaving his face.

"Me of course, I knew it the moment I laid eyes on you. God whispered it in my ear."

God? So he was one for the fairytale too. No way something that isn't real, could whisper anything to anyone.

"He must've because I've never been happier."

I watched the two of them show so much love and adoration for each other throughout dinner, I barely ate a thing. I've never seen Sharon so ... so excited and full of life. Not even when it came to me. She never acted like this when I was a child, especially with the men she dated back then. She seemed to be a different person now and I couldn't help but wonder what the reason was behind it. What happiness could she truly have, knowing her child was out in the streets alone?

"So Kole," Corey started as he neared the end of his meal.

He relaxed in his seat, sipping on a glass of water.

"Sharon tells me she's taking you up to the school tomorrow to sign up for classes."

My eyes widened, looking towards her; she was already looking expectedly back at me.

"She didn't tell me that."

Her brows furrowed, "Oh, I didn't? What about the talk we had in the car?"

"You said I had to attend school but you didn't say anything about that starting tomorrow."

"Well, spring quarter starts in a week and a half. I'm sure all of the classes are getting picked over at this point. And that reminds me, you need to get online tonight and complete the FAFSA information so it can already be submitted when you sign up tomorrow."

I frowned, placing my fingers to my temple. All of this was too much for one day and I could barely manage. I was ready to explode.

Corey frowned at the sight of me before looking to Sharon.

"Why don't we give her a day to rest baby? Let her get adjusted to just being here and then talk about it after that. FAFSA needs a few days to process anyway before they'll let her do anything."

Her eyes softened at the advice of her husband before she nodded and began to pick at her food. "You're right. I'll take you in a few days. Just please Kole, don't forget to fill it out tonight."

I looked to Corey with thankful eyes as he smiled back knowingly with a soft nod.

I liked him.

"I won't."

I sat on the front porch, inhaling a cigarette as the afternoon sun beat against my mocha brown skin. My hair was freshly washed and straightened, cascading against my shoulders. I just sat – relaxed in a tank and sweatpants, just taking everything in. Sharon and Corey left for work this morning and I was appreciating the silence and freedom of just having time to myself. The past couple days still seemed hazy.

I sighed, taking another draw of my cigarette and pulling my notebook into my lap to write down a few thoughts. Maw Maw told me years ago to just start writing my thoughts on paper since I had a hard time expressing myself. She said, if I wasn't going to speak, I might as well talk to the paper. It was going to be the only thing that wouldn't respond and I could have the freedom to say whatever I want without judgment.

I was preparing to jot down my thoughts when I heard laughter coming from across the street. I looked up to see Jesse and some Asian looking girl, smiling together. She was leaned up against a car and he was standing in front of her, playfully poking at her. Her long brown hair was swaying with the movement. It made me smile a bit, it reminded me of the happiness that Sharon and Corey also had.

I'll forever wonder what that's like, thinking I'll never know that feeling for myself.

I pulled my eyes away from the happy couple before tending back to my writing. Before I knew it, I had two full pages of thoughts and my wrist had grown tired. I released a breath, setting the pen down and flicked my wrist to relieve the tension.

"Yo."

I jumped and my eyes darted quickly to meet Jesse's stare. He was looking intently at the pack of cigarettes at my side.

"You smoke now too?" he questioned, never taking his eyes off the pack. I shamefully moved them from his view.

What was he doing here? Did I not make myself clear yesterday?

I kept my eyes on him, waiting for an explanation as to why he was now in front of me and not with his girlfriend. I looked past him, noticing the car that was parked on the street just moments before was now gone.

How long was I writing?

"That's bad for you, you know? Bad for ya lungs."

I shrugged, "Keeps me calm."

He nodded, accepting my answer for what it was before motioning his head towards the front door.

"Ms. Sharon here?"

I shook my head, "She's at work, why?"

"Oh," he replied, shoulders slouching in disappointment.

"I usually cut her grass when I come to cut my mom's. You think she'd mind if I got started anyhow?"

"I doubt it. If you do it all the time then do ya thing." I answered softly, looking back to my notebook. I noticed he hadn't made any motion to leave, so my eyes fell back to his after a short moment. He seemed conflicted as to what he wanted to say next. His lips twisted in every which way while staring into my eyes.

"Your hair – it looks good," He finally spoke before turning to walk away.

I ran my fingers through my soft, clean tresses before snorting and began to write everything that came to mind.

Jesse's smirk was imprinted in my memory.

"Well there's my beautiful daughter." Sharon cooed as she approached me on the front porch. I studied her for a moment, not allowing my expression to match hers as she smiled at the compliment she just gave. She looked nice, dressed in her business attire. She seemed to be in a lighter mood than yesterday.

I probably have Corey to thank for that.

She stepped closer and ran her fingers through my hair, watching as it fell back against my shoulders gracefully.

"You did an amazing job on your hair honey. You look nicer today," she commented stepping back before glancing at the yard.

"Jesse was here?" she questioned, noticing the fresh cut grass.

"Still is." I murmured as her eyes looked to mine in confusion.

"Is he?"

Before I could respond, Jesse himself came into view. He was busy sweeping the grass from the sidewalk on the other side of the house. He saw Sharon and smiled bright, waving his hand in the air.

"W'sup Ms. Sharon!" he called as she waved back.

"Hey baby, thank you for stopping by!" she said sweetly while I continued to watch the exchange between the two of them.

Jesse stopped sweeping, allowing the broom to fall unceremoniously on the sidewalk and began trudging through the freshly–cut grass, towards our way. Here we go, another awkward moment between the two of us but now ... now we have a witness.

"S'not a problem at all. You know I always have to take care of you when I take care of momma," he grinned charmingly as Sharon blushed under his gaze. I couldn't help but to roll my eyes.

"I truly appreciate that baby! Did you and Kole get re-acquainted yet? I'm shocked the two of you aren't in some type of trouble already!" she said, gesturing between us as I felt the heat rise to my cheeks at the attention now suddenly directed towards me.

Jesse stared softly at me before nodding with a shrug, "Yeah, you know ... things change."

"Mmm, a friendship like the one ya'll had never changes. You were simply inseparable. Kole would talk nonstop about you every day, even when she left from what her Grandmother told me."

"It wasn't even like that," I spoke quietly, watching his gaze leave from me and back to Sharon.

"Yeah ... but hey, where's Corey? He knows we gotta re-match that one-on-one game he cheated me in, right?" He didn't know it but I mentally thanked him a thousand times for changing the subject.

Sharon laughed, "He'll be home from work soon. If you're still hanging around just stop on by, he would love to play."

Jesse chuckled too, rubbing his chest. A habit I remembered him always having when he was amused.

"Aye, he really fooled me man. I swore white men couldn't jump till' we played. I was sad to lose that money that day. I'm ready now though. Double or nothing."

"That's funny! He used to play in high school and college. I guess he still had some skills that didn't leave with age," she giggled as Jesse made his way down the driveway, still smiling.

It seemed like no matter what, that smile never left his face.

"Man, I believe it. Let 'em know I'm looking for him. I'm about to finish up the yard though."

"Okay baby. Thank you again and tell your mom to call me!" Sharon replied with a small wave back, watching Jesse retreat to the sidewalk.

She shook her head, "Jesse is fine ain't he Kole?

I turned my lip up looking at her as she looked back to me.

"What, am I lying? You guys would be cute together!" she said, poking at my shoulder.

I shook my head, "He has a girlfriend."

Like it even mattered. Jesse wouldn't even look at me in that way.

"Who – that little tiny girl that's over there sometimes? Oh, she's new. I'm sure you would trump her any day as much as that boy loved you. He would be over here every day wondering when you were coming back."

I never knew that he asked about me!

"You never told me this."

She shrugged before pinching my cheek, "You weren't too keen on talking to me much back then."

She stepped past me to head into the house.

"You should get your friend back, Kole. Everybody needs a friend."

I heard the door open then close shortly after her words. My eyes fell back on Jesse while he finished up the sidewalk.

I shook my head at the thought.

CHAPTER
-TWO-

I blew the smoke from my cigarette as I looked over my new class schedule, along with a map they gave me to help locate my classes. I sat on the steps of the admissions office, legs shaking. I'm going out of my mind.

I was never really a school person. I got bullied when I changed schools in middle school and the teasing continued all throughout high school.

It wasn't until the day all my clothes got cut up in gym class and I got jumped on the way home, that Maw Maw finally decided to pull me out and allow me to attend a virtual high school so I could graduate. She used to tell me prior to the drama that girls were just jealous of how beautiful and smart I was and that I was different.

I was different all right ... never the good kind.

I was beginning to feel the anxiety of being in a new environment all over again along with the stress of not knowing anyone. I didn't want to have the same problems I had during my adolescent years. My plan was to stay out of the way and get an education, even if it was against my will.

I truly just wanted to cope and find some type of peace within all of this.

I heard the doors to the admission office opening and I scooted to the side so I wouldn't be in the way of any passerby's.

Heavy footsteps soon followed before they slowed to stop next to me. I didn't dare look up, not wanting to cause problems just by looking at someone the wrong way.

"They really gave you a map? That thing actually gets you lost," I heard the raspy twang of a seemingly familiar voice call.

He reached down and took my schedule from my trembling fingers before slowly walking down the steps scanning it over. He turned his body to face me, my eyes climbing up his tall build to watch his eyes darting from left to right.

"Looks like we got a class together, Nic." Jesse smirked, meeting my stare. He held the schedule up, "Lemme help you with this."

I huffed before putting out my cigarette. I stood to my feet and adjusted the backpack Corey had given me.

"No, I think I got it."

He frowned, "Come on, man. I've been going here for a year already and I know where all of your classes are. I can already tell this is stressing you, just let me help you."

"I got it. I don't need your help."

"What happened to you Nic? Like ... why are you so ... cold and dark now? You never used to be like this."

His voice was desperate for an answer, like he had been trying to wrap his brain around why I had been acting the way I was for a while.

I shrugged before looking down, "Life happened. I went through shit when I moved."

"Then why did you? Why didn't you just stay or come back when things got crazy?"

I shifted on one foot, stepping forward to take my schedule back from his grasp. I didn't want the questions to continue and he seemed as if he wasn't going to let up on helping me.

"You gonna show me where the classes are or what? Sharon will be coming to pick me up soon."

"Well since now I have to go off photographic memory," he replied with sarcasm. "I think ya first class on Mondays and Wednesdays is

Tiffany Campbell

in Thompson?" he questioned, looking back at me for confirmation before I looked to the schedule.

I nodded, "Yeah it is."

"Okay cool, well that's this way." I picked up my pace to fall in sync with his while we walked across campus.

The grounds were still pretty lively as classes were still carrying on from winter quarter. I watched several students lounge around at different tables; others were scurrying off to their next destination.

"Why do you still want to help me, Jesse? Even after how I've been acting towards you?" Somehow I found the courage to ask. I just couldn't take it any longer.

He shrugged. "That's what friends do."

The answer sounded so simple and effortless leaving his lips but it made zero sense to me.

"What? We're not friends"

He laughed, "What you mean we ain't friends girl? That stuff you was talking the other day? That was ya hurt talking. I ain't ever do anything wrong to you so you couldn't have been talking to me and actually mean it."

Why was he being so kind? It was something beyond my comprehension, so I left the topic alone ... for now.

Another question came to mind and I was already on a role with this courage thing. "Was that your girlfriend?"

He raised a brow and looked down at me. "My girlfriend? The girl from the other day?"

I nodded.

"You were watching us?" he smirked, running his tongue quickly over his lips as I rolled my eyes.

"I saw y'all. That was it."

He chuckled at my dry response before nodding. "Yeah. That's my girl. Name is Phi."

My nose wrinkled, "Phi, as in pay a fee? That's ... different."

He grinned. "Her momma is Vietnamese and her dad is Black. Phi is short for something crazy that I can't pronounce."

I hummed in response to the information. "Well, she's pretty."

"Thank you. I think so too," Jesse said, as we reached the building named Thompson.

I waltzed in, looking around the corridor as Jesse spoke from not too far away.

"So the numbers for the classrooms are based off the floor they're on. So like 100 is the first floor, 200 is the second and so on." he explained briefly as I nodded in understanding looking around.

"Cool."

He grinned at me before shaking his head. "Next building?"

I looked down at my schedule, "After this class I head to Morrison for English Comp. I."

He snapped his fingers in recognition before heading through the doors while I was quick to follow his lead.

"That's the class we got together," he shared. My nerves began to settle a bit. At least there would be a familiar face somewhere.

"English?"

He nodded, "Yup, you good with words?"

He looked down at me and I up at him. No words were exchanged between the two of us.

"Yeah," he murmured after our weird silence. "That tells me all I need to know."

I snorted a bit at his humor, shaking my head. "I can write."

His brow rose, "Oh? Fooled the hell out of me. You barely act like you can talk now."

"Well I never have too much to say these days," I answered softly, watching as my feet made each step on the sidewalk.

"Nah, I don't think so," he said, brushing me off.

"I think you have a lot to say, just have to find your voice again. What you have to say matters. Believe me," he replied confidently creating a peaceful silence to follow.

––––––––––––

"So like ... you bleeding ... down ... there?" Jesse questioned looking down at me as I sat on the base of one of the jungle gyms at school. I was holding my stomach tight, while other kids from our fifth grade class were running around us enjoying recess. I was in too much pain to enjoy anything at the moment.

"So what's that mean, you dying?" he questioned with curiosity, taking a seat next to me.

I shook my head softly. "I thought I was. I was gonna leave you all my Pokémon cards in my will."

His eyes widened looking at me, "Yo, forreal? C-Can I still have 'em?"

I flashed him a dry look, "No."

His shoulders slumped in disappointment. "Oh. Well ... what's all that mean then?"

I shrugged, "It's called a period. My mom said I'm becoming a woman and stuff. That's why my chest and hips hurt too. She said I'm developing early."

"Well, isn't that good? You growing up right?" Jesse tried to soothe as I shook my head.

"It's bad Jes. Becoming a woman is bad for me."

"Why? You don't want to be a woman?"

I put my head down, shaking it softly, doing my best not to let him see me cry. "No ... I don't want Larry to know I'm a woman now."

"Hey kiddo." The sound of Corey's sudden voice nearly made me jump out of my skin. I turned my head quickly, watching him walk carefully towards me after closing the front door.

I hurriedly put out my cigarette, "Uh, hey."

He leaned his shoulder against the left side post on the porch, looking down at me worriedly. "You okay? Did I interrupt something?"

I shook my head no, internally thankful that he had, in fact, interrupted my memory.

He nodded, accepting my answer. "Okay. How was signing up for classes today, cool?"

"Yeah, it didn't end up so bad. I uh ... ran into Jesse and he showed me where all of my classes were."

His brows climbed his forehead, "Jesse, huh?"

I grinned a little before giving a nod in response.

Corey chuckled, "Ha! Yeah, Jesse's a good guy. From what Sharon told me, the two of you used to be like best buds back in the day?"

I nodded, rubbing my shoulder and looking at my feet, "Yeah, something like that."

"Jesse's cool. If there's anybody you should stick to here, it's him. He's got a good head on his shoulders."

I shrugged, not really wanting to think about Jesse much longer. A part of me still felt like I couldn't bring him anything but harm, but the other part of me wanted my friend back. It was very conflicting.

"How are you feeling about school and stuff now, any better?" Corey questioned, breaking my internal battle about my friendship.

I sighed a little before picking up a leaf to pick at. "I feel a little better about it. I think it's good to keep me busy. Back home, I worked long hours at my old job to keep my mind busy. I never really gave college a try so, why not?"

He nodded taking in my words. "I just didn't want you feeling a particular way about Sharon pushing this on you. She truly wants the best for you Kole, she just has a hard time expressing it."

I scoffed, "You think?"

He grinned at my reaction. "Look, I know you guys have been through some very trying things that strained your relationship but I need you to understand that she really does love you and honestly wants to make things right between the two of you."

I rolled my eyes, "I get that. It's just that her approach is all wrong. She comes off telling me what I'm going to do rather than try to get understanding about where I'm coming from."

"And I understand that as well," he agreed. "She slips up by thinking you're still her 11-year-old girl, not realizing that at the end of the day … you're an adult. Your choices are your own but she loves the heck out of you kid and the strain the two of you have; pains her to no end. She's spent many of nights praying for you, hoping that one day you would reach out to her to let her know that you were still alive after your Grandmother passed. The day we got your message from jail, she cried all night."

My eyes widened at the confession. "She-she cried?"

He smirked. "After calling and cursing out every guard in the county and the girl you beat up. Yeah, she laid in my arms and cried herself to sleep."

I was in shock. "Wow."

"I know this transition is different for you," he continued. "It's different for her too. I just … want you to be open to everything, you know? Give it a chance. Everything happens for a reason."

"That's the part that's hard to grasp," I answered. "The reasoning behind it all."

He smiled, looking ahead at the setting sun. "Not everything is meant for us to understand baby girl."

I squinted up at him. "How do you do that?"

"Do what?"

"Remain so positive? Seems like nothing bothers you."

He chuckled a bit, turning his gaze back to the sun set. "Sure, stuff bothers me. It's just all about perception."

His words rang true; using a phrase I consistently would use with others.

"Where does your perception stem from?" I questioned with genuine interest.

"To be honest, my faith. The day I gave my life to God was the day my views on the world and how it operated changed."

I try to take his approach and his mindset in everything I do. It keeps me balanced and life more manageable."

My heart fluttered at the thought but my brain wouldn't allow me to accept the concept. How can I believe God exists, when so much has happened to me throughout my life? No way an all-knowing God could just sit and watch all that happened and be okay with it. There's no way.

Corey watched me closely. "You know I heard about the rule about you attending church with us every Sunday and I must say that I disagree with Sharon's stance on that."

My eyes shot to his in surprise, "You do?"

He nodded. "Yeah sure. A relationship with God is not something you should be forced into. It's something you have to want for yourself more than anybody else wants for you. You don't have to come Kole, but when you have questions, feel free to ask. And if you're ready to experience a service, you're more than welcome to join us.

A sense of calm washed over me at Corey's warm words. I was actually saddened to see him head towards the front door. "I would love to stay and chat but the new episode of Scandal is coming on and Sharon doesn't play when it comes to Scandal."

I couldn't hide my amusement as Corey looked back at me, "Wanna join us?"

I raised a brow, pondering the thought before shrugging. Why not? Having company wasn't half bad today.

"Sure."

"Dammit Sharon!" I groaned, closing the refrigerator door in frustration. Her ass still doesn't buy groceries until right before she's about to cook. I sighed, rubbing my stomach in hunger.

I wasn't getting my last check from my old job, Walmart, until next week so I was broke until then. I didn't even have the option of ordering a pizza if I wanted.

I rolled my eyes, walking out of the kitchen towards the living room to at least keep myself asleep until either Sharon or Corey got home, hopefully with some food.

My eyes closed while I scoffed and shook my head.

Some things about Sharon never change.

> I sat alone at my usual lunch table in the cafeteria, watching as other kids happily ate their sack lunches around me. Mommy had forgotten to pack my lunch again this morning and I spent all of the change I found lying around the house last week to get food.
>
> This was becoming a usual thing that I was growing accustomed to. Not eating. It seemed like feeding me was becoming the least of her worries ever since Larry started coming around more.
>
> I didn't like Larry. He was always saying weird things and talked to me like he talked to Mommy sometimes. He scared me. Even though she forgot to pack me lunch, I didn't care since she was out, meaning he was nowhere near me. I looked down, clutching my stomach, feeling it growl. I sighed, hoping no one could hear it.

The moment I looked up, I saw a sandwich wrapped in plastic being pushed in my face, and Jesse's smile behind it.

"Made this special for you," he grinned, waiting for me to take the sandwich from his fingers. I gave a smile, taking the food as he sat directly across from me, flipping his paper bag upside down to release all of its contents.

"We can split my chips too Nic. My mom was watching me close after she caught me making another sandwich."

"How'd you know to pack me one?" I asked softly. Jesse opened his bag of Doritos and began pouring some onto the plastic baggy my sandwich had just been removed from.

"You never have lunch anymore and you need to eat. I heard your stomach last week during reading time," he confessed easily.

I smiled, more than grateful that I had Jesse. He made everything that was happening at home, not seem so bad.

"Thank you Jesse."

He waved me off, devouring into his peanut butter and jelly.

"Don't worry about it. I got you."

―――――――――――

The sound of the doorbell ringing snapped my eyes open in wonder, vanishing the memory from my mind.

I blew out a breath before standing to my feet and trudged slowly towards the front door. My eyebrows met at the center of my forehead when I saw Jesse standing on the other side. He gave me a once over before clearing his throat.

"Hey, what's up?" he greeted, as I looked questionably back at him.

"Nothing much, what's up?" I asked in return, waiting to get the reasoning on his sudden arrival.

I glanced past him to see a black Acura parked in the driveway. He came straight here?

"You eat today?" he questioned, raising a brow.

I shook my head, "Nah, but I'm not hun-"

He cut me short, nodding his head towards his vehicle. "Come on. Let me take you to get some food."

"No, I'm cool." I declined. "I'll just eat something here."

He gave me a knowing look, "There's food in there?"

I debated back and forth about whether not I was going to lie. Knowing Jesse though, he would test to see if it were the truth. I decided against it. "No."

He frowned at my honesty. "Then how you gonna eat something here? Let me take you to get some food Nic, come on. Get ya things, I'll be out here."

"Jesse, you don't have to take me to get anything. I don't have any money and I'll be okay ... really.

He cut me off with a wave of his hand in annoyance. "Ah, quit all that talking. Don't worry about it. I got you."

A smirk graced my lips before it disappeared just as fast as it came. "I'll be right back."

He nodded, "I'll be in the car."

I guess some things never changed about Jesse either.

I chewed on my fry slowly, looking around the seemingly empty Cheddar's restaurant while Jesse ate his food greedily. I snorted a bit at the way his jaws worked furiously while he chewed.

He stopped mid chew, "What?"

I grinned, shaking my head, looking back to my plate of chicken fingers and fries.

"You eat like a bird and not like a gorilla now? So much about you has changed," Jesse teased, shaking his head before taking a sip of his water.

"I don't eat like a bird," I defended. "I'm just – I don't know." I sighed, unsure of what I was trying to say.

"I know you're not shy around me. At least you shouldn't be. I'm still the same for the most part," he assured, setting his glass down, piercing his eyes into mine.

I shrugged, "I wish I was too."

Jesse looked at me curiously before he spoke.

"Why do you go by Kole now?"

I licked my lips of any salt residue from the fries before clearing my throat, "When I got to my new school the kids used to tease me about my name."

His eyes widened, "Why? Dominic is dope!"

I smirked. The name always sounded angelic coming from his lips.

"It's not dope when kids are telling you that you were born with a penis because your name is for boys. So I just decided to reinvent myself altogether. Kole wasn't much better but I didn't get teased for it. They just thought it was short for something."

Jesse nearly spit out the water that he was sipping before covering his face to hold the laugh in.

"I'm sorry, but dang! Kids are evil yo!" he giggled as I couldn't help but chuckle too.

"Whaattt?" Jesse stretched in surprise. "You still laugh? Never thought I'd see the day."

I blushed, shaking my head and tending back to my meal, "Whatever."

It was quiet for a few moments before Jesse spoke again.

"So what are you doing back? Weren't you staying with your granny out in Greensboro?"

I nodded, feeling a small pang in my chest at the mention of my late grandmother.

"Aw ok. Well how she doing? I remember seeing her like once or twice."

I forced myself to swallow the food I was chewing, "She passed away about two years ago."

Jesse hissed with a pained expression plastered on his face, "I'm sorry Nic. I wouldn't have asked had I known."

I smiled, tucking some hair behind my ear. "S'not your fault. You didn't know."

"May I ask what happened? That is – if you're comfortable talking about it."

Was I? I hadn't really talked about her out loud to someone in a long time. Jesse seemed to be someone I could still trust.

"She just went to sleep one night and didn't wake up." I explained as he gave an understanding nod.

"Man that's tough."

"Is it bad to feel like it's my fault?" I blurted, releasing the pained secret I had kept all this time.

Jesse looked to me with so much concern in his eyes, "What do you mean, how could her death be your fault?"

I blew out a shaky breath, realizing I would have to explain what I meant since I went so far to express my inner most thoughts.

"The night before she passed, we got into a huge fight about this guy I was dating. She really didn't like him and I didn't like that she didn't like him. So I said some very hurtful and ugly things to her – things I would've never said had I been in my right mind. I never got to apologize to her or say that I didn't mean it."

And there it is, I confessed, refusing to meet Jesse's stare.

I could feel the emotion in the bottom of my throat, begging for freedom. I swallowed it. I just wasn't ready.

"Sometimes I feel like … her heart stopped beating because … because I broke it beyond repair."

Jesse shook his head.

"You can't live with that kind of guilt on your heart. What happened was not your fault, it was out of your control."

I cut him off, "How do I know that?"

"How could you think otherwise is the question. People fight, Nic. They say things they don't mean to the ones that love them the most. It's human nature. You can't look at that situation like that or it's going to destroy you, if it hasn't already. You have to let it go, and forgive yourself."

He paused a quick moment before he continued, "It was just her time. Everyone is going to have their time. It's the only thing promised in this life. You didn't know her time was coming, because if you had, that conversation would've gone differently. The biggest lesson you need to learn is to appreciate people while they're still here. Appreciate those that got your back and your best interest at heart. That weight of her death is just too heavy for you to carry, Nic. It's not meant for you to."

I took in his words, sniffing back the tears that wanted so badly to fall. Crying wasn't going to be an option right now.

"You got some healing to do baby," Jesse said stuffing a fry into his mouth. "It's all in your demeanor that you're hurting and carrying the past with you everywhere you go."

I shook my head slowly, "I really don't even know where to start. I feel like I'm just too messed up."

"You start by being willing. It's all going to take time but be willing to open up to the process. Be willing to be better and feel better. Change your perception. I'm here for you, Sharon here for you and even Corey. Just ... accept us and accept the fact that we're here. We all wanna see you win, I promise." he assured, as I began to feel a small tinge of hope. Jesse talked with so much ease and confidence. I wanted to possess that same confidence one day.

And with his help, I'm sure I could.

———————————

"Thanks for feeding me." I said softly to Jesse as he pulled into the driveway of Sharon's house.

He nodded, turning down the volume of the music. "It's no problem man. I missed kicking it with you."

I smiled at his honesty. It's been a while since I've been missed by anyone.

"We should hang again, like for real. You're weird as hell now but you're good company regardless." he added, causing me to chuckle.

I shrugged, "Sounds like a plan."

He grinned, before putting his car in reverse. "Aight, well I gotta go see what Phi up to. I'll see you Monday for class, right?" he asked to make sure, as I nodded in response.

"I'll see you Monday and thanks again." I said, closing the door behind me.

Jesse waited until I was fully inside before he took off down the street.

I grinned to myself, walking down the hallway towards the kitchen. I had a good afternoon with Jesse and just being around his positive energy. It just felt good to be back in the presence of someone I knew I could trust, knowing they truly cared about me in return.

I stepped into the kitchen seeing grocery bags filled with food spread across the counter. Sharon was bent over in the refrigerator putting some away. She popped her head up noticing me and pointed her finger over to the counter.

"Hey baby, can you help me put some of this away?" she requested politely as I moved my feet over to start taking food from the bags.

"I'm sorry I didn't go grocery shopping sooner. I'm not used to making sure food is in the house since it's usually just me and Corey that I have to worry about."

She shuffled over to another filled grocery bag to remove its contents. Her words stung, even though I knew it wasn't their intended purpose.

"It's cool. You never really used to have food in here so I wasn't surprised," I replied nonchalantly as her body froze next to mine.

"Yeah, but that was different," she answered shortly, taking out the items much slower now.

"What's different? You didn't really care if I was fed then. The difference is that you care now?" I questioned, trying to keep the sarcasm out of my voice.

I tried to remember Jesse's and Corey's words but right now the emotion was getting the best of me.

"I cared then ... " Sharon said quietly, walking over to the fridge to put the food in her hands away.

"Just not more than the high? Or the men?" I asked, quickly turning my body to lean against the counter and face her.

She looked up from the refrigerator at me before sighing, "Why are you picking a fight with me Kole? I'm not that person anymore and I've been trying since you've been back to just be okay with you and you won't let me."

"Why do you think you deserve it?" I shot back, keeping my voice as calm as my mind would allow.

Her face fell a bit, "Because I'm your mother! That's why I deserve it."

I shook my head, "The only mother I ever had is dead. You try for a few days and bail me out of jail and think that just erases everything? Like it's all fixed? You may be different and better and happy and shit Sharon, but I'm not!"

She clenched her jaw, shaking her head slowly. "You're so ungrateful and bitter Kole. I could've left you there to rot in that cell or in those streets but I didn't! I bailed you out and brought you back to your home."

"This isn't my home!" I shouted. My tears betrayed me as they slipped from my eyes. My heart was cracking down the middle all over again at the thought.

"This isn't my home." I repeated softer. "A home is where you feel safe and protected. I could never feel that here."

Sharon was quiet as she looked at me with glossed over eyes, biting the inside of her cheek.

"I just wish you would've listened, Sharon," I breathed, doing my best to contain the sob. "I wish you would've cared ... when it mattered."

I finished, wiping my dampened cheek and exited the kitchen.

CHAPTER
- THREE -

I was relieved to be at school the following Monday, to say the least. Since my conversation with Sharon, things were awkward in the house all weekend. Even Corey couldn't slice the tension between us. That's typical Sharon though. She hears a bit of how I feel about her and wants to be mad at *me* for it. I didn't mean to hurt her feelings or whatever. I was just being honest and said how I felt. I know me and her need to have a serious talk soon, but I'm just not ready. All of this is weird and new and I'm seriously just trying to cope until it all gets better. That's it.

"Aw hey can I bum one of those?" A girl requested referring to my cigarette as she approached me, setting her bag down at her feet.

I was standing outside of Thompson after my first class, waiting around until it was time to head to English.

I shrugged, pulling a stick from the pack and handed it to her. She looked grateful, her blonde hair bouncing wildly against her shoulders when she stepped up to take it from my fingers.

"Wow, thanks. Typically, people are assholes around here."

"It's cool. I'm trying to quit." I shared, earning a chuckle from her while she placed the cig between her lips, digging in her pocket for what I assumed was a lighter.

"Yeah? I've been saying that since I was 15. Now I just make sure I don't buy any. But if I see someone smoking, I just can't help myself sometimes."

I studied her carefully. She had a head full of bleach blonde hair with dark roots and stood just a few inches taller than me. Her skin was pale but she didn't seem purely white, she had to have been mixed with another nationality, I was sure of it. Her button nose wrinkled a bit while she lit the cigarette then blew the smoke through her full painted red lips. Her style was edgy, much like my own.

She seemed cool to me.

"I'm Lucy by the way," she introduced, sticking her cigarette-free hand towards my own.

"Kole." I greeted, lightly returning her handshake.

"Dope name. You new here? Haven't seen you around before."

I nodded, "You can say that. New to the school, not the city. I moved around a bit but I'm from here."

She sighed shaking her head, "Why on earth would you come back? The world is so much bigger than Raleigh. I swear, I'm ditching this place the minute I get my degree and I'm never looking back."

I smirked at her comment as I observed the campus. Just as I was scanning the land, I spotted Jesse not too far away, posted under a tree with his girlfriend. She was leaning against the trunk as he towered over her. They seemed to be in an intimate conversation so I chose to wait before I made my presence known so we could go to class together.

I continued to scan the yard, watching all of the different people as they headed towards different directions. It wasn't until my eyes landed on a boy walking through, that I felt everything around me stop.

He was ... beautiful.

He was tall and walked with a sense of command as if the world were beneath him. He smirked cockily at several girls that made eye contact and he seemed to greet every male that crossed his path.

Who is he?

"Who?" Lucy asked as my eyes darted to hers. She was focused on the boy I was staring at prior.

I said that out loud?

"Oh him? That's Devon. Walks around here like he's God's gift," she said with an eye roll.

She grinned knowingly at me, "You think he's cute or something?"

I shrugged, "He's alright." I lied.

He was one of the finest men I had ever seen.

"Well I know a few people that run in his circle. Maybe I can introduce you at the block party ... if you come."

"Block party?"

She nodded her head before digging in her purse, pulling out a flyer.

"Yeah, the University is throwing it on campus to kick off spring quarter. I went last year and it was pretty fun. You should tag along."

I bit my lip, looking at the flyer and then back at Devon who stopped to talk to a few guys.

"You can roll with me if you want since you're somewhat new here. I don't run with many girls so it would be cool to have a tag along that's as cute as you," she urged with a wink. I looked down at the flyer again, scanning over the details.

It had been a while since I had done anything that was even remotely fun and seeing how Jesse had a life of his own, it would be nice if I had one as well. Just to keep me busy and out of the house.

"Here, put your number in my phone." Lucy handed me her phone and I quickly punched the numbers in the key pad before handing it back.

She grinned with satisfaction. "Dope! Thanks again for the cigarette, Kole! I'll text so you can have my number and we can link up for the party."

She leaned in to give me a quick hug before heading off.

I watched her disappear further on campus.

Did I just make a friend?

"Yo Nic!" I heard none other than Jesse call out from behind me while I was walking to English.

I turned my head, watching him jog up with that smile plastered on his face.

"You're always smiling."

He flashed me a puzzled look before chuckling. "You say it like it's something bad. Dude can't be happy around you either?! Sheesh!"

I couldn't help but laugh at his reaction.

"I'm not saying that ... "

"What is it then? You wanna know my secret?"

"Well, yeah I guess."

He smiled. "I got peace."

He said it like it was just so simple to obtain. He made everything seem much simpler than it really was.

"I can see that. But how?"

He smirked, "I got the kind of peace that only Christ can give me. If I ain't have Him, I'd be shook up."

I gave him a look of unsurety, "You mean God or something?"

He nodded, "Sure do, or something," he mocked.

"This is the most God has ever been brought to my attention in the last 22 years. It's weird," I said, adjusting the strap of my book bag.

"What's so weird about it?" Jesse asked.

Tiffany Campbell

"I just ... don't think He's real."

"Well what do you know about Him to not think He's real to you?"

I paused, trying to think of the best way to answer his question. "I know He must not have been around for most of my life."

"Well ... did you want Him around?" Jesse asked, my eyes snapping to his.

He continued, opening the building door for me. "How real can someone be to you if you always thought they didn't exist? Would you be around someone that constantly showed you they didn't want you back?"

"I have and it was complete torture on my heart."

He sighed at my revelation.

"I'm sorry you had to go through that because you didn't deserve it. That pain you felt? He feels the same, just probably ten times as hard. Imagine not being wanted by the very person you created," Jesse finished, leading the way to class, leaving me speechless behind him.

"So do you have any more classes after this? I can't remember." Jesse asked, opening the door for me as we exited the building after class.

My eyes squinted at the bright afternoon sun while I shook my head, "Nah. My next set of classes are Tuesdays and Thursdays."

"Aw ok, I won't be around those days. I work. You remember where they are right?"

I nodded with a smirk, "I'm a big girl, Jesse. I think I've got it."

He crossed his eyes, "Well whatever. I'm just trynna look out for you. Make sure you're good."

I shrugged, "I'm surviving. Getting a little more adjusted to being here. I made a friend today."

His brow rose, "A friend? Who?"

"A chick named Lucy. We're going to the block party together this weekend." I said proudly. Last acquaintance I made was Gina. I just hoped this friendship would go a lot smoother than that.

He looked surprised. "Lucy? Lucy Taylor?"

I shrugged my shoulders unsure of what her last name was.

"Are you going to the party?" I questioned as he bit the inside of his cheek in thought.

"I typically don't do parties. If I do go, it's because I like being around people. I wasn't really stressing the block party too much but I may go now," he answered looking ahead of him before his eyes lit up.

I followed his gaze to find his girlfriend; the object of his affection. She was grinning wide, heading our way, her deep dimples revealing themselves.

She was even more gorgeous up close.

Jesse greeted her with a sweet and gentle peck on her lips before tucking her small body underneath his arm. She smiled up at him before her eyes landed on me.

"Hi!" She said brightly, making me fidget a little under her gaze.

Why was everyone just so damn happy and friendly all the time here?

"Hello," I replied awkwardly, causing Jesse to stifle his laugh at my nerves.

"Babe, this is Dominic. Nic, this is my girlfriend Phi."

I extended my hand to her, "It's Kole actually. Nice to meet you."

Her smile never left her face as she shook my hand, "Oh right! Jesse has told me so many stories about the two of you from back in the day. You're so beautiful! So you're back now, officially?"

She seemed genuinely interested and Jesse was eyeing me carefully, waiting for my response.

I nodded, "Officially for now. Just trying to get used to the city and everything again."

"Well hey, if you ever need someone to shop with, definitely hit me up! Your shirt is   really cute!"

I looked at her appearance, then back to my own. Wasn't anything special about what I was wearing, in my opinion but I appreciated the compliment nonetheless.

"Thank you." We grinned at each other before she looked up at Jesse.

"Where you headed?" She asked, causing him to finally remove his eyes from mine.

"I'm about to take Nic home and then head over to Mom Dukes. What you getting into?"

My eyes widened. I was just going to hang around until Sharon got off work to pick me up.

She frowned a bit before recovering quickly, "Okay. Well just call me then. I have one more class and then I'm heading home. Come see me later?"

He nodded before bending down to peck her lips, "Of course. Call me after class."

She smiled before standing on her tippy toes to give him one last kiss, removing herself from his embrace. "It was nice meeting you, Kole! I'm sure we'll be seeing a lot of each other, girl."

Phi gave me a friendly tap on my elbow before waving at the two of us and heading in a different direction.

"She seems nice." I spoke, watching after her for a moment before Jesse nudged me in my side.

"Ready to go?"

"Yeah."

The car ride was quiet initially. It wasn't an awkward silence, just a quiet one. It was comforting in a sense. Jesse's radio was playing softly, adding to the peaceful atmosphere.

"So how long have you and Phi been together?" I asked, earning a grin from him while he kept his eyes on the road.

"About three months."

"That's it? Seems like ya'll have been together for years."

He shook his head.

"Nah. I've known her for a little minute but that's it. We decided to start dating a few months ago though."

"What made you take the leap of commitment?" I questioned, getting more comfortable in my seat, happy to be getting to know more about Jesse.

He chuckled, gripping the wheel smoothly, steering the car onto the freeway. "I'm not afraid of committing to nobody, girl. Phi was just real cool and somebody I felt a connection with. So I locked her down, made her mine."

"You love her?"

His eyebrows rose a bit before releasing a soft chuckle, "I got love for her cause she's my girl and most importantly my friend. But like in love though? That's deep. I don't feel that for her yet. Not now."

Tiffany Campbell

"Think you ever will?"

He shrugged, "Maybe, who knows? I don't worry about the future too much. It'll take care of itself. Whatever happens, happens. I like her right now, I enjoy my time with her and we have fun. That's what matters most to me."

I nodded, "So you're a live-in-the-moment kind of guy then, huh?"

He smirked, "Yeah. I gotta think that way. Appreciating every moment as it comes, not taking anything for granted."

I hummed, ending my series of questions.

"What about you?" he inquired after a short silence. My eyes shot to his side profile.

"What about me?"

"What's your love story? How things work out with that guy you mentioned the other day?"

"Oh." I slouched in my seat a bit at the thought. "Things were crazy with him." I answered softly.

"Word? What was so crazy about it?" he asked while my eyes gazed out of the window.

"Everything." I breathed, before dusting the thought away. "But it doesn't matter. I'm single now. Have been for a while."

Jesse smirked, easing the mood. "Single huh? So you tryna mingle or nah?"

I chuckled before giving a shy shrug. Devon's face instantly coming to mind. "Maybe."

I looked over my outfit in my bathroom mirror, making sure everything was in place. I fluffed my hair a bit, adding body to the feathered layers I had just curled, checking for any random specs on my face. I studied the roundness of my cheeks, the almond shape of my light brown eyes, the bridge leading to my small yet slightly pointed nose and the fullness of my lips. I was surely Sharon's child, that much was obvious and of course the combination of a man I had never met.

I always wondered who my father was and what he was out doing in the world. Sharon got pregnant with me at 16 and she would tell me that the man she referred to as my father was much older than her and married with his own kids. He supposedly wanted nothing to do with her or the pregnancy and Sharon was much too afraid to get an abortion, so here I was. Still questioning if abortion would've been the better option for us all.

My phone vibrating against the bathroom countertop snapped me out of my dark thoughts. I saw Lucy's name appear on the screen and quickly picked it up to answer.

"Hey." I breathed, hearing music blaring on the other end.

"Hey girl! I think I'm pulling up to your house now."

I texted her my address earlier in the morning so she could GPS the directions.

"Ok, I'll be out in a sec." I hung up the phone and gave one last look over in the mirror before heading down the stairs.

I hurriedly glided down the hall to the foyer to let someone know I was leaving. I found Corey in the kitchen, chomping on an apple while reading the newspaper. He looked up at me and smiled.

"You look nice!" he complimented as I smirked.

"Thank you. Sharon here?" I asked, earning a headshake from him.

"Nope. She left out about a half hour ago. You going somewhere?"

I nodded, "Yeah. I'm heading to a block party with a girl I met from school. I may be in a little later than midnight possibly. I don't know how long these things last."

He chuckled, waving me off. "Go have fun baby girl. We'll be here when you get in. Just try not to be too loud," he winked as I let out a breath in gratitude.

"Thanks, Corey. Tell Sharon for me okay?"

"Sure thing."

———————————

"You look cute, boo!" Lucy complimented the minute I got into her grey Honda Civic. I grinned, buckling up my seatbelt.

"Thank you, you too." I returned, giving her a once over. She was so eccentric and wore red lipstick every time I saw her. I loved it.

She blushed, fluffing her hair. "Thanks girl. You ready to turn up? You seem like you need some fun in your world."

I nodded, releasing a sigh. "I really do. I haven't had fun in such a long time."

She smirked, reaching into her purse, "Well you're in luck, chica." She pulled out a personal bottle of peach flavored Ciroc, handing it to me.

"That's you." Lucy told me, putting her car in reverse to back out of my driveway.

I studied the bottle for a second before looking at her, "The whole thing?"

She shrugged, "Sure. I drank before I came and got you. You gotta be tipsy at these type of functions. Takes the edge off."

I smiled a little, staring back at the bottle. It had been a while since I had any alcohol, and I did always feel a bit better when I did drink. I twisted the top open, sniffing the liquor before I took a sip.

"Aww," Lucy whined. "You gotta drink more than that! Take a shot!" she encouraged as I chuckled and took a larger gulp of the liquor. The liquid burned while making its way down my throat.

"That's my girl."

I coughed, wiping the corners of my mouth. "S-so what typically happens at a block party?"

Lucy relaxed in her seat while she drove. "Um, they typically have a DJ playing music loud enough for the entire block to hear. There are food trucks and different booths set up for people to purchase food and drinks and everybody just hangs out. Sometimes there are live performances. It's just a really cool and laid back time to socialize with fellow students all while getting drunk."

I nodded, looking out of the window as we traveled through the streets.

"You'll have fun though. Even more fun if you take another shot."

I guess one more shot couldn't hurt.

I held Lucy's hand as she led us through the large crowd of students. The liquor had given me a calm that I hadn't felt in a while, so I wasn't as bothered or uncomfortable being surrounded by so many bodies. Everyone was talking amongst friends while dancing to the music blaring over the loud speakers.

"You want a drink or something?" Lucy yelled, turning her head to look at me. I shook my head no.

She nodded, "Ok, well stand in line with me. I want a beer."

I agreed, stepping in line next to her bobbing my head to the music. My eyes danced over every face I saw, until they landed on Jesse standing not too far away with a group full of guys.

He was laughing hysterically at something, while leaning his arm on the nearest body to him. I grinned – intrigued to see him in a different element. This really didn't feel like a place I could ever picture him at, but he seemed to be enjoying himself around his friends.

He looked cute.

As if he could sense me staring, he turned his head, locking eyes with me. Jesse's smile grew before saying something to his friends and then leaving to come my way.

"This line is slow as hell," Lucy grumbled, taking a tiny step forward while I did the same. I looked up to where I had last seen Jesse, realizing that he was only a few feet away now.

"What's up, Nic!" he greeted, leaning in to give me a hug.

It was the first time we had physically made this kind of contact and I felt my entire body tense up the moment his intoxicating cologne hit my nose. I closed my eyes for a brief moment, taking in his scent before letting go.

I gazed shyly at him while he grinned back, "You turnt up?"

I caught the real meaning of his question before I nodded shortly.

He chuckled, "I can tell. You ain't a statue today. Not looking evil and all that, you look more loose," he teased, nudging me while I playfully rolled my eyes.

"Are you?"

He shook his head, "Nah, I roll off a natural high. I don't drink," he replied, instinctively placing his hand over his stomach.

"Oh, so how long have you been here?" I asked, stepping out of line with Lucy who had barely noticed. She was too pressed wondering why it was taking so long.

Jesse gently grabbed my elbow, moving me out of the way of a couple of dudes wildly running through the crowd. I looked to him thankfully, even though his eyes were still trained on the guys that just passed.

He shook his head before gazing back down at me. "What you say, baby?"

"How long have you been here?" I repeated, trying not to pay attention to how the way he said baby so effortlessly made me feel.

"Oh. I've actually only been here for like twenty minutes. I came with a few of my boys." He gestured his head in the direction he had originally came from.

I nodded, never taking my eyes off his and the smile never leaving my face.

"You goofy, man," he chuckled at me. "What you smiling for girl? I ain't never seen you smile like this before. Them dranks got you feeling it."

I giggled, before quickly covering my mouth to hide my grin. Jesse snorted before grabbing my wrist, removing my hand.

"Don't do that, I like ya smile," he grinned before shaking his head.

"You got so many layers, Nic."

I was preparing to ask him what he meant before I felt a light arm draping itself around my shoulders.

"What up, JP! You meet my new friend Kole?" Lucy's voice boomed excitedly, pulling the two of us from our moment.

Jesse gave her a head nod, "Sup Lu. How you been?"

I looked at my new friend, smiling flirtatiously at my old one, biting her lip. "Better now that I see you. Where ya eggroll at?"

Jesse gave a light groan, rolling his eyes. "You always do that, man ... "

Lucy giggled innocently, "What? I can never remember her name!"

He shook his head, keeping a polite grin. "You know her name, Lucy. Be respectful. Why you playing?"

"Because it should've been me," she smirked boldly as my eyes shot open looking between the two of them.

"Yeah, so you say." Jesse replied before glancing at me, giving a look. It was the same look he would give me whenever he was put in an awkward situation by a female.

I chuckled quietly before he tapped my arm, "Find me later okay? I'm about to head back that way."

I nodded, watching Jesse give Lucy one last head shake before he turned to go his own way.

"JP always playing, he knew he wanted this," she said turning to face me the minute he was out of earshot.

"You like him?"

"Girl, I've had the biggest crush on Jesse's fine ass since we had a political science class last year. He's always playing me off though."

"Well he has a girlfriend." I explained as she looked at me impassively.

"So? He's been with her for five minutes and he ain't married so he's single to me."

She shrugged as she took a sip of her beer. "Even people like Jesse can't resist a little sexy temptation."

Jesse seemed to be very sure of himself and solid. It was clear he was not interested in Lucy in any way.

"Anyway," she said looking at me. "How you know JP? I thought you just moved."

"We used to be friends when I lived here and we got back cool when I moved back." Lucy nodded, glancing behind me before her eyes lit up. She shot a devilish grin in my direction, poking my shoulder.

"Looks like your crush just showed up," she smirked as I turned my head.

My eyes instantly landed on Devon.

He was standing with a friend, talking to a group of females. I chuckled, shaking my head before turning back to face Lucy.

"He seems busy, I'm cool." I shrugged.

"So ... we go interrupt what he's doing."

I declined, "Nah. I usually don't approach guys anyway. S'not my thing. I typically just wait to see if they're interested."

She nodded in agreement, "Ok, I feel that. Guess since I'm so damn bold I never take that approach. It hasn't helped thus far, as you can clearly see with Jesse."

I grinned, thinking about the look Jesse had given me in regards to Lucy. She was a character for sure but I liked her. She balanced me out and kept things fun for me; something I hadn't experienced in a while.

"Let's just keep drinking and see where the night takes us." I suggested as she instantly beamed.

"Yesssss! My kind of girl!" she said giddy, locking arms with me.

"I gotta ... I gotta pee." Lucy slurred next to me as I sat in a daze.

We were posted on a bench, people watching and secretly taking swigs out of the Ciroc bottle. I was definitely feeling the effects of the shots I took in the car and the ones we had been taking back and forth for the last hour. We kept each other good company, laughing and discussing the different characters we witnessed so far.

"Where you gonna go?" I questioned, watching the many people walking past our bench.

She pointed directly in front of us, "Right there in one of the outhouses."

My eyes found the spot she had pointed to, realizing for the first time a long line of outhouses posted there where people were standing awaiting their turn to use the restroom.

"Ok ... Im'a wait here."

She nodded to my reply before standing to her feet, slightly uncoordinated. I chuckled, watching her frame disappear wobbly into the sea of people.

I took a moment to scan the crowd to see if I saw Jesse anywhere. He seemed to have kept a safe distance from me all night. He would be off doing his own thing but not too far to the point where I couldn't see him. I figured he was doing it intentionally to keep an eye on me and I appreciated him for it.

I spotted him soon after my initial search; Phi nestled under his arm while they stood in a large group of friends. Throughout the last hour he motioned for me to come and join them any time we locked eyes but I would decline every time. I'm much too shy to be the new girl in the group.

My eyes were so trained on Jesse that I hadn't even noticed another body sitting next to me until they spoke.

"Mind if I sit here real quick?" a deep country accented voice questioned, causing me to snap my head in surprise.

All of the blood rushed to my cheeks the moment Devon and I locked eyes.

He looked at me expectedly, awaiting an answer to his question while I froze.

I couldn't even find my voice.

"So ... is that cool?" he asked again, never taking his eyes off mine.

I nodded my head quickly, forcing myself to look away. "You're good."

I could hear him snicker at my response but my heart was rushing too fast for me to even process. I hadn't felt like this in a while when it came to another man. All of the emotions I suddenly had inside felt foreign.

"You go the University or something?" Devon asked me after a short pause, my eyes nervously meeting his.

He was just so gorgeous up close. His caramelized skin tone gave off a glow, while his lips were so full and moist. I just wanted to kiss them.

I shook my head, "The community college."

His eyes widened at my confession, "Oh word? I go there too. I've never seen you before though."

He squinted his almond eyes, as if that would give him a clue to who I was.

I grinned bashfully, "I just started this quarter, so you probably haven't."

He nodded, getting more comfortable on the bench, giving me his undivided attention.

"Aw okay. Well, I'm Devon."

He extended his hand towards me and shyly I shook it, lost in the softness and warmth of it. "Kole."

"Kole, huh? I like it." he smirked, revealing his dimple.

"You here waiting on ya boyfriend or something?"

I blushed, realizing he was trying to figure out if I was single. *He's interested?*

I shook my head, "I don't have one of those."

"Yeah, me neither," he joked.

"Who are you here with then? Somebody I know?"

I shrugged, "Came with my friend Lucy."

He nodded in recognition. "Yeah I know her, she's cool. I guess you're in good hands."

We grinned, looking at one another. He was getting ready to say something else before we heard his name being called not too far away. He looked past me and cursed under his breath as his friend called him over.

"Aye, I gotta go. You got classes on Monday?" he asked, preparing to stand up.

I nodded, earning a smile from him.

"Cool. Well if we don't run into each other again tonight, find me then aight, Kole?" he winked before completely removing himself from my company.

I finally released the breath I felt like I was holding the entire time.

I placed my hand on my chest, trying to calm down from the brief moment I shared with Devon, already trying to come up with an outfit in my head to wear on Monday. He had to see me looking better than I had tonight.

"Nic!" I heard and turned my head to find the voice that belonged to Jesse.

My head spun with the sudden movement and with that I became aware of how much I had to drink. I wasn't as tolerant to alcohol like I used to be since it had been a while.

Jesse gave me a look of concern when I placed my fingers against my temple to settle the dizziness. He sat by my side quickly, placing a hand on my shoulder.

"Yo, you alright? Did I scare you or some'n?"

I shook my head, "Nah, I'm cool. Just got a little whiplash."

He giggled, "Whiplash from what girl? Turning that big ol' head of yours? It does look heavy," he teased as I gave him a dry look.

"Ha-ha." I responded sarcastically earning a laugh from him.

"What you doin' over here anyway?" I questioned, looking past him to see the group he left, still in the same spot. Phi would occasionally glance our way.

He shrugged, "Saw you over here talking to Devon."

His brows rose. "What was that about?"

I grinned, shrugging my shoulders. "He just needed a place to sit for a second. No big deal."

He looked at me close. "You sure?"

I nodded, becoming curious of his questioning. "Yeah I'm sure, why? What's wrong with Devon?"

Jesse sighed, shaking his head.

"Ain't nothing wrong I guess. Just ... just keep yourself guarded Nic. That's all I ask."

My face scrunched, "Don't I always?"

He smirked, running his tongue over his lip and shaking his head. "Nah, you don't."

"What do you mean I don't?"

He grinned, scratching the hair on his chin. "I mean you're guarded, sure. You keep yourself guarded from people that hurt you and people you don't want to hurt. But when it comes to these strangers though, you open yourself quick."

I grew offended, "No I don't!"

Jesse raised a hand in defense, realizing I was growing upset.

"Chill. I'm not tryna piss you off. I'm just being honest. You don't know what these people are capable of doing and yet you don't try to protect yourself from them like you do from the people that care. You do that in your last city too? How'd that turn out?"

My mind instantly went to Gina, getting mad all over again from what she did and because he was right.

I stood to my feet, "You don't know me anymore, Jesse."

He stood up too, watching me intently.

I pointed at him; "You think you got me all figured out because you knew me when I was a kid. Well newsflash, a lot of shit changed since then! I'm not that same girl."

He shook his head, stuffing his hands in his pockets.

"Nah you're not. But you wanna be though and that same girl is still in there somewhere. She's tucked underneath that heart of stone you got."

I rolled my eyes before looking away, running a hand through my hair. "Just-"

He stepped closer as I stepped back, feeling the dizziness surge throughout my being. I felt my stomach churn in response, causing me to clutch it tightly.

"Nic? Nic, you good?" Jesse called as I looked to the ground beneath me, wanting it to desperately stop spinning.

"I got-I gotta throw-"

Before I could finish, the surge of vomit shot up through my throat and out of my mouth, landing unmercifully onto the pavement.

"JP, what the hell happened?" I could hear Lucy yell, while I stood weak with Jesse's strong arm tucked underneath me.

"I dunno! We was talking and she just threw up. Every dang where! What all was ya'll drinking?" he questioned, voice laced with concern.

"We were just drinking a little bottle of Ciroc, nothing heavy. If I would've known she was a lightweight, I wouldn't have let her drink so much but she was cool before I went to the bathroom. I come out and she's looking like she needs life support!" Lucy screeched, her voice sounding just as concerned as Jesse's did.

"Well look man, I'm about to take her back to my crib. She can't walk into her momma house looking like this. Imma just text them from her phone, let them know she good and that she's with me. They should be fine."

I could see Lucy nodding, looking panicked at me through my blurred vision. "Ok. Just please look out for her, JP. I feel like shit for doing this."

"S'not your fault Lu. You ain't know, she'll be good, just gotta get it out her system. You know, sleep it off. She's good, you're good," he soothed as she nodded in response, running a hand through her wild blonde hair.

"Okay. Text me and let me know ya'll made it back and tell her to call me when she wakes up."

He gripped me tighter, feeling my body beginning to drift. I felt weak all over. "Aight, I got you."

"Babe, what's going on?" I heard Phi say after Jesse and I had walked a few steps. "What's wrong with Kole, she okay?"

"Nah, she drank too much. Throwing up and stuff, I gotta get her home," he told her, grunting as he lifted me up to keep me on my feet.

"Ok, do you want me to come with you?"

"Nah Phi, it's cool. Just lemme take care of this and I'll call you when I get home, aight?"

It was quiet for a moment before Phi finally spoke, "Alright, babe. Make sure you get her home safe and don't forget to call me. I want to be sure everything is okay."

"I got you, don't worry. I'll call you."

Not long after, we were moving once again, walking briskly through the crowd.

I groaned, feeling my feet wanting to give out.

"Jesse just let me go," I begged softly, just wanting to lie down.

"We're almost there Nic, I promise," he said gently, wanting me to keep my cool.

"It just hurts. Everything hurts." I whimpered, meaning more than my body. Alcohol always brought out the emotion.

"I know, baby and I'm sorry for even bringing it up. It's all my fault," he replied. I could hear how mad he was at himself.

"Everything hurts." I repeated, feeling the tear at the brim of my eye.

––––––––––––

It was going on about 1 a.m. "I feel so much better." I sighed in relief while I snuggled more onto Jesse's couch underneath the quilt he had given me.

I showered and was dressed in one of his gray sweat suits since my clothes had regurgitated alcohol on them.

Jesse snorted at my comment from the loveseat. "I bet, you threw ya whole life up in the bathroom earlier."

I could still sense the sadness in his voice so I sat all the way up so I could see a clear view of him. We had been at his house for over an hour since leaving the block party and he still seemed troubled about the entire situation.

"It wasn't your fault that I got sick Jes-" I was quickly cut off.

"Yeah it was. I should've just kept my distance and let you chill. You were having fun and I came messing it up because I wanted to open up my mouth about something that could've waited." He was picking at his nails, refusing to look at me.

"Since you've been back I just got this overwhelming need to just keep you safe. I can tell you've been hurt so much and I don't want nothing hurting you anymore. I don't want you to get hurt so bad that you end up leaving again."

There it is. The real reason he was so troubled. Jesse didn't want to lose me all over again. I could see now that he was genuinely glad to have me back, no matter how I had treated him since.

"I never realized ... me moving affected you so much." His eyes darted up to mine.

"Why would it not? You were my best friend, Dominic. Back then all we had was each other because we were both being neglected by our parents."

I remember Jesse's dad used to work crazy hours and his mom was a stay at home mom but she was always so paranoid about what her husband was doing and keeping the house clean, she never made time for him. We were literally all we had at the time.

"What happened with you? You know, after I moved?" I questioned softly, seeing the vulnerability and his own hurt lying deep within his eyes.

He shrugged, wiping his face clean of the sad emotion, covering it up with a small smile.

"A lot happened. I went through a few things but I made it. I'm still here, still breathing."

I shook my head, "It seemed to have hurt you though. How'd you cope?"

His smile grew. "I already told you, God. He was my only method of coping."

My face fell at his confession, not understanding.

He continued, "The day I learned about God, everything changed for me Nic and that's real. I ain't grow up in church or nothing so I ain't really understand it at first. The whole ... I wouldn't say religion but ... the relationship. The more I learned and the more I loved, the better life got. I still go through things, don't get me wrong, but having God on my side makes everything not seem so bad. I understand life's true purpose."

All I could do was admire the way he spoke so highly of it all.

"And what's that?" I questioned, referring to life's true purpose.

A small chuckle erupted from his chest, "That life isn't about me. None of this is about me. It's all for a greater purpose. Seek and save the lost."

"Guess I'm one of the lost ones, huh?" I questioned, partially joking.

"Nah, I wouldn't say that. I ain't here to convert ya beliefs or nothing, just sharing my experience. When you're ready to experience love, in its purest form, you will." he answered simply, leaning back into the couch.

My eyes never left him as I watched him bend his neck back to rest it on the top of the couch, his eyes peacefully closed.

"I'm sorry I left you Jes." I said softly into the calming atmosphere.

His eyes opened slowly to look at me, never uttering a word.

"After what happened to me, I just – I just couldn't be in that house anymore. I couldn't look at Sharon the same and having only you was no longer enough. I couldn't – "

He stopped me, raising his hand. "It wasn't your fault Nic. Being a man now, I understand whatever it was that caused you to go, was for good reason. I was hurt then but I was a child. I didn't get it. I just wanted my friend."

I nodded, sniffing back the emotion. "I know. You got her now, I promise. Damaged as all hell but I'm here."

He grinned softly before lifting himself completely off the couch and coming to sit next to me. He wrapped his arm around my shoulder, pulling me more into his chest.

"It's all good now. Just get some sleep. It's been a long night. Just relax."

His raspy voice was so soothing and his physical comfort is exactly what I needed in this moment.

Before long, I rested my head against his legs, closing my eyes and allowing the sleep to take over.

CHAPTER
- FOUR -

" Man, don't scare me like that ever again! No more Ciroc for you bro, that's done!" Lucy ranted as I chuckled at her antics.

It was Monday afternoon, both of our morning classes had let out and she and I were hanging out on a picnic table on campus until our next class was due to start.

"I'm serious! I'm thinking you're a pro, but you had me completely fooled. My heart nearly jumped out of my chest watching Jesse hold you up and you looking half dead! Never again," she sighed, blowing out the smoke from her cigarette. I had given her the pack I had, no longer desiring to keep the habit for some reason.

I shrugged, "I'm good. I just drank too fast. I typically mix my liquor but it's been a while." I answered shortly.

It was a beautiful sunny spring day.

"So how'd ya night go with JP? Or did you pass out the moment you got to his crib?" she questioned after a short silence between us.

I grinned, "Nah. We just chilled and caught up. I missed my friend."

That was the first time I admitted that for the first time out loud.

Allowing Jesse back into my life wholeheartedly was probably the best decision I had made since moving back. I was still working on my guard with him, but it was because I truly didn't want to hurt him. He meant too much.

"Wow, so the two of you were really tight back then huh?"

I nodded, "Best of friends. He was my neighbor, so I literally saw him every day."

She tapped a few ashes off to the side. "And you never saw him in like a different light? Like more than a friend?"

"No," I lied. "It was always just a friendship. That's all I really see for us now anyway."

I tried to downplay as best I could. Truth was, at one point in time in my younger years, I thought Jesse was going to be the boy I married. Now though? I'm extremely too tainted. Jesse is a good soul and Phi seems like one too.

He and I would be a horrible fit. I wasn't even fit to love myself; no way could I love him the way he deserves.

"Kole!" I heard a voice from a short distance, both Lucy and I directing our attention towards it.

I saw Devon with a charming smile on his face walking in our direction. He gave me a short wave, as I smiled and waved back.

"Oh snap, love connection." Lucy murmured and began to gather her things. "I'm about to head over to my next class, girl. Text me and let me know how this goes."

I chuckled, shaking my head before giving her a hug. Lucy waved at Devon when they crossed paths, before turning and giving me a goofy look. I blushed, attempting to hold my laugh in when Devon approached. He took a seat next to me on the picnic table.

"I found you." He grinned, taking his book bag off his back and sat it down beside him.

"Sup, beautiful," he greeted.

I felt the nerves in the pit of my stomach at the compliment but tried to brush them off. "Hi."

He chuckled, "Aw you getting shy on me now, Kole? You was so cool at the block party the otha night. What's different now?"

I smiled, tucking some hair behind my ear. "I'm sober."

Devon laughed at my comment before nodding his head, "I would have to agree that is the difference. I was under the influence too."

"I just couldn't forget about you though. You come off different than the other girls around here," he added, my eyes snapping to his.

"How so?"

He shrugged, "I don't know. You're a mystery to me. I can't figure you out. I'm usually good at reading girls the first time I come across them. I can't read you."

I rose a brow, "That a bad thing?"

He squinted his eyes a bit, "I don't know. I'm still trying to figure that out."

I felt a tinge of bravery, "You want to?"

His eyes perked at the question before he licked his lips and smiled. "I would love to. If you let me."

I smiled before pulling out my phone to look at the time. I had ten minutes to get to English.

"Walk me to class and I'll think it over." I offered, hopping off of the table and grabbing my bag.

Devon was quick to follow.

"So what you getting into after this class?" Devon questioned, resting his back against the brick siding of the building.

I slowed to a stop in front of him, studying his every feature.

I adjusted the strap of my book bag before shrugging, "I'm not too sure, probably just homework. You?"

"I gotta work, unfortunately. Maybe we can link tomorrow, you got classes?"

I nodded, "Yeah, from 10 a.m. – 3 p.m."

"Aw word? My last class lets out at 2:30 p.m. tomorrow. You wanna chill?"

My heart seemed to be caught in my throat. He wanted to hang out somewhere together outside of school? Already?

Devon chuckled, pulling me out of my mental crisis. "Why you look so surprised? You don't think I wanna hang with you or something?"

I shook my head, "No, it's not that."

"Then what is it? It don't gotta be major, just wanna get to know you a little better. See what you about and you can see what I'm about," he stared into my eyes, awaiting an answer.

I shifted my weight on one foot, "My last class is in the Jefferson building tomorrow. Meet me there after, and we'll take it from there?"

He smiled, pushing himself off the wall with his foot. "Cool. That means I still don't get your number then?"

I chuckled, turning my head to see Jesse heading our way with Phi by his side. They stopped a short distance away from us, bidding each other goodbye with a kiss.

"I have to get to class." I told Devon slyly, heading for the door.

He grinned, nodding. "Yeah aight. See you at 3 p.m. tomorrow, Kole." he replied, walking backwards. He and Jesse flashed each other a look before Devon turned on his heels and walked off.

Jesse met me at the door, pulling me in for a side hug. "Sup, shorty?"

"What's up?" I replied letting go of him and walking inside the building, Jesse on my heels.

"Nothing, trying to prepare my mind for this class. This teacher is weird," he breathed, referring to our English professor. He was super quirky and strange.

I raised my shoulders, heading towards the staircase. "Most writers are."

"Yeah, after dealing with you lately, I'd have to agree." He teased as I smacked his arm playfully.

"Hey," I began after a few beats. "You and Devon not cool or something? Ya'll gave each other an awkward look out there."

Jesse chuckled, following me up the steps. "It ain't that. We just never vibed well for real, our personalities don't mesh."

"Why is that?"

He shrugged, reaching the second floor with me. "You know how you just meet people and ya'll have nothing in common? That was always us. Plus, dude always wanted to compete with me like he had something to prove. I'm not really competitive; I like peace. So, we ain't click."

I nodded, processing the information while we entered the classroom. There were only a few other students in the room and our professor typically ran late. Jesse and I took our usual seats in the front.

"I'm hanging out with him tomorrow," I blurted, opening my bag to take out my book and notebook.

Jesse paused his movements, looking over at me. "With Devon? That's what y'all was talking about?"

I nodded. "You think I should?"

"Girl, you're grown, do what you want." He smirked, continuing to place his items for class on his desk.

"I know, but I'm asking for your opinion as a friend. Do you think I should?" I questioned again, staring at him patiently.

Jesse looked ahead for a moment like he was thinking it over before he smiled and glanced at me. "Yeah, I do."

I don't know why I was surprised by his answer. "Really?"

He chuckled, "Yes Nic, dang. What you think, I was gonna say no? I don't know dude enough to tell you it's a bad idea. Just go and feel him out for yourself. I'm sure after you hang with him you'll know if you wanna see him a second time."

I nodded slow, sitting back in my seat.

"You just like the man, that don't mean you gotta marry 'em," Jesse continued as my neck snapped in his direction.

"What? I don't like him!"

He grinned, "Yeah you do. You get this dorky smile on your face when you talk to him and ya eyes twinkle. You like him."

I rolled my eyes, watching our teacher waltzed through the door. "Whatever."

———————————

"So am I taking you home today?" Jesse asked as we exited the building after class.

I shook my head, "Nah, Sharon picking me up. Plus, I don't think Phi would like that too much."

His brows furrowed, "Huh? What you mean Phi wouldn't like it?"

I shrugged, "I don't know, Jes. I've been getting this vibe that she doesn't like sharing your time."

"But why would it matter when it comes to you though? You're my best friend."

My heart fluttered. He still considers me his best friend, even after all this time.

"I don't think she gets that yet. She hasn't even been talking to me as nice like she did the first day. Your girl wants your attention; it's cool. I'm not tryna step on any toes."

He scoffed, shaking his head. "She's going to have to learn to deal. I mean, I see where you're coming from but I've never given her a reason to be insecure. That's me. She knows that."

I stopped in my tracks once we reached the parking lot. "Well, she's not too sure right now. Go assure your lady. I'm cool, Sharon will be here."

He nodded, leaning in to give me a hug goodbye. "Whatever you say. Call me tomorrow after your little date and what not. I wanna know how it goes."

I snorted, "You're such a girl."

He rolled his eyes, preparing to walk off. "Shut up. You sure you don't want me to wait until she gets here?"

I shook my head, seeing Sharon's car pulling up in the distance. "Nah, she's here now actually. I'll hit you up."

He nodded, "Aight bet. Peace."

I watched Jesse disappear amongst the cars in the parking lot, before Sharon pulled up in her BMW. She didn't even look my way as she waited for me to get in.

It was still awkward between us, and this was the first time we had been forced to be in a closed space since the tension started.

I just hoped this didn't end badly.

"I gotta go in and do my homework, Nic," Jesse told me as we stood in his driveway. We spent all afternoon drawing different characters on the sidewalk with chalk.

I frowned, looking at the car in my driveway before looking back to my friend.

"Do you have to? Right now?"

He sighed before nodding, "Yeah, Im'a get in trouble if I don't. I can come over when I'm done if the streetlights aren't on yet."

"Aight Jes. I'll see you later."

"What's wrong, are you mad at me now?" he questioned sincerely, walking me down the driveway. Jesse always walked me home, even though he could just watch me from his house.

"No, It's not your fault. Just wasn't trying to go home yet."

"Is it because of Larry? Is he there?" he asked, the moment we reached my driveway.

"Yeah. He's here with my mommy."

"Why don't you just tell her that Larry is weird? Maybe she'll stop having him come over." He suggested as I shrugged.

"I'll try, but she really likes him. She doesn't care."

"Just talk to her, Nic." He urged, standing in front of my porch.

I turned to face him, doing our handshake before walking up towards the door. "I'll see you later."

"Ok, later." Jesse replied, defeated, turning to jog back towards his house.

I was about to step inside before the front door opened. Larry's tall, black and bald figure was the only one to appear.

He smirked.

"Sup, pretty girl." He greeted, standing right in front me.

I kept my head down, attempting to walk around him but he stepped to the side to stop me.

"What's the rush? You not happy to see me today, pretty girl?" He bent lower, attempting to come to eye level with me.

I was mute, afraid to speak. He made my skin crawl each time he was near.

"Ya momma told me that you a woman now but I don't believe her. Wanna know why?"

I was shaking, just wanting the moment to be over.

He leaned his lips closer to my ear. "You can't be a woman until I make you one."

I gasped before running past him and into the house, hearing Larry's laughter in the background.

"Mommy!" I screamed running down the hall, tears threatening to fall from my eyes.

She was slouched, barely conscious on the living room couch. Her eyes opened slightly to look at me.

I shook her, still shaking myself from the encounter with Larry. "Mommy, wake up!"

She snarled, smacking my hand away from pushing her any further. "Girl, what?! Stop shaking me and yelling like you crazy!"

I backed up a moment, attempting to catch my breath while watching her slowly sit up, rubbing her temples. "What is it, girl?"

I sucked in air before speaking. "Mommy I don't like Larry! He said-he said something outside about making me a woman! Please Mommy, please don't let him back here!" I begged, tears falling down my face as she gave me a crazy look.

She paused for a moment before laughing.

"Mom-mommy?" I questioned, shocked she was sitting here taking me for a joke.

She stopped laughing before finally looking back at me with an amused expression.

"Girl, are you crazy! What Larry gonna want with you when he got me? Why would you sit up here and tell that lie!"

I was shocked. "Wh-what? I'm not lying! I swear!"

Her face turned serious. "My man don't want you little girl! That's nasty! And there's no way he would ever talk to you like that! Ever! You don't even got nothing he want! He's getting it from me!"

My heart was breaking the more she talked to me like it was my fault.

Was it?

She shooed me off, "Go upstairs and do ya homework and get out my face! I can't even look at you right now, saying something sick like that," she spat, turning her head away.

I wanted to speak, but the words wouldn't come out.

I just turned my back, doing as she asked.

Maybe it was all in my head.

"Therapy." Sharon spoke in the silent car shortly after we had pulled off from the school, snapping me from my distasteful memory.

My brows furrowed before looking at her side profile. "What?"

She took in a deep breath, gripping the steering wheel. "You asked me what's different this time around and it's because after you left, I went to rehab and got some therapy. I got help."

I said nothing, continuing to stare, wondering what she was trying to say.

Her lips folded in before releasing a shaky breath. "After what happened to you Kole, I just … I couldn't accept the fact that I failed you. I failed you as a mother and protector."

She shook her head, "How could I, as your mother, allow a pedophile into my home and around my daughter and not listen to you when you tried to tell me about what was going on? I was that gone off a man that I left you wide open to get hurt by him. And did nothing to stop it. You know how bad that hurt me? Do you know how bad I was destroyed from that?"

She blinked, releasing a lone tear from her eye. "You wouldn't talk to me anymore. You couldn't bear to look at me and I couldn't even live with myself. It wasn't until I got some help, and got myself together did I find the power to forgive and find healing from it. I've grown from that experience and didn't allow it to ruin my life."

She quickly glanced at me before looking back at the road, "I don't want that for you. It's made you so bitter and I don't want that for you baby. I want you to find your healing and your peace. Maybe therapy – "

I scoffed, shaking my head. She was losing me. "How am I gonna make peace with that, Sharon? How am I gonna make peace with you? Talking to someone ain't gonna change the type of mother you were to me. It ain't gonna change what happened … "

"But it could change your perception. You don't have to view it so negatively."

"What good came from it Sharon, huh?! I'm not like you or Corey or even Jesse! I can't look at the bright side of shit, when it's really just messed up! It's all so messed up! And some fictional character is not gonna make me think otherwise! I don't believe I can be fixed, I don't believe I can change!" I bellowed, voice cracking.

I huffed, attempting to contain the anger that was boiling in the pit of my stomach. "I just want ya'll to just let me be, that's it. Let me keep finding my own way to some peace. I'm maintaining now and I'm trying to give all this a chance. Just let me – on my own time." I pleaded, not wanting to continue with the discussion any longer.

I was tired of people wanting something for me that I didn't even want for myself. I was just tired, period.

She nodded slowly, biting the inside of her lip to refrain from saying what she truly wanted to.

"If that's what you want, Kole, to just wallow in your brokenness, then fine. I won't stop you. Just know if you need me, I'm here."

I rolled my eyes, "Believe me. I won't ever need you."

———————————

"You're much cuter when you smile," Devon said, watching me stroll out of the building of my last class for the day.

He was right. I was wearing a scowl on my way out here, simply because I was still mad at the talk I had with Sharon.

She just doesn't get it. She doesn't get that this isn't something you can put a band-aid over and call it healed. I'm a person – I have feelings. And unfortunately, I'm hers.

It'll all work itself out in time, but for now, Devon was the perfect distraction.

I fixed my expression, putting on a genuine smile of relief for him.

"Much better. Hey, beautiful," he complimented, pulling me under his arm.

"Hi, Devon." I replied shyly, clutching onto the strap of my book bag.

"So you think it over today? You gonna give me a chance or what?" he asked, peering down into my eyes.

I pretended to debate, placing a finger to my chin. "Hmm ... "

He smacked his lips before groaning, "Come on. I'm a cool guy, I swear."

I giggled, rolling my eyes. "Finc, where are we going?"

He smiled widely, "You hungry?"

I shrugged, "I could eat."

"Cool, I know the perfect place."

"So you were born here?" Devon asked as he poured a pool of ketchup all over his fries.

We were sharing a booth at Dave and Busters. Devon thought this would be the perfect place to eat and then play games right after. I never really got into games much as an adult, but the idea sounded fun so I appreciated the effort.

I finally nodded to his question, using my fork to shuffle around the lettuce in my salad. "Yeah, I was. I moved a little upstate in middle school though."

His brow perked, "Really? What brought you back?"

I shrugged, not wanting to get too deep. "Just wanted a change of scenery, Greensboro got kinda tired."

He grinned "Well I, for one, am glad that you're back. Would've never met you if things had worked out differently."

I smirked, "And what makes you think crossing my path was a good thing?"

His eyes traveled up my frame until they met mine. "What makes you think it could potentially be bad? You're interesting, Kole."

"And the girls around here normally aren't?"

He grinned, licking his lips. "To be honest, girls around here don't make it too hard for me. Usually if a girl is feeling me, she makes herself known and it's up to me to take the bait or not."

"And you usually take the bait?"

He shrugged, wiping his hands of any crumbs. "If I'm bored, sure."

I took in his words, careful about my next question. "So what makes me different?"

He paused, staring at me for a moment. "You were just somebody I couldn't take my mind off of. I wanted to be the fisherman this time."

"Mm, so you pulled the bait out for me this time, think I'll take it?"

He smiled, sitting back in his seat. "You're nibbling thus far. We'll see."

I chuckled, allowing that conversation to float in the air before changing the topic. "What are you looking for? You know, from this?"

His eyes darted to mine. "What do you mean?"

"Like ... what do you want from me? What's the chase all about?"

He chuckled, "I just wanna get to know you Kole, that's all. If you think I'm after sex or whatever, that's not the aim. I just wanna get to know you and see where it goes. I don't have an agenda."

I accepted his answer, finally taking the initial bite of my salad.

"I got a question for you though," he blurted after a short moment of silence.

"What's up with you and that dude JP?"

My brows furrowed, waiting for him to explain.

"Like, do y'all talk or something? I mean I be seeing him hugged up with Phi, but every time I see you around I see him too."

I smirked, shaking my head. "Jesse is a friend of mine, nothing more."

He nodded, "Oh ok. I just ain't wanna start trouble if I started being around and stuff. Didn't want dude grilling me like I stole his girl or somethin."

I chuckled, "Nah. We're cool and Jesse isn't sweating it. I promise."

Devon seemed to relax a little more in his seat, as I eyed him.

"Is there anyone that you're talking to that I should steer clear of?" I questioned, just wanting to hear his reply.

"Nah, ain't nobody been on my radar until I took a seat next to a pretty girl at the block party," he said smoothly, causing me to blush.

Hearing that I'm pretty didn't sound so bad coming from his lips.

"Good."

"You in a rush to go home?" Devon questioned the minute both of us got comfortable in his car.

I shook my head, looking at the radio to see it was only 8 p.m.

He grinned. "Cool, I wanna show you my little spot," he said, starting the car as I became more relaxed in the seat.

"It's not real far from here, should be there in a few minutes." He explained pulling out of the Dave and Busters parking lot.

We had a good evening thus far, playing all of the games the restaurant had to offer. Devon is competitive, but it was all in good fun. He was surprised to see me beating him in the racing games and air hockey, pretending to be a sore loser.

It was fun. The most fun I had in a while without puking at the end.

Before long, Devon pulled up in a High School parking lot, in front of the football field entrance.

I looked puzzled once he put the car in park. "What are we doing at a school?"

He smirked, looking over at me. "How daring are you, Kole?"

My brows rose.

"You in the mood to walk on the wild side with me tonight?"

I was intrigued with what he meant so I nodded, causing him to smile wide.

"Cool! Come on."

He opened the car door and I was quick to do the same.

I followed him until we reached the large metal gate entry to the football and track field of the school.

"Look out for me, baby." Devon instructed as I cautiously scanned our surroundings.

"What am I looking out for?" I asked quietly, surveying the parking lot and the passing street.

"Cops." He said from what seemed like a higher altitude. I quickly turned my head to find Devon scaling the fence.

"Devon, what the hell?!" I whispered as harshly as I could, causing him to chuckle while continuing to climb the fence.

"This the only way I can get us in! Look out." He said again, as my heart rate picked up but I couldn't hide the large smile on my face.

This was scary, yet exciting.

I kept a close eye on our whereabouts while also trying to keep watch of him to make sure he didn't fall. He reached the top, and jumped down on the other side with ease.

He smiled triumphantly before fidgeting with the handle on the gate and opening it for me.

"Right this way, beautiful." He smirked, leaning against the door as I strolled through.

We sat at the very top of bleachers underneath the moonlit sky.

"This is one of my favorite spots to be. I swear I can see the sky so clear from up here." He explained, taking his jacket off and wrapping it around my shoulders.

"You used to go here?" I questioned, shrugging the jacket on for more coverage. I was appreciative of his gesture.

He nodded shortly, "Yeah, this was my school. And this used to be the field I owned."

"You played sports?"

"Yeah, I was a running back. Got a full ride to Duke and everything."

"Really? What happened?"

He chuckled lightly, looking down below at nothing particular. "Everything was cool until I tore my ACL my sophomore year. Cost me my scholarship and my relationship with my father."

My eyes widened, "How is that? With your dad I mean ... "

He shrugged, "All he cared about was the game. He stayed on me hard, wanting me to go pro. I did it to make him proud, you know? And even after I tore my ACL, he wanted me to get healed up and go at it again, but I chose not to."

"Why?" I asked softly, sensing the sensitivity of this topic.

"To be honest, I was afraid. Getting an injury like that really messes up the way you view the sport. You start seeing the injury before it even happens. Not to mention, it makes you more likely to re-injure or even your other leg. I refused to give it another shot, and he couldn't forgive me for that. He went so far to calling me a coward."

I was taken back by the confession, not thinking that Devon would have a life-changing story. It saddened me that he was too afraid to conquer his fears, yet it was comforting how relatable he was. It made me realize we weren't so different.

"So," he breathed after a short pause. "I decided to come back home and just get a job and enrolled at the college. At least finish my education. Most kids on campus just remember the man I used to be, that's why I got clout. I ain't that dude anymore though."

He continued, "This field is real special to me. Every little problem that bothered me, I took it out here, on that field. Hell, I even slept here some nights when it was warm enough to."

My eyes widened, "Seriously?"

He grinned, "Yeah. My parents used to argue a lot. My little sisters could sleep through it but not me. I would just hope they would break up one day. Save us all the heartache of watching them be so unhappy."

"You would never assume that's your story by looking at you. You always seem to have everything so well put together, and happy." I said, looking down below at the empty field.

It really was calm out here.

"Never judge a book by its cover, Kole. You never know what kinda pain lies behind someone's smile." Devon said, leaning back to rest his elbows on the bleachers behind him.

"I like you." He blurted. My head snapped to look at him.

"I never really open up with females but with you it's different. Comes natural."

I chuckled, shaking my head, "I don't feel like I did anything special …"

"You don't have to, you just are." He sat up to scoot closer to me.

I felt the goose bumps that I had been feeling all night return; the closer his lips inched towards mine.

This was it. We were about to share our first kiss and I quickly began to regret having Italian dressing on that salad from earlier.

Devon gently placed his fingers underneath my chin, slowly bringing my face towards his ...

"Hey!" A strong voice bellowed from down below, causing both of our faces to turn from each other.

There looked to be an overweight elderly security guard standing in the middle of the field, holding a flashlight, looking directly at us.

"Hey! What are you doing up there?!" He yelled again, realizing he had our attention.

Devon had a wild, yet excited look on his face before grabbing my hand. "Hope you can run, Kole!"

"Wait," I started before being pulled up to my feet. "What!"

"Hey! Get down here!"

He laughed, looking back at me as we ran towards the opening we had walked through to get up there. "Run girl! Or we getting caught!"

He seemed thrilled about this entire ordeal, causing all of the fear of getting caught to leave.

Devon was exciting, that was for sure.

And excitement is just the thing I need right now.

———————————

"You're so corny for having that goofy smile on ya face all day, man." Jesse teased, snapping me out of the daze I'd been in all morning.

I was still reeling in excitement from my date yesterday with Devon. It was the most carefree I had felt in years it seemed and I was glad he was the one to grant me that happiness. It's like he could sense my need for adventure buried deep and he pulled it out of me with ease. Everything seemed much easier with him.

I looked at Jesse impassively as he sat next to me, jotting notes from his textbook. Our professor had finished his lecture a few minutes ago and gave us the rest of the time to get started on our weekly essay assignments and to ask questions if needed.

"Whatever." I huffed, feigning annoyance while opening up my own textbook.

"It went that good yesterday, huh? You never hit me up," he said with a playful smirk at his lips.

I nodded, "It was a lot of fun and he's cool so far. No complaints."

He hummed a response before flipping a page in his book. "That's good. I'm glad to see you smiling again, Nic. That scowl was annoying."

I stared at his side profile, making note of the freckles scattered upon the bridge of his nose and cheeks. "No warning this time about guarding myself and what not?"

He chuckled with a shake of his head. "You're a big girl, like you said. I gotta give you room to find ya own way and discover people how you see fit. How I personally feel is irrelevant, to be honest."

I took in his words, happy that was someone's answer for once. Jesse understood, I needed to do this my way or it wouldn't be genuine.

"He thought you and I had something going." I confessed, watching him grin at the revelation.

"I don't think you and I give that kind of impression. Plus, he knows I'm with Phi. That was made known months ago."

I raised a brow, "Why you think that?"

"Because, he was trying to get at her right before me and her made things official. She chose to be with me and he ain't like that too much." Jesse explained as my eyes widened.

"Really? Why didn't you tell me this the other day?"

He shrugged, "Because it wasn't important and still isn't now. I mean, that wasn't the initial reason I ain't rock with the dude and I really never let the thing with Phi get to me. It wasn't that big of a deal. We both liked her; she just wanted to be with me more than him I guess."

I decided to let the initial conversation drown out, not wanting it to change how I felt about Devon. He didn't seem to be too phased by the situation anymore either. "How are things with you and her now? Did you talk to her?"

He nodded quickly, running his tongue over his lips. "Yeah, we talked. She's good now. She admitted that she was getting a little jealous of our relationship, but now she says she gets it and apologized if she came off rude or whatever."

I sighed, "Good. I've had drama in the past when it came to girls and their men and I just don't want those kinds of problems now."

Jesse perked a brow up at me, "Word?" He shook his head, looking back to his book. "I swear man, layers."

I chuckled at the way he said it. "And you still have yet to explain what that means."

"Means you got a lot of depth; a lot of layers to who you are and what made you that way. I just be wanting to peel 'em all back at once to discover what I'm dealing with. But you reveal something more each day. It's kinda dope though because I'm patient."

I nodded slow, understanding what he was saying. "What if – what if you peel back all the layers, and don't like what you see?" I questioned softly, afraid of the answer.

Jesse's opinion was the one that always mattered most.

"Nah," he responded shortly. "I'm sure I'll love what I find, because it's you entirely. Now whether or not *you* like what you find is the real question."

I bit my lip in uncertainty, "I don't think I will."

"Welp, it's good that there's such a thing called change. Whatever you don't like about yourself is fixable, Nic. It's just up to you whether or not you want it bad enough."

"You sure you don't mind taking me home today?" I asked Jesse, realizing our class time was preparing to end within the next 10 minutes.

He nodded quickly, reading over the text in his book. "Yeah sure, Ms. Sharon gotta work or something?"

I sighed, shaking my head. "No, it's not that. We're just not on the best of terms right now."

His head quickly turned in my direction. "Huh? What for?"

I grunted, "She just doesn't get it, Jes. She thinks everything is gonna be all peachy just because she brought me home and fake apologized for being a shitty parent."

"So you've been being foul to her?" He questioned, waiting patiently for an answer, an unreadable look on his face. Disappointment maybe?

"Not foul," I defended. "Just ... I'm not in a place to act like she's my mother."

"But she is your mother. Even with all her imperfections she's your mom, Dominic."

I rolled my eyes, "You don't get it. She's at peace now with everything that happened, but what she doesn't get is that none of this happened to her. It happened to me."

"So, what? You ain't think she wasn't affected too? Like she wasn't hurt she lost her daughter, her only child? You really be thinking you ain't mean nothing to her and that's not fair, not fair to her."

I scoffed bitterly, "So we're not gonna talk about what wasn't fair to me?"

"I'm not saying it was fair to you either but she got something that you so desperately need right now. She got closure and she's trying to make it right. You just can't let go."

"I- I just can't forgive her right now, Jesse. I won't." I answered quietly, feeling the familiar pang of hurt in my chest.

He smacked his lips, sitting up straight in his seat to give me his full attention. "When are you gonna realize that forgiveness ain't about the other person? The only person you hurting in this is you. Not forgiving someone is like you drinking poison, but you waiting someone else to die."

My brows furrowed, "What you mean?"

"You think anybody that's hurt you in the past still thinking about that time they hurt you? I'm sorry to say it to you like this baby, but they're not. They're out there living their life, just like Sharon began to live hers. She forgave herself and got her peace and even found happiness with a good man. Yeah, I'm sure she's hurt that you're still upset with her, but believe me, it ain't hurting her like it's hurting you and that's real."

He sat back in his seat at my silence. "Everybody gets their karma for what they do, Nic. Good and bad, it comes back around but that ain't for you to worry about. Seeing them hurt won't give you any restitution cause' you're still gonna be hurting. And honestly, right now, you're choosing to. It's not a good look, for anybody." He finished, just as our professor dismissed us for the day.

I quietly began putting my items in my book bag, taking in everything Jesse said.

I hated how he was always right. I just couldn't pull myself out of it. It always sounded so easy coming from his lips, but so hard to do in my heart.

I watched my feet, following Jesse out of the building. The sun warming my face caused me to look up once we exited the doors, surprised to see Devon standing in the walkway with his hands in his pockets.

He smiled softly when his eyes landed on me, stepping forward. "Sup, Kole."

Jesse stood not too far away, texting on his phone. I pulled my eyes from him and back onto my handsome surprise.

This was my first time seeing him today.

Devon walked up, wrapping both of his arms around my short frame, engulfing me in his comforting scent.

"Hey, baby," Devon greeted a little softer, peering down at me. "Mind if I take you home today?" he questioned as I peeked past him at Jesse.

I looked back to Devon before nodding my head. "I would love to. Give me a sec, okay?"

He nodded shortly, taking a step back. I swiftly left his presence to approach my friend.

"Hey, Dev is gonna give me a ride home," I said. He squinted at me before looking over my head at Devon.

After a short moment he finally nodded, "Ok be safe, bum," he replied using a teasing nickname he gave me when we were kids.

I leaned in to give Jesse a hug goodbye before happily turning to walk back to Devon.

"All set?" he asked, watching Jesse's retreating figure.

"Yes, so ready to get out of here and I have too much homework to do." I sighed just as Devon draped his long arm over my shoulder.

"Coo, let's do it together?" he suggested smoothly, causing my grin to spread wider if it were at all possible.

"Sounds like a plan."

Devon and I sat on the front porch with books and papers in our lap. Sharon and Corey weren't home from work yet, and I figured it would be rude to have someone in the house they had never met without them being here.

Devon didn't mind though. He enjoyed doing his homework unorthodox like we were.

"Yo, that was too funny watching that fat ass chasing us last night, man." He laughed, placing his fist to his mouth. We spent most of our time together reminiscing about our outing yesterday.

I chuckled, shaking my head. "I can't believe he actually thought he was going to catch us. That's the funny part."

He grinned widely, "Man, my bad about that. I forgot they got security scoping the place some nights ever since the field got vandalized during a senior prank."

"Nah, it was fun. Definitely a night I'll never forget." I replied calmly, reading over a chapter from my sociology book.

Devon looked around, "So where ya folks at? You sure they gonna like my black ass? I ain't never been good with parents." He said nervously, rubbing his neck.

I giggled, "I wouldn't care if they liked you or not."

"Really? Isn't that like a big deal for girls; what their Mom and Dad think?"

I shrugged, "I wouldn't know. I never met my dad and I could give a damn how my mom feels about anything."

His eyes widened, "What, Mommy issues? Would've never guessed. I mean ... I guessed you probably been through something cause everybody got a story, but usually mom's don't mess up as bad as dads do."

I scoffed, "You haven't met my mom."

"Aye, I'm sure whatever reason you got to be mad at her is legitimate," he said simply, looking back down at his book, tapping his pencil against the page.

"How do you feel about grudges, Dev?" I questioned, wanting to see how his response differed from Jesse's.

He smirked, never taking his eyes off the page he was reading. "I hold 'em. The way I see it, if you hurt me, you don't deserve my forgiveness. You took me for weak once, won't take me that way again. I assure you that."

"So you get revenge?"

He chuckled softly, looking me in my eyes now, "Baby, I get even. Then maybe after that, I'll let it go but nine times out of ten, I feel a lot better knowing you're hurting like me. I feel like that's how it should be. All that letting it go, and letting life deal with it stuff they try to tell you about is bull."

I sighed with a bitter smirk, "That's how I feel sometimes."

"Ain't nothing wrong with it, Kole. I personally think it's healthy. I've been feeling that way my whole life and ain't nothing wrong with me, I'm happy. If people can hold grudges against my ass and keep living then I can do the same," he said, looking back down at his book.

I stared at him for a moment, watching his eyes reveal the small tinge of sadness before it disappeared. I saw a car pull up out of the corner of my eye – Corey was home.

He walked up to the porch with a confused yet amused look on his face. He smiled softly at me first.

"Hi, baby girl," he greeted gently, the kindness only Corey possessed. I couldn't help but feel warm in his presence.

"Hi, Corey."

He looked down at Devon next, putting his fist out to him. "What's up, man?"

Devon smirked, bumping his fist. "What's up bro- dude- sir," he stuttered awkwardly causing Corey and I to chuckle in response.

"Devon this is my stepfather, Corey." I shared with a sense of pride.

I never referred to anyone in my life as a paternal figure but it felt good and it felt right since it was someone like Corey I was referring to.

"Aw shit, I mean shoot!" Devon hissed, standing to his feet, dusting himself off and sticking out his hand.

"I'm sorry sir, I didn't know. I'm Devon, Kole's friend," he said, shaking Corey's hand firmly.

Corey grinned before looking over at me, "You didn't tell him I was white?!" he asked, feigning shock and disappointment. "You racist or something kid?"

"Uh-" Devon shifted uncomfortably between the two of us, not sure what to say to my stepfather's teasing.

I chuckled, shaking my head. "I didn't think it mattered and he's not racist!"

"I swear I'm not sir!" Devon defended, raising his hands as Corey and I both laughed at his expense.

Corey was hilarious.

Devon began gathering his books and notepad, shoving them in his bag while Corey and I watched his sudden movements.

"Well, Im'a get going Kole. I gotta finish the rest of this work, call me aight?" he said softly, avoiding Corey's stare as he put his book bag on his back.

I nodded in response, giving a wave. "I'll hit you later," I replied watching him walk down the steps.

"It was nice meeting you sir," Devon said, bowing slightly in Corey's direction, earning a laugh from him.

"See ya later, man." Corey said to his back, grinning before coming to take a seat on one of the porch chairs.

"So, Devon, huh?" he asked, tipping a brow at me.

I blushed, "He's my friend."

"Mm hmm," he hummed playfully, getting more comfortable in his chair.

"So how's it going kiddo?" Corey asked after a peaceful moment of silence. "You liking school?"

I nodded, pointing down to the book in my lap. "Tackling homework now."

"Good, you look good – a bit happier," he commented, looking me over carefully.

I released a soft sigh, "I'm adjusting, Corey. It gets a little easier each day."

"Yeah me and ya mom were talking-"

I cut him off quickly, putting my hand up. "I really don't want to talk about the conversation Sharon and I had … "

Corey flashed me a strange look, "Who was going to talk about that? I heard about it, but that's not what I'm here to talk about."

My face fell, "Oh."

He chuckled, "Yeah, we were talking about letting you redecorate your room. You can change it up exactly how you like. Paint it a different color – just make it more … you."

I smirked, "Whoever that is."

He shrugged, "Whoever that is. You just need a change and although you can't change your location at the moment, you can at least change your room."

My heart warmed at the thought; changing my room may be just what I need to stomach being in there better.

"You can have your friends come over and help you. Jesse and maybe the girl you went out with on Saturday, whoever you want. I'll give you my credit card and you can buy all of the materials you need."

I thought it over. Lucy doesn't seem like the type that would even enjoy redecorating and I liked the way Jesse's apartment was laid.

"Thank you, Corey. I appreciate this."

He smiled, looking softly over at me. "Anything you need, baby girl."

"Ain't this what Lucy or ya mom 'sposed to help you do?" Jesse whined, pushing the shopping kart behind me as we walked through Lowe's. "This feels soft."

I snorted, rolling my eyes while I continued to look over the different cans of paint. "I wanted to do this with you."

He huffed behind me, "Yeah? Well this is not how I pictured my Saturday, bum."

I looked over my shoulder impassively, "What else did you have to do?"

One of his arms flapped in the air dramatically, "Not this! When you called me over to chill, I thought that's what we were doing. I ain't think I was gon' have to work."

I rolled my eyes, looking over the paint, gravitating towards a burnt orange color.

"No." Jesse said flatly as I looked over the card that a sample of the color rested on.

My eyes snapped to his, "What? Why not?"

He fanned me off, "You gonna have a headache waking up to that color every day. What's ya favorite color?"

I pondered for a moment, "Black."

He crossed his eyes with an annoyed smirk, "Figures. What was ya favorite color when you were still Dominic?" he cracked, causing me to chuckle.

I thought it over, "Hmm. I dunno, probably something pretty and soft like yellow."

He walked over in front of the array of colors, looking them over. "Well, I agree. You should go brighter. It'll keep ya mood light when you're in there."

I agreed, my eyes dancing over each option. They widened when they reached a particular color and I picked up the card. "What about this? Another favorite, olive green."

Jesse looked it over, turning his nose up slightly. "Like dookie?"

I couldn't hide my amusement, shaking my head. "Man, what?!"

He snatched the card out of my grasp, looking it over. "This is the color of dookie, bruh."

I giggled at his juvenile choice of language, taking the card back. "Its olive green, dumb dumb and I like it! It will make my room look like a forest or something. I can make the drapes a nice shade of brown or tan and get a new comforter set to match."

He chuckled, shaking his head, watching me put a couple cans of paint in the cart. "You're so weird Nic, I swear. Witcha room looking like boo-boo."

I snickered, ignoring his displeasure.

I watched from the hallway, chomping on an apple as Corey and Jesse carried the last of the furniture from my room into the guest room to store it while Jesse and I painted. I watched Jesse carefully, his face red and chest heaving desperately for air.

"You ok, Jes?" I questioned, eying him as he came out of the room breathless and coughing. Corey walked out shortly after tapping Jesse before he headed towards the stairs.

"I'm gonna order us a pizza, guys. I'll let you know when it gets here," he told us before disappearing down the steps.

I looked back to Jesse, watching him catch his breath while digging in his pockets. An inhaler appeared, gripped in his fingers and he took a couple puffs from it before placing a hand on his chest.

My eyes widened, "You have asthma?" I asked, not remembering him ever having it as a child. All we used to do was run and play.

He shook his head quickly, wiping his reddened eyes. "Nah, not exactly. Just have trouble catching my breath sometimes," he explained, shaking it off and walking into my empty room.

I followed him slowly, taking another small bite of my apple. "Why? Is something wrong– "

He cut me short, smiling wide. "I'm good, Nic, I promise. I'm just like an obese man on the inside sometimes. I just lose my breath – been like that for a while. I just overworked myself, I'm alright though."

He tried to keep his voice steady and calm to not worry me, but it didn't keep me from being curious. I wouldn't push it for now, I was enjoying his company too much and I could tell the questions were bothering him.

"Let's lay out this plastic so we can start making ya room look like diarrhea," he grumbled, grabbing the roll of plastic on the floor.

I scoffed, taking another bite of my snack. "Hater."

"How you and ya boy been lately?" Jesse asked casually, pouring paint into an aluminum container.

I smiled, "Good. We talk just about every day, he's cool."

He took a peek at me before chuckling to himself. "Over there, blushing. It's cute."

I sat back against the wall, watching Jesse grab a roller to dip in his freshly poured paint. I ensured all the windows were open just to make sure he could breathe okay even if he downplayed his shortness of breath.

"Is it ... weird, seeing me in that light now? Watching me date and stuff?"

He shook his head, "Not really. You're a woman now, so I wouldn't expect anything less."

I nodded, "Did you ever think you were going to see me again?"

He stopped mid roll, before he continued. "Yeah."

My eyes widened, "Really?! How'd you think that?"

He shrugged, "I just knew the last time I saw you then, wasn't going to be the last time ever. Eventually we were gonna cross paths again, plus ya mom was still across the street. There was always a chance."

I just loved the way Jesse talked. His voice was smooth as velvet, with a raspy twang. He didn't seem to put too much thought into what he had to say, he just always had the right words.

He looked over his shoulder at me as I was in a crouched position on the floor, "You gone help me paint this room or nah?!"

I giggled, standing to my feet and grabbing a roller. I dipped it in the paint before joining Jesse at the wall.

"I think it's really cool Corey and Sharon suggested that you did this," he breathed, stretching his long arm up and down.

"Yeah," I agreed. "It really is. I couldn't thank them enough when they gave me the credit card this morning."

"You have good parents, Nic," he stated, bending down to fill his roller with more paint.

"H-how are your parents?" I asked.

He chuckled, "Trying to stay together, I guess. I don't know, honestly. I only come to help around the house."

"What happened to them?"

"They just couldn't find the reason why they loved each other anymore, I assume. They were only really together initially 'cause of me anyway. Pops used to mess around back then, you know that. So, they never really got past it."

"Why stay together then?"

Jesse huffed. "I used to ask the same question when I cared. They're like roommates, miserable roommates. Pops ain't never there. That's why I started coming around more after I moved out. I had to get out of there though, the energy was toxic."

He paused for a moment before continuing, "That's why it's refreshing to see Corey and Sharon sometimes. That dude really loves ya mom – he adores her. I ain't never seen that before."

I bumped his shoulder with my own, "You adore Phi."

"I mean yeah but in a "you're cute and you're my girl," type of way. The way Corey looks at Sharon though? He has that undying love for her, like he would give her the world on a platter if he could. Ain't no way I look at Phi like that."

"You think we'll ever feel that?" I asked innocently as Jesse smiled looking down at me.

"F-for someone we care about one day?"

His light brown eyes looked into mine for what seemed like an eternity before he pulled away, licking his lips, focusing on the task at hand.

"Sure, one day."

CHAPTER
- FIVE -

It was a lazy Monday afternoon after classes had finished up and I stayed around with Lucy, not in any rush to head home.

We were sitting at a picnic table on campus, enjoying the warm weather while getting ahead on homework for the next day. Jesse wasn't too far away from us, hanging out with Phi and their friends and Devon was still in his last class of the day.

"You and Devon have sex yet?" Lucy blurted randomly, never looking up from her assignment.

"What?! We've only known each other a week!"

She looked up at me questionably. "Wait, so this is serious? Not a hook up?"

I gave her a duh look, "Um, would think. I mean, I think it's more than just sex. I hope ... "

She nodded, "Oh ok. You didn't catch me as the relationship type Kole, my bad."

I raised a brow, "I didn't?"

She shook her head, "Nah, you're just real chill. Doesn't seem like you get connected to people too much. You ever have a boyfriend?"

I shifted in my seat before looking down at a random word in my textbook, "Yeah, kinda."

She snorted. "What's kinda?"

"I thought he was my boyfriend but it just wasn't that."

"Then what was it?"

I scoffed bitterly, "A mistake."

"I'm heading to work Maw Maw! I'll be home later!" I yelled to the top of the stairs while shoving on my shoes.

I could hear my grandmother shuffling up above me on the second floor of our duplex. "Ok, baby! You don't need a ride?!"

I shook my head like she could see me, "Nah, I'm good. I get off at 11 though. Pick me up then, okay?!"

"Ok honey, I'll be there. Have a good shift." I could faintly hear her and rushed out the door.

I locked up behind me before stepping off the porch and began my daily trek to work. This had become routine since I graduated high school a year ago. I refused to go to college and found a job at the McDonalds a few blocks from my house. It wasn't much, but it bought me better clothes than Maw Maw could afford and kept me busy since I didn't have much of a life outside of home.

Don't get me wrong, I enjoyed my grandmother but she was literally all I had. I desperately wanted more. I needed more.

At least back at hell ... I mean home, I had Jesse. I wonder what he was up to these days? If I had social networks I would try to find him but I'm sure he's forgotten all about me by now and I definitely wouldn't be somebody he would want to find him. Our distance was probably all for the best. I was sure of it after what happened all those years ago –

"You too cute to be walking, girl."

I heard a voice call from a car as it slowed down to my pace.

I ignored it, feeling my heart race. There were always random men trying to holla at me on my walk to work and it made me uncomfortable each and every time. I don't know what they even wanted me for. I was damaged goods.

"Aw, come on sweetheart, don't play me like that," the voice said as I quickly glanced to my left to see his face.

I wish I hadn't because he was too damn fine to be talking to me.

I turned my head, his chocolate skin and perfect smile imbedded in my memory just that quick.

"Yeah, you see me, baby!" he shouted cockily as I rolled my eyes. Now I'm annoyed.

"Can't you see I don't want to talk to you?!" I snapped, looking at the handsome stranger's face again, already wishing I hadn't because of how much I was drawn to it.

He smirked, licking his lips.

"Nah you wanna talk to me. Where you headed, to work?"

I rolled my eyes. Of course he can see I'm wearing a McDonald's uniform. Why is he playin?

"If you rolled with me baby, you'd never have to work another day in your life – believe that. I wouldn't have your pretty ass out here walking neither! Melting and shit!" He taunted with a confidence I couldn't ignore.

I could see my job appearing in the distance, still not bothering to address the stranger.

"Aye, you keep ignoring me, Im'a roll up in there and order 30 McChickens. Think I'm playin!" he clowned, causing me to finally crack a smile.

I looked over at him, still driving the car slowly to keep up with my pace. His smile was wider than before, now.

"What you want, man?" I asked, annoyance heavy in my tone.

"To be yours. Take my number!"

I blushed in embarrassment. "I don't have a phone."

He pulled his car to the side, placing it in park before getting out.

I froze in nerves, watching as he walked towards me in long cool strides. He was even more handsome up close.

He dug in his pocket before pulling out a cellphone and handed it to me.

"Here, now you do," he said smoothly, before gently grabbing my wrist to place the device in my palm.

His eyes scanned my nametag quickly before he began to back up. "I'll call you later, Kole."

He turned, heading back to his car and pulled off without another word while I looked at my new cell phone in shock.

"Damn."

———————————

"Sup ya'll." Jesse's smooth greeting snapped me out of my memory and I looked up to him and Phi with thankful eyes.

"Hey, guys," I smiled, actually happy to have some more company.

Jesse set his book bag down on the table before taking a seat next to me, Phi on the other side of him. I looked across at Lucy who was eying Phi with an amused grin.

This should be interesting, or at least entertaining.

"Sup, Lu?" Jesse asked with a grin, catching the looks Lucy was giving his girlfriend.

"Hi, Jesse baby, how you?" she responded with obvious flirtation.

My eyes darted to Phi who was staring impassively back at my friend.

"I'm good, just chillin for real." Jesse smiled, looking down at me and bumping my shoulder. I giggled, keeping my eyes on my work and not this awkward bubble Jesse's presence had created.

"Hey, Kole. Hi, Lucy." Phi greeted politely as Lucy's eyes went into thin slits.

She cleared her throat, looking up at Phi with a devious smirk. "Sup, Ming Ming, how are you on this lovely Monday?"

I tucked my lips in to avoid the chuckle that wanted to escape as Phi scoffed in response before rolling her eyes.

"Wow, how racist of you."

"You shouldn't expect anything less from me at this point." Lucy shrugged calmly, flipping a page in her book.

Jesse chuckled before speaking, "Aye ya'll chill. Can't we all just do our work in peace?" he said trying to be the mediator between the two catty women.

Phi kissed her teeth, "I don't know why you even suggested for us to come over here. You know that girl is just jealous!" she barked, as Lucy's eyes snapped to hers.

"Jealous of what, the chest or the ass that you don't have? Girl, bye." Lucy replied, flipping her wild blonde hair.

"Lucy!" Jesse called sternly, attempting to get her to calm down.

For her to be Puerto Rican and White, she had a lot of sass about her nature. It was always fun to witness.

"Stop it, you know you like Jesse!" Phi bit, ignoring Jesse's mediation. "It's the only reason there's an issue!"

Lucy crossed her eyes, brushing her off. "Stop talking to me, Ming. I'll call you when I need my nails done. Until then, we have nothing to discuss."

Jesse frowned, looking at Lucy, not at all fazed by the behavior in front of him. "Lucy, knock it off. You do this every time we come around."

She shrugged, "Well, learn to start speaking to me by yourself."

"Learn to be respectful," he stated firmly, a serious expression on his face now. Lucy looked up at Jesse, noting the tone before glancing over at Phi.

"Sorry," she mumbled before looking back to her work.

"Yeah, whatever. Don't worry about it," Phi responded, finally putting her book and laptop on the table.

I looked at Jesse surprised yet impressed. He gave a wink. I guess he knew how to keep the girls in check. He's grown up for sure.

Things calmed down between the two ladies the more we concentrated on our work and shared small talk with one another.

Phi lightened up and actually shared quite a few laughs with the three of us. This was something I never shared back in Greensboro. I was never surrounded by groups of people like this that actually enjoyed and wanted my company. I was treated like such an outcast at my old schools and after graduation, the only friend I thought I had was my boyfriend ...

"So I've been around you every day for the last month and still don't know your name, yet you know mine and everything about me. Why is that?" I questioned as we sat in an Applebee's booth before my shift.

He smirked, resting his arms at the top of the booth, looking me over. "I told you what to call me, girl. Call me Daddy."

I rolled my eyes, picking at my fries. "I ain't never called no man daddy in my life. Definitely not starting now, tell me your name."

"Come stay with me, and let me take care of you ... then I'll tell you my name."

I didn't know much more about the handsome stranger than I did a month ago, except the basics but I knew he had money and plenty of it. Every day he would take me to and from work. He would always have a gift and a little bit of money waiting for me. Such things typically didn't move me; at least I thought they didn't until he started presenting them to me on the regulur.

I had never known anything like what he was beginning to show me. I had never been pursued or chased by a man before. I had only seen it in movies or for the popular girls at school. This must be what it felt like, and it felt good – really good.

"Tell me first," I said quietly, looking down.

I felt his warm fingers touch my chin to lift my head up.

"None of that with me. You keep ya head up, baby. You're too beautiful to hide that face."

I looked into his soft brown eyes, trying to picture my future with him. I was so infatuated by his being; I truly never wanted to leave his company. He was the only one that made life not seem as bad as it has been anymore. He made me feel beautiful and like a woman. He was my escape. So I figured, why not have that escape every day?

"Tell me your name," I urged again, never taking my eyes off his.

He smirked, "You know what you gotta do if I tell you, right?"

I nodded, already prepared for the lecture from Maw Maw I was bound to receive once I told her I found somewhere else to live.

"Terrance. But trust me, after ya first night with me, Daddy will suit just fine."

———————

"Get out ya head," Jesse said quiet enough for only me to hear to snap me out of it.

I furrowed my brows, "Huh?"

He chuckled, jotting some notes down in his notebook. "Get out ya head. You zone out sometimes and I think you get lost in there. You used to do it a lot when we were kids."

I smirked before shaking my head and looking back into my book. "You remember so much about me."

He shrugged, "You don't make it hard. A lot of things about you are still the same."

"You think?"

He nodded softly, "I know."

We smiled softly at each other before my name being called caused both of us to look in search of who was speaking.

I saw Devon not too far away, motioning for me to come talk to him. My smile widened at the sight of his face before I hopped up from my seat.

"Be right back," I said to Jesse before removing myself from the table.

I strolled with happiness but once I got to Devon, his expression however, wasn't as pleasant. He kept his eyes trained hard on the table I had just left from. I walked up, wrapping my arms around him. He finally looked down at me, face growing softer and kissed me sweetly on my forehead.

"Hey, gorgeous," he greeted, causing me to blush.

"Hi. How was class?" I asked, receiving one last peck on my forehead before removing my arms.

He shrugged, "Long and boring like always." Devon motioned his head towards the table. "What's going on over there?"

I smirked, "Awkward study group, come join us," I suggested, grabbing his hand to pull him towards the table but his body didn't budge. Instead he used our conjoined hands to pull me back towards him abruptly.

"Just come study with me. I don't want to go over there and I want you with me now."

I could hear the pleading in his voice as I looked back to my table of friends.

Lucy and Phi were still busy with their work but Jesse was looking back at Devon and I. When I caught his stare, he looked back down at his book calmly.

I bit the inside of my cheek, not really wanting to leave them just yet, before looking back to Devon. "Let me go get my stuff, ok?"

He nodded, letting me go as I turned and headed back to the table. I began to gather my belongings, getting a confused look from Lucy.

"Yo, where you going? I thought I was taking you home," she asked, garnering the attention of both Jesse and Phi.

"Devon's out of class now, I'm about to go do some homework with him."

She scoffed before rolling her eyes, "Damn. Ya'll ain't even had sex yet and he already got you dropping the world for him? I ain't mad, just text me and let me know if you still need a ride, if you get a minute to breathe from Devon's suffocating grip on your free will."

I rolled my eyes at her rudeness in before stuffing the last book in my bag.

"I'm sure he'll take me home, it's cool."

I noticed the couple began tending back to their studies. I don't know why, but I was expecting some type of reaction from Jesse like him telling me I should just stay with them or something, but he didn't seem to care if I left or stayed.

For some reason, as I walked further away from them, it bothered me more and more.

Tiffany Campbell

"Midterms are ruining my life!" Lucy groaned, letting her head fall on her kitchen table. I began to laugh.

We were four weeks into our spring semester and midterms were coming up within the next week. She and I were in her house that she shared with her sister and mother. Thursday night, we studied after our classes. Lucy and I had grown a bit closer since we first met. We had fun together and we always made casual conversation. She was rough around the edges and had her moments where she irked my nerves, but I liked her as a friend. I never got too deep with her and she never got that deep with me either but our trust in one another was slowly building.

"It's not that bad if you make note cards," I said as I completed my Sociology study guide.

She rolled her eyes. "Yeah, I'm not doing that. I barely have the patience to look over these weekly quizzes. This came too fast."

I listened to her groaning before watching her stand to her feet and walk to the kitchen. She reached in one of her cupboards and pulled out a large bottle.

"Want some tequila? It gets your brain flowing, helps you memorize the stuff better," she grinned, placing the bottle on the counter and removed two cups.

I frowned knowingly at her, "That's not true."

She kissed her teeth, "So ... it sounds good, right? Come on, we don't have classes tomorrow and a little turn up never hurt nobody."

She poured me a glass of tequila anyway while mixing both of the drinks with lemonade. She carefully brought both of the cups over to the kitchen table, placing one in front me.

"Ghetto margarita, drink up!" she said excitedly, holding her glass in the air. I chuckled, clinking my glass with hers before taking a sip.

"Hey, watch how you drink that this time. We don't need another one of your episodes," Lucy warned after taking a sip of her liquor.

I rolled my eyes, taking another small sip and placing the glass down.

"I'm shocked you're even chilling with me tonight. Lately all of your nights have been filled up with De-von," Lucy teased.

She wasn't very fond of my relationship Devon anymore and I had yet to truly understand why.

"Well I like spending time with him. Devon gets me."

She scoffed, "Ha! That's what you believe?"

My nose turned up, "What's that supposed to mean?"

She chuckled, shaking her head. "That boy just telling you whatever he needs to get in your pants and keep you controlled."

I shook my head, "Not true. Devon doesn't try to control me. I know what real control is and how people get … "

My mind drifted to Terrance before Lucy spoke up.

"Yeah? Well what about manipulation, do you know when people do that?"

My mouth dropped in offense, "Devon is not manipulating me!"

She grinned, "Oh he's not? How's Jesse been, Kole?"

My mouth opened, preparing to tell her exactly how my best friend had been, until it snapped closed. I had no idea. I had only seen Jesse in class the past few weeks and since midterms were coming up, our professor was cutting off our open class time. Not to mention, Devon made sure to walk me to English and took me home when it was over.

We barely had a conversation that possessed more than a few sentences and I hadn't noticed.

Lucy smirked at my silence, taking another gulp of her drink. "Just what I thought, you're whipped by Devon's charm."

I rolled my eyes, upset that she was right. I needed this drink after all.

Devon was nothing like Terrance. At least I knew that was for certain.

> *"Man Kole, you better hurry up before Daddy comes up here!" My roommate, Lisa hissed at me in a hush tone.*
>
> *I waved her off, taking more gulps of Hennessey straight from the bottle. I was numb to everything as of now.*
>
> *"Ain't nobody scared of Terrance." I spat, wiping the corner of my mouth with the back of my hand.*
>
> *She growled, "You better be with that ass whooping he handed you last week! Wake up, Kole. You ain't his bottom bitch no more! You can't say and do whatever you want these days. You work, just like everybody else in this house." Lisa scolded, as I continued to look out our bedroom window.*
>
> *I longed for the days I used to be free and longed even more for the days Maw Maw was alive. The bank took the duplex, due to all the money she owed on it and I was trapped here because I refused Sharon's offer for me to live with her after the funeral. I planned on moving back with Maw Maw shortly after moving here once I realized Terrance's occupation. This was nothing like I thought it was going to be and I was a fool to think I was in love and in a real relationship. I was truly*

believing Terrance was my happily ever after like I heard about.

Naïve and stupid is what I was. But I really didn't know anything else, I just wanted happiness.

I used to watch him run these girls, all coming from battered situations; similar to how mine used to be living with Sharon. All of them were in love with him and all of them thought they had something special. That is, until he put them to work just like he did to me two weeks ago.

I had nowhere to go and nowhere to turn, so I was stuck here until I found a way out.

If hell is real, this must be what it's like. Every. Single. Day.

———————

"Lucy! Take me to Jesse's house!" I slurred, feeling the effects of the ghetto margarita. I kept trying to call Jesse, but his phone would go straight to voicemail like he turned it off and my heightened paranoia was getting the best of me.

"Why? He probably hates you right now," she chuckled drunkenly, leaning back on the couch.

I shook my head, standing shakily to my feet. "Nooo. He can't hate me! He doesn't have a hateful bone in his body!"

Lucy giggled, her eyes still closed. "Yeah, but Devon hates him and you're always with Devon sooo ... "

My brows furrowed, "Devon doesn't hate Jesse."

"Girl, how blind are you? Do you ever open your eyes to see what's real ... like ever? I think you might be missing a few in that department honey."

I rolled my eyes before stumbling towards the kitchen table to gather my things. I placed all of my books in my bag before sloppily throwing it over my shoulder and heading back to the couch.

"Come on Lu, please! I need to go see Jesse, it's an emergency." I begged, stomping my foot a little as she huffed before standing up.

"Ugh finnnneee! Do you know where he lives?"

I nodded, remembering from the last time we stopped at his house before he came to help me paint.

"Alright," she yawned, stretching out her skinny limbs. "Let's go."

"Dominic?" Jesse questioned sleepily, rubbing his eyes as I stood at his front door, relieved to see him.

"Jesseeee!" I squealed opening my arms wide, losing my balance and stumbling through the entryway. Jesse was quick to catch me.

"Nic, what the heck man? You been drinking? How you get here?"

His voice was filled with exhaustion and that rasp that I had grown to adore. I rested in his strong hold for a moment, growing tired from all of the alcohol I consumed.

"Nic!" Jesse shook me in his arms a bit, causing me to wake up fully.

I looked up at him with a wide grin, "Lucy brought me."

He smacked his lips, closing the door and pulling my body over to his couch. He placed me gently on it before sitting next to me.

"She must've been just as drunk as you to think it was a good idea to bring you over here wasted like this and without a warning," he grumbled, followed by a yawn.

"Uh uh! I called you, you didn't answer."

He chuckled, resting his head back and closing his eyes.

"I turn my phone off when I go to bed, bum."

"Oh," I responded, feeling slightly dizzy.

"You mad at me, Jes?"

He snorted, opening his eyes to look at me. "Why would I be mad at you?"

I shrugged, "Because I've been hanging with Devon a lot and haven't made time for you."

He smiled, shaking his head. "You got ya own life Nic, just like I got mine. I ain't gonna be mad at you for that."

I sighed, twiddling my fingers. "Yeah, but I can tell you don't like Devon for me ... "

"And what would give you that impression? I've always supported your decision on seeing him. What ya'll got going isn't any business of mine."

I sighed, flapping my hands in the air. "But I want it to be your business! I dunno, before I would get kinda annoyed that you were preaching at me all the time, but now I miss it. I miss you checking me and telling me what the right thing to do is."

He frowned, sitting all the way up.

"Why? You don't need me doing that all the time. Live with your decisions ... "

I blew out breath, slouching my shoulders. "I just always tend to make bad ones sometimes. It's like I always need somebody in my corner, telling me to do right."

"You have that and you do the opposite though. What good is that? Live with what you choose on your own, out of your own free will and see if that's how you want life to go. Seems like that's the only way you're going to find solace."

I pouted, too drunk to keep going back and forth with Jesse and I rested my head heavily on his shoulder, realizing for the first time he was shirtless.

My head snapped up, looking over his toned upper body, covered in body art.

"You sleep with no shirt on?"

He cackled at my reaction, "You just now realizing I ain't have on a shirt, girl?" he questioned, the toothy grin never leaving his face.

I studied him slowly from his head, down his jaw line to his neck and then his chest. My eyes squinted at the long scar on his left peck that started at his collarbone and ended right above his nipple.

I reached my hand slowly out to touch the abrasion, before Jesse gently grabbed my wrist to stop me.

"Wh-what happened there?" I asked softly, seeing the expression on his face begin to fade.

He shook his head, still gripping my wrist. "Had surgery a long time ago. It's noth-"

"Was it on your heart?"

He shook his head no, "Don't worry about it Nic, for real. It was a long time ago."

I huffed, snatching my wrist from his.

"You never tell me about the things that pain you, ever! It's frustrating!"

He smirked, licking his lips. "Because it doesn't pain me anymore. I ain't gonna talk about things like I want them to still be relevant."

"Well you can talk about them just to let me know more about you. Let me know more about what happened when I left."

He frowned, rubbing a tired hand down his face. "We ain't gotta talk about it. Just like we don't talk about why you left – "

I could feel the frustration bubbling in my chest. "Why can't you just tell me?!"

He rolled his eyes growing annoyed, "Why you wanna know so bad? Like seriously. What's my pain gonna do for you?"

My hands flew every which way, "Make you real! Relatable! Make you human Jesse, damn! You act like nothing affects you, like nothing bothers you. Nothing! And I know that's not true! I know it."

Jesse snorted, "I get it now, it all makes sense."

My eyes snapped to his side profile; he was looking straight ahead at the TV that was off.

"Get what?"

"Your liking to Devon. Pain is all that makes sense to you and that dude is made up of nothing but that, just like you."

He finally turned his head to meet my stare. "You scared to rock with me because you're hurt and I'm not. You ain't comfortable."

"That's not true ... "

He smacked his lips, "I'm sick of you calling me a liar too. You came over here to wake me up, call me a liar, and make me hurt just like you. If that's what it's gonna take for me to have your friendship now, I don't want it Nic. Stick with Lucy and Dev. They match that Kole persona you got."

I sighed, looking to the floor. "I knew I was going to push you away."

Jesse groaned, "You still don't get it. That's the only thing you'll even take responsibility for is keeping someone that cares about you at a distance. All those other choices you make though? You'd rather someone make 'em for you so you don't gotta take the fall for how your life is. But nah, you unhappy now because that's how you want it to be."

"No its not! You don't understand what happened to me! You don't understand how hard life has been for me!" I shouted, voice cracking with every word.

"No, but I do understand you've chosen to stay there. You've chosen to wallow in it, and kill your spirit. You need new life, Nic. You need to be born again," his breathing became exasperated.

My frown deepened. "This is why. This is why I didn't want to be back in your life. I know how much trouble I can cause."

He sighed, "It's not that, baby. I just … I can't carry that weight you got on your shoulders. I ain't strong enough for it and it's not meant for me to. I just pray you wake up and get it one day, I really do. Until then … I just have to keep giving you the space to do so. Find it on your own. I can tell you 'til my face turns blue, like I've been doing. Look where it's gotten me. Nowhere, and I'm tired as hell."

I slowly laid down to rest my head in his lap, wrapping myself up in my own arms. After a few moments, I felt his fingers running through my hair, bringing the warmth I always felt in his presence.

"I'm sorry, Jes."

A small bitter chuckle erupted from his chest, "Me too."

"Babe," Devon called, looking back at me with a concerned look on his face.

We were in his room, sitting on his bed. He was sitting at the edge playing a video game while I sat behind him, resting my back against the headboard. My mind hadn't even been tuned into what he was doing, I was too much in my head about my conversation with Jesse yesterday and the things he said about my relationship with Devon and Lucy. Basically saying all three of us were miserable and that's why I could tolerate them.

Was he right?

"Baby," Devon called again, regaining my focus.

I shook my head a bit, before giving him my full attention. "Yeah?"

He chuckled, "What's with you? You've been quiet ever since we got home from dinner. Everything okay?" he questioned softly, pausing the game and crawling towards me.

Devon was perched on all fours, crawling his way between my knees until our noses were inches apart. He looked me squarely in my eyes before gently placing his lips against mine.

My eyes closed at the softness of his lips, relishing in the feeling of his affection. I was growing to love these kisses more and more.

He pecked me one last time before pulling back, taking in a deep breath as my eyes fluttered opened.

He searched them quickly before speaking, "What's going on with you? Is everything okay?"

I ran my tongue over my lips, still tasting him there before nodding. "Yeah. Yeah, I'm fine."

He smirked knowingly, rubbing his nose against mine. "Don't lie to me," he said softly against my cheek as I sighed.

I pushed my fingers through my hair, scratching my scalp to find the words.

"It's just this conversation I had with Jesse the other day."

Devon snorted before he shook his head and sat back on his knees. "Really, this about Jesse? You can't be serious."

My brows furrowed, "Not necessarily about him, just about something he said."

He rolled his eyes, "And what he say? Something about how I'm not good for you or something?"

My face grew confused, not sure how to respond.

"Wh-what? What no – "

He released a bitter chuckle, running his hands over his short bed of curls.

"What I say about lying to me Kole? I know him, man. I know he said some stuff to get in your head. Wow, I can't believe he's tryna run the same game on you that he did on Phi … "

I shook my head quickly, not able to process all he was trying to say.

"What? No babe, Jesse isn't like that. He doesn't even look at me like that, we're just friends – "

"Don't tell me!" Devon snapped, before inhaling a deep breath, preparing to calm himself down.

"Don't tell me how he looks at you, Kole. You don't see it. If I didn't know any better I would say he loves you."

My eyes widened. Love? Jesse? Me? No, never.

It was quiet between us. I didn't even want to look up, afraid of him losing his temper over the conversation again.

"Look, I'm sorry for even bringing it up. It's nothing really."

He bit down, revealing his strong jaw line before scooting back to the front of the bed, grabbing the controller of his game.

"You like me, Kole?" he asked quietly after a few beats, not yet starting the game.

I nodded first, "You know I do."

He sighed, "Then please, don't let Jesse come between us. You say it's not like that, then he shouldn't be a friend that you're afraid to lose. Just please; give us a real chance with this babe. I care about you too much to lose you over something petty."

I bit the inside of my lip, thinking about all he was asking. Basically requesting that I choose between him and Jesse.

The thought of losing either one of them was unbearable but I just couldn't decipher who would hurt me more.

Who would I hurt more by staying may be the better question. After thinking that through … the choice was obvious.

"Hey, so, uh," Jesse started the minute our professor ended his lecture.

I was doing my best to try to ignore him all throughout class, but he kept trying relentlessly to get my attention it seemed like. Even though I know he wasn't doing anything but being himself.

I never turned to look his way but he continued talking, "You wanna go to the library after class to finish up our midterm paper together?"

"No." I said quickly, trying to sound as unbothered as I could.

His eyes burned holes into the side of my face, "Oh, you finished it already?"

I shook my head. "No, I haven't. I just ... I just wanna work on it alone."

I could hear his sigh.

"Man you've been acting shady towards me since you came over. Look, I'm sorry if I offended you – "

"You didn't offend me, Jesse. I don't care about what was said."

"Look, Nic, I'm not trying to give up on you."

"Why not?" I asked louder than I intended to, gaining a few stares from a couple of students.

I softened my voice, keeping my eyes facing the ground. "Just give up on me, Jes. You said it yourself. I wanna surround myself with pain and your happy go lucky ass is just not what I need right now."

He chuckled, shaking his head, "You sound so crazy right now."

"Well then let me sound crazy. Let me be crazy! I can't even mean that much that you won't even open up to me. You don't even trust me with you, Jesse. How could you expect that same trust in return?"

He huffed, looking ahead with a set face. "I'm not tryna hurt you."

"But I'm going to hurt you, don't you get that? I'll hurt you. You never heard a person can weigh you down quicker than you can pull them up? That's me. A weight, an anchor."

I frowned, trying to keep my emotion steady. "I'm not dragging you down to my hell, Jesse. You're too good for that."

He smirked in disbelief, shaking his head. "I can't believe this. I can't even believe you're saying all this right now."

"Believe it. It's who I am. I warned you day one. I told you, I'm just passing through and I told you not to bring me back in but you insisted. I could barely even stand to be around you with how warm you are and cold I am."

He tucked his lips in before releasing a heavy breath through his nose. "This what you want? You wanna be Kole forever, huh?"

I rose a brow tossing him a confused look, "What?"

He shook his head, "Do you know why I call you Dominic and refuse to call you Kole? Do you even know what your name means?"

I shook my head no.

He snorted, rolling his eyes and beginning to pack all his books away. "Look it up."

"Where are you going? Class isn't over yet."

He shrugged, "It's over for me."

"Jesse – "

He stopped me, shoving his book bag over his shoulder. "Save it, Kole. You wanna keep 'saving' me from you? Well you got it."

He called me Kole and I hated the way it sounded leaving his lips.

He stood tall, looking down at me before glancing away. "You got it. Sorry I ever walked back in your life."

My heart dropped watching Jesse jet down the steps and out of the classroom.

Jesse powered through the building doors, feeling an unwanted emotion of anger creep through his being. He didn't understand it. He couldn't grasp why Dominic kept rejecting him time and time again. What has he ever done but try to help her and be there for her?

He began to pace in front of the building, attempting to calm his nerves. Upset that she had struck one. He released a shaky breath, looking up to the sky for answers.

"What you want me to do, God? I'm trying; I swear I'm trying. She doesn't see what I see. How can I get her to see? Please, help me. Help her." He prayed, desperately needing a word from the Lord at this very moment.

Deep in his heart, he knew the reasoning for Dominic's return and what she desperately needed to grasp. The responsibility he had in her life was heavy; he just didn't understand how to go about it. He needed guidance. He needed strength. He needed her to wake up for her to get it.

He just didn't know how that was going to be possible.

"Aye, JP!" He heard a voice call, snapping him from his inner turmoil.

His eyes landed on Devon and immediately he felt the anger rise up in his flesh again.

He stared at the object of Dominic's affection, walking casually towards him.

"Hey, I was just wondering where Kole was." Devon finally said, standing a few feet away from Jesse.

"Still in class," he answered flatly, turning his eyes away from the reason of his current anger.

Devon's eyes widened at Jesse's reaction. He always knew JP to have a level head and positive attitude even towards his enemies. Something must be bothering him, or someone.

"Is something wrong?" Devon asked, trying his best to imitate sincerity.

Jesse released a breath, flicking his nose before looking back at Devon.

"What you want with her, man? Like what's ya aim?"

Devon smirked, gripping the strap of his bag.

"No aim. I really like Kole, she's special."

Jesse rolled his eyes to the answer, "Cut it out, man. You tried to run the same game on Phi, bruh. Tryna make her shut me out. What is it? You after everybody I talk to or somethin?"

He furrowed his brows, an amused grin was set on his face.

"What you mean? I thought you ain't like Kole like that. Ain't y'all just supposed to be friends from back in the day?"

Jesse smacked his lips. "You know what I mean, man. Don't get funny."

Devon mocked an empathetic sigh, frowning at his nemesis.

"Look JP, you may got this thing for Kole that she's completely oblivious to. But even if she wasn't, she wouldn't want you. She doesn't want you now and didn't want you back then. Whatever thin line you're hanging onto, to keep this friendship alive isn't going to work so cut ya losses. It's over. She's not gonna be the person you want her to be for you."

Jesse gripped his fist, doing everything he could to refrain from punching Devon in his mouth.

But for what? Dominic made it clear she didn't want him in her life anymore. She made it clear that this was the path she chose.

He just knew it was the wrong one. But he had to let her go, he had to let her fall so hopefully she could get back up.

He just had to trust God on this. It was out of his hands now. All he could control was his prayers.

"Baby!"

He could hear Dominic's cheery voice call out for Devon behind him.

He closed his eyes for a moment before stepping closer to Devon.

"You don't get what she means to me so you don't wanna know what's going to happen to you if you hurt her." he warned; tone icy and thick, allowing his flesh to rule in the moment.

Devon laughed, backing up a little and placing his hands in his pockets.

"I'll take my chances," he replied with a smirk.

Jesse looked over his shoulder, watching Dominic approaching with a mixed expression before he just shook his head. He walked off, making to run into Devon along the way.

CHAPTER
- SIX -

"Babe, you cool – you seem stressed," Devon asked, pulling my eyes away from looking at Jesse and Phi across the yard.

Devon, Lucy and I were standing outside of the Thompson building after our classes ended, waiting on our next class to start. I hadn't talked to Jesse since our falling out in class a couple of weeks ago and it was starting to eat away at me. We would constantly lock eyes but he would give me this look of disappointment that irked me to no end.

I missed my friend, but what could I do now? I made it obvious who I'd chosen. He would be better off without me, I was sure of it.

I flashed Devon and Lucy the best smile I could muster and shrugged, "I'm fine, really. I'm just not looking forward to this next class."

Lucy gave me an empathetic look, rubbing my shoulder. "Still on the outs with JP, huh?" she asked as Devon smacked his lips.

"Who cares? You don't need him. That's already been made clear. You got us, ya real friends," Devon assured, never taking his eyes off mine.

My eyes danced quickly from Jesse back to them, before Devon stepped into my view.

"I got something that will ease ya stress," he suggested quietly as my brows furrowed.

"Like what?" I questioned, both Lucy and I waiting for an answer.

He looked cautiously around us before grabbing my hand. "Follow me to my car, ya'll."

"Yo this is crazy, I haven't gotten lifted in forever!" Lucy giggled from the backseat as I looked from her back to Devon.

He was in the driver's seat, carefully concentrated on rolling the blunt as I bit my lip in nerves.

"You ever smoke before, Kole?" Lucy asked.

"Nah, never. Drinking was my vice."

Her eyes widened, "Damn for real? I would've thought you did since you used to smoke cigs. Weed is much better for you than nicotine."

"What? How?"

Devon chuckled, "You ever heard of any marijuana related deaths, babe?"

I paused, thinking for a moment. "Um, no. I don't think I have."

He grinned, licking the paper and rolling the blunt tightly.

"Exactly. Weed ain't bad like the feds try to make it seem. It does more good than harm. That's why it's used for medical purposes. Cigarettes could never do that for you."

I nodded, watching the flicker of the lighter Devon used to light the drug. Lucy was squealing with excitement as he took the first inhale. The smoke instantly filled the car.

"You don't think we're going to get caught, do you?" I asked as both of them groaned in annoyance.

"Relax Kole, we good. I do this all the time," Devon explained passing the blunt my way. I looked hesitantly at the drug before my eyes darted to Lucy who was smiling with encouragement.

"Do it, girl. It ain't gonna hurt you," she told me as I carefully took it from Devon's fingers and placed it to my lips.

"Yeah, God placed weed on the earth for people like us to enjoy. If not, why else would it be here?" Devon asked rhetorically while I finally took a few puffs. I could feel the smoke instantly filling my lungs.

I began to cough uncontrollably, regretting taking such a deep breath while Lucy laughed patting my back.

"It's a marathon, not a sprint girl," she teased while I continued to cough, passing the blunt to her. She happily took it from me.

I wiped my watery eyes, still thinking about the last statement Devon made.

"You believe in God?" I questioned, genuinely interested in his response.

He smirked with a shrug, "Eh, sure. Why not? I may not believe like others believe per-se but I believe something like Him exists somewhere."

Lucy growled from the backseat, passing the blunt to Devon.

"Ugh, let's please not discuss religion while smoking.

"You don't believe in God, Lu?"

She huffed, "Are you kidding me? What's there to believe? All this bad shit happening in the world and there's someone or something out there that can fix it and they choose not to? All for some big ol' lesson or something? I'm good."

Devon chuckled, blowing out smoke. "What happens if you die and find out He real and then you end up in hell ... then what?"

She smirked, "I'll take my chances. It can't be too much worse than living on earth, right?"

I could tell neither one of them were taking this conversation seriously. It was strange hearing the way they talked about God versus how Jesse and Corey did. It made me wonder who was right.

Somebody had to be.

"What about you?" Devon asked, taking me out of my thoughts while also passing the blunt to me.

My lungs were still burning from the first time and I could feel my body being taken over by the effects already. It did kind of make me feel more relaxed, and I'm sure being high would take the edge off from thinking of Jesse.

I took the drug from him, "What do you mean?"

He smirked, watching as I inhaled. "What do you believe?"

I shrugged, watching as I made circles with the smoke.

"Nothing."

I was in English class higher than a kite, reading the same sentence over and over.

I couldn't focus on one thing, I just kept finding myself staring at the back of Jesse's head.

Smoking before this class was becoming a ritual for Lucy, Devon and I. It was the only way to keep my mind off everything that had to do with life. It kept the pain away, even if it was only temporary.

This class in particular, I couldn't stop staring at Jes. Wondering how he was and what he was up to. I was craving just a piece of his intellect and wisdom.

I was missing him more and more each day. I missed the warmth and comfort that only he could provide but I couldn't take it back now. We were how we were because that's how I wanted it to be.

Why was I so messed up?

I jumped, startled as everyone began packing their things to exit class for the day.

I had zoned out the entire time?

I noticed Jesse packing his things up quickly, not even looking back my way. I gathered my things just as fast, trying to catch him before he reached outside, knowing Devon would be waiting to take me home.

I flung my bag over my shoulder, walking briskly out of the classroom to catch Jesse in time.

"Jesse, wait!" I called, unsure of what my entire plan was for speaking. We had barely spoken in three weeks and before that it had been a month.

He stopped in his tracks, turning slowly to look at me with wonder. I smiled softly, happy to have his attention if only for a moment before slowing my pace just a little. He watched me carefully the entire time as I walked up to him, waiting to see the result of my call.

"Hi," I greeted shyly, looking up at Jesse. He was beautiful, just like I always knew him to be.

"High is right. That's what you do now?" he questioned, squinting his eyes at me.

I shifted my weight from one foot to the other and shrugged shamelessly.

"It takes away the pain."

He sighed, "For only a moment, until the next high. Natural pain relievers are the way to go."

He slightly smirked at the end, causing me to release a breath. Jesse was still the same man. There was no judgment but that didn't mean he ever kept his opinion to himself.

"How you been?" he questioned after a few moments of silence.

"I've been kinda worr – "

"Kole!"

Both of our heads turned at the sound of my name being called in the corridor.

Devon was waiting by the door with an expecting look on his face. I cursed to myself before looking up at Jesse.

"I gotta go," I said quietly, placing my head down.

"No you don't," he responded, attempting to block me from leaving.

I looked beyond him to see Devon's patience wearing thin. I wanted to avoid an argument and a potential shuffle with him and Jesse.

I had to do this to keep everyone out of harm's way by my own doing.

"Take care, ok?" I told him before moving around his body to meet Devon at the door.

Devon grabbed my arm roughly, dragging me through the doors and outside before I snatched my arm away.

"Chill out!" I barked, rubbing the spot where my arm was now a bit sore from how tightly he had squeezed.

"Chill out?! How disrespectful can you be? We agreed you wouldn't talk to that dude no more and you purposely stay inside so I wouldn't see?! You do that every day or something?!" His eyes were fiery, looking down at me for an answer.

I glanced up, noticing Jesse watching the scene from a safe distance. He gave me a look, but with that look, I knew he was asking if I was okay. I nodded shortly, before looking back up at Devon.

"It won't happen again, can you just take me home?" I begged. My high was completely gone.

He rolled his eyes, making to walk ahead of me. "Gladly."

"Baby, you're not focused," Phi said, gently placing a hand over Jesse's.

He sat at his kitchen table bouncing his knee uneasily, thinking of his run in with Dominic earlier. He couldn't get the image of Devon roughing her up and then him not doing a single thing about it.

It was eating him up. How was he supposed to just sit and watch? How could he do nothing, watching her destroy herself intentionally when he knows exactly what she needs to get better?

He wondered then, how God does it? Every single day, watching the souls He created, deny Him and refuse His love, every day.

This was practically unbearable for Jesse.

"Babe ... " Phi called again, pulling her boyfriend away from his thoughts.

He sighed, before taking in a deep breath, unable to form any words.

"What is it?" she asked, searching his eyes, desperate for an answer.

"Is it Kole?"

He closed his eyes at the mere mention of her name, giving Phi every indication that she was right.

She huffed a little, sitting back in her seat. "Jesse, you've been worrying yourself sick over her and personally, knowing what's going on, I don't think it's in your best interest –"

He cut her off, emotions beginning to run high.

"How am I not supposed to care, Phi? It's different when she was missing for 11 years and I wasn't around to see what was happening for myself. Now, it's in my face and it's hard to watch."

"Then turn a blind eye to it. Kole made it clear she doesn't want you in her life."

He shook his head, "She only said that because she's afraid."

Phi scoffed shaking her head, "Afraid of what?"

He groaned, throwing his hands up, "Afraid of growth, love, positivity, I don't know! But she's afraid to have it. I just don't get it."

He sat back in his chair, closing his eyes and rubbing his temples. Phi watched her beau and shook her head with sadness.

"This isn't healthy."

"What I'm supposed to do Phi, huh? Just be ok? You don't get it cause you don't know her."

"You don't know her either!" she shot back, not meaning for her voice to carry the way it did.

"Like you said," she continued softer. "It's been 11 years. She's different. She's grown. You can't just look out for her anymore, she doesn't want you to."

He disagreed, closing his eyes once more.

"I've always looked out for her. No matter how hard she's pushed me away."

> *"Why won't you tell me what's wrong, Nic! You don't wanna talk to me no more, you never come outside and play and every time I see you, you're crying! What's going on? Talk to me!" An eleven-year-old Jesse begged, sitting next to his best friend on the bus on their way home from school.*
>
> *Dominic sat against the window, holding herself tightly with her arms, head pressed against the glass. A single tear fell as she refused to look in Jesse's direction.*
>
> *"Nic –"*

"Just drop it, Jes. I'm fine, alright," she replied, voice cold and tight.

Jesse frowned, refusing to accept that answer.

"Whatever's going on just let me help you."

She turned up her nose, "You can't help me."

"How you know?!" he asked, only wanting to be her savior in this moment.

"Because it's too late!" she cried louder than intended.

It was all becoming too much. Knowing she would be home in just a few minutes, and Jesse's constant pleading of her time. It was too much. She wasn't a little girl anymore, not in the world's eyes.

She had been robbed of it. No one could save her now.

"It's never too late, Nic. I promise, it's never too late to get help." he spoke softly, placing an arm around her shoulder, pulling her close, as she sighed and continued to cry silently to herself.

If only he knew you could only lose your virginity once, no matter how it happened.

It was too late, she'll never be pure again.

How was she going to get help for that?

"Why did you decide to date me over Devon?"

Jesse asked randomly after their initial conversation had died.

It was a question that had been on Jesse's mind to ask ever since Devon and Dominic had become more serious. He noticed that's when Devon kept ensuring Dominic would stay clear of him and he couldn't figure out why.

Phi froze for a moment before looking at Jesse with question.

"What kind of question is that? There was never a choice."

Jesse looked at Phi impassively, "Are you forgetting we were friends first? You were really into dude before you and I really got started."

She frowned nervously, tapping her pencil against her book.

"Promise not to say anything? Because I swore I wouldn't."

Jesse's jaw clenched, upset she had never said anything about it until now, realizing she was about to say something serious.

"Jesse, promise –"

He cut her off, patience wearing thin. "Out with it, Phi."

She blew out a breath, running a finger through her honey brown locks.

"Ok … well back when Devon and I were talking, he told me that he lost his scholarship at Duke because of an injury."

Phi paused a moment before she continued her story.

"Well there was this time we went to a party together at A&T and this girl recognized him. Dev had left to go to the bathroom and she pulled me to the side saying that I need to be careful dealing with him."

Jesse's brows furrowed, "Careful how?"

"She was saying that the injury story was just a cover up for why he really lost his scholarship. She said he was expelled."

His eyes widened, "Expelled for what?"

"Supposedly over a girl. She pressed charges on him for domestic violence, possibly rape."

Jesse's heart sank. *Rape?* He always had a feeling that was the cause of Dominic's move and possibly her self-destruction. He grew angry at the mere thought.

Before he could catch himself, he slammed his hand on the table, causing Phi to jump in surprise.

"Are you kidding me? Why didn't you say anything?!"

She breathed, attempting to collect her thoughts in a panic, never seeing Jesse so upset. He rarely got angry at anything.

"It wasn't my place! And when I called him out on it, he begged me not to say a word and that the stories weren't true which I kind of believed because the girl dropped the charges. I looked them up myself."

Jesse rolled his eyes, not wanting to even look at her.

"If you ain't think they were true, why did you stop messing with him?"

She sighed, "Because he started bugging after that and it was just a complete turn off. I didn't trust him so I cut him loose."

"Why didn't you say anything when you saw that Kole was into him then if you knew he couldn't be trusted?"

She huffed, "Because honestly, I was just happy someone other than my boyfriend was taking up her time. He seemed to be making her happy so why would I block –"

He cut her off, unable to hear the sorry excuse she was giving him.

"Because he's dangerous! You think people go pressing charges for no reason, or cause they're bitter?!"

"Kole is not my problem, nor my responsibility, Jesse! And she's not yours either! She's grown!" Phi fired back, growing tired of being the receiving end of his anger.

He growled, running a hand down his face, "What about being a decent human then, Phi?! You see how much she means to me. Does that not mean anything?!"

Her body tensed before sitting back in her chair, shaking her head.

"It meant everything, which is why I didn't say anything. She started pulling you away from me, even emotionally, the moment she came back. How am I gonna compete with that?"

Jesse's brows furrowed looking at his girlfriend. "Compete? Compete, Phi? You're my girl. I make that known to you and everyone around us."

"But I'm not in your heart. I'm not in there like she is."

Jesse had to pause to gather himself. Here Phi was, making this about something other than what really mattered.

"She's an old friend, man. An old friend that meant a lot to me back then."

"But it's not the same now! You can't let go of the past just as bad as she can't. That little girl you were in love with is no more, Jesse. She's gone! You see who she is now."

He frowned before looking Phi in the face. "Yeah? Well I see who you are now too."

He shook his head before grabbing his phone.

"What are you doing?" Phi questioned exhausted, watching as Jesse searched in his phone for something.

"I'm going to try to call her, stop her from messing with Devon."

Phi instantly grabbed at his phone, snatching it from his grip.

"Babe, it's too late! What do you not understand? You can't save her. It's on her now to save herself!"

She wanted desperately for him to understand, for him to let this go emotionally like he had already done physically.

"It's going to be better this way, I promise. She has to go through this or she won't learn." She pleaded, searching his eyes for agreement.

He sighed, holding back the emotion that rested deeply in his throat at the thought of his friend. "So I'm just supposed to sit here and let her get hurt by an abuser or possibly worse?! To damage her worse than she's already been?"

"All you can do at this point is pray, baby. God can take care of her way better than you ever could. You have to understand that and trust it."

Jesse's heart cracked down the middle while placing his head down on the table in surrender.

Please keep her safe. He prayed in his head, having trouble believing in his heart that it would be answered. Failing the test of faith once again.

———————

Soft knocking at my bedroom door caused me to look up curiously from the English assignment I was working on. I placed my pencil down before clearing my throat, "Its open."

My eyes widened seeing Sharon appear in the doorway, peaking her head in.

"Hey, mind if I come in?" she asked softly, awaiting my answer.

I shrugged, not really bothered by the company at the moment.

"Sure."

Her smile widened a bit more before she stepped in, closing the door behind her. She looked around my room, nodding in approval.

"I actually like what you and Jesse did with the room. Looks a lot better in here. Feels cozy." she admitted, wrapping her arms around herself in comfort while studying the changes.

I smiled, "Thanks for allowing me to do so. I really appreciate it."

Her eyes snapped to mine in surprise, probably shocked at the first kind thing I uttered to her in a while. I'm sure it had been years.

She finally caught herself, clearing her throat once more, "How are you, Kole? Is everything ok?"

I could hear the sincerity, but I couldn't pin point where it was coming from.

"Why do you ask?"

She shrugged, "You just seem ... I don't know, different. It seemed like you were getting a bit better but now you just seem sad most days. Even when that boy drops you off ... "

Sigh. She was talking about Devon. I had been avoiding him since that incident after class the other day, him grabbing me up. It reminded me of Terrance so much and it pissed me off. I really liked Devon and I was disappointed he allowed himself to get upset over something so small. He's been calling me, trying to apologize but I just wasn't sure how to feel.

Everything and everyone was making me feel some kind of way at this point and I felt like I had nowhere to turn, nowhere to find peace and solace. It used to be Jesse but I swear my entire existence is causing stress his way; I can feel it.

"I'm fine, Sharon. School just has me stressed is all," I lied, running a hand through my straightened tresses.

Sharon studied me for a moment, biting the inside of her cheek in search of words, the right words even.

"What?" I asked, feeling strange about the silence passing between us.

"I don't want you to be like me, Kole. When it comes to life and people, don't begin to realize things when it's too late, after being naive to it for so long," she shouted, pleading in her tone. She was concerned for me; that much was evident.

I snorted, looking back to my book. "Kinda too late for that type of talk don't you think? I've already started living from the examples that were set."

She sighed, "What about the good ones? What about the good examples, like the ones Maw Maw used to set?"

I shrugged, "What good did that do her? She died long before her time."

"But she lived a good life, Kole. I need you to see that. Corey and I, we have a good life together. We're happy despite what we've been through."

I huffed, realizing where this conversation was going but I was in no mood to entertain it. Even the mention of my grandmother was enough to bring the emotion to the surface.

I could just feel myself breaking more and more as the days carried on and I didn't know how much longer it would be until I shattered into pieces. Shattered to the point I'd be un-repairable.

I noticed Sharon's large brown eyes begin to gloss over as she stared at me but she quickly looked away, blinking back the tears.

She released a shaky breath, staring at the wall before wiping her cheek and looking back to me.

She straightened up, "I wanted to tell you that Corey and I have a conference to attend in DC on Friday and won't be back until late Saturday evening" she announced, my brows furrowing in curiosity.

"Oh yeah?"

She nodded shortly, "Yeah. We'll leave late Thursday night after work. Are you going to be okay, staying here by yourself?"

I would be lying if I said the thought didn't bring me chills, but I brushed it off. "I'll be fine. I'm 22 now, think I can handle it."

She smirked knowingly, "Well you know Jesse has his own place so if you get uncomfortable just call him and have him pick you up. I would let you keep one of the cars, but you not having a license worries me."

I chuckled softly, "It's cool, Sharon."

She watched me for a moment, preparing to utter something else until Corey's booming voice sounded from downstairs.

"Kole!" He shouted, my ears perking up.

"Yes!" I shouted back, looking to Sharon for some type of answers. She shrugged in response.

"You have a visitor! – "

"Will you cut all that damn screaming in my house!" Sharon yelled, stopping our shouting match.

I giggled at her antics before hopping off the bed.

Who would be visiting me, unannounced?

A part of me hoped it was Jesse waiting for me at the bottom of those stairs.

I saw Corey at the bottom, alone. Sharon brushed by me to head to her room, only pulling my attention to her for just a moment before looking back to Corey.

"Uh ... visitor?" I questioned, slowly coming down the stairs.

He revealed a charming smirk before nodding his head towards the door.

"Porch," he answered, pulling me into a soft embrace once I reached him.

It couldn't be Jesse. He would gladly come in.

"Thanks, Core," I said, earning a gentle kiss on my temple before he made to walk off.

"Be careful, Kole," he replied, turning the corner and disappearing down the hall.

I took in a breath, opening the door and seeing Devon standing on the porch, rubbing a hand through his short bed of curls.

He looked relieved at the sight of me, while I softly closed the door. I pressed my back against the screen, eyeing him with my arms crossed.

"What are you doing here?"

He stepped forward a bit, pleading evident in his eyes.

"Kole, I'm sorry. I swear I didn't mean to grab you that way."

"You didn't?" I challenged.

He sighed, "I didn't. I got carried away. I don't know what got into me."

"Jesse. Jesse gets to you and I don't get it. I don't get why he makes you so upset."

Devon huffed, looking away from me. "He don't get to me."

"Yes he does –"

"He doesn't, Kole! Drop it." He hissed, keeping his hands by his side to calm himself.

I rolled my eyes. "Why are you here, Devon? I didn't make it clear that I don't wanna talk to you?"

His eyes slowly began to climb up my body before they met mine.

"You don't mean that. You don't miss me?"

"It's been a few days, what do I have to miss?" I asked, watching as he slowly began to walk in my direction.

I kept my back pressed against the glass as Devon's intoxicating scent came closer and closer until we were chest to chest. He bent his neck, planting kisses on mine as my eyes closed from the feeling.

"Come over ... "

I shook my head, not daring to open my eyes. "No. I'm mad at you still."

He snorted against my cheek, his sweet breath beating against my ear. "Well stop."

I groaned, attempting to push him off as he chuckled, resting his hands on my hip to stay put.

"I'm playing, babe! Alright, for real, I'm sorry about the otha day. I swear to you it won't happen again."

I searched his eyes for sincerity.

I bit my lip, rethinking his request. I glanced back at my closed door before meeting Devon's stare.

"My parents are leaving tomorrow night. If I want you over I'll let you know, ok?"

He licked his lips before smirking flirtatiously. "Ok. You gonna talk to me at school tomorrow or keep dissin?"

I shrugged. "We'll see."

He released a soft chuckle before quickly sneaking a small peck on my lips.

"Until tomorrow then, Kole."

He smiled, turning to step off the porch.

I watched him walking to his car in silence. I kicked myself for giving in so easy but really, who else did I have to lean on for support staying in this house by myself?

I needed someone, and right now Jesse wasn't an option.

"Mommy, please. Please let me stay at Jesse's tonight."

"Dominic, no! How many times you gonna ask me to keep hearing the same answer?" Mom scolded, only turning her head slightly from the dishes she was washing.

I stood behind her, pleading for an escape. I couldn't go through another night of this, I refused to.

"But Mom! Jesse's mom said it was okay. You never said no before," I replied softly, giving it one last effort.

She slammed the pot she had just finished washing on the counter, causing me to jump in surprise.

"No! You're getting too old to be staying the night with boys! What are you not getting about that?!"

I felt the anger bubbling in my throat. I had no choice but to utter my next choice of words. "But you do! Every damn night Larry is over – mmph!" I grunted, as the sting of the wet slap she just rendered to my face cut me off.

She bent down, eye level with me, finger pointed in my face. Her eyes were cold and dark now. I could tell I made her mad.

"What I do with my man is my got damn business, not yours!" she spat as I took quick shallow breaths, trying to contain myself.

"What about what he does with me? Is that your business too?!" I shouted, tears burning my eyes, before shoving her out of my face and running up the steps.

I was patiently waiting for the whooping I knew I would receive later for talking back.

My head shot up at the sounds of chairs screeching against the tiles. I must've dozed off in class. I sighed, sitting up and rubbing my eyes, still exhausted from the lack of sleep. Ever since knowing I would be in the house by myself, it just put me on edge. It brought back constant flashbacks from the last fateful evening I spent in the house before leaving to stay with Maw Maw.

I swung my bag over my shoulder, sluggishly dragging my feet out of the classroom. I still had about a half hour until Lucy was out of class and would take me home. Corey and Sharon had already left the city for DC.

I just have 48 hours, 48 hours to survive and not be driven crazy from my own mind.

I stepped out of the building and immediately felt the warmth of the sun's rays beating against my skin. I scanned the quad, looking for a familiar face, desperately hoping to spot Jesse somewhere.

My eyes soon found Phi, standing not too far away with a friend. She would have to know where Jesse was.

I took in a deep breath, carrying my feet over to where she stood. Her eyes widened a bit at the sight of me, realizing that she was in fact, my intended target. She said something quickly to her friend and soon after she was alone.

"Hey!" I greeted as warmly as I could, earning a short yet confused smile from her.

"Hey Kole, what's up?" she asked, shifting from one foot to the other.

"Nothing, have you seen Jesse around here or know where I could find him?"

She opened her mouth before quickly closing it and shaking her head.

"Um ... no, I haven't talked to Jesse in a while actually."

My brows furrowed, "Is-is everything okay? Is he hurt or – "

"We broke up, Kole. He – he didn't tell you?" she asked, surprised that I hadn't known.

I shook my head, "No. I haven't really talked to him in a while either. Sheesh, I'm sorry. I wouldn't have asked if I knew."

She grinned, revealing a dimple before fanning me off. "Not your fault. I just figured you would've been the first to know. I guess he was serious."

"Serious about what?"

She quickly shook her head before looking away. "Nothing. But umm look, he typically works on Thursdays so he normally isn't around."

My shoulders slouched; knowing Jesse probably wouldn't even answer my call. Catching him in person would've been my best bet.

"Is everything alright?" she questioned, realizing my disappointment.

I sighed, running a hand through my hair. "Yeah, I guess so. I'll catch you later, Phi."

I was turning to walk away before feeling a gentle hand on my shoulder. "Kole, wait."

I stopped in my tracks, turning to look at her waiting to hear what she wanted.

"There's something I've got to tell you –"

"Yo Kole!" The calling of my name caught both of our attention. We saw Devon standing not too far away. I rolled my eyes, while hearing Phi hiss to herself.

"He can wait," I answered calmly, giving Phi my full attention. "What is it?"

She released a short breath before shaking her head, "If I uh, hear from Jesse I'll let him know you were looking for him, ok?"

I barely got a chance to respond before Phi was out of my sight, quickly walking past Devon with her head down. I watched her strangely, not even realizing Devon was a few feet away now.

What was that about?

Tiffany Campbell

"Hey," Devon called, forcing me to pull away from Phi's retreating figure. I had to admit, even though I had an attitude with him, he was still a gorgeous face to admire.

"What's up?" I asked, trying to sound as calm as I could.

He shrugged, placing his hands in his front pockets.

"So, what's the plan for tonight? You still want me to roll through?"

"Lucy will be there, so I guess that's fine." I answered shortly, darting my eyes around campus to see if I saw her anywhere. Sometimes her class lets out early.

Devon smacked his lips in response, "Why you gonna have her there like we need supervised visits? It's me we're talking about. Me and you done been alone plenty of times."

I rolled my eyes, already annoyed, "Fine if you don't want her there then don't come. I don't care." I made to walk away until Devon grabbed my arm to stop me.

It was tight at first, but turned gentle once he realized. I looked up at him questionably.

"Let go."

He quickly dropped my arm.

"Sorry, I just don't like when you do that walking away thing when we're not done talking."

I crossed my arms with a huff. "I'm not going to beg you to come over, Devon. It's not like you ever come in when they're home anyway so it really wouldn't make a difference."

He grumbled, "Man, ya parents just make me feel funny, aight? Something about their presence I just don't rock with. I get strange vibes but now that they're gone I'll feel a little more comfortable."

He stepped closer placing his hands on my hips.

"Maybe you'll feel a little more comfortable too," he said flirtatiously.

I tipped a brow, "And in what way are you referring to?"

"You know what I'm talking about baby. That thing we always get close to doing but never do."

He bit his bottom lip, while his brows climbed his forehead.

I scoffed, before moving out of his grasp.

"The last place I wanna do that is at my house. And besides, I told you I wasn't ready."

Devon dropped his head shortly in defeat before picking it back up, "Come on, Kole, it's been two months. I know you ain't a virgin."

"So!" I shot back, already feeling my skin crawl at the thought.

"So, why you ain't tryna go there with me? We like each other and been kicking it for a long time. I don't ever wait this long for no damn body man. That don't show you nothing?"

I grew frustrated with the way this conversation was going and was beyond grateful that I could see Lucy approaching in the distance.

I then looked back up at Devon's confused face and sighed, "We'll talk about this later ok? I'll be home, just – come through."

He released another defeated breath before nodding. He leaned down, placing a heavy kiss on my cheek and walked off.

Jesse sat idle on a Thursday night, flipping through the channels of his television. He didn't watch TV much but tonight he couldn't shake the eerie feeling he had, so he did his best to distract himself.

He prayed but heard nothing; worked out, but grew tired with how hard he was pushing, and none of his friends had been available when he had tried to contact them.

His leg shook as his foot tapped against the carpeted floor, trying to keep his mind off the gut wrenching feeling in his spirit.

His eyes darted quickly over to his phone before looking back at the TV, resisting the urge to reach out to Dominic to see if she was safe. He was doing his best to keep his mind off of her but somehow it always drifted back to wonder how she was doing.

Why?

A sudden knock on his door pulled him away from his thoughts, thankfully. He looked at the door like he possessed x-ray vision, wanting to know who it was before he tended to it.

The knock came again, more urgent and desperate this time, causing Jesse to stand to his feet and glide over to the front door. He looked through the peephole, tipping a brow at the unexpected guest before opening.

"What you doing here, Phi?" he asked genuinely confused, watching as she let herself in, shutting the door behind her.

She paced a bit in front of him while Jesse watched patiently, arms crossed over his chest.

"I should've said something," she finally stated, frustrated.

Jesse's brow tipped even higher than before. "Said what?"

"To Kole. She stopped me today, looking for you and I was going to tell her about Devon but then I saw him and I just got choked up. But I've been having a weird feeling since I left school that I should've said something."

Her voice shook with each word she spoke. She flopped down on Jesse's long couch, breathless. Jesse walked carefully to his living room area, taking a seat across from Phi on the other couch.

"You were right, babe and I'm sorry. I should've said something in the very beginning; it just didn't seem like my place. You were right to break up with me. I'm just messed up, I don't even – "

"Stop." Jesse sighed, unable to listen to Phi talk down on herself any longer.

"I didn't just break up with you because of that, Phi. I broke up with you because I wasn't being fair to you by not being honest with myself," he admitted as she hung on to his every word.

"Honest with yourself about what?"

Phi was almost afraid to hear the answer.

Jesse took in a deep breath, unsure of how transparent he should be.

"Honest with the fact that I was never going to love you the way you love me. Realizing that what it was between you and I was just a season. Temporary."

Phi shook her head, unwilling to accept what he was telling her.

"Stop it, Jesse. You're just saying that because of everything that's going on with you right now."

"No, I'm not, Phi. I'm saying it because that's just what it is."

Phi swallowed the emotion daring to reveal itself before she spoke, "I know I messed up, but I also know that she can't love you, Jesse. She can't love you like I can. She can barely love herself."

Jesse huffed, placing his head down realizing that Phi was missing his entire objective. "This ain't about Nic."

She nodded, "Yes it is. You didn't feel this way until she came back."

"Phi, I've been feeling like this. Seeing how you reacted with all that just put the nail in the coffin. There's no way I can think about a future with someone who's willing to put another at risk because of their own jealousy. That was too hateful and it left a bad taste in my mouth, sure. But more than anything it just showed me who you are and how I'm different from that."

"She's no better than me though."

"Stop making this about her! This isn't about her, Phi! With or without Nic, we would've still crossed this road. We would've still broken up," Jesse stressed, doing his best to keep his voice mild.

"Was this ya real reason for coming over here?" he asked, rubbing his forehead after it had been silent for a few moments.

Phi sighed, attempting to muster up every bit of pride she had left after hearing Jesse's heartbreaking truth.

"I just wanted you to check on Kole. It seemed like she really needed you today. She was disheveled, more than she usually is and she seemed really uncomfortable when Devon called for her. I don't know – something is going on with her, Jesse. And I was wrong for pushing tough love on the situation. You should talk to her."

He blew out a breath, slowly opening his eyes. "S'not why I did it. She has to fall or she won't ever get back up and get out of her pain."

Phi scrunched up her face, "How is that going to help? How is more pain going to cause more good?"

Jesse smirked softly, "The most beautiful creations are crafted together from broken pieces."

———————

I sat on the couch in a daze, pretending to watch the television. Lucy and Devon were in the dining room, playing a drinking game and laughing loudly while I sat in my own world, too overpowered by weed and alcohol to participate. I barely felt here, just about numb to everything and everyone at the moment. I thought having my friends around would help but I've never felt more alone in my life.

"Aye yo, Kole," Lucy called, walking to stand in front of me, blocking the view of the television.

I looked up at her through low eyes, smiling softly.

"Sup?"

She chuckled, "Man, you are gone, girl. I'm about to head out. Im'a let you and Dev be alone," she told me, as my brows furrowed before looking back to Devon who was currently cleaning up the mess he and Lucy had created on the table.

I looked back in her direction, "What? I thought you were going to stay the night with me?"

She giggled, plopping down on the couch next to me, turning her head to meet my eyes. "Yeah, I was but now I feel like I'm blocking. You don't want alone time with your boo?"

I frowned, shaking my head softly, earning a laugh from her.

She pushed me in my shoulder playfully, "Aw, don't be a baby, Kole. I heard he's crazy good in bed. You're not a virgin are you?"

I sighed, shamefully shaking my head no.

"Okay then! You're good, mamas. Just be relaxed, let it happen. Weed makes it even better so you should be cool. But for real, I gotta go. You gonna be getting it in tonight and I'm on my way to get me some myself," she smirked, hugging me from the side.

"Hit me up tomorrow and let me know how everything went. I wanna know all the details."

I sat up on the couch watching as she left out of the living room and gave Devon one last wave. The two of us watched her disappear down the hall before hearing the front door open then close.

Our eyes instinctively landed on the other. Devon smiled small before looking away, continuing to clean up the mess.

"And then there were two," he said quietly to himself as I felt the nerves build in the pit of my stomach.

Jesse pulled into his mother's driveway, placing his car in park then stepped out. He looked curiously across the street, studying the car parked in Dominic's driveway. He found it odd that both Sharon and Corey's car were missing yet this car was there. He felt the ominous feeling he had been feeling all night return heavy but chose to push it to the side, wanting to check on his mother.

He walked into the dark house, his nose instantly filling with the smell of nicotine that this house seemed to be forever plagued with. He sighed, walking down the dimly lit hallway.

"Momma?" he called out, hearing coughing not too far away. He picked up his pace down the hall, before coming face to face with his mother. She was quickly putting out the cigarette she had been smoking, attempting to fan away the smoke.

"Jesse baby, why didn't you tell me you were coming over? I wouldn't have been smoking in the house," she said apologetically, wiping off her hands and walking to the sink to wash them.

Jesse released a soft sigh of relief, glad to see she was okay before walking over to the back patio door to open the screen to ventilate the house.

"You picked it back up?" he asked quietly in regards to the habit, adjusting the screen door to ensure it was closed completely.

He looked up at his mother, her skin seeming paler than usual. Her long brown curls were matted and worn. The bags underneath her eyes gave away that she had been missing nights of sleep. Her hazel eyes still seemed to glow somehow, no matter how exhausted she looked.

She released a breath, rubbing her sweater clad arm and taking a seat at the table.

"Only when I'm stressed, baby. I promise."

Jesse huffed softly before taking a seat across from her.

"What you stressed about, Momma?"

She smiled bitterly, shaking her head and looking away from her only child.

"What am I not stressed about? Between you and your father … "

Jesse frowned, "Stressed about me? Don't be."

"How can I not, Jesse? You are my son. I still can't help but feel responsible."

His heart sank at his mother's confession. It hurt him that she had trouble forgiving herself after all of these years. He stretched his arm across the table, gently placing his hand over hers.

She gratefully took it, smiling through her own pain. She felt better in his presence, like she always did – appreciative that he had come to visit her.

"What brings you by this late? I know it wasn't just to check on little ol' me," she joked, looking at her child knowingly.

Jesse sighed, "I was gonna stop and check on Dominic first. But I don't know what she got going across the street."

His mother raised a brow, "There are people over there? Sharon told me she and Corey would be out of town this evening and to keep an eye out."

His eyes widened. "Yo, for real?"

She nodded, "Yeah. She called me earlier. I forgot all about checking over there. I'm sure Dominic has a pretty good handle on things. She was always a good kid back then. Very smart and beautiful," his mother cooed, thinking of the little girl she once knew.

Jesse bit the inside of his lip, tapping his foot repeatedly against the hardwood floor of the dining room, the feeling in his gut stronger than ever.

What you want me to do God? He thought to himself, needing an answer.

What you want me to do … ?

> *I tiptoed quietly down the steps when I was sure mom and Larry were sleeping. My mouth had been dry all night, desperately needing water but I refused to come out of my room so I wouldn't have to be faced with him. I was dressed in as many clothes as humanly possible, trying to come off as unattractive as I could. He would tell me every time that it was my beauty that drew him to me, but that no one else but him would ever find me attractive after what we've done. No one would ever want me now that he's made me his. The thought alone would make me sick; the thought of never being able to be with Jesse made me feel even worse.*
>
> *I quickly took my drink of water, careful not to make a sound as I stood gulping it in the kitchen. Once I was*

refreshed, I placed the cup quietly in the sink and turned around to head back upstairs.

A solid body instantly blocked me, coming face to face with Larry.

He smirked evilly down at me, "Going somewhere, pretty girl?"

I shook to my core.

"P-please. Just let me go back to sleep," I begged quietly, my chest heaving for air, the tears touching the brim of my eyes.

He smiled, grabbing my arm tightly, "No problem. Let me help you with that first."

"No please!" I shouted, feeling the pee begin to run down my leg from fear.

———————————

"So we staying down here or ... going upstairs?" Devon asked suddenly, snapping me out of my thoughts.

We had been alone for a while now and he kept trying little slick moves but I would find every reason to put a halt to his advances. I had even suggested that he leave a couple times but he insisted on staying and 'keeping me safe'.

I looked at him strangely before shaking my head, "No. I would rather stay down here."

I began rubbing the back of my neck, feeling uneasy at the thought of him being alone with me in my room.

Devon smiled, scooting closer to me on the love seat. He replaced my hand with his and started to ease the tension coming from my spine.

"Let me help you with this, baby."

I rolled my shoulders, relaxing as best as I could in his touch. The feeling wasn't as comfortable as it used to be. He was giving me all types of unwanted vibes and I couldn't tell if it was the drugs that brought my anxiety to the surface, him or a mixture of the two.

After a few moments, Devon leaned his lips near my ear, placing a gentle kiss there. The feeling made goose bumps rise all for the wrong reasons and I moved my head away from his lips, annoyed.

"Devon, cut it out," I hissed, as he only snickered and leaned closer, starting to kiss me along my jaw now. I tried swatting his face away.

"Stop Kole, you know you like it."

He continued to kiss me as I kept trying to brush him off.

"I'm not in the mood for real. Cut it out."

He ignored my warnings only pushing up on me more.

"Quit teasing me," he replied sternly, only pressing his body hard against my own and wrapping his arms tightly around my waist locking me in.

I groaned, "Devon, stop. I don't want to do this."

He smacked his lips, only squeezing me in his arms tighter. I turned my head to look at the fire resting in his eyes. I could see now, just how angry he had grown.

"Why, why don't you want this? Why you keep rejecting me like you too good or something, huh?! You think I can't have any chicks prettier than you? You don't think Lucy been tryna smash me ever since she found out we was talking? I could've had ya friend but instead I'm stuck tryna be with you! Tryna respect yo ass!" he yelled furiously in my face, as I instantly filled with fear and panic.

All of this was too familiar.

"Devon – "

"No!" He growled pinning me down on the couch, pressing both of my arms back. "You gonna want me, Kole! Want me more than weak ass Jesse. And when I'm done, he ain't never gonna want you back. Believe dat, imma make sure of it!"

I felt the tears come to the brim of my eyes, realizing what he was about to do to me.

"Ple-please, baby. Please don't do this to me," I begged, before the hard sting of a slap graced my face.

Devon was huffing hard; pinned over top of me, looking like a man I didn't know. Better yet, a man I used to know all too well.

"You're leaving me no choice. You should've wanted me when I gave you the chance. Should've wanted me more than him. If I can't have you, neither can he. This gonna be the last time he try to come for what's mine," He spat, tugging at my jeans as I squeezed my eyes tight. Praying that if there was a God, He wouldn't allow this to happen to me all over again. I wouldn't be able to handle it.

Jesse walked out of his mother's house, realizing the unfamiliar car was still parked in Dominic's driveway. His feet began pulling him down the pavement and towards the car, wanting to see if he could figure out who it belonged to.

He walked up onto the Chevy Malibu, looking inside for any clues. Judging by the gym bag and baseball cap he observed in the back seat, it couldn't have belonged to Lucy.

Devon?

I was pinned underneath Larry, one of his hands covering my mouth as the other furiously began to grab at my clothes. I kicked underneath him; doing anything I could to break free.

"Shut up! This ya own fault for trying to hide from me! All of this is your fault! You think I want to do this to you, pretty girl? Huh?! You think I want to do this? You make me do this! You make me fight! You gon learn to just start giving it to me," Larry hissed as quietly as he could, struggling with the many pairs of pants I was wearing.

"You done pissed on yourself. Pissing me off." He rambled as I cried underneath his hand, just wishing my mom would wake up. Wishing she would care for once in my life.

I looked around frantically for anything that could save me from this situation. He never did this to me in the living room before, so there were more objects in near reach. I saw the glass lamp sitting right above my head resting on the end table.

Larry removed his hand from my mouth to use them both to pull my pants off my body. I screamed loudly before grabbing the lamp above my head to smash over his.

Jesse sighed at the realization and made to walk off – realizing that his friend had made her choice and he should respect her space no matter how bad it made him feel. He would be sure to check on her later. He couldn't keep himself from doing that even if he wanted to.

He turned on his heels but froze when he heard a loud scream and a crashing of glass coming from inside the house.

He turned back around, running as fast as he could up the porch steps, "Dominic!"

Jesse reached the door, jiggling the handle and thanked Heaven when it was unlocked. He could hear tussling coming from the living room and immediately carried his feet to the noise.

He found Devon and Dominic wrestling with one another on the living room floor; Devon bleeding from his forehead.

Anger sparked in Jesse's soul like never before and he was quick to pull her from Devon's aggressive grip.

She was belligerent in Jesse's strong hold as Devon struggled to get up from the ground. "Mom! Mom! He – he tried to rape me. He's been raping me, mom!" she cried, scratching at Jesse's arm desperately and pointing at Devon.

Jesse placed her on her feet, turning her body to face him. He cupped her cheeks in his hands, trying to get Dominic to snap out of her trance. Tears were streaming down her face as her teeth chattered and her hair was shuffled all over.

"Look at me, baby! It's me. It's Jesse, I'm here," he said, searching her eyes that were wild and filled with panic and fear. He scanned her body, seeing her jeans were ripped at the zipper and her lip was busted. He bit down hard as the anger came back as he looked behind Dominic to see Devon was standing up tall now, a smug expression on his face.

He sat her down in a nearby chair, "Stay right here and keep trying to breathe, baby. Take deep breaths; can you do that for me?" he asked her calmly as she nodded through her shivering state. She was having a panic attack and he could see that. He just had to take care of something first.

Jesse turned to face Devon, "You touch her?"

Devon chuckled, wiping at his lip, "She's lying."

Jesse stepped closer, "Oh, she lying now? She lying about you trying to rape her?!"

Devon smacked his lips, waving his hand in Kole's direction, "Man, you heard her! Calling for her mom and shit! She's drunk and hit me for no reason! I ain't do nothing she already ain't want me to."

Devon's words were cut off by Jesse's fist colliding with his face, causing a full on fight to spark between the two. Jesse knew all that he was risking by fighting Devon in his condition, but he couldn't help but defend his friend's honor since he never had the opportunity to do so all of those years ago. He would save her, or die trying to.

Kole watched the two boys fight, feeling the weight of the world pressing heavy on her shoulders, time seeming to stand still. All of this was because of her. All of this trouble and chaos was because she kept ignoring the signs and warnings of the people that cared about her most. She turned a blind eye to it all, like she did constantly, just hoping it would all play itself out.

Well it wasn't playing itself out. Things had only gotten worse, and she wanted more than ever to not be a part of this world anymore. She had been nothing but a burden since the moment she was conceived. What truly did she have left to offer? What more could she give?

While Jesse and Devon continued to render blows to one another, Kole stood slowly to her feet and walked unnoticed into the kitchen. She opened every drawer until she found a knife.

Trembling she picked it up, holding the knife to her wrist.

"Nic!" She heard from a short distance, snapping her head to the body the voice belonged to.

Jesse stood there, breathing heavy, looking at the knife in her hand with wild eyes.

"What are you doing?!"

"Wh-where's – "

Jesse shook his head at the question she was about to ask,

"He out cold in the living room. What are you doing?!"

She blinked, allowing the tears to fall freely from her eyes. She looked between her wrist and back to Jesse shaking her head vigorously.

"I-I can't do this Jesse. I can't, I can't live any longer."

Jesse tucked his lips in; doing everything he could to regain the air in his lung.

"Give me the knife, Nic ... please."

His hand was shaking as he reached in her direction.

She took a step back, not wanting to give it up. "No! Look what I've done! Look what I did to you! Look what keeps happening to me! I don't deserve to be here anymore! I cause nothing but pain! That's all I feel ... that's all I feel every day."

Jesse sighed, placing his head down, unable to look at her. "Please just give me the knife and I'll help you, baby. I'll help you get through this."

"No!" she shouted causing Jesse to flinch. "No! You can't help me, Jesse! You never could! You can't save me from me!"

"But I know somebody who can! Just trust me, Dom please!" The tear had pricked the surface of Jesse's eye, daring to fall. He couldn't blink, afraid that if he might, Dominic would do the unthinkable.

"Don't be selfish like this, Dominic," he pleaded as she tossed him a confused look. "Don't be selfish tryna take ya life."

Her brows pulled together at the center of her forehead.

"Selfish? How can this be selfish?!"

"Cause there's people out here fighting for a life to live and you just tryna end yours! You're healthy – you can get through this! People out here don't have those kind of options!"

She scoffed at his words, "Yeah? People like who."

Jesse couldn't take it anymore, he couldn't hold it in, "People like me … people like me, Nic."

She stilled, feeling the wind knocked out of her body. "Wh-what? What are you talking about Jesse, what are you saying?"

Jesse took in a deep breath, swallowing hard. His glossed over eyes looked into Dominic's pain stricken face. "I'm in remission. I've been battling cancer since I was a kid. That scar you noticed? It was from when they had to remove one of my lungs."

Jesse stopped his sentence when he noticed Dominic's eyes rolling to the back of her head. The knife dropped first then her body began to fall lifeless to the floor. Jesse caught her in his arms before she could hit the ground, panic spreading throughout his being.

"Nic! Dominic!" He called, shaking her before her body began to convulse. He placed her gently on the ground; worry began to take over as he watched as she had a seizure on the kitchen floor.

CHAPTER
- SEVEN -

My eyes slowly fluttered open. I didn't feel any pain, I wasn't crying and everything was still intact. I was standing on my feet and finally glanced at my surroundings. Nothing but white engulfed me and I was suddenly confused ...

"Hello?" I called out into oblivion, hoping for some type of response. I received nothing.

I looked below my feet and gasped at the sight underneath my body. I could- I could see myself, convulsing on my kitchen floor with Jesse's body hovering over me. Looking further down, I noticed Devon lying unconsciously on the living room floor. I was standing on what seemed to be an invisible barrier between my feet and the current happenings in my life.

Why was I up here? Was this an out of body experience?

Within moments, paramedics charged into my home, tending to a hysterical Jesse while my body stopped it's jerking suddenly. I couldn't make out the words being said and tapped at the barrier with the soles of my feet, desperately trying to get back down there to let everyone know I was okay.

At least I think I am.

"You can't get down there right now," I heard a voice say from behind my back, startling and shaking me to my core.

It couldn't be her. It couldn't be.

"It is," she chuckled warmly, hearing my thoughts I suppose.

"Turn around, baby."

I felt my body shake at her words but I couldn't turn around. I was in shock.

I must be dead.

She giggled again, her footsteps nearing me. "Child, turn around, now."

I turned slowly, coming face to face with my grandmother. Her brown face glowing, dressed in an all-white gown. She looked happier than I had ever seen her before. She looked much younger than she was when she died.

"Hi, beautiful," she greeted, smile bright and bringing a calm over my soul.

I released a scoff in disbelief before the tears began to drop from my eyes, one by one. "Maw Maw," I choked, being wrapped in her tight embrace.

She laughed happily, holding me in her arms. "It's so good to see you," she smiled. I squeezed her tight, not believing she was real.

I took a step out of the embrace, looking at her and then our surroundings once more, confusion washing over me. "What are you- What am I – "

I glanced down again, noticing that Devon and I were both on stretchers now, faces covered in oxygen masks, being wheeled out of the house. I could see Jesse and his mom standing outside talking to a police officer.

What was happening down there?

"Come," my grandmother called, forcing me to tear my eyes away. She wrapped her arm lovingly around my shoulder, guiding me away from the scene.

"Walk with me. Let's talk."

Maw Maw and I were walking together in this peaceful space of white that only contained the two of us. It seemed no matter how far we walked, we never reached the edge. I was just happy to be in her presence again. I felt safe, just like the day I finally left Sharon's house when she picked me up, promising I wouldn't have to go back if I didn't want to. She would take care of me. And she's still taking care of me now, even in her death.

"Am I dead?" I asked my grandmother, breaking the comforting silence that had consumed us.

I peeked over at her, a set grin on her face. The same one she used to wear daily.

She slightly shrugged, "Physically, no. Your heart is still beating in your body right now."

"Why did you specify physically? Am I dead another way?"

She nodded. "Yes. Your spirit has died, baby. What happened just now took everything that was left, that's why you're up here."

My heart began to race. "So-so what does that mean? I can't go back to my body?"

She opened her mouth to speak, but I cut her off by continuing. "I don't even think I want to go back honestly. I'd rather stay here with you."

Maw Maw stopped in her tracks, turning to face me. I stopped as well, mirroring her actions. It made perfect sense for me to stay here with her. This is where I belonged – I could feel it.

"This peace that you feel now, you know where that comes from?" she questioned softly, not removing her eyes from mine.

I shook my head puzzled, "From being here with you, being in your presence."

She smiled, shaking her head. "No. It's here because you feel God, you feel Heaven."

My mouth dropped, as I glanced around quickly. "Heaven? Is that where we are right now?"

She shrugged softly, "This is only a small part, where we can have visitors during times like these. Heaven itself is far too beautiful for mortals to experience. Only when your spirit completely leaves your body could you experience such a thing."

I ran my fingers through my hair, which I just realized was straightened and curled to perfection. And like my grandmother, I too was wearing a beautiful white gown. I hadn't even noticed.

She gently tucked a curl behind my ear, allowing her fingers to travel along my jaw and stop at my chin gracefully. I relished in the feeling of her warm touch.

"Well, can I go to Heaven with you?" I asked sincerely, earning a chuckle from her.

"Baby, if you die … this is not where you'll be. You won't be with me. This is only a place where believers dwell." she explained as the realization hit me hard.

"So..so it's real. Heaven, God, the devil, hell … it's all real?" I asked in a soft whisper, looking down at my bare feet before looking back to her.

She nodded with a smirk, "All real."

I shook my head in denial, "Then how can everything that has happened be justified? How could my life be the way it is? How –"

She shushed me softly, realizing I was working myself up.

"Some things are far too complicated for us to ever understand. One day, it will make sense, baby. I promise. But this peace, this peace you feel right now? You can have this with you every day that you live moving forward. You just have to accept Jesus, accept Him as being real to you and continue to work to learn more about Him. Learn how to love and be loved by Him."

I huffed, taking a step back from my grandmother. My chest felt as though it were ready to explode.

"I can't do that."

She sighed sadly, looking to me. "He brought you to Heaven. He gave you one more chance to experience His love before you would've sent yourself to an eternal hell and you still can't? You don't realize the grace you have on your life? You have something special on the inside of you, Dominic. You wouldn't have been named that if you didn't."

My brows furrowed, hearing the mention of the meaning of my name for the second time. "What does it mean?"

She smiled, "Belonging to God. You're His, you always have been. When are you going to walk in His purpose for you and stop rejecting His call?" she asked sincerely and my lip trembled, feeling the tears come to the surface.

She cooed softly, stepping up to me and placing her hands on my dampened cheeks. "Don't cry, baby."

I sniffed, shaking my head. "What if I fail Him like I've failed everyone else?"

She smirked, kissing me softly on my cheek before looking me in my eyes.

"You will fall short daily but in God's eyes you can never fail. What's so great about Him is that He loves you anyway, and He'll teach you every day how to love yourself as much as He loves you. He'll even send others to help you … if He hasn't already."

My eyes widened as memory washed over me, "Jesse."

I remembered then, the confession that sent me into shock, learning of Jesse's battle with cancer. He said he was currently in remission, which I get means the disease wasn't actively attacking him but knowing that he went through something so traumatic and remained as positive as he is about life … I couldn't process.

"I have to get back to Jesse. He needs me, I need him," I answered, searching my grandmother's eyes frantically as she only smiled softly in return.

"You're right," she answered proudly. "Are you ready to go back? Ready to start living?"

I swallowed before nodding, "I'll try, I'll try for you."

She blinked, allowing the lone tear to slide softly down her full brown cheeks.

"Don't try, baby just do and do it for *you*, Dominic. Do it because you deserve all the peace, joy and love our God has to offer. It rests in your Father's hands. Free of access, just for you. Don't take the grace He's given you for granted another day."

I nodded before she pulled me into an earth-shattering hug. I clung the cloth of her gown for dear life, afraid to let go.

"It's going to be okay, I promise. I'll be watching over you," she told me in my ear, as I nodded into her shoulder.

"I'm sorry." I whispered, feeling her arms squeeze me tighter.

"Close your eyes," she instructed as I closed them tight, tears falling constantly on her shoulder.

"I love you, baby. Please don't ever give up on yourself again."

I released a shaky breath, knowing this was our goodbye.

"I won't."

My eyes slowly pulled open, squinting at the bright light shining over my head. I made to squirm, but the IV in my arm put a halt to that. I was in the hospital?

I blinked a few more times, adjusting to the light. I glanced around, realizing I was in fact in a hospital room. My eyes traveled from the monitor, to the large window, to the bathroom, to the TV and finally landed on something that brought a relief I never thought I could feel.

Jesse was asleep awkwardly on the couch, covered in a hospital blanket. His inhaler rested on his chest, moving up and down as he breathed.

He was breathing. He was okay. He was here, with me.

I smiled, lying back on the bed, looking to the ceiling. I remembered my grandmother's words and hung on to them with everything in me.

I was given a second chance. A second chance to live life the way I was meant to.

"I can do this," I said softly into the quiet before hearing a stir next to me.

My eyes darted to Jesse who was stretching and rubbing his eyes like a small child. "Nic?" His voice was thick with exhaustion.

I smiled softly at him, relaxing my head more into my pillow.

"Hi," I greeted shyly as he cleared his throat and leaned towards the bed.

He began touching a few buttons, and before long my bed was moving upwards, putting me in a more comfortable and upright position.

I smirked, getting better adjusted. "Thanks."

He grinned tiredly, sitting back on the couch.

"No problem. I've spent a lot of time in here so I know the best spot for the bed."

I frowned at the thought, but the smile never left Jesse's face. His eyes scanned me over before asked, "How you feeling?"

I sighed, "Better, surprisingly. I feel a weight lifted to be honest."

His brows furrowed, "Really? How so?"

I shrugged, "In a sense, I feel like tonight was just what I needed. You know, to wake up. Like for everything to click. It hit me that the way I think and how I look at life is just ... so wrong and so unhealthy."

I could feel Jesse's stare. He cleared his throat again before speaking, "So what does this mean?"

I pulled my eyes away from my hands to stare in his sleepy orbs. "It means I'm starting over with everything. My outlook, the way I treat people, the way I treat myself. I'm going to give it a true effort."

Jesse smiled with pride looking at me before nodding.

"Okay, I believe you. I'm gonna be here for you every step of the way."

I relaxed back into the bed. "What time is it?"

He stretched before looking at the watch on his wrist, "3:28 in the morning it's been a long night."

I nodded in agreement, blowing out some air. Jesse looked at me close.

"You need some water?" he asked, standing to his feet. I realized for the first time how dry my mouth was.

"Uh, sure. Wh-what happened after I passed out?"

I don't know why I even asked. I didn't really want to know the answer.

I watched Jesse as he walked over to a bag sitting on the ledge of the window and pulled out a fresh bottle of water. He walked near the sink to grab a cup to pour the water for me.

"Well when you started seizing, I called 911. I've witnessed one before and I know you're not supposed to touch the body in the middle of it and you had like three of them back to back. By the third one, the medics arrived and you blacked out completely. I was scared." He handed the small cup to me.

I thanked him before taking a sip, feeling the relief the water instantly provided.

Jesse took a seat back on the couch, "So when they got there the cops were asking about what happened and I told 'em what Devon tried to do and I admitted that we fought. They said they'll be here later to talk to you to get a statement and see if you or Devon want to press charges."

My eyes widened, "What? What could Devon press charges over?!"

He shrugged, "He can press them on me. I hit 'em first."

My heart sank, "And you're not the least bit worried that he'll do so?"

Jesse chuckled, shaking his head.

"I mean I wouldn't put it past him to try. But I don't take back what I did Nic, at all. That dude is sick, man. He deserved more than what I could give him."

I couldn't help the smile that slowly appeared on my face. A man had never defended my honor before. I was more than happy that it was Jesse doing it and I was relieved that he wasn't upset about the whole thing.

"But yeah, they brought you here. They said they wanted to monitor you for a day to make sure your brain levels and vitals are good. They don't know what triggered the seizures. I called ya folks, they're worried sick. They're on their way back, not even attending that conference."

I instantly felt guilty for all the trouble I had caused in just one night. "I'm sorry for all this, Jes."

"It's not your fault."

"It is." I cut him off, shaking my head in shame. "It is. I was just scared to be in that house alone because of what happened and it ended up nearly happening again. I had a bad feeling about Devon – I just didn't want to be by myself. Is that stupid?"

He stood to his feet and stepping towards my bed.

"Scoot over, bum."

I chuckled softly before scooting over to do exactly what he asked. He joined me in the bed, wrapping an arm around me and pulled me close.

"It's not stupid, baby. You just had the wrong company. Lucy and Dev? They're toxic people. They always have been which is why they never kept friends. You don't gotta end up like them, Nic. Bitter and lonely like that? That doesn't have to be your life."

I sighed, nestled into the warm embrace, hearing Jesse's strong heartbeat. It was comforting.

"H-how'd you get cancer, Jes?" I asked softly, hoping I wasn't ruining the moment between us.

He shifted a bit, getting more comfortable.

"Remember how my parents used to be smokers? And how our house always smelled like it and my clothes?"

I nodded as I remembered

"Well all them years of second hand smoke caused it. I was playing a baseball game and my lungs started burning while I was running and I couldn't breathe. I passed out on the field and was taken to the hospital. The doctors found a tumor in my left lung. I went through chemo for a few years to shrink it but it only grew so they did surgery to remove it."

"Damn, Jes."

"I know right – some of the most painful years of my life, especially since I was the one that got cancer and my parents didn't. It made me angry with them for a while ... until I got saved of course. That's where I learned about forgiveness and all that. I learned to live with the cards I've been dealt. Now I've been able to help other kids that are going through it. I go and talk to them during their treatments, keep them uplifted. I pray for them and make sure they know God if they're terminally ill. It's rewarding and beautiful."

I grinned at the thought, picturing Jesse talking with kids and brightening their day like he brightens mine.

"Is it going to come back?" I dared to ask, feeling his chest heave in a sigh.

"I dunno, baby. I try not to think about it. I just continue to enjoy every day I'm here, and appreciate every moment, big or small," he relaxed a little more.

"Let's not worry or talk about none of that. It's been a long night, you need to get some rest," he said quietly, resting his cheek on top of my head.

I wrapped my arms around Jesse's torso, feeling exhaustion suddenly take over me.

"Thank you Jesse ... for everything."

Those were the last words I uttered before drifting into a deep sleep.

"Got any fours?" Jesse asked drily as he sat across from me with his legs hanging off the side of the bed.

I smirked before shaking my head, "Go fish."

He grumbled, throwing the cards down.

"Man I can't teach you Tonk or nothing?! Go fish is so lame man and we been playing this for hours!" he groaned as I couldn't help but laugh at his arms flailing everywhere, being all dramatic.

"We could at least play I declare war, slap jack or something!"

I grinned, "Come on, Jes. Go fish used to be our favorite!"

He rolled his eyes, "Yeah when we were like 6 and were just excited we knew how to play some cards."

I laughed and tossed my cards to the side. "I'm tired of playing anyway."

"What did Sharon say again when you talked to her?" I asked, looking out of the window.

"She said they were almost here. They got hit with some traffic on the way down," he explained, stretching his long limbs. I could see the exhaustion on his face.

"You can go home Jesse," I offered, feeling guilty for his lack of sleep.

"Clean up, get some rest."

He flashed me a goofy look, "What, you tryna say I stink or some'n?" he asked sniffing his armpits as I chuckled.

"No, stupid. I'm trying to say you look tired and I know a hospital is not the most comfortable place to sleep."

He smiled, shaking his head, "Nah I'm cool right now. That breakfast we ate kinda helped. Plus, I'm tryna wait till ya folks get here. You know, make sure you good," he assured,

I leaned back against my bed, watching as the sun beam against Jesse's light brown skin, forming a healthy glow. He resembled an angel. My angel.

"God is real, Jesse." I blurted with a smile, picking at a loose thread on my hospital blanket.

Jesse flopped on the couch, getting comfortable in his original spot, rubbing his eyebrow. "What makes you say that?"

My grandmother's face came to mind, bringing a warm feeling to my heart.

"When I was passed out I talked to my Maw Maw in Heaven."

"Word? That's really dope!" he said excitedly as I smiled.

"Yeah, it was crazy. But she was telling me how God and all that is real. It got me thinking."

"Aw yeah? Thinking about what?"

I shrugged, "Just like if God is real ... where has He been, you know? Like why didn't He come and stop all the stuff that happened to me?"

Jesse sighed before shaking his head softly. "I understand where you coming from, Nic. I had the same questions when I learned more about it too. But what I've come to understand is that God ain't gone be nowhere, where He ain't welcomed or invited. He's not like that. He's not here to force Himself on us. He wants us to want Him just as much as He wants us. Plus, earth is the devil's playground. Some people be so consumed by the enemy all they do is hurt people." He explained as I nodded.

"God has been keeping you though. That's why you're still here and why you're stronger than you think. You just gotta tap into your potential and be the woman you were always meant to be. You can overcome all of this. I'm one hundred percent sure of that."

I smiled, taking in a deep breath. "I just love the way you talk about it all."

He smirked, looking up at me. "For real?"

I nodded, "Yeah. It's the most attractive thing about you."

Jesse looked a bit surprised at my choice of words and opened his mouth to speak before the door suddenly opened, revealing a heart broken Sharon and Corey in the doorway.

Jesse stood to his feet quickly to greet Corey as Sharon rushed to my side looking me over. The fresh tears still rested in her eyes.

"Oh my God, baby are you ok?" she asked, pecking me all over my forehead and cheeks before she sniffed and looked me over one more time.

"Did-did he hurt –" she began but I was quick to cut her off with a shake of my head.

"No." I groaned softly, slightly embarrassed at her worry. I met eyes with Corey and Jesse who were looking uncomfortably at the scene before them.

Corey cleared his throat first, looking to my friend. "Jes, you wanna show me to the cafeteria real quick?" he asked cheerfully, as Jesse was quick to nod his head.

"Uh, yeah, sure. Of course."

Jesse opened his palm, showing Corey the way out. I looked to them both with thankful eyes as I watched the men leave our presence.

Sharon blew out a breath before plopping down on the couch next to me, shaking her head softly. She covered her face with her hands. She seemed more stressed than me at the moment.

"What's wrong?" I asked softly, hearing her sniff.

She released a shaky breath, removing her face from her hands.

"I-this happened again and I wasn't there. Again. I knew I shouldn't have left you there alone. I knew something was off about that boy. I had a feeling and I ignored it. I should've let you come with us to DC, or I should've made sure you were staying with Jesse or something I shoul-"

"Mom." I couldn't hear any more of what she was saying.

She stopped at my calling of her name and looked to me with slight confusion and surprise.

"This wasn't on you this time. This was my fault." I admitted as her mouth dropped.

"Kole, how can you say that? This wasn't your fault, baby. It never has been."

I felt the emotion bubbling in my chest, just thinking about all of the actions that led up to last night. "It was. All of you tried to warn me not only about Devon but about the direction I was heading in. I knew I was scared to stay at home by myself and you gave me the chance to speak on it and I lied and told you I was fine. I was the one that invited him inside without your consent and knowing I had a bad feeling about it. It was me this time, all me. And I can't sit here and let you take the blame for not being there for something you had no idea to be there for."

The minute my mother blinked, the tear escaped her eye and also mine.

"I really wanted to take this time to say thank you," Corey spoke, as the two men breezed down the hospital hallway, in no rush to get to the cafeteria.

Jesse's brows met at the center of his forehead before turning to look the elder in his eye, "For what?"

Corey smirked, looking ahead, "For being there for Kole. She really needs someone like you in her corner right now, and I can see how much the two of you mean to one another. I just want you to know I appreciate you being there for my daughter to protect her in a time when I wasn't there to do so. The kid's been through a lot."

Jesse smiled, "We all have."

Corey agreed, "Which is why I think you guys should definitely lean on one another during this time. You have a lot you can teach her and I think there are some things she can teach you too. I'm just truly thankful things weren't as bad as they could've been and I have you and God to thank for that."

Corey stopped, facing the young man and outstretched his hand. "Just take care of her, alright? She's going to run to you quicker than she'll ever run to us and I want to know I can trust you with her? Trust you with her heart?"

Jesse grinned bashfully, taking Corey's hand into his own for a firm handshake.

"Thank you sir but you're talking as if Dominic and I are going to –"

"Date?" Corey finished with a charming smile, releasing his hand from the young man in front of him.

He nodded feverishly, running his tongue over his plump lips. "Well, yeah!"

Corey grinned before stuffing his hands in his jean pockets, "Do you love her, Jesse?"

Jesse paused, surprised at the question being asked.

"I really don't like you blaming yourself, Kole. Those things you said may be true, but when you don't want it, that's just it. No man should force himself on any woman. It's disgusting," my mother said sternly, wrapping her arms around herself shaking her head.

"Jesse called me, I wanted to come down here and rip off that boy's head. I knew I ain't like his narrow behind when I would see him dropping you off. Didn't even have the nerve to come in and speak? I just ... " she stopped, collecting her thoughts from continuing to go off, causing a small chuckle to escape my lips.

"I'm sorry, baby. You remember what I did to that demon Larry. Cops lucky they got there when they did because I was going to kill him dead. Dead," she spoke with a bitter huff, causing me to cringe slightly at the memory.

She was right. She did try to murder Larry with her bare hands. And she would have if she were given the chance. It was things like that I chose to forget which I was now starting to regret. My mother did love me the best way she knew how and it was wrong of me to continue to penalize her for her past mistakes.

We had to start somewhere, why not start now?

"I'm sorry for how I've been treating you. I never thanked you for bailing me out and giving me a place to stay," I spoke genuinely after a few moments of silence.

Her eyes widened looking over at me, before a soft laugh of disbelief came from her. "Ok, who are you and what have you done with my daughter? Thanking me, apologizing?"

I grinned, "I owed you that much."

She smiled, "No seriously. What happened? Those seizures cause something to connect in your mind or something? This is hard to believe."

"I uh. – I saw Maw Maw. We talked," I admitted to her, watching her smile slowly increase.

"You see her too?" she questioned quietly, peaking my interest.

"So I'm not crazy because I saw her?" I asked hopeful, as the most joyous laugh I've ever heard burst from her lips.

"Of course you're not crazy, baby. I talked with her a little after she died. She was warning me about you, saying you needed me. That's when I tried to get in contact with you, find out where you were. But anytime you called, you would call from strange numbers and kept our conversations short. It was hard for me. Really hard."

Her voice was sad at the recollection of the time I was staying with Terrance. I never imagined how she would've felt not being able to contact me. I truly didn't think she cared. I underestimated her true feelings for me.

I smirked, "Going to jail might've been the best thing to happen for us, huh? Brought me home?"

She smiled, shrugging her shoulders before clasping her hands together. "Whatever it took. I'm just … really happy to have you back with me and with Corey. He really loves you. We both do, so much. I just need you to understand that."

"I do," I answered, running my fingers across the blanket covering my lap. "I'm grateful for you guys. It's the first time I've felt like I had a family, a whole one."

"Ah," Corey raised his hand, stopping the young man from even speaking if he wanted to. "Say no more."

Jesse's mouth fell, quickly following Corey as he continued to walk down the long hall full of rooms and nurses walking briskly all around them.

"Wha- I didn't even say nothing!" Jesse squeaked, only causing Corey to laugh.

He smiled, hands stuffed in the pockets of his jacket. "Exactly, you didn't have to."

"I mean," Jesse started, his eyes darting back and forth. "I know I love her, like I really do. I was willing to die for that girl. But like, love – love? That's real. That's what you and Ms. Sharon got. Me and her don't got that yet."

"Yet?" Corey quipped amused, with a risen brow. Jesse blushed under his gaze, feeling his cheeks get hot.

"I mean ... I don't know, maybe! You never know what the future holds. Plus, I'm single now."

Corey's brow rose, "Single? You and that cute girl broke up?" he questioned, genuinely intrigued about Jesse's love life.

Jesse sighed, placing a hand in the middle of his chest; a habit he always had over the years. "Yeah. She wasn't right for me. She didn't have her heart in the right placc."

Corey hummed in response. As the two men reached the hospitals cafeteria, he looked at the large crowd of people eating.

"Is the food any good here?" he questioned his younger counter part.

Jesse shrugged, "Man, anything's good when you on chemo and can keep it down. I would be in here grubbing on all dis!" Jesse expressed amusingly.

He patted the youngster's back, "Well lead the way my friend."

———————————

"Does it feel weird being in here?" Jesse asked.

I had to stay longer than anticipated due to a psych evaluation since the hospital knew about me wanting to commit suicide. By the end of my stay, all of those thoughts were gone. I just wanted to get back to somewhat of a normal life.

I shrugged in response, walking further into my room, stepping towards the neatly made bed. My mother must've been in here to clean it up before I arrived.

"I don't know. I don't feel as bad as I used to. It still stings a little but nothing happened up here, so I'm okay." I answered truthfully, taking a seat on the edge of my mattress.

Jesse watched me from the doorpost for a moment before using his shoulder to push himself off the frame. He slowly walked in my direction, standing in front of me.

"You're more than welcome to stay with me for a couple days. Until the sting is gone." He offered, trying to lift my mood.

I chuckled softly, shaking my head. "It may take more than a few days for that. I'm just nervous about going to school. Corey told me Devon was on the news for what he did. His old case got reopened too, I feel horrible."

Jesse sighed, taking a seat next to me. "Don't worry about Dev. He made his own choices."

"Yeah but people know him and not me. He was idolized at school and people loved him. They're probably going to think I was lying or trying to set him up."

"Shh," Jesse shushed, placing an arm around my shoulder. "Don't worry about all that right now. Worry about you and getting healthy. Your teachers already said you can finish up the rest of the quarter online so you don't even have to be worried with the kids at school. Transfer if it bugs you that bad. Just don't let it stress you."

I nodded, taking in Jesse's advice, looking down at my feet.

"You need some fun in ya life, Nic," Jesse stated into the quiet, as my eyes shot to him in wonder.

"Fun? What is that?" I joked poorly, his expression never changing.

"I'm for real. You need some good, genuine fun. Not that stuff you and Lucy used to be about."

I rolled my eyes at the sound of her name. "You know she hasn't even attempted to reach out to me? Like at all?"

Jesse revealed a dry expression, "You expected her to? She doesn't have the capacity to care about anyone but herself, Nic. You need genuine friends, people that actually care."

I nodded in agreement, "That's why I got you. You're all I need right now, Jes. It's always just been me and you." I smiled, bumping our shoulders together softly.

"I'm really glad to have you back. I really missed you when you left, more than I've ever missed anyone," he confessed.

"You don't understand how it was when I saw you in ya driveway. It felt like I got back that piece that was always missing, that spot in my heart only you could fill," he continued, causing my heart to swell at his honesty.

I wrapped my arms around him, igniting an emotional embrace between the two of us. I lifted my head, pecking Jesse softly on his cheek.

"I missed you too. More than you can imagine."

We stared at each other for a moment before I cleared my throat, releasing him from my hold.

"So about this fun you were talking about. What you got in mind?" I asked, watching Jesse's smile grow wide.

"Something cool," he smirked before standing to his feet. "Get dressed. I'll be downstairs."

———————————

"This is ... beautiful," I said breathless, looking at the scenery of trees growing plush green leaves. A flowing creek was replenished from the two waterfalls, falling from the cliff. It was a gorgeous sight. I had never seen anything like this in my city, or even knew it existed.

Jesse had taken me to a secluded wooded path, not too far outside of the city and I couldn't have been more grateful for him bringing me here.

"This is the most peaceful place I think I've ever been," I said, wrapping my arms across my chest, studying the waterfalls. I had never seen one in person before.

"Yeah, this was the place I always used to come to just clear my head and think. I always found solace here. I thought you might enjoy it too."

He took a seat on a large boulder that sat not too far away.

I continued to stand, allowing the warmth of the sun to heat my brown skin, enjoying the serenity.

"How'd you find this place?"

Jesse cleared his throat before speaking, "My uh- my therapist brought me here one time during one of our sessions. He thought I would enjoy it and I did. I've been coming ever since."

My eyes darted to his side profile. He was staring ahead of him, refusing to meet my gaze.

"You were in therapy?"

He chuckled before shrugging, "Yeah. Cancer has a way of messing with you mentally. Like I said, I was full of a lot of anger and a lot of questions. My therapist was the one that invited me to church for the first time too. I trusted him, ya know? He helped me through the hardest period of my life."

My mouth was agape, listening to Jesse share more of his past. I walked slowly towards the boulder he was perched upon. I took a seat next to him.

"How is it?"

He turned his head slightly to look at me, "How is what?"

"Therapy, what's it like?"

Jesse smiled, looking ahead of himself once more.

"It's really good if you take advantage of it. I mean, you're talking to someone completely unbiased that's trained to help you through ya issues and teach you how to cope in a much healthier way. At first I was rebellious to it. It was mandatory in the hospital that you went through it because of how the disease can be. But after I warmed up, I enjoyed it. It became something I looked forward to after chemo."

I could still hear the peace that rested in Jesse's heart and I knew he wasn't still bitter about what he had gone through. He was getting more comfortable with sharing himself with me and I appreciated it.

"Do you think that's what I need?"

"Therapy?"

I nodded.

"To be honest, I do. You've been through so much Nic, and kept it bottled up for so long, I think it would be of good use. With them, you can share what you want them to know and they can help you, help you at least release it and put it all out there. It couldn't hurt."

I nodded softly, taking in his words. "I think you're right."

His head snapped in my direction, "You do?"

I laughed, touching my shoulder against his. "Yeah, dummy. I'm not knocking your advice anymore. You're just trying to look out for me. I can't help but to respect that."

He grinned, giving a nod before looking ahead at the beauty before us.

"Looking at this makes me want to draw."

"Can you?"

I shook my head, "Nah."

Jesse laughed at my short response, causing me to smile. His laugh was still young and boyish just like when we were kids.

"Why did you break up with Phi?" I asked randomly, never hearing Jesse's side of things.

"You know about that?"

"Yeah. She told me when I was looking for you that day everything happened. She was kind of shocked that I didn't know already, thinking you would've told me first."

He smirked, leaning forward to pick up a few pebbles by his large feet. "Oh, well no. You weren't on my list to tell first. I wasn't really harping on it that tough."

My eyes widened, "Why? You really cared about her."

He nodded, quickly running his tongue over his dry lips. "Yeah, I still do. She just wasn't who I thought she was and I wasn't going to lead her on when I knew I would never fall for her like she wanted me to."

"Why not? Phi is beautiful."

"So, beauty fades, Nic. I'd be superficial to think that's the most important thing about a person. I see past that, I see the heart. Is that beautiful? That's what I wanna know."

I sighed quietly. I knew my heart was all but beautiful. It's probably as black as coal.

"What's wrong?" Jesse asked, pulling me out of my saddened thoughts.

"Remember," I started, looking for the words. "Remember when you told me Kole was befitting when you saw me for the first time?"

His face remained blank as he nodded quickly, "Yeah."

"What did that mean? You saw my heart?"

Jesse smirked, I'm assuming because he realized the point I was trying to make.

"That wasn't ya heart I saw, that was the block around ya heart. It was that aura you were trying to pull off with me, pushing me away. I could just tell you was letting your pain get the best of you. I could understand why you wanted to go by your middle name."

It was quiet for a few moments before he spoke again, "How you feel about ya name now? Still wanna go by Kole?"

"I don't know, I don't mind you calling me Dominic but I've gotten so used to Kole. I just think I may start outgrowing her soon."

"You might but she's apart of you and it's not necessarily a bad thing. It's your name, It's who you are. It just doesn't have to be negative."

I smiled at his words, instantly feeling warmth in my soul. Jesse always had that effect on me.

"And by the way," he added, "I think you're beautiful Dominic. Beyond that really – inside and out so don't ever question that, especially not with me."

I watched in awe as he stood up, standing near the edge of creek skipping rocks across the water.

The butterflies in my stomach started doing flips.

––––––––––––––––

I strolled through the hallway towards the dining room and kitchen area of my house, still in complete bliss of my afternoon with Jesse. I could hear noise coming from the kitchen the closer I approached and to my surprise, Corey was standing in front the countertop cutting up what appeared to be tomatoes.

"Corey?" I questioned, voice full of wonder and surprise.

"Kole?" he returned, playfully mimicking the way I had called for him.

"You cook?" I asked, watching as he skillfully diced the tomatoes.

He revealed his charming smile while nodding, "Of course, my mother is Italian and my father is Polish."

I shook my head slowly, "No idea what that is supposed to mean."

He chuckled at my response before scooping up the tomatoes he had diced and placing them in a large bowl. "Cooking is in my blood, baby girl. That's what that means."

"Well," I smiled. "What are you cooking for us tonight?"

"Penne Alla Vodka with breaded chicken breast. Ever had it?"

"Never. Vodka though, is that safe to cook?"

Corey smirked at my inquisitiveness. "Of course it is and it's not so much the vodka being the reason it's called that, it's the type of sauce. There is actually very little alcohol involved, you'll love it."

"I hope so. I've never seen a man in the kitchen cooking before." I said, my eyes following his every move.

"First time for everything," he quipped, pealing the outer layers of an onion now. "Anyway, how was your afternoon?"

The blush instantly returned to my cheeks at the thought of Jesse and my head tipped lower to hide the bashful smile.

"It was fun. Jesse and I had a good time exploring nature." I spoke quietly, feeling Corey staring at me.

"Jesse, huh?" I could hear the taunting smile in his voice. "You guys uh – "

"No!" I answered abruptly seeing where Corey was heading by the lead in his voice.

His laughter filled the room as I rolled my eyes.

He placed his hands up in surrender, "Hey, forgive a concerned step-father for asking."

I smirked lazily at his choice of words.

"When did you and my mom get married anyway?"

A grin came to his face as he began to chop up the onion, "About two and a half years ago. Not long after your grandmother's funeral."

I nodded slowly, remembering that was the last time I saw my mom before now.

Corey cleared his throat before speaking, "To let you in on a little secret, I didn't know about you until after we got married. I was livid to find out that you weren't apart of the wedding or barely her life. We had a gray area in our marriage for a while until we got past it."

"You didn't know about me? How did you find out?"

He sighed, "Sometime after I had initially moved in. I lived about an hour away from here and even our job. I would commute every day, which is why we chose your mother's house and not mine to live in. Plus, hers was already paid off. It would be more cost efficient. But anyway, when I was cleaning out one of the rooms to create an office, I picked yours first. I came across all of your things, your pictures and paraphernalia. I thought you had died or something. But to know you were still alive and out there without a mother made me truly upset. She had kept that from me the entire time."

"So-so what was her reason?" I stuttered, finally having answers as to why I wasn't really a part of her marriage.

He shrugged, "Said she didn't want me to judge her for the choices she made when you were younger. She said you hated her, and didn't really listen to her when she told you about the wedding at the funeral. I explained that you had lost the only mother you ever knew, why would you care about your mom's new relationship? But, I'm thinking around the time she had finally confessed to me, she made more attempts to reach out to you and didn't receive much in return. So, I just had faith that one day I would meet you, on decent terms."

I nodded slowly. I was a bit pained to know my mom had kept me a secret, but at the same time I didn't blame her. I wasn't too keen on acknowledging her existence back then either.

"Are you glad you met me?" I asked softly, too ashamed to look him in the face for an answer.

"I am more than glad I met you, honey. It's a blessing that you are a part of our lives right now. I'm thankful you're still here with us. You had us scared there for a moment though," he breathed with a quick shake of his head, as if he were reliving the moment.

A peaceful quiet engulfed us as I watched Corey begin to cook his sauce on the stove. He was concentrating on what he was doing and it was starting to smell really good.

"Do you have kids, Corey? Like from another marriage?"

"Nope. No kids, no previous marriage. I was a bachelor in my old days before I met your mom," he explained.

"Do you and my mom plan to have kids then?"

He shrugged, "We got you kiddo. I mean, we're still young so if it happens, it happens. We're not preventing it, but not trying either. Just letting the cards fall where they may. If it's meant to happen, it will."

I smiled, "I think you'll be a great father, Corey. You're already a great one to me," I confessed before standing to my feet.

Corey turned his head to look at me, a soft smile on his face.

"I'm going to go get cleaned up before dinner," I finished, heading towards the steps to wash up.

There was a weird silence at the dinner table but I didn't confront it; I was too busy eating Corey's delicious pasta.

"Baby, the food isn't going to leave your plate," my mother teased, taking a sip of her wine.

I stopped my fork midway up to my mouth and blushed in embarrassment. "I'm sorry, it's just so good. I haven't had real food in days."

She chuckled, "I was just kidding, Kole. Eat up. This is my favorite dish of his."

They looked lovingly at each other as I began to chew slower, not wanting the way I was eating to gain any more attention.

"So how are you feeling?" my mom asked sweetly, giving me her undivided attention.

"I feel okay, not as heavy as I used to."

She nodded in agreement, "You already look much healthier. Your eyes are light and your skin seems richer," she studied.

I smirked. "Thanks," I said softly, my attention shifting back to my plate.

It had been quiet most of dinner and I was starting to think I was the reasoning for it. It seemed like they both had a lot to say to me but neither knew where to start ... as a family.

I couldn't take it much longer. I had to say something to break the ice, since they were unsure of how to do so. I understood they wanted to be careful with me after everything that has happened but I needed them to know that they didn't need to be.

I put my fork down, causing a clang against the glass plate, catching both of their attention.

"I want to go to therapy," I stated firmly.

Corey's eyes widened as my mother was quick to take another sip of her wine before looking to her husband and then back to me.

"What?" she questioned, speaking for the two of them.

I sighed softly, "I want to start therapy. Is that not a good idea?" I questioned nervously, unsure of how to take their reaction.

My mom was caught on her words before she finally managed to form some, "Why-n-no! I think that's an awesome idea, Kole. It's what we wanted to talk to you about. How did you come to that conclusion?"

I looked down, slowly picking my fork back up to pick at a few noodles. "Well Jesse and I were talking and he said therapy helped him and he thinks it'll help me too."

Corey cleared his throat quickly before speaking up, "Is this something you truly want for yourself, Kole? Do you think it'll be beneficial?"

"I'm not just doing this because Jesse thinks I should. I'm doing this because I want to get better. I don't want to be the same girl I turned into. I want to be ... myself whoever that is. I want to start figuring it out and I think this is a good place to start," I answered with more confidence, causing a small smile to grace both of my parent's faces.

"Well I, for one, am proud of you sweetie and I'll help you find a good place."

I nodded to my mother's support. "Thank you. I want to get in as soon as I can. I'm ready to get started I'm ready to move on – ready to just be happy."

Her big brown eyes never left mine as I spoke; I could see the emotion building in them. She looked to her husband, who returned a warm glance.

She sighed happily before looking back down to her meal. "Thank you, God."

"So they found you a place?" Jesse asked, typing away on his laptop.

We were at his apartment, doing homework and I had just finished talking about the appointment I made with the therapist my parents found for me.

I nodded, flipping a page in my sociology book. "Yeah, my appointment is on Monday. I'm kind of nervous."

He fanned me off, "Ah don't be, just be open, that's all they ask for. Be honest and just share whatever comes to mind and answer the questions. They ask all of those questions for a reason."

I nodded to his explanation, reading the same line in my book over and over. I couldn't concentrate like I wanted to.

"How's school? Has campus been awkward since everyone found out about Devon?"

It wasn't like people really knew me anyway but they knew him. I hope I didn't change the atmosphere with something coming out so dark about their admired pupil.

Jesse exhaled, scratching behind his neck, "I mean I dunno. He's out on bail right now until the trial in the fall. People ain't really been treating him no different from what I can tell. The court issued a restraining order so I haven't really been around him that much."

"What about Lucy, have you seen her?"

Jesse looked at me with an unreadable expression, twisting his lips to the side before glancing away.

"Yeah, I seen her."

My eyes widened, feeling the anger boil in my chest, "And she didn't ask about me? Nothing? She was the last person to see me before everything happened! She-she left me! She left me there when I asked her not to and she's not even the least bit concerned?!"

I don't know why I was so surprised by Lucy's lack of caring, but I thought we were really friends. She was the only other person I had here besides Jesse, at one point.

"She with Devon now, Nic. She's on his side with this," he told me carefully, waiting for my reaction.

I felt my heartbeat begin to quicken at the news. "What do you mean she's with Devon now?"

He blew a heavy breath through his nose, sitting back in his seat, "They're together it seems like. They walk around campus, holding hands, kissing. Acting like nothing ever happened."

"Like I never existed."

"Wow," I scoffed in disbelief. "I was really getting played. It's like they targeted me or something."

Jesse shook his head, "Nah they just foul and Lucy always been a jealous individual. She never wants something for herself, she only wants it cause someone else has it. That's just how she always got around and why she can't keep friends. You didn't know."

"But you did," I spoke sharply, cutting Jesse off.

"Now wait a minute –"

"You knew and didn't tell me! You didn't warn me or anything," I replied, getting hot and wanting to take my anger out on something.

Jesse frowned, his eyebrows pressed in the center of his forehead. "I told you to be careful, Nic. Remember, at the block party, I told you then don't be quick to open ya self up and you made it clear you ain't want me to pry and to let you live. So I let you! Don't put them doing you wrong on me. I was speaking on deaf ears."

I sank with shame, realization hitting me. He did try to warn me and at the time I wasn't trying to hear it.

"I'm sorry, just hearing that rubbed me the wrong way."

He sighed, "I knew it would. I was just hoping you would never ask so I wouldn't have to tell you."

I rolled my eyes at the thought of the two of them.

"Well it's good to know they can just live care free, not thinking about the way they impacted my life in the worst way."

Jesse shook his head, "They'll get theirs. Revenge just ain't yours to seek, they'll get dealt with but just don't focus on that. It ain't your burden to carry."

I ran a hand through my hair, knowing Jesse was right.

"It's just easier said than done ... it hurts."

He nodded, "As expected and it's okay to hurt for a little, just don't stay there. Don't stay trapped in that pain, baby, that's what the enemy wants."

My brows furrowed in wonder. "The enemy? You talking like the devil or something?"

Jesse gave a nod, looking back to his laptop screen.

"Yeah. It's his spirit operating behind Lucy and Devon to hurt you and others. They're just letting him take over freely. It's always a choice and they made theirs."

There was a silence as I tried to process what Jesse was explaining so effortlessly. When he talked about God, it all sounded like facts. It flowed so freely from his lips that it was hard not to believe what he was speaking of was truth.

Maybe it was?

"Can I go to church with you one day? I want to know more about the things you're talking about. You know, understand it for myself," I blurted as his eyes darted to mine in surprise.

"Yo, you serious or are you messing with me?"

I chuckled at his astonishment. "I'm serious, I mean ... I ain't tryna go on Sunday. I wanna have more talks with you before I make a step like that but I do wanna go with you, one day. Just when the day comes, will you take me?"

He smiled softly, reaching out to place his warm calloused hand over mine.

"Of course I will, baby, whenever you're ready."

I blushed at the softness in his tone and the genuine care resting for me in his eyes. He was happy about this and surprisingly, so was I.

"Thank you, Jesse," I replied, already missing the touch of his hand after a reassuring squeeze.

What would I do without him?

I sat in a chair in the waiting room of the therapy office. I had filled out all of my new patient paperwork and was instructed to hang tight until my appointed time.

I couldn't sit still. I kept crossing my legs over the other, uncrossing them then repeating the action in the opposite direction. My palms were clammy; goose bumps were running up and down my spine. I was nervous, to say the least. Nervous for what was to come and trying to pin point what I was going to say to not come off crazy. The last thing I wanted to be labeled was crazy. If I hadn't gotten dropped off, I would leave but I was stuck. Stuck to come face to face with my issues.

Truthfully? That's what scared me the most.

"Kole Sommers?"

My name being called nearly made me jump out of my skin. I clutched my chest slightly, trying to calm myself as the woman who spoke my name smiled somewhat amusingly in my direction.

"It's okay, sweetheart. Dr. Tracy will see you now." She said sweetly, gesturing her hand for me to follow her.

I stood slowly to my feet, glancing down before meeting her stare. Once I got close enough, she began to walk, leading me from the sitting area to a narrow hallway full of doors. We walked down to nearly the last one before she opened the door for me.

"Have a seat on the couch, honey; she'll join you in a minute." The kind receptionist spoke as I nodded quietly, taking my seat and studying the room.

It looked like something from a movie, you know, the typical shrink's room. There was a long couch and a large comfy chair resting adjacent from it. The office had three large shelves full of books and a desk with a computer sat right next to one of the shelves near the window.

I gripped the edge of the couch in nerves, waiting until my shrink joined me. I looked to my left, watching as a tall, pale brunette glided in the room, happily taking a seat across from me in the chair.

She took off her thick-framed glasses, crossed her legs and smiled at me.

"Well hello, Kole. I'm Dr. Tracy, how are you today?" she asked brightly as I sat further back on the couch. The nerves began to slowly leave.

"I'm fine, how are you?" I returned softly, studying her every movement.

She was getting more adjusted in the chair and grabbed a pen and large clipboard with a paper on it. She quickly jotted something down before drawing her attention back to me.

"I'm wonderful today sweetie, thank you for asking," she beamed. "Are you nervous?"

"A little. I've never done anything like this before," I responded.

"I understand, it can seem a little intimidating at first but I can assure you, I'm only here to help and to talk. If you only want me to be a listening ear some days, I can be that. On the days you really want to walk through the emotions that you're feeling, I can do that too," she explained as I nodded in response, sitting more upright.

She sat back in her chair, resting an elbow on the armrest.

"So for this first session, I just want to get to know more about you and why there isn't a smile on that beautiful face."

I smiled at the compliment, waiting for her to continue.

"What brings you in today, why did you come here?" Dr. Tracy questioned sincerely, piercing her green eyes into mine as if she could see right through me.

I blew out a heavy breath, unsure of what to say. I clasped my hands together, unclasped them then clasped again, searching for the words.

"I don't know," I stumbled. "I just- I just want to be better. I feel like I'm so messed up and I'm trying to figure out where to start. I figured this is where I start."

She nodded in understanding, while jotting down a few notes.

"Why do you feel like you're messed up, when did that begin?"

I chuckled bitterly with a shake of my head.

"Hmm … let's see. Do I start at the part where I was raped repeatedly when I was eleven or when my boyfriend turned into my pimp?"

Dr. Tracy's eyes widened as she dropped her pen. "Wow, I am … I am so sorry to hear that you were raped, Kole. You said repeatedly, so you knew who it was?"

I huffed, "Unfortunately. It was my mother's boyfriend at the time. I can't even say his name out loud without wanting to throw up."

She hummed softly, setting her notepad to the side.

"That must've been awful, unimaginable really. Did your mother know?"

I shrugged, "Not exactly. I had tried to tell her but she was so strung out on drugs that she wasn't hearing me. Half the time when it would happen she would barely be conscious. You know, looking back, I think he did that on purpose just so she wouldn't hear the screams."

I watched as her face dropped while listening to my story.

"Honey, that is horrible – "

"To me, that wasn't even the worst part about it," I admitted.

Her brows furrowed in wonder.

"Really? Then what was?"

I sighed, "The fact that I had to lose Jesse in the process."

"Jesse, who is that? Tell me about him."

The smile began to spread across my face at the mere thought of him. I was thankful for the shift in conversation to something, or someone positive. I hated reliving the haunting parts of my past and most of it was just something I was not ready to open up about on this first session.

"Jesse ... is my best friend. He lived across the street from my mom with his parents. We grew up together, did everything together but the moment I lost my innocence, I knew I couldn't stay there. I knew he would never be able to look at me the same. I had experienced something I thought I would only experience with him."

"Sex?" she questioned as I shook my head.

"Yeah, but not just that. Love in its' entirety and all that came with it. I wanted him to be my first everything because ... because –"

I caught myself, realizing I was revealing more than I ever would with anyone else.

Dr. Tracy already had a way of making me feel comfortable talking to her and I appreciated it.

"You were in love with him," she finished with a smirk.

I couldn't speak; I just placed my head down in response. I was too fearful to admit that out loud.

"Where is Jesse now?" she asked curiously.

"He's back in my life. When everything happened initially, I moved in with my grandmother until she died a few years ago. Now I live back with my mom and her husband so Jesse and I got back in touch," I explained as she nodded.

"You still love him?" she asked.

I froze.

"What?"

She smiled softly, "You still love him now as much as you did back then?"

I sighed, looking to the ceiling for some type of refuge.

"I don't know, sometimes I think I do more now than I did before, if that makes sense. He's just always there and so compassionate. He cares about me so much and he just has it all together. I feel like I'm too broken to even receive love or even reciprocate it."

"Is that why you're really here, Kole? Not because you're messed up but because you want to be better to love, you want to be free to receive love?"

I finally met her eyes, feeling the emotion prick at my chest.

"I don't know, maybe? Just … fix me? Please."

She grinned, leaning in a little. "I'm only your therapist, Kole. I don't have the power to actually fix you. What I can offer you are tools to help you to help yourself. That power lies solely in your hands. But I tell you what, you've chosen a great place to start. We can spend this time each week helping you to get stronger and let go of your past issues, one by one. I'll be here to show you how your past, no matter how dark, can help you to have a great future. It's all based on your perception."

Her words rang true and showed me that I had made the right decision by choosing to get help. My perception desperately needed a change.

CHAPTER
- EIGHT -

"Does therapy always make you feel ... heavy?" I asked Jesse after we both had gotten more comfortable in the booth.

He took me out to get some dinner after picking me up from my appointment. The rest of my session went well with Dr. Tracy as she asked more about my upbringing and life with my grandmother and the events that led me to her office. She was excited for us to continue our weekly sessions.

Jesse opened his menu, "What you mean?"

I sighed, "I don't know. It's not like I feel bad after therapy. I'm just ... thinking about everything, you know, about my life."

Jesse nodded in response, "Aw, yeah I know what you saying now. I mean, therapy don't always make you feel like sunshine and rainbows after. Some sessions are really good and light and you can laugh and then some are just ... heavy but you gotta get deep. That's what they're there for, to pull that out so you can deal with it. Thinking is good though, you should be thinking things through."

I felt a little more at ease after he answered my question. I was finally able to look through the menu, realizing how hungry I was.

"Man this steak is looking RIGHT though!" Jesse exclaimed in a goofy tone while holding his fist to his mouth. I laughed at his mannerisms just as the waitress approached our table.

She was looking directly at Jesse, not paying me any mind. "Good evening, welcome to Marco's. Can I start you off with something to drink?"

I smirked to myself at the girl's tone. It was the most flirtatious I had ever heard someone take an order.

Jesse looked directly at me, not even bothering to look at the waitress.

"What you want, baby?" he asked, waiting for my answer.

I smiled before looking up at the waitress, whose smile had left.

"I'll have a raspberry tea, please," I answered; smile widening as she just nodded shortly at my request.

Jesse grinned, finally locking eyes with her, "Sounds good, so I'll have the same please, thanks."

She blushed, "Okay sweetie, sure thing. Be right back with your drinks."

She paid him one last look before leaving our table.

I chuckled, shaking my head, "I don't think she likes me very well but you though? I see you, Jes."

He playfully rolled his eyes, "Ain't nobody checking for that girl, she's rude anyway. She should've been asking you first."

I smirked, "Must you be perfect in everything you do?"

I could tell he was amused, "I'm not perfect, Nic."

I shook my head. "I disagree. If there was such a thing as a perfect man, I believe you are damn near close."

He grinned, "Ain't nobody perfect, girl. I'm human just like everybody else. I mess up all the time."

"Oh yeah, how so?" I asked drily, earning a chuckle from him.

"With my attitude, my faith sometimes. My thoughts ain't always the best. I don't always have the best judgment when making certain decisions. I've got my sins. They may not be the next mans, but I got my flaws. It's just when I get down, I don't stay down." he admitted strongly, not even sounding the least bit bothered by it.

It was quiet as I stared at my friend, admiring his features and the beautiful person he was. He didn't even notice, still glancing over his menu, reading the items carefully. He would scrunch his freckled nose at the food that seemed to disgust him.

"So you're not going to ask what we talked about in therapy today?" I questioned as he gave me a puzzled expression.

"Why would I do that? What you get out of that is for you and solely you. I'm just here to witness the growth, I already see it."

My eyes widened, "You do?"

He nodded confidently, "Of course. I saw it before you went today. Just the decisions you've been making and the positive attitude you've had since everything went down. It's truly surprised me but it's been a pleasant surprise. I love it to be honest."

My heart fluttered to hear Jesse use the word love while talking about me. I knew he would never love me in a romantic way but the thought of it was always nice.

"That means the world coming from you, Jes," I said softly, closing my menu.

"Well someone like you deserves the world. Any way I can offer that to you, I will," he responded smoothly just as the waitress appeared back at our table.

"Man I swear, if she leaves my cup empty for five more minutes, we're not tipping!"

I giggled, masking my annoyance, watching Jesse's shoulders hop in amusement.

We had our food and the waitress was being even colder to me now than she had in the beginning. She couldn't accept Jesse's rejection so she continued to take it out on me each time she passed our table.

"That's mean, Nic!" Jesse tried to defend as I shook my head in response.

"Nah man, I'm over here thirsty as hell! Mouth dry as fu-"

"Language!" Jesse scolded with a laugh, turning red from how humored he was.

"I'm sorry, Jes but she sucks!" I spat, turning up my nose and pushing my empty cup away from me childishly.

"Here, you can have some of mine," he offered sweetly, pushing his full and replenished drink in my direction.

I smirked, pulling the drink closer and taking a sip through his straw, relieving my thirst.

"Big ol' baby," Jesse teased watching me suck on his drink happily.

I pushed the cup back towards him when I was finished, before picking up another fry to chew on.

"Okay anyway, where were we?"

"You were about to ask me another 'first'," he reminded as I nodded.

We were asking each other questions about the time we spent apart, wanting to get to know more about the other. These questions had been the most entertaining part of my entire evening.

"Okay, let me think," I pondered out loud, playfully tapping my chin. "First … kiss?"

My heart was beating heavily in my chest. Before we were just asking innocent questions, but I was ready to turn it up, just a little. I only hoped that he would answer whatever I asked with an open mind.

Jesse seemed to have blushed at my question, putting his head down only slightly before lifting it back up, running his tongue quickly over his bottom lip.

"Don't tell me you don't remember. It was with you."

My eyes nearly popped out of my head at his revelation. "W-what?!"

He grinned, shaking his head.

"Man you don't remember?!"

My mouth was agape, as I tried to think it over but couldn't place it. "We kissed?"

Jesse chuckled, "Yeah bum, we kissed. I was s'posed to be ya first too but now I'm not too sure … " He eyed me questionably as I laughed.

"No, I'm sure you were. I'm tryna dig deep in my memories. A lot has happened since then."

He snickered, "Dig deep in them memories, girl. I thought my kiss was unforgettable!"

I smiled, shutting my eyes tight; wanting desperately to remember this kiss we shared.

Suddenly, the memory came.

> *"That party was so stupid," I complained, kicking at a rock while walking down the neighborhood street with Jesse at my side.*
>
> *He had been quiet most of the walk home since we left Kristin's 12th birthday party. We were the youngest kids there, everyone else was in middle school already but Kristin invited Jesse. He just brought me for comfort since I didn't really like Kristin that much.*
>
> *"And Kristin likes you, you know. She doesn't even care that you're a fifth grader," I told him, the attitude clear in my tone.*
>
> *I hated that I could see how much she liked him. She gave me the rudest look when she greeted us at the*

door but only let me in because Jesse said he would leave if I couldn't stay.

The girl didn't have a choice at that point.

"So!" Jesse finally responded, causing me to be taken back with his tone.

"What you mad at me for?"

"Because!" he shouted, cutting me off. "You're telling me Kristin likes me like I care."

My brows rose at how mad he was getting while talking about her. I didn't want to be the cause of it I and was more annoyed that I was. "Well sorry for pointing out the obvious! She's older and she's pretty, why wouldn't you care?"

He rolled his eyes, stopping in his tracks. I stopped too, seeing our houses not too far away in the distance.

"Why did you keep leaving me at the party?" Jesse asked sincerely, voice calmer now.

It was then that I could see the hurt.

"What do you mean? I didn't keep leaving you. Everyone wanted to be around you and I didn't feel like I was fitting in so I was letting you have fun."

He shook his head, looking down at his feet.

"Ain't nothing fun without you, Nic. I didn't care about none of them middle schoolers at that party. I just wanted you around, that was it. You were my whole purpose for even being there. Without you, I wouldn't have even went."

My shoulders sank at his words, not realizing how much me coming meant to him.

"I thought," he stumbled, looking for the words. "I thought you were embarrassed by me or something like you didn't want us to be seen together."

My mouth dropped, placing a hand on my chest. "Me? You thought I didn't want to be seen with you? Jesse you're my favorite person in the whole world! I'm proud to have someone like you as my friend!"

He finally looked up, smiling at my confession. "You mean that?"

I nodded quickly, "Every word, pinky swear."

He smirked, beginning to walk again as I trailed along.

"I, uh," I started after a few moments of silence. "I saw you go in the closet with Kristin too, for that dare. What happened?"

I was so nervous to hear the answer.

Jesse began snickering, only making me more nervous and kind of upset.

"That great huh?" I replied with sarcasm after he only continued to chuckle to himself.

"No, dummy. Ain't nothing happen in there, that's what's funny. I overheard her lie and tell girls we were kissing and stuff but ain't none of that happen." he replied nonchalantly as I grew even more confused.

"But ya'll had to be in there for seven minutes and the dare was to make out!"

Jesse turned his head towards me.

"Man we sat in there in silence for five of those minutes. Then she asked me if I thought she was pretty and why I wouldn't kiss her."

"And what did you say?" I was nearing the edge, wanting to know the full details of what went down in the closet. I almost wanted to throw up watching them go in there.

He shrugged, "I said she has pretty eyes and that I was saving my first kiss for someone special."

My heart dropped, eyes darting back and forth trying to figure out who that special someone could be.

"Wha- I don't get it. Who could be even more special than Kristin?" I asked, thoroughly confused.

Jesse stopped walking, just before we reached my house and turned to face me. I turned to face him as well and my face still twisted.

"You're way more special than Kristin could ever be." he said softly, his eyes holding an emotion I had never seen before.

"Huh? What do you –"

Before I could say another word, Jesse's soft and warm lips were pressed against mine.

They were softer than I ever imagined and he used the tip of his index finger to bring my face closer to his. He pecked my lips gently several times, his eyes never daring to open as I continued to stare at him in complete shock before finally closing my own in bliss.

He pecked me one more time before pulling away. We looked at each other, slightly breathless and in awe of the moment.

He sighed happily, revealing the dimple in his left cheek.

"I saved it for the right girl."

I shook my head at the memory, coming back to reality. "I can't even believe something like that slipped my mind after all these years."

"Probably because we both swore each other to secrecy that following Monday on the bus, saying we'd never speak of it again."

"Why did you kiss me?" I asked suddenly, still trying to process it all, coming up short with an answer of my own.

He scrunched his nose, "What kind of question is that?"

"A valid one," I returned. "Why did you?"

He smiled, shoving a fry in his mouth, "You really must not have known me too well back then."

I grew offended. "What? I knew you like the back of my hand, you know that."

He shook his head, dismissing my words.

"You couldn't have, not if you couldn't see how much I cared about you."

"Well yeah, we cared about each other, we were best friends –"

"More than that," he cut me off. "More than a friend it was deeper than that. I didn't even really realize it then, how much I cared about you until you left."

It was quiet and I was at a lost for words. It never crossed my mind that Jesse cared about me as much as I did him when we were younger. I used to map out my entire future with him, secretly name our kids – the whole nine.

"What about now?" I asked bravely. I needed to know for sure now, I needed to know if those feelings were still there.

His eyes never left mine, giving me a feeling that he was picking apart my soul.

"What do you feel now?" I dared to question again, breath caught in my throat.

His expression was intense, before he broke eye contact, revealing a small smirk.

"I care now just as much as I did then, maybe even more than that."

"So then what happened?" Dr. Tracy questioned, with a playful smirk. She seemed to be on the edge of her seat, waiting to hear what I had to say next about my dinner with Jesse last week and his revelation.

I took in a deep breath, hands clasped together.

"I don't know … I panicked, I freaked. I wasn't expecting him to answer that way."

She chuckled, jotting down some notes on her pad. "So let me get this straight. You dared to ask the question and then became afraid when he gave you the exact answer you wanted?"

It sounded so stupid coming from her lips. "Well, yeah."

She snickered more, shaking her head amusingly before setting her pad down and putting her glasses on.

"So what's happened since? Have you two talked about it?"

I quickly shook my head no. "Not at all. It got awkward real fast afterwards and we were about done with dinner anyway so we left. He tried to talk to me, but I just kept spacing out. I've been avoiding his text since then."

Dr. Tracy grinned at me with a sweet sigh.

"Oh Kole, you are one interesting young woman to figure out."

I blew out a breath, running my hands down my thighs. "Tell me about it, what have you discovered thus far?"

She seemed to be pondering a bit before she answered, "What I've come to understand about you is that you are someone who has been through a traumatizing experience, not once but nearly twice. Not to mention, your stint of prostitution ... yet you sit here in front of me as beautiful as can be and somehow able to not have completely succumbed to the brokenness you feel on the inside."

Dr. Tracy paused and then continued, "What I really want to discover about you, is how you're able to sit here in front of me and be able to talk with such strength. Do you know that you possess such a thing? Strength, resilience?"

I was quiet for a moment before shaking my head softly. She seemed to be surprised by my confession.

"And how could you not? Where does that strength and courage to press through come from?"

I felt my heart pounding in my chest, my face becoming hot with emotion that was starting to surface. I was afraid to blink, thinking it would cause fresh tears to fall.

My shoulders rose briefly before falling back to my side. "To be honest, it comes from Jesse. Being around him, being with him and knowing all of the things he has been through and the pain he has endured, it makes my problems not seem so big. They seem manageable. Everything is just so easy and free. His presence alone makes me feel at ease. Safe."

She nodded in understanding, "And I truly admire the love that the two of you have for each other. I know one day, when it's time, the two of you will share a love and bond so strong that'll be so beautiful to witness. But for now, I want to focus on Kole and her alone."

My brows furrowed, trying to process what she was saying to me.

"Kole, you depend a lot on Jesse in regard to your emotional state. Even though he sounds like an amazing man and an even more amazing friend to you, he is only human. His presence isn't always promised to bring you peace or to make you feel safe. You need to learn how to be that for yourself, how to be whole. So when that day comes that Jesse wants to love you with everything he has within him, there will be someone there for him to love."

It felt like my heart had dropped down to my toes. My head shook in disbelief.

"I can't … I don't know if I can do that. I don't know if I can –"

"You can cope without Jesse, it is very possible," she said gently, cutting me off.

"You have to learn, Kole or you'll start to feel like you don't know how to breathe without him there. Jesse is great; believe me but he cannot be all you have. You have to have yourself, sweetie."

I looked to the floor; unable to face the truth I was hearing.

"Some people," she continued, "depend on a higher power, or their faith to help them cope, to have that inner peace, to learn how to love themselves. Their religion gives them that."

When I didn't utter a word, she spoke up, "Do you believe in a higher power?"

I lifted my head then, "You mean God?"

She nodded.

"Do you?" I asked her, earning a soft smirk.

"I do. I believe in God with everything that I have," she answered truthfully as my lips parted at her honesty.

"It's like," I stumbled. "I know that He's real. I just don't know how to find Him in reality, if that makes sense. It's hard for me."

She nodded, carefully listening to my words. "Sometimes people just need a push in the right direction, some guidance. Have you ever gone to church?"

I shook my head. "I went a few times when I was little and the last time I've been inside a church was for my grandmother's memorial. I've mentioned it to Jesse before and my step-dad has talked to me about going a few times. I plan to go, I just don't know when."

"I understand," she assured with a kind smile. "This conversation doesn't mean that church is the only answer nor should you feel forced to go. What I really want for you is to love yourself, really discover who Kole is beyond everything that you've been through."

"I wouldn't even know where to start, Dr. Tracy. Loving myself? That just seems so ... "

"I know it seems strange or foreign to you but it's important. You can't expect someone else to love you genuinely if you don't know how to love yourself by yourself. It's the most important piece."

I sighed, nearly exasperated, "But where do I start?"

She grinned, ripping a piece of paper from her pad. She placed it on the coffee table before me then handed me a pen.

I looked at her questionably, "What's this for?"

"It's to make a list."

My brows connected at the center of my forehead. "A list of what?"

"Of all of the things you love about yourself."

I scoffed.

"Well, this paper will remain blank. I don't love anything about myself."

She frowned, "And there lies the problem but I'm sure there are some things you love about yourself. It doesn't matter if there are five things on that piece of paper or fifty, before this hour is over but we will come up with some things together. Each week we will continue to add more, until that paper is full of beautiful things that you love about yourself."

"Ok!" she sighed happily. "Let's start with number one!"

I rolled my eyes at her excitement before looking back to the blank sheet of paper.

This was going to be a long session.

———————————

I sat on my bed, listening to soft music while trying to study for my final exams a few days after my last session with Dr. Tracy. They were coming up and I wanted to be prepared. I begged my counselor to allow me to just take my test online but he said it would be too easy for me to cheat and that the rules were for all online students to take all final exams at the center. My nerves were through the roof about that, but I chose to push it to the back of my mind for now.

I rubbed my eyes, preparing to read yet another page in my book before there was a soft knock on the door. I looked up, questionably, clearing my throat.

"Come in" I called, expecting either my mother or Corey.

I waited patiently as the door opened and nearly gasped at the person walking through.

"Jesse?" I looked at him strangely as he only grinned in response.

"Surprised to see me?" he asked mockingly, closing the door behind him.

I sighed, "What are you doing here?"

"Are you avoiding me?" he responded with a question of his own.

"Yes."

He was taken back before chuckling softly and took a seat at the edge of my bed, not too far away from where I sat.

"Well at least you were honest," he shrugged as I shied away from his eyes.

"I wouldn't lie to you."

"But you would ignore me instead like I did something wrong? You almost made me wish I would've lied to you just to have my friend around a little bit longer."

I picked at a loose string on my comforter, "You never answered my question."

"What, about me being here? You know why I'm here. I shouldn't have to answer that for you."

I looked up now, "Well why are you here even after I ignored you?"

"Because I don't operate that way. We clearly need to talk and get on the same page about some things. We're too old to go about this so childlike."

"Go about what?" I challenged as he flashed a dry expression.

"This," he gestured between us with two fingers. "Our feelings, what's happening between us and I know I ain't alone. I was just the first person brave enough to admit it."

I released a short breath, "So, so you meant it. You meant what you said?"

He chuckled softly, putting his head down before picking it back up.

"Of course I did. I said it didn't I? With no shame."

The nerves returned, forcing me to catch my breath and look down again. I could hear a small snicker from Jesse before he spoke up.

"Look at me," he demanded softly as I continued to keep my head down. I couldn't look at him; I was afraid that I would crack.

He placed a delicate finger underneath my chin lifting my head up.

"Look at me, baby."

My heart fluttered, like it always did when he showed me affection causing me to be a magnet to his charm. I couldn't look away even if I wanted to.

He removed his finger from my chin, not daring to remove his eyes from mine.

"These feelings I got for you Nic, are real. It's something more real than I've ever experienced. I thought, when you moved, they would go away. They did for a while but the moment you returned, they rushed right back, stronger than ever. You had grown and yeah you had been through some things but you were still that same girl, still my best friend, still a part of me."

I couldn't find the words, only giving Jesse more room to speak. He stood tall to his feet, beginning to pace slightly.

"And trust me, when you came back, I kept ignoring it, ignoring my heart because I wanted to be true to Phi but deep down, I knew I could never love her like she wanted because ... because my heart was already spoken for. That's part of the reason why I had to end it. I prayed and asked God for guidance on the relationship I had with her, and He showed me exactly who she was and why I had to stop wasting both of our time."

He stopped mid pace to stare down at me. I was frozen in my spot, hanging on to every word he was saying for dear life.

"I feel for you, baby. It's real and it's the strongest thing I've ever felt for anyone in my life. I just know that we need time. You've been through a lot and you're just now starting to heal from your past and I need to respect that space. I'm going to respect that space, because it's not for me to fill at this very moment."

He stepped towards my bed slowly, my eyes following his every step. "But just know, please know that when the time is right, we're going to have a love so deep and so strong that nothing on this earth can break it. I see it, I feel it, please tell me that you feel it too?" he dared to ask me, nearly catching me off guard.

I took in a shaky breath, blinking slowly.

"Yes. I feel it every day and ... and even more when I'm with you," I admitted. He grinned softly.

He sat down on my bed, taking my shaky hand into his, kissing it gently.

"What does this mean then, for us?" I whispered, my eyes traveling from his torso up to his beautiful light brown face.

"It means, we continue to remain the best of friends, we continue to learn more about ourselves and each other. We grow together, laugh together – just have fun together and when it's time for us to transition into more, we will. Just don't ... don't run from me anymore,

Nic. Don't ever be afraid to be real with me. Don't ever be afraid of … me."

He sighed, "I can't rush this with you because I can't afford to lose you again. I need you here, I need you in my life and I can't risk that. I don't ever want to hurt you."

I shook my head, "I don't want to hurt you either Jes."

He nodded, "Which is why we're going to take our time. I just couldn't go another day without you knowing how I truly feel, setting the record straight with where I stand with you. No more guessing, no more wondering if I care about you more than a friend or thinking I never could because I do. I always have."

I released a short laugh of disbelief, "I just don't understand, why me?"

He smirked, moving some hair from my face then placing his hand behind my neck and pulling me in to place a soft gentle kiss on my forehead. He backed away only a bit, his sweet breath beating against my cheeks.

"That's what I need you to get before we take this any further than friendship. I need you to start asking yourself the question *why not you*? Once you see the beautiful person I see, we can go somewhere. Until then, it's time to focus on Dominic. Fall in love with her first, before you fall in love with me," he answered, rubbing the hairs on the back of my neck.

"It may already be too late for that."

———————

I was standing in the kitchen, singing an old New Edition song to myself while washing dishes.

"Because I need somebody who will stand by me. Through the good times and bad times you will always … always be right there." I sang softly, in a groove, washing a pot.

"Sunnnyyyy dayysss! Everybody loves them!" My mother busted out, dancing along side of me, nearly making me jump out of my skin in surprise.

She laughed happily, attempting to bump hips with me playfully. "Aww come on Kole why you stop singing?! I wanna join in!"

I giggled at her antics, placing the now clean pot in the drying rack to my left. "You scared me!"

Her laugh simmered down to small chuckles as she walked over to the refrigerator. "Well you seemed to be in a zone, singing and what not. I wanted to get in on that. I haven't heard you sing in years."

I grinned to myself, trying to finish up the last of the dishes in the sink.

"I'm in a good mood I guess. I don't know."

She stopped her movements to stare with one hand on her hip and a playful smirk on her face.

"Mm hmm. I know that look," she teased, pointing at me before leaning against one of the counters.

I shrunk under her stare, the heat coming to my cheeks, not sure of what she could see in my face. I didn't want to give anything away.

"I'm just … content, Mom. I'm in a better place," I explained, avoiding her eyes.

She snickered, "Uh huh, I'm sure you are. I have a feeling Jesse has something to do with that too."

I crossed my eyes in annoyance, placing the last dish in the drying rack and pulling the plug to empty the sink full of water. I dried my hands against my sweatpants, preparing to leave her company in haste.

"Aww come on Kole! Don't leave. I was just kidding, baby. I know ya'll are just friends," she chuckled, coming up behind me and grabbing me by my shoulders to pull me back into the kitchen with her.

I smirked, leaning against the counter across from her, "What ma?"

She shrugged, the smile still evident on her face.

"Nothing. What's going on, how are you?"

I sighed happily, shrugging as well, "I'm good. I can say that."

She nodded in understanding, "Even after everything? Are you sure you're okay? Is going to school next week going to be a problem at all?"

I frowned a bit, raising my shoulders, "I'm just taking it as it comes but as far as everything that has happened, I'm just ready to move forward from it, that's all. I've just been taking it day by day."

She grinned, happy with my answer. "That's wonderful to hear baby. I am truly proud of you, more than you could ever imagine."

"Thank you," I shifted on my feet. "I think when school ends, I want to start working. I kinda miss it, having something to do every day and making my own money. I want to start saving up to get my own car."

Her eyes widened in surprise, "Well, okay. You know Corey and I can get you a car –"

I shook my head, "No, it's something I really want to earn. I've never had the opportunity to save up and buy something that's really important. I think it'll be good for me."

Tiffany Campbell

I watched my mother continue to watch me with pride before she slowly nodded her head, "Okay baby, sounds good."

She made to walk off, but I stepped forward, not wanting her to leave just yet.

"Ma, wait," I called as she turned, revealing an inquisitive expression.

"What do you love most about me?"

My heart was racing, awaiting her answer. I was trying to work on my list and I figured hearing positive reinforcement from others would help me.

She grinned softly, "Your smile and your laugh. When you're genuinely happy and smiling, your cheeks touch the tips of your eyes and you just have this radiant glow about your beautiful brown skin. It's my favorite thing and it's exactly what I love most," she finished before turning and heading up the steps.

———————————

"So like, do you even know how to drive?" Jesse asked from his couch while he flipped through the channels on his television.

We were taking a break from studying for our exams and decided to find a mindless show to watch until we were in the mood to study again. I was sitting on the floor, my back pressed against the loveseat.

I snickered, "Yes I know how to drive dork. I used to drive my Maw Maw's car all the time back in the day."

His shoulders hopped with amusement, "Back in the day, what's that mean? You still ain't have a license."

"So? That doesn't mean I don't know how to drive, it's like riding a bike."

He smirked, rolling his eyes, "Yeah? Why'd you never take a test then?"

"Because I'm a good driver. I never got pulled over, not once."

He chuckled, shaking his head. "Whatever bum. So where you trying to look for jobs at?"

I shrugged, "I don't know. I was thinking somewhere in the mall or something. I used to work at Walmart, so anywhere would be fine with me. I just want to make some money and get some hours."

He nodded, running his tongue over his lips quickly. "Aight, cool. We'll go looking after finals. Plenty of places are hiring."

I relaxed looking at the show Jesse landed on. I wasn't really paying attention to it, my mind beginning to run wild with thoughts of working again. I missed the feeling of independence desperately.

"Hey," Jesse said into the quiet, my eyes traveling lazily to him.

"What's ya plans for ya birthday? It's coming up," he reminded as I shrugged at the thought.

"I haven't even been thinking about it. My birthday has never been a special event. I've never really had friends besides you, and my grandmother would just make me a cake every year. It's just never really been something to celebrate."

He turned his nose up, "What you mean? There's a lot to celebrate because you're still here. You've been blessed with another year to share ya world with others."

I smirked, shaking my head. "Yeah, that sounds good and all but it's just never been my life for real. You remember; we didn't have parties or anything as kids. It was always another day."

He smacked his lips, "Well, we changing that this year. I'll plan something nice for you."

"You don't have to do that Jes," I said softly.

He fanned me off, "Too late. I was already starting to get you gifts."

My eyes widened, "What? You did not start getting me gifts!"

He chuckled, "I swear. You want one of them?" he asked, tipping a brow.

I was stuck, not sure how to answer. I couldn't even believe he got me a gift. He watched my expressionless face before pushing himself off the couch. I followed his tall, slim built frame with my eyes, watching as he disappeared out of the living room and into his bedroom. I looked ahead, waiting patiently for his return, nerves picking up wondering what he could possibly have for me.

After a few short moments, he returned with a short box in his hand. He walked up to me with a bashful smile, stretching the box in my direction.

I reached up hesitantly, "What is it?"

He snickered, "Open it dummy and see."

I playfully rolled my eyes, taking the box from him. It was slightly heavy so I placed it on the ground between my legs. I opened the top, my eyes widening at what was inside.

It appeared to be a black leather Bible with gold stitching. I ran my fingers across the smooth casing, in complete awe of the holy book. My eyes traveled from the top down to the bottom.

"It … it has my name on it."

He cleared his throat, "Yeah. I remember you telling me how you wanted to learn more about God and I figured what better way to start than with His word? I ordered the best one I could find online and had your name engraved on it. I thought it would feel more personal."

I smiled softly, "This is beautiful, Jesse. I love it."

I pulled the Bible from the box, opened it and flipped through the delicate pages, noticing some red lettering.

"What's with the red letters?" I asked, looking to Jesse for an answer.

"That's Jesus talking. Whenever you see red, He's speaking." he explained as I nodded.

"What's your favorite scripture?" I asked with intrigue, skimming over the words on the page, somewhere in Mark.

Jesse was quiet for a moment, "1 Corinthians 13," he answered with ease as I skimmed through the Bible trying to find what he was talking about.

"Is it in the front or back? I can't find it." I said getting slightly frustrated. I had never even opened a Bible before but I didn't want to look so immature in front of Jesse.

"It's in the back, baby, after Romans."

I nodded in remembrance because I had seen that word before. I kept skimming through the pages until I found it.

"Chapter 13 you said?" he nodded.

"What part?"

"It's verse 1 through 7."

I swallowed preparing to read, "If I could speak all of the languages of earth and of angels but didn't love others, I would only be a noisy gong or a clanging cymbal. If I had the gift of prophecy and if I understood all of God's secret plans and possessed all knowledge and if I had such faith that I could move mountains, but didn't love others, I would be nothing. If I gave everything I have to the poor and even sacrificed my body, I could boast about it; but if I didn't love others, I would have gained nothing."

I took in a breath, "Love is patient and kind. Love is not jealous or boastful or proud or rude. It does not demand its own way. It is not irritable, and it keeps no record of being wronged. It does not rejoice about injustice but rejoices whenever the truth wins out. Love never gives up, never loses faith, is always hopeful, and endures through every circumstance."

I released the breath I had been holding in astonishment. "Wow."

He grinned, "My absolute favorite. It's tatted on my arm."

I looked up to him, "Why?"

His brows furrowed, "Why what, is it on my arm?"

I shook my head, "Is it your favorite?"

"Oh," he smirked. "It explains exactly what love is supposed to be, who God is. God is love and it describes Him perfectly. How He loves us, and how we're supposed to love others. It's like a blueprint; it states how important love is and how nothing else matters without it. We could possess the whole world, but if we don't have love? It means nothing."

I nodded, remaining quiet. I couldn't help but think that this scripture not only explained God perfectly, but Jesse too. The way the Bible talks about love is exactly how Jesse expresses his love for me.

Maybe it can also be the blueprint to how I need to start loving myself.

"What you staring at, girl." Jesse asked, never taking his eyes off his laptop.

We resumed studying after our mini bible study. I was finding myself distracted, staring at his every feature. The slant in his honey brown eyes, the perfect arch in his eye brows, the way his freckled nose wrinkled out of habit when he was stuck on a problem and how he would dampen him plump lips every so often for moisture.

Why was this man so beautiful?

"Nic," he said again, looking at me now, only causing a small smile to spread across my face.

"What?" I asked, feigning innocence, never taking my eyes off his.

"Why are you being the biggest weirdo right now? You studying me and not ya Sociology?"

I shrugged, "This is all the sociology I need."

He snickered, shaking his head and looking back to his computer.

"When did you get so corny, dude? This how you act when you like somebody?"

I playfully rolled my eyes, "I wouldn't know, maybe. There aren't too many people I've liked other than you."

I could see his head nodding out of my peripheral vision, choosing not to comment on my statement.

"H-how many girlfriends have you had?" I boldly asked, unable to keep quiet about it any longer.

Jesse grinned to himself, "You are random."

"And you are avoiding an answer." I shot back with a smirk, locking eyes with him again.

He sat back in his chair, not taking his eyes off of mine.

"Three: one in high school, one when I first graduated and then Phi. I didn't really date much."

My eyes widened, "Didn't date much?! That's two more than I've ever had."

He chuckled, "What you want me to say, Nic? I dated. I liked girls ... a lot. It's not like I knew when I would see you again, or you had Facebook or something. I had to move around and find some fillers in the meantime."

I chuckled at his response, finding amusement in our conversation.

"How long were these so called relationships before Phi?"

He looked up to the ceiling with a thoughtful glance before raising his shoulders.

"Not long. No longer than a year I don't think. I think the girl I dated in high school was the longest. We were digging each other long before we made it official so I don't really know the dates."

I nodded, taking it in. "Did you love her?"

He scoffed, "Pft, nah. I mean, she was cool and we told each other we loved each other and what not but we were young. I wasn't in love or anything."

My heart eased a bit, but still held a pang of jealousy. It was in the past so there was nothing I could do about it but it didn't mean that I liked the thought of Jesse being with anyone else.

"What's that look?" Jesse asked.

I was debating about asking the next question.

"Are you a virgin?" I blurted, before I could catch it, unsure if I really wanted to know the answer ... yet again.

His mouth dropped a bit along with his brows. He was quiet for a moment before he cleared his throat, preparing to speak.

"No." he answered softly, avoiding my eyes now which were practically popping out of my head.

"What?! You're not? Why am I so surprised by that?" I asked more to myself than to him.

He snorted, "Because you think I'm perfect and like some nun over here. I'm not a virgin though."

"So who was it, Phi?"

He grinned, shaking his head.

"Phi and I never had sex. I lost my virginity to my first girlfriend but after we broke up that's when I got more serious about God and became celibate. It's been a while for me and it wasn't like I knew what I was doing back then."

I nodded, in genuine surprise. "So why didn't you take things that far with Phi then? It seemed like ya'll were intimate."

He shook his head, running his tongue over his bottom lip quickly. "Nah. Intimacy doesn't always involve sex, baby. Intimacy is being completely naked with someone with all of your clothes on. It's knowing their heart, their thoughts and sharing your feelings and your full self with the other person without being afraid of the consequence. I want to share that with someone before I ever share my body with them again. I only want that with my wife."

I was quiet for a moment, processing his words and what intimacy really was. I had never known it for myself in the physical or spiritual sense.

I could feel his eyes on me but I refused to meet his stare. I was starting to feel ashamed when it came to my own so-called sex life. I shared my body with so many people, people I didn't even know and all of them had a piece of me, leaving me practically empty. Even though Jesse has been with someone else, he was still more pure than I ever will be.

"The cool thing about your virginity though is that spiritually it can be renewed so that when you decide to give yourself to your soul mate it feels like the first time all over again. Completely, brand new," he spoke, my eyes darting to his.

"Don't let your past define you baby, everybody has one. Just move forward from here. You'll have your moment to feel true love and intimacy in the physical sense. You just have to heal first," he assured me, as if he was reading my thoughts.

I released a breath, feeling comfort swallow me whole. He always had a way of giving me back the pride that I felt was lost.

"Are you nervous?" Corey asked me from his driver's seat, while I looked out of my window at the college campus.

It was buzzing with students like it normally would on a Wednesday afternoon.

"No," I lied, feeling my face flush with fever as my heart quickened. I sat frozen in my seat, earning a chuckle from Corey.

"Well ... we've been sitting in the car for about ten minutes now, just looking at everyone else going to their class."

I sighed a bit with a slouch of my shoulders. "I'm scared, Corey." I finally turned my head to meet his kind eyes.

"Yeah, kinda figured that much kiddo. What's really bugging you?"

I shrugged, "I don't- I don't want to see him."

He nodded, "You shouldn't. Sharon talked with your counselor and they said that he shouldn't have any test scheduled for today based on his classes. Remember, 100 feet. The minute he breaks that, you call the police."

"Seems like such a cowardly thing to do. I don't want to cause a scene. I just want to finish up this quarter strong."

"Well you've already proven to be strong baby girl by maintaining a 3.7 GPA despite all you've been through this quarter. Will Jesse be on campus today?"

I shook my head, "He had his test this morning. I'm solo today."

He sighed before following up with a nod. He leaned in, grabbing my head softly and pulled me in to place a kiss on my temple.

"I'm just a phone call away. If you need an escape, call me and we'll work it out with the school later. Don't put yourself through this if you think you can't handle it," he assured strongly as I nodded meekly.

"I'll be fine … thanks Corey," I replied, finally finding the courage to open the passenger door.

"I should be done by four," I told him, holding the door open.

"I'll be here by 3:30, promise," he said. I gave a nod and shut the door closed.

I turned to face campus, sucking in as much air as my lungs would allow.

"I can do this," I told myself, before taking my first step.

I had just finished my Introduction to Business exam, waiting patiently in the courtyard for my next final exam to start. I hadn't seen any familiar faces yet and I was thankful for that, but I was noticing stares and whispers as people walked past.

It wasn't that my name was released in the news when everyone had found out about Devon but they had seen us on campus together prior to the incident and I'm sure they assumed that I was the girl in question and seeing how I never returned to school afterwards, it wasn't hard to put two and two together.

While I waited, I texted Jesse back to keep me company.

So everything is cool so far?

Yeah. No run ins yet. Just trying to stay calm.

Take your mind off of it then. Think about how you're going to this party with me on Saturday.

Party? Whose is it and for what?

My dude that I've known since high school. It's like an end of the year type thing. It should be fun, wanna go ... ?

―――――――――

I was walking now, debating if I wanted to step out with Jesse and be surrounded in his element. I was getting used to our one on one time that we shared. It wouldn't be much but I always left learning just a little bit more about him and even myself. Before, I used to despise Jesse's wisdom but I was growing to love every bit of it ... and him.

"Oh!" I yelped, surprised I had suddenly bumped into someone, "I'm sorry."

My phone had dropped out of my hand upon our collision and so had the other persons. I was picking up mine, just as she was picking up hers and I instantly noticed the bleached blonde hair and the faint smell of cigarettes.

Lucy.

She was looking at her phone in dismay before she cut her eyes at me.

"You should be sorry, you broke it," she spat, turning the now cracked phone in my direction.

The nerves I had about running into her had quickly turned into anger.

"It was an accident!"

She rolled her eyes, shifting on her foot. "Sure it was Kole. I'm sure you heard about Devon and me. If this was the revenge you wanted it was pretty pathetic of you."

My eyes turned into thin slits as I stepped closer to her; she didn't know the type of game she was playing, messing with me. I've gone to jail for being disrespected. I wasn't afraid to go back.

"Oh what?" she taunted, an amused smirk on her lips. "You stepping to me like you couldn't step to Devon? Lying because he didn't want you, even more pathetic than I thought!"

My eyes nearly bucked out of my head, "Lying on him?! Is that what he told you to clear his name? Are you kidding me?"

"It's the truth!"

I scoffed, "The truth? Lucy you were there! You know how it was and you knew I didn't want to be alone with him and you left me! You left there to get ... to get – "

She cut me off before I could even get it out.

"I didn't leave you! You're grown, you're a grown ass woman! If you ain't want him there then why you invite him? Your whole story is just bogus and it won't hold up in court! I'm on his side with this, not yours! Should've known better than to be cool with a nobody that just strolled into town. You just came to drag people down with you in that gutter you call a life!"

Her words were cutting like daggers and I couldn't believe she had the audacity to talk to me this way, especially when I knew deep down she knew better. At least I thought she did.

My hand was wrapped so tightly around my phone I was sure my knuckles were turning yellow with rage. I wanted so bad to use it to pummel Lucy's pale face in.

It was the sudden vibration in my palm that took my eyes off of her and the fire that was building up on the inside of me.

Jesse sending another text – that's right, I had him to think about. I had someone in my corner who still believed in me, a true friend. I didn't need to entertain this nonsense with Lucy. She wasn't worthy of my time or the beating that she truly deserved.

I took in a deep breath, training my eyes back on hers, watching the sinister smile that rested on her face. She was getting a rise out of the trouble she was causing me internally and I know that to be true because I could feel it. She wanted me to snap, just to prove Devon's case.

Well not today Lucifer.

"God bless you, Lucy," I said as easy as I could, earning a scoff and an eye roll from her. I chuckled at her reaction, before bumping her hard as hell in her shoulder when I made to walk past.

I shrugged at her calling me out of my name in the distance.

It wasn't the full *What Would Jesus Do* type moment, but it was a start.

God wasn't through with me yet. He was just getting started.

CHAPTER
- NINE -

"You should've seen me Jes!" I ranted, doing my hair in the mirror of my bathroom as Jesse sat patiently on the toilet.

He was watching me with an amused grin in the reflection of the mirror as I straightened another piece of the natural poufy chaos called my hair. I loved my hair because it was full, thick and wavy in its natural state but I hated it at the same time because it was just too much to do.

"Like everything in my right mind was telling me to slap that girl and drag her face across the concrete, everything! But ... instead, I took the high road. I shocked my damn self." I was still surprised at my actions from the other day. I finally had the chance to tell Jesse about it in person.

"Well I, for one, am proud of you Nic! You told me about ol' girl that you used to live with that you beat up and I'm sure this hurt a little bit worse than that."

"Man you don't even understand! Like I was utterly offended and disgusted at her whole being! She pissed me off to another level but I just didn't think she was worth it. I'm just ... better off."

He nodded, "You're better than that."

"I am."

The words rolled off so effortlessly I barely caught what I said. I *was* better than Lucy's actions, so much more.

I caught Jesse's eye in the mirror and blushed at the look he was giving me.

"What?"

"Nothing you're just ... pretty."

I quickly looked away.

"Shut up, I look crazy right now," I said, attempting to down play his words.

He shrugged, "So, your skin just glows and it looks just as soft as it is. I kinda wanna touch it right now just looking at it," he admitted, causing me to giggle.

"You can touch my face any time Jes. Just go for it."

He put up a mocking excited face, sitting up on the toilet seat.

"Oh gosh Dominic, you really mean it?! Any time I wanna? My golly I'd be honored to do that!"

I laughed out loud at his ridiculous tone as he chuckled too, easing back on the toilet seat.

"You're not helping this process move along being corny like this. We're never going to make it to the party at this rate."

I smiled, shaking my head.

"We'll be fine. My boy won't care, his parties typically go for a while."

I nodded in response, sectioning off another row of hair to straighten. "Does he have an apartment or ... "

"It's a fraternity house down on campus, him and his bruhs are throwing it."

My eyes widened, "A frat party? This is serious, I can't even believe you're going!"

He shrugged with a set grin on his face. "Don't treat me like some holy roller that sits in the dark quoting scriptures like rain man or some'n. I like being around people, girl, you knew that. Block parties weren't really my thing, but house parties are cool. It's in a more condensed space."

"You think your friends will like me?" I questioned genuinely, wrinkling my nose.

"I know they will. I like you, so they will too, just be yourself."

I rolled my eyes, "Like that's so simple."

"It is. You put too much thought into learning about yourself, Nic. You're a really cool person. Just relax, breathe and allow it to just be and it will. Don't make it complicated baby."

I tried to hide my smile at his usual term of endearment but I couldn't help the butterflies it always gave me.

"Do you call all of your female friends baby?" I asked trying to keep my blush to a minimum.

He shook his head, "Nope, just my baby."

"And I assume that's me?" I replied smartly, earning a soft smile from him.

"Always been you."

"Wow this party is packed," I stated, standing in front of the hood of Jesse's car.

He parked across the street from his friend's house and there were students everywhere; on the porch, in the front yard, on the sidewalk, and wall to wall in the house. Everyone was holding red cups, smiling and laughing amongst one another and you could hear the music blaring from indoors. What was crazy is that his house wasn't the only one having a party tonight. It seemed like most of his neighbors were throwing something as well.

"And this differs from a block party?" I asked Jesse with sarcasm.

He smirked, playfully rolling his eyes before interlocking his hand with mine, "Come on, It'll be fun."

I wasn't even paying attention to what he said; my orbs were fixated on our hands being interlocked as he led me across the street and up the walkway towards the house. I would randomly lock eyes with other girls, all who looking curiously at the two of us. I avoided their stares as best I could until Jesse and I reached the front door of the house, music swallowing us whole.

I watched Jesse's head nod at a few dudes, dapping them up with his free hand and holding me tight with the other. He said something inaudible to one of the guys, who then pointed towards the kitchen. Jesse thanked him and continued to lead us through the crowd of rocking bodies until we arrived to the intended destination.

My eyes instantly landed on a guy that seemed to hold the attention of everyone in the room. He was about Jesse's height, darker in complexion with a short haircut and the biggest country smile. He was attractive, that was for sure.

The handsome stranger locked eyes with Jesse, throwing his arms up high. "JP! What up boy?!"

I looked up at Jesse's smiling face as he unlocked our hands to join his friend in a brotherly embrace. They went in to slap hands before wrapping their arm around the other's shoulders. Everyone in the kitchen watched the exchange with happy faces. You could tell the two really had a strong bond.

Jesse took a step back by my side, "Aye Jamie bro, I want you to meet my good friend Dominic. Dominic, this is my boy Jameson," he introduced as Jamie's eyes widened looking at me.

He pointed at me before looking to Jesse in surprise. "This is the infamous girl you used to talk to me about all the time from way back when?!"

My eyes darted to Jesse who was nodding with pride, "This is the one."

Jamie looked back to me, arms open wide.

"Damn. You're more beautiful than he even said. I feel like I know you already! Gimme a hug!"

He pulled me into a warm and gentle squeeze as I took in his scent before letting go. He smelled as good as he looked. He and Jesse had that in common.

"You drink, Dom?" Jamie asked, pointing over to the counter full of alcohol. I looked at the arrangement briefly before shrugging.

"Not too much."

Jamie nodded in respect before looking to his friend and then fanning him off.

"I know yo holy ass ain't drinking nothing unless you somehow have to turn this water into wine to keep the party going," Jamie cracked, causing Jesse to laugh.

"Man shut up. You know why I don't drink bro," Jesse cackled earning a nod from his friend.

"Yeah I know I know. I'm just playing," Jamie said, tapping Jesse lightly in his chest. "Come on, let me show ya'll around, introduce you to some people."

Jesse and I were standing off to the side, watching Jamie participate in an intense game of Beer Pong against a couple of his frat brothers. I kept finding myself laughing at all of the yelling, chest hitting and chugging of the beers as Jamie's team was in the lead.

I would occasionally take peeks up at Jesse. He was tuned in, but his eyes would drift off, bouncing from different people scattered all over the room. He had been getting approached by people he knew all night, boys and girls alike and he made sure to introduce me to everyone. I bumped him lightly with my shoulder, getting his attention.

"W'sup baby?" he asked, bending down to hear.

"You ever wish you could fully be a part of this?" I asked, trying to over talk the music.

His eyebrows connected at the center of his forehead, genuinely confused by my question. "What you mean, be a part of what?"

"The drinking, letting loose completely and just enjoying the intoxication? You've never experienced that, right?"

He smirked, finally catching on to what I was asking. He licked his lips coolly before shaking his head. "Nah not really. My health is the most important thing to me and like I've told you before, I have a natural high. I don't need the liquor to have fun."

I nodded. "I would love to see you drunk, just one good time."

He chuckled, rolling his eyes playfully. "Yeah? Well I think you've been drunk enough for the both of us, hacking ya life up all over my crib."

I scoffed, pushing him in his side as he chuckled, trying to block my hits.

"Yooooo!" Jamie slurred walking up to us and hanging off of Jesse sloppily.

"I'm sorry ya'll. I might be just a littttttlllleeeeee tipsy. Not much though."

Jesse and I laughed at his friend before I felt the sudden urge to pee.

"Where's your bathroom again Jay?"

He put on a calculating face, pointing his finger in every which way. I chuckled, shaking my head and patting him on the shoulder.

"Don't worry about it, I'll find it," I joked, as Jesse gave me a concerned look.

"Need me to go with you?"

I shook my head. "I'm a big girl Jes."

He nodded, "Aight. We'll be in this area, just look for me."

"Will do." I smirked, heading in a different direction.

"Man, real talk, JP," Jamie said to his friend as they sat next to one another on the living room couch as the party continued around them.

"Dom is super cute. I know I don't know her or nothing yet, but I can tell you like her."

Jesse grinned at his best friend's words, "Thanks man."

"Nah like seriously. I ain't know you was gonna bring her and I saw Alana, thinking I was gonna try to hook ya'll back up but – "

His face scrunched up hearing the name of his ex-girlfriend. "Yo what? Alana is here?"

Jamie nodded, meeting eyes with Jesse depicting his reaction. "Yeah man, you knew her and her sorority were gonna roll through. I thought they were outside, you ain't see her?"

Jesse shook his head in response. "Nah. I was too focused on Nic."

He nodded, "As you should've been. I can tell you care way more about Dominic than you ever did Alana. I just knew ya'll were like the 'it' couple back in the day and there wasn't any bad blood. She was looking for you. It was before I knew you weren't coming alone, so I told her I'd let you know."

Jesse sighed, shaking his head, ridding his mind of all things Alana. "I'm good, fam. I'm just tryna chill and look out for Nic. She's where my head is right now."

"Respect. How you feeling these days though, everything good?" Jamie's tone had grown a bit more serious as he gave his friend a once over. He earned a toothy smile in response, allowing his spirit to be more at ease.

"I'm good, man. Healthy. That's all that matters."

Happy with the news, Jamie dapped him up, "Good, good. I'm happy to hear that. Now that schools out we gotta kick it, get back to the old days. I miss the days of just sitting back and playing 2K, talking about life and feeding off one another. The crew has been wanting to link up."

Jesse's eyes widened, "Word? Man I don't know, ya'll dudes is crazy. I've been living right, ain't got time for ya'll hellish ways."

Jamie smacked his lips, earning a laugh from his friend. "Man shut up! We got our shit together with Jesus too! Don't judge us."

Jesse held his stomach in laughter, "I'm just messing witchu. I miss the crew, ya'll gotta come through my crib. I'm sure Nic would love everybody."

"Yeah, they'd love her fine ass too," Jamie teased earning an eye roll. He paused, squinting a bit around the room. "Speaking of, where is she?"

Jesse paused too, searching around the room, "I dunno. I told her we were staying right here. Should we look?"

Jamie shrugged about to sit up before he unceremoniously fell back into the couch. Jesse laughed at his antics.

"Let's give it five more minutes," Jamie groaned, sitting still and waiting for the room to stop spinning.

I stood in the bathroom after washing my hands, studying my every feature, wanting to see what Jesse and Jameson were seeing whenever they call me beautiful.

I ran my fingers through my long and soft brown hair, fixing a few loose strands that strayed from my middle part. My rich brown skin was glowing from the light's reflection and I dabbed at the tiny beads of sweat that were forming on the tip of my short yet pointed nose. I pulled the Carmex from my pocket to gloss my full lips and did a double take of my almond shaped eyes to make sure there were no specks on my eyelashes.

I *was* beautiful. It had been so hard to see it for myself but I see it now. I see my beauty. I just wondered so strongly how beautiful I was on the inside. How radiant was my soul?

The hard knock on the door took me out of my thoughts, forcing me to realize how long I had been in the bathroom.

"One second!" I called, straightening out my high waist shorts and adjusting my crop top.

I gave myself one last look over before stepping out of the bathroom, rushing past the agitated stranger just as my phone vibrated in my palm.

It was Jesse wondering where I was. I sent a quick reply letting him know I was coming to him as I shoved past people while heading down the congested stairs.

Just as I reached the bottom, a group of girls burst through the front door, all wearing some form of green or pink and holding up their pinky and chanting a shrieking sound in unison. I watched them curiously as they walked through the crowd with a sense of entitlement and everyone allowed them to.

I crossed my eyes at the scene before searching for Jesse and sighed in relief when I noticed him and Jamie standing up from the couch.

I was preparing to head their way until I saw the ringleader of the group of girls that just walked through, stop in front of the two of them. She squealed before wrapping her arms tight around Jesse, pulling him as close as humanly possible. After a few moments, she pulled back and whispered something in his ear and then kissed him on the cheek. He frowned a bit at the action, which brought some ease to the current pang in my chest.

I was frozen in my spot as the girl engaged him in conversation while Jesse appeared to only be half paying attention and searching the room. I'm sure for me.

I was just too embarrassed to go and say something to interrupt them. She had a swarm of chicks surrounding her, all acting superior and very nicely dressed. What would I look like approaching all of them? I didn't want the attention.

I struggled with my debate for a few more seconds before lifting my head high. Yeah, social settings make me extremely nervous and awkward but I wasn't about to punk myself before anyone even had the chance to.

I flipped my hair, retaining all of the confidence I had just moments before and eased my way through the crowd towards my intended target.

I slipped in, right next to Jamie who seemed happy to see me, while mystery girl was explaining something to Jesse.

"Man did you get lost?! What the hell yo?" Jamie exaggerated, causing me to laugh. His sudden announcement of my appearance caused Jesse's eyes to snap towards mine, revealing his relief.

He reached out and pulled me towards him in the midst of ol' girl's speech, tucking me underneath his arm.

"You had me tripping, next time I'm going with you," He scolded in my ear as I snickered at the thought.

I looked up, the girl's eyes on both of us in pure surprise. I wasn't sure if it was because of me or because she was interrupted. Jesse noticed her face too and began gesturing between us.

"Oh, Alana this is Dominic. Nic, this is Alana." I nodded at the introduction, as Alana only glanced my way before looking to Jesse putting on a fake smile.

"JP we were talking ... " she hinted, slightly annoyed. I furrowed my brows before looking Jamie's way, who was doing a poor job of trying to hide his laughter.

Alana's minions were all watching me now, cold looks in their eyes.

There must be something going on that I don't know here.

"I believe *you* were talking when you asked what I was up to, I told you I was looking for someone and here she is," he grinned down at me as I smiled.

"I guess here I am," I joked with sarcasm, looking Alana in the face, noticing for the first time that her eyes were blue.

She was pretty, I wasn't going to downplay that. She stood tall, almost nearing Jesse's height and she had the slender figure of a super model. She appeared to be biracial as her skin was a tanned complexion and her light brown hair was wild with full bouncy curls.

"Can we talk?" she almost demanded, not taking her eyes off of him.

"Sure, what's up?"

She rolled her eyes, shifting on one foot. "Alone, please. I don't deserve that much respect from you?"

From the tone, I could tell she was one of Jesse's ex-girlfriends ... but which one?

Jesse looked down at me, almost like he was asking for permission that he didn't need.

At this point, we were only friends and he was free to talk to whoever he wanted.

I looked from him over to Jamie who was watching this whole thing in complete awe. I almost wanted to laugh at his expression.

Almost.

"Jamie, you wanna go fix a drink with me?" I asked sweetly as he made a face almost like he didn't want to leave and miss the action before realization spread across his face.

"Aw. Yeah. Ok, let's go!" he said, failing miserably to hide the obvious. I snorted before looking up to Jesse, whose arm I was still tucked comfortably under.

"Be right back," I told him before he nodded and placed a gentle kiss on my forehead. I relished in the feeling of his lips against my skin.

"Don't leave me for too long," he said loud enough for everyone around us to hear.

I smirked, removing myself completely from his hold before Jamie sloppily threw his arm around me, leading us away from the group, ignoring the holes being singed into my back.

"I can't believe you're treating me like this!" Alana shrieked as she and her first love stood outside of the house away from any prying ears or eyes.

Jesse stared back impassively, unsure of what the problem was. He and Alana had been broken up for years but always remained in touch. It was nothing that ever went farther than platonic conversation in most recent months.

"Treating you like what, Lan?" he questioned, tipping a brow as she flung her arms in the air.

"Like I mean nothing! Like … like we meant nothing."

Jesse frowned, scratching the back of his head before allowing his hand to fall to his side.

"Now you know that ain't true – "

"Then what is it?!" she shouted, desperate for an answer for his rejection of her.

"Man, we haven't been together in years."

"But we were working towards it, last year when we saw each other, we talked the possibility of a future – of picking up where we left off and everything, just last summer!"

He sighed, putting his head down and then picking it back up. "That was last summer."

"And what changed?"

"I moved on," he breathed, drained from the conversation already.

She shook her head in denial, "No. You never do really. Yeah you've had girlfriends since me, but none of them ever came close to what we had."

Jesse chuckled in disbelief before shaking his head, "When you get like this?"

Alana's brows furrowed, ignoring the crack she felt in her chest. "Like what?"

He shrugged, "So arrogant? You think telling me all this is gonna win me over? You don't know me at all, Lan. You can't possibly think you're taking me away from what I got going."

She crossed her arms in anger, "Yeah? Well why are you out here with me and not in there with her then?"

Jesse's eyes widened before he snickered some more. "Girl, what? She allowed you this time because you seemed so desperate for it. Trust me, Nic ain't tripping off you right now."

———————————

"I get good vibes from you Dominic." Jamie blurted, while we stood against his kitchen counter, sipping on a light drink he fixed the both of us.

My brow peaked, looking in his direction. "Seriously?"

Jamie chuckled at my reaction, "You seem surprised."

I shrugged, "I've never been good with new people. I think I read people wrong."

He shook his head, disagreeing. "You probably just see the best in people until they prove you wrong, we all do it."

I nodded in reply, "So you think I'm misreading Alana by thinking she's way too full of herself?"

Jamie laughed, "Nah. You're pretty on the money with that one. She never used to be like that though, believe it or not."

"Yeah?"

"Yeah. She used to be really sweet and humble; the girl next door type. She was always pretty but never arrogant. The sorority makes you like that, plus all the dudes around here act like they ain't never seen a pretty girl before. The attention gets to you."

"It didn't seem to get to you." I said as Jamie met my eyes.

"Pft, girl I always had attention! What you thought?" he clowned.

"So when did you and Jesse meet?" I asked, changing the subject all together, wanting to know more about the friendship they formed.

Jamie's face contorted in thought, "Hmm, it was middle school. We were both on the same AAU basketball summer team and then we realized we would be going to the same high school. He's been like a brother to me ever since. We don't really see each other too much during the school year unless it's at like a mutual function. But summer time though, we click tight."

I smiled, listening to the story of their friendship.

"He used to mention you a lot though," Jamie continued. "Would try to recruit me to help him find you and what not, especially when everything went down with him ... "

His tone was softer at the end, causing me to believe he was referring to Jesse's battle with cancer.

"I wish I could've been there for him ... you know, through that," I said quietly, taking a sip from my cup.

Jamie was quiet before he shook his head, briefly looking down. "Nah, you really don't. Those were hard times, even harder to watch. Just be glad you're around now. He always wanted it that way."

"I don't know what else you want me to say. I'm not apologizing because truthfully, I did nothing wrong," Jesse explained, not taking his eyes off of Alana. He could see the hurt there; he just didn't understand why he was the cause.

"Then why are my feelings hurt so bad?" she dared to ask, unable to mask the emotion any longer.

Jesse sighed, looking away from her momentarily.

"I'm not trying to hurt you. You know that's never been my aim with you, ever. You've always been a good friend to me, what's wrong with that?"

She scoffed, shaking her head. "The plan was to never just remain friends. We were supposed to find our way back to each other after you got your life together. You let me go so that you and I could focus on ourselves and when that was done, we were supposed to get back together."

He frowned, running a hand down his face, "Lana we were 17!"

"And you were my first!" she shouted in return, equally as frustrated as him.

"You've been my only." she continued, her voice calmer now. "No one comes remotely close to the way you used to make me feel and it's not fair that I'm stuck feeling these feelings alone. It's not fair that it's so easy for you to replace me. It isn't!"

Jesse bit the inside of his cheek, guilt eating at his spirit. He always regretted his decision to take things to the next level with Alana after realizing the weight a soul tie holds. He created one with her, knowing he didn't have the strength to stay when life became too hard to bear.

"I didn't mean for none of this to happen but what do you really want me to do? I was a kid, we both were. You're acting like I've just been taking advantage of you since then or something."

She shook her head, "I just still love you Jesse. What am I supposed to do about that? What do you want me to do?"

His shoulders slouched, "Let me go and not only for me but for you too. Just let me go."

"Man what on earth could they be talking about?!" Jameson whined as I chuckled in response.

We were in the living room now, on our second mixed concoction, doing a little two-step to the song that was on.

The party was still going strong around us. Girls were grinding, dudes were behind them, and everyone was just having a good time being in the moment.

"Her feelings," I answered simply, taking another sip. Surprisingly, I wasn't the least bit intoxicated and felt only a buzz. I could tell Jamie put as little alcohol in it as possible.

Jamie smacked his lips in response; "Man it's never that deep. She needs to let that hurt go."

I giggled at his comment, feeling his eyes looking at me. "It doesn't bother you that he's still out there with her?"

I shook my head calmly, "Not at all. Jesse's not trying to hurt her and it seems like all she needs is some closure."

Jamie blew out a breath, "You're better than me. Let that be MY girl out there talking to her ex about his feelings. Not to-damn-day, believe that."

I covered my face to hide my laugh. He was so serious, which made it all the more funny.

"Well Jesse isn't my man, so I really don't have anything to trip over," Jamie rolled his eyes, fanning me off.

"What the hell ever. Ya'll gonna be together eventually, that's a given."

I smirked, allowing my eyes to dance all over the room at the many drunken faces. I was having a good time, enjoying Jamie's company while Jesse cleaned up loose ends with his past. I missed his presence, but I knew he would be back to join me soon.

"I wanna do something daring," I blurted randomly, getting a side eye from Jamie.

"Daring like what?" he questioned curiously. I shrugged.

"I don't know, something to make this night memorable but something I won't regret later," I said meeting his much-confused stare.

He seemed to be thinking over my words before his eyes darted to the front door and a smile appeared across his handsome features.

He nodded his head towards the door, "Well I dare you to do something memorable with him."

I turned my head, eyes landing on Jesse as he smiled the whole way towards the two of us. I turned back to Jamie, handing him my cup.

"Hold this."

He took my cup with ease, a sneaky grin plastered on his face before I turned and began walking towards Jesse, nerves filling me to the brim.

It seemed like the more I wanted to get to him while I had the confidence, the more different bodies tried to block me from doing so. By the third person I was almost fed up until a strong hand grabbed my wrist, pulling me in his direction.

Jesse.

He pulled hard enough for my body to press against his and there was a look in his eye I had never seen before; one of intensity and passion, yet soft with love.

This was my chance, my moment.

Tiffany Campbell

"Miss me?" he said loud enough for only my ears, placing his hands on either side of my hips.

My eyes were slanted, zeroing in on the tiny freckle resting on his bottom lip.

Before I could back out, I placed my hands firmly on the back of his head, pulling him in eagerly for a kiss.

After a few blissful moments of our lips connecting our souls, I pulled away. My fingers clutched the jean material of his button up, looking down in shame.

"I'm so sorry Jes," I apologized, refusing to meet his gaze.

"I shouldn't have –"

Cutting me off, Jesse placed his hands on my cheeks lifting my head up so I could see him. His brows were connected at the center and he stared into me so deep, it took my breath away. Within an instant, our lips were connected again, more passionate this time, deeper, as if it were the moment the two of us had been waiting for our entire lives.

I wrapped my arms around Jesse's neck, opening my mouth to allow him more access. Our tongues swirled careful and slow with the other while Jesse continued to hold my face in his warm and loving hands.

This had to have been one of the best decisions I've ever made in my life.

I had forgotten a whole party was circulating around us and eventually it caused me to limit our kiss down to just a few tiny pecks. I removed my face from his, my hands sliding from his neck down to his shoulders, staring at the top button of his shirt.

I peeked up, hesitant and shy, to meet his gaze. His arms were now wrapped around my torso and if it were at all possible, he pulled me closer.

"I won't forget this one, I promise." I smirked, earning a chuckle from him.

"I needed that," he confessed as my face grew slightly puzzled.

"Why?"

"Needed to know that what I was feeling was real … and mutual. I just ain't wanna make the move first, out of respect."

He released a nervous laugh, causing me to grin.

I looked around us, happy that no one was paying attention to our little moment and realized we still had the rest of a party to enjoy.

"You wanna dance?" I asked softly, Jesse's eyes widening.

"You dance?"

I rolled my eyes, turning in his arms and grabbing his hand, "Let me show you."

"Man JP I'm so glad you came out tonight bruh!" Jamie called, reaching over to dap his friend up.

We were posted against a wall, my back pressed against Jesse as his arm was draped loosely around my neck and he was using his free hand to show love to Jamie.

We spent the rest of the evening dancing, meeting more of Jamie's friends and even a few of Jesse's. After our kiss, we sunk into normalcy. We were showing more affection to each other, laughing and just enjoying the moment of being young and free. I enjoyed my night and it was good to see Jes in high spirits.

"I'm glad I came too. You gotta come through man, next weekend or something and definitely help me celebrate this one's birthday." he told Jamie, referring to me.

Jamie looked at me with widened eyes.

"Yo, ya birthday coming up, Domo?!" he asked as I giggled at his new nickname for me.

I nodded, "Sure is."

"Aw, well we turning up then, I got you! I know how to throw a party." he informed as I looked around pleased.

"Yeah, you sure do. I would love for you to be there." I expressed as he grinned and nodded.

"I got you, you're family now. It's nothing." he leaned in and gave me a hug before showing love to Jesse one last time.

"Y'all about to head out right?" he asked. I could feel Jesse affirming his words.

"Yeah, baby you ready?" he bent his neck to look at me as I nodded.

I stepped out of Jesse's hold, allowing the two of them to share one last embrace.

"Aight man," Jamie said. "Hit me up bro. I'm serious."

Jesse smirked, taking a hold of my hand and beginning to lead us out of the house that was slowly starting to clear out.

"I got you Jay," he replied, tossing up the deuces to his friend before the fresh warm air of the late night greeted us.

"Thank you for bringing me here. It was just what I needed," I sighed with happiness, following Jesse's lead down the walkway.

"Yeah no problem. Just what I needed too."

"Where to now?" I asked as both of us reached his passenger door.

"You tryna go home?"

I shook my head, "Only if that means with you."

A smile formed across his face as he opened the door for me.

"Aight then. Let's go."

————————

"Can I ask you a question?" Jesse spoke into the peaceful quiet.

We were lying on top of the covers of his bed, both on our backs, staring aimlessly at the ceiling as only the moon illuminated our faces. I changed into one of Jesse's black crew necks, secretly sniffing the cologne on the collar. I loved his smell.

Jesse was stalk still, his hand resting comfortably over his belly, while he ran his tongue smoothly over his bottom lip. He appeared to be in deep thought about something.

"Sure," I answered finally, turning my cheek to the cover to view his gorgeous face. "What's up?"

A smirk twitched at his lip but he still refused to meet my eyes, "Why you kiss me tonight?"

I chuckled, "Should I not have?"

"No, no," he answered quickly, shutting down my question all together. "I told you I needed it. I just wanted to know why, why tonight?"

I shrugged, turning my head to face the popcorn ceiling once again.

"I felt courageous. I've wanted to do that for a long time."

He snorted, "What's a long time when we've done it before?"

"I mean being eleven when we first kissed counts but at the same time, it doesn't. This kiss ... was different. I'm not good with words like you are. My actions have always spoken for me."

"I can see that." I could hear the smile in his voice, but my cheeks were too hot to face him in the moment.

"I ain't want you to pull away," he confessed, as I tucked my lips in to hide the blush.

"I know you were probably worried about all those people," he continued.

"But I ain't care. I ain't care who was watching. You was igniting something in me, girl, and I never wanted it to end."

"So I didn't cross any boundaries?" I asked nervously. He grinned.

"What boundaries we got? I mean we're friends, the best of them. But we both know what we want. It's just all about timing with this."

I sighed, releasing the breath I was holding, "I don't want to rush, but I don't want to wait forever for you either. I feel like I've already waited half my life. Literally."

Jesse turned his head and I mirrored his actions, staring into his soft brown eyes. He then reached his hand over, caressing my cheek the way only he knew how. My eyes fluttered closed, relishing in the comfort the action brought.

"I refuse to hurt you." he spoke, only causing my eyes to shut tighter at his words.

"I need you to understand that baby."

I bit the inside of my cheek, taking in a deep breath. "How could someone like you hurt me? You bring too much joy to ever come with pain."

I was breathing short and ragged breaths. The thought of not being able to have Jesse like I wanted almost become torture to my heart. Before I knew it, I felt the warmth of his lips pressed gently against mine for a sweet and loving peck. Slowly, I opened my eyes, once again meeting his.

"Can you trust me? Trust that I know what's right and that I'm not going to leave in the process? Trust our growth and our connection?"

I nodded, the emotion bubbling in my chest at his words.

"You're too sacred and too precious to rush," he said with passion in his eyes, desperate for me to understand him.

"I'm taking my time with you because I don't want to miss a moment. I don't want you to miss a moment. I'm taking advantage of every minute we have together. You got me, I'm not going anywhere," he assured, stealing one more kiss before pulling away.

"Just me and everything that could potentially come with me, can't be the thing I allow to break you. I couldn't ... I couldn't live with that."

I felt like Jesse was talking in riddles. Speaking of something unknown that had yet to happen, if it ever did.

"You don't think I have the power to break you?" I asked. "My life used to seem like it was prone to pain. I'm scared that even with this little happiness I do have, something is bound to destroy it."

He shook his head, "Don't talk like that."

"Same for you," I challenged right back.

"Truths."

He held out his pinky for me to interlock with his. I snorted before doing so, pushing him playfully in the head afterwards.

"Watch it man, this fade too crispy for your grimy hands to be touching all on it!" he teased, rubbing his hand over the top of his hair.

I giggled, rubbing my hands all over his head as he laughed, trying to move out of my reach. I stretched my hand his way one last time before he was quick to snatch my wrist and pull me into him. He wrapped me up into his arms, holding me close as I rested my head against his chest right above his heart. I could feel the thumping against my ear, and knowing that it was still beating brought a peace over my soul.

I was content and I never wanted it to end.

I couldn't picture life if it did.

CHAPTER
- TEN -

It was a relaxing Sunday afternoon and I was at our kitchen table on Corey's laptop filling out different jobs applications. I was serious about my quest to find a job.

Now that school was officially over, I needed something to fill my days. Jesse was going to be working more and I wanted to as well so I could start affording my own personal luxuries, without having to ask my parents.

Speaking of, I could hear them giggling with each other as they approached the front door. My brow tipped, wondering what on earth had them so happy.

My mother's heels clicked down the hall until she reached the foyer, smiling at me while setting her purse down on the table.

"Where are you two just getting back from?" I asked, giving Corey a wave. He was just as happy as her.

"Church, girl. It's Sunday," she said as if I had asked the dumbest question in the world.

I smirked in realization, nodding my head. "How was it?"

Corey took a seat at the table, while my mom walked to the kitchen.

"It was so good Kole, like crazy good," he breathed, as my brows climbed my forehead.

"What was it about?"

"Today he was talking about just knowing your identity and how everything we need to know and to understand about ourselves has already been given in the Bible. He talked about how the key to really knowing who you are and why you're here, is in God. He has all the answers and has given us an unlimited amount of resources to obtaining them. He – being our ultimate source. It was eye opening for me," he said, before shaking his head at the thought of his own words.

I nodded slowly. It *was* after Jesse had given me the Bible and I started to read a little bit more on my own did I start getting more confident in myself. What he was telling me now made perfect sense and that came as a surprise.

"Can we all go together next Sunday?" I asked, looking to my stepfather and feeling my mother's eyes on me. "Us and Jesse? I want to go."

I could hear my mother's heels entering back into the kitchen, her eyes were nearly bugging out of her head. "Wh- are you sure?"

I chuckled, "Yes I'm sure. I wouldn't ask if we could all go together if I didn't want to go."

She blew out a breath of air, still in disbelief it seemed like.

"Well just a few months ago, you called it a fairytale and had a conniption when I wanted you to go."

I shrugged, "Maybe I'm starting to believe in fairytales."

––––––––––––––––––

"You're going to be proud of me," I spoke to Dr. Tracy's smiling face as I dug in my pocket.

She crossed her stocking clad legs, one over the other, adjusting the end of her pencil skirt. "Yeah? And why is that?"

Excited, I pulled out the folded piece of paper and slapped it down on the coffee table in front of me. She tipped a brow at the paper before looking back at me over the brim of her glasses.

"And what that might be?" she inquired with a playful smirk.

I bent forward, unfolding the paper I had been carrying with me for two weeks, fingers shaking. I was so confident walking in here with my big reveal, but now nerves were getting the best of me. My soul felt like it was on this paper.

I spread the bent edges, straightening it out.

"It's my list."

Dr. Tracy's eyes widened in surprise, "The things you love about yourself? You started working on it?"

I nodded slowly, the grin spreading. "Yeah. I got like fifteen now."

She chuckled, "Oh wow! I must say I am pleasantly surprised."

I smiled shyly, looking over a few of the things I wrote on the list.

"I've just been writing some things as I go."

It was quiet before Dr. Tracy spoke up, "Would you like to share some with me?" she asked sweetly as I thought it over for just a moment before agreeing.

"I love that -" I started, taking in a small breath. "I love that I've started to learn how to adapt to change."

My revelation earned a nod from the therapist, "I like that one."

I cleared my throat, feeling self-assured.

"I love that I can identify with beauty ... because I can see it in myself."

She was silent, allowing me to continue. I shifted in my seat, preparing to read one more.

"And ... and I love how I can now say and be confident in the fact that ... my life isn't over. It's only the beginning."

Her grin was so wide, eyes twinkling with pride. "That is one beautiful list you're working on there."

I smiled, folding the paper back up and shoving it into my jeans. "It's starting to be. I'm amazed at the things I'm learning each day. I never thought I would be here."

Her brows furrowed in question, "What's here?"

I took in a breath, adding a shrug of my shoulders. "Just … in a good place. My life had been so dark for the last eleven years, I couldn't see past the heartache and pain. I'll admit, some things still hurt, most do actually but I can … I can cope, I can breathe. I can wake up each day with a newfound hope and happiness. It's crazy to me."

She nodded in understanding, briskly writing on her pad.

"What's crazy about it?"

I sighed, "Maybe that I think it's all too good to be true. I think with every good thing has to come something bad, like clockwork."

She frowned a bit, "What you focus on expands, Kole. Keep thinking about all that's positive going around you. Focus on that."

I shook my head, "As good as that sounds Dr. Tracy, that's just not real life. If I only focus on what's good, I'll be devastated when bad happens because I didn't see it coming. I didn't see it possible. Isn't that a false sense of hope and reality?"

She smirked, "It's called faith, honey and you need to strengthen it now, so that if the bad does happen, your faith will be strong enough to know that everything will get better."

I nodded slow, allowing that conversation to stay where it was. My faith was only in the beginning stages of developing. Maybe when I go to church on Sunday, this feeling in the pit of my stomach would go away. Until then I would just have to brace myself for whatever was next.

"So," Dr. Tracy said after the silence had consumed us. "Tell me about your week."

"Thanks for stopping through, bro," Jesse spoke to Jamie, while they played video games on his living room couch.

It was a lazy Saturday afternoon and both friends were off from work and decided to spend the time catching up and enjoying one of their favorite pastimes together.

"It's all good man," Jamie answered, pressing aggressively on the controller. "It's never a bad day to beat you in Madden, since I'm the Madden gawd and all."

Jesse snickered at his remarks, continuing to focus on the game at hand.

"You still helping me with Nic's party?"

Jamie nodded quickly, "Of course, that's the homie and a lot of people had been asking about her since the party. She left quite an impression."

Jesse grinned at Jamie's confession, knowing that Dominic had the capability to leave a mark. Her presence was larger than she would ever realize and he knew that.

"What you think she's going to want to do?" he inquired.

Jesse thought it over for a moment, "Pool party. She's been asking me to go swimming for like the past two weeks since it started getting real hot. I figured we could do that, make some food on the grill and have music. Just do something real cool at the pool here at my complex. They have a nice pool house too."

Jamie nodded in response, liking the idea. "I think that's dope. Real simple, and something people will definitely come out for. She looking to do something big?"

He quickly shook his head, "Nah, she's just getting warmed up to people so I guess just invite the main ones that we were hanging with at the party, I'll invite her fam and then maybe some more females. I know we know plenty of girls she could start hanging with that'll be good company. She doesn't read women real well on her own."

Jamie chuckled, "Why you say that?" he asked.

"Every female I've ever seen Nic befriend, they always fall out in the worst way afterwards and it's only because she's real nice and accepting. She's always wanted a female she could really hang with, so she trusts them easily."

Jamie shook his head, "Quickest way to get you messed up, these broads are evil."

Jesse blew out a breath, "Tell me about it."

A calm silence had passed over the two of them while they continued to play against one another. Jamie peeked over at his friend, building the courage to turn the conversation in a different direction.

"So we didn't really get to talk like I wanted to at the party," Jamie spoke, slicing the silence in half.

Jesse hadn't noticed the seriousness of his tone and continued to play the game without a second thought, "Word. What's up?"

"That's what I want to know, what's up with you?"

"Ain't nothing up with me. You see what's up with me."

Jamie smacked his lips, "You know what I'm talking about, health wise." he watched as his friend paused momentarily before noticing the roll of his eyes.

"I told you man. I'm good, I'm healthy."

Jamie nodded, eying him carefully.

"Yeah? You still do ya checkups every six months?"

"Of course."

"When was ya last check up?"

Another silence passed between them, this one more uncomfortable.

"Jes –"

"What?"

The patience was running thin and Jamie could sense that this was a conversation that Jesse didn't want to have. He would push because he loved the man he had grown to know as a brother and he had to make sure he was okay at all cost.

"When was it Jesse?"

"Eight months ago."

Jamie paused the game completely before tossing his controller to the side so he could face him.

"What? Eight months ago? You're always on top of this. Why you ain't schedule ya follow up?"

Jesse's breathing had quickened and he was doing his best to calm the beating in his chest. This was a conversation that was never easy to have, whether he was praying, talking to his therapist or even the doctors.

"What is it? Do you feel sick or something?"

He shook his head, "Nah."

"Then why you stalling with it? It ain't like you don't know the routine by now."

Jesse released a breath of frustration, running his hand over his hair.

"I'm scared man. This time for some reason I'm just ... truly scared."

Jamie frowned deeply, upset to see the strongest man he knew crumble at the seams. "What, what you scared of? These test been running flawlessly for years."

"Yeah but this time – this time I'm scared because I really feel like I got something to lose. Dominic just came back in my life and I honestly haven't been happier. I've been missing her and needing her this whole time and now that she's back, I don't want to lose her over anything and I don't want to hurt her. Before, when I would get tested I never really cared how the results came back because I knew everything happened for a reason. This time ... "

Jamie shook his head, "That can't be why you allow ya faith to shake JP, you know this. You know the enemy just tryna use your love for Domo as a trick to get you to live in fear. I know you bro and I know you don't fear nothing, so don't start now. Just pray, pray for ya health. See the test coming back negative for everything. Envision it and it'll happen."

Jesse nodded, knowing Jameson was right. It had been something he had been battling within himself for over a month when he realized it was time to schedule his appointment. He was having anxiety about it like he never had before and he knew he couldn't allow that to take place. He had to be strong, regardless of the outcome, not only for himself, but for Dominic too.

"Don't let that eat at you dude." Jamie said, placing a reassuring hand on his friend's shoulder.

"Schedule ya appointment so you can put both of our minds at ease."

"You're a good friend," Jesse spoke. "You've always been the one to get me in check when it comes to this. It just never gets easier. Cancer sucks and I just don't want to go through it again."

Jamie nodded, hearing the emotion behind Jesse's words. It was causing him to feel it too. He remembered when Jesse was going through his surgeries and treatments. He remembered always being there to make him laugh even when he felt the worst.

"Well just don't talk like it's already here because it's not. You said it yourself, you feel good and you look good. There ain't nothing to worry about. They just want to make sure you're good too, that's all."

Jesse sighed softly, reaching out his hand to dap his brother up, feeling better about it than he had in weeks.

He made a mental note to make an appointment on Monday.

———————

"Kole! You almost ready?" I could hear my mother calling from the hallway, but I was frozen. Looking at my closet as if the clothes I needed were just going to pop out at me.

It was Sunday morning and time for me to be ready for the first church service I would be attending with an open heart. I was nervous to say the least, but more nervous about how I would come off. What do people wear to church? How do they carry themselves? How should I?

The knock on my door pulled me from my dilemma.

"Ma if it's you, come in."

I could hear her snickering as she opened door, and then shutting it quickly behind her when she realized I was standing in my underwear.

"Oh Kole you have a nice body! Almost like the one I had when I was your age," she said, studying me as I rolled my eyes.

"Almost? Are you trying to say yours was better?" I asked, already knowing the answer.

She gave me a duh expression causing me to laugh.

"Whatever."

She smiled, before waving her hand in my direction.

"But seriously, why aren't you dressed yet? We have to leave in like fifteen minutes."

I sighed, my shoulders slouching, "I don't know what to wear."

"It's come as you are, wear whatever you want. It doesn't need to be fancy."

I frowned looking from her and back to my closet. Looking at my small array of clothes was making my head spin. Who was I kidding thinking I was ready for church?

"Hey," my mother soothed, walking up behind me and placing her hands on my shoulders.

"What's really the matter?"

I huffed through my nose. "God might smite me the moment I walk in His house."

She smacked her lips, causing me to chuckle. "I'm serious. All the things I used to say about God and religion? It's just –"

She shushed me, "Don't focus on the religion, that's man made. Focus on the relationship, that's what you and God share in your heart. That's what He's after. That's what He's always been after, is your heart. He's a relational God. It's His whole purpose of creating us, just so we can spend time with Him. He loves us, and only asks for love in return. Love for Him and love for His people, don't ever be intimidated by love baby. It's too beautiful to ever be afraid of."

I nodded, as she kissed me on my temple. It was one of the first times she had brought calm over my soul, easing every tension I felt before she came in.

"Now hurry and get ready. Jesse will be here any minute so you can ride with him," she said walking to the door.

The sound of Jesse's name caused my heart to flutter and I quickly began to pick out an outfit that he's never seen before.

Jesse kind of has that effect.

"Girl, it's just God!" Jesse teased me as I sat in his passenger seat, trying to keep the shaking in my legs to a minimum. We were getting closer to the church because I could see the building in the short distance.

"You say it like He's an ant," I smarted.

"I'm saying it like His love isn't intimidating," he replied sweetly as I crossed my eyes.

"Now you sound like my mom."

"Well she's a smart woman."

I groaned at our back and forth only causing Jesse to be even more amused.

"Relax baby, seriously. I'm going to be there and your parents are going to be there. It's just a service. It's nothing to be nervous about."

I nodded, "I know. This is just … a big step for me. The fact that I even invited myself after the way I used to feel when I first got back. It's just all a huge transition, and I'm trying to adapt the best way I know how."

"Don't adapt, Nic," Jesse spoke, pulling into the church's parking lot.

"Evolve."

He parked the car smoothly as I eyed the churchgoers walking through the lot towards the front doors. People were smiling with each other, even singing a little because the music could be heard from a short distance.

I clutched my Bible tightly, feeling my palms beginning to sweat. Jesse turned off his ignition and unbuckled his seatbelt before he paused to look at me.

"It's going to be okay," he spoke softly, covering my hand with his own. "I'll be there with you the whole time, right by ya side. There's nothing to be afraid of. This is one place you'll realize that you feel the safest."

I nodded slowly, unbuckling my seat belt. Jesse pecked my temple before stepping out of the car. He met me in front of the car, interlocking our arms. Corey and Sharon were walking in our direction.

I smiled at my parents, before being escorted to the front doors of the church, where a smiling older gentleman opened the doors for us.

"Good Morning ya'll," he greeted sweetly, as Corey and Jesse allowed my mother and I to step ahead to enter the foyer first.

We walked through another set of doors, entering the main concourse. There were several members standing around conversing quietly as soft music and singing could be heard coming from the sanctuary.

Jesse led us to one of the entrances into the sanctuary where we were greeted by a woman and a gentleman in a suit. He approached our group expectedly.

"How many?" he asked softly as my mother held up four fingers, earning a nod from the usher. "Right this way."

He led us to four open seats in the middle and I felt the heat come to my cheeks as several eyes landed on us. My mom and Corey waved to some, but Jesse's only concern was assisting me to my seat. He sat down, scooting over so there would be enough room for me close to him. My mom sat next to me, then Corey on the other side of her.

"You okay?" Jesse asked softly as I nodded, in awe of the bright lights coming from the stage.

There was a large choir of robed singers, singing a soft gospel. Some members were standing up, some had tears in their eyes and others were singing along with everything in them.

I sat back in my pew, getting comfortable as my family joined in on the song. For that moment I wished I knew the words so I could sing too. Everyone around us seemed to be locked in, emotionally attached to everything happening. It was a beautiful sight to see and it stirred up mixed emotions within me.

I was here, in church. A place I never thought was meant for someone like me. A place I never thought I could be accepted. A place I barely even understood ...

Yet here I was, yearning for understanding and secretly praying that before I left, I would have some.

"Can I be honest?" the Pastor's voice boomed as he walked slowly across the base of the altar.

The praise and worship portion of service had ended and everyone was in their seats, watching the man of God intently as he spoke.

"No really," he continued. "Can I be honest?"

You could hear numerous responses from the congregation; all beckoning him to say what was on his heart.

"Sometimes … not only as a Christian … but as a human being, this thing called life gets hard. Like … it gets really, really hard. Can anyone here agree with that?"

There were a few responses, but everyone I could see was tuned in to where he was going with his statement.

"Now I know more people than that have had a bad day or two. If I can admit as your Pastor that this walk hasn't been the easiest, then I know it's hard for ya'll," he teased in a light manner, earning a few chuckles.

"But you know what I think about when I have a bad day? When the devil seems to be hitting me from every possible angle, attacking my family, attacking my church, attacking my friends, attacking ME. You know what keeps me up when all I want to do is quit?"

He paused, standing in front of his podium, locking eyes with a few members.

"It's a five letter word called faith, say that with me."

"Faith!"

The congregation shouted together as I remained mum, looking around curiously.

"Faith is the one tool that you'll need to be equipped with as a believer because trust me, there are going to be trials and there are going to be tribulations. This was never something that was promised to be easy. Even without God, life isn't easy. But with Him? I promise, it's so much sweeter and faith is the added sugar that makes it so."

There were nods of agreement as he carefully walked behind the podium, opening his Bible. "Don't believe me? Let me prove it in the word. Turn with me if you will to Hebrews, Chapter 11 verse 5," he said patiently as I opened my Bible up.

I bit the inside of my cheek, searching anxiously for anything that said Hebrews. I could feel my body get hot with frustration before there were gentle hands lightly grabbing the book and opening it right to where I needed to be. I looked to Jesse with thankful eyes before tuning back into the service.

"And it is impossible to please God without faith. Anyone who wants to come to Him must believe that God exists and that he rewards those who sincerely seek him," the Pastor read aloud as I read silently along with him.

"Before I explain what that scripture is saying, some of you might ask what is Faith? I'll tell you, it's the belief in something that can't be seen, the belief in something that has yet to manifest. Something that has yet to reveal itself or show to be true, but you believe it's true already without having to see it."

He stepped away from the podium a bit, continuing his sermon. "You might say, how am I to believe in something I can't see? It's called faith. I don't need to see my heart to know that it's beating in my body. If it wasn't, I'd be dead, right? I've never seen my brain but I've been told that it's there. I have faith that it's there. If I sat right here and told you I didn't have a brain because I can't see it, ya'll would look at me like I didn't have one! Right?" he asked jokingly earning chuckles.

"Well how do you think God feels, being told he doesn't exist, being told that prayers don't come true, being told that He's never there, He never listens, that what you believe isn't real and He's asking where is your faith? How are you using your faith? What you have to understand is that faith can work for you or against you. All depending on what you're putting your faith into."

I watched several heads nod in understanding.

"No really, what are you putting your faith into? Faith is the evidence of that unseen right, in something that hasn't happened yet? So say you need your rent paid, you don't have the money but you're believing and expecting financial help. You can activate your faith two different ways: by believing and speaking that your rent will get paid no matter what. You may not know how, but it'll happen. May not be on time, but it'll happen. It'll get paid, you believe that with your whole heart."

"Or, you can activate your faith to work against you and that's by worrying. That's by fear, thinking, "Oh man how is this gonna get paid? I don't have the money. I don't think I will have the money. There's no way possible for me to have the money to pay my rent." And then what happens? You don't have the money and for whatever reason, you're surprised! Guess who you're blaming for that? You're looking up like 'God why didn't you come through for me? You knew I needed my rent paid and now I'm on the verge of eviction!' And He's looking down like, you didn't have faith in Me. You didn't have faith it would get paid. You believed whole-heartedly that it wouldn't more than it would. And that's the outcome you received."

He walked easily across the altar, looking lovingly at us all. "It's going to take faith for this, people. Unshakable, undeniable faith! It says it right in the text. It's impossible to please God without faith. Why? Because He is the evidence of what we cannot see! We can't see God but He dwells within us. He's in our everyday life. He's real, and He will exist to you if you believe. He rewards those that genuinely seek Him! Blessings! Manifestations! The relationship we have with the Lord is built on FAITH! It's going to take faith for this!"

His voice boomed throughout the church causing a feeling I've never felt come into my soul. It's like I could connect the dots and understand fully what he was desperately trying to explain. It was starting to make some sense.

"Faith isn't the easiest thing to obtain, which is why the Bible talks about it so much. And if you take the time to read Hebrews, it explains the numerous times that faith is mentioned in text. It took faith for Moses, Abraham and Jesus to complete God's will for their lives. They had to have faith in Him and also themselves."

"What are you believing for? What are you hoping for? Do you have the faith to carry it out or do you have fear, the opposite of faith? We can't have faith and fear at the same time. One cancels out the other."

He paused, "Or, do you even believe? Trust me, there are Christians that have not one lick of faith. They say they believe God. They say they believe what He says in His word, but their lives don't match. Their words don't match. They struggle with their faith more than a non-believer. At least a non-believer has a stance, they don't believe. That's faith right there, they have faith that what I'm saying right now is complete garbage but they're not the only ones."

He looked curiously out at us all.

"Ask yourself, where is your faith? Where has it been or what have you been putting your faith into? Without faith, this life and this walk CAN be hard. It's guaranteed but it doesn't have to feel that way. You can have joy, you can have peace even in the midst of your trial because you know this is not the end. You have FAITH in what you cannot see! God is still God and He'll never leave you nor forsake you. God never walks away from us, we walk away from Him during our times of little faith. Do you know how weak I've felt when I didn't have God? How empty and alone I would feel? You ever felt like that, like something was missing, that one piece to connect you to something so much greater? Don't get disconnected from the vine that leads you to the root that's in Christ. Get connected – STAY connected. That connection is through the power of faith. It's so real and it's so strong. I couldn't function if I was disconnected."

The emotion was bubbling in my chest at his words. I've never felt like this before. An overwhelming sense of compassion and love came over me. It was swallowing me whole, like a hug, bringing tears to the brim of my eyes. What was I feeling?

"I don't know who I'm talking to in here but I know life hasn't always been easy for you. I know you've been through some things you don't understand. You ask yourself, if God is so real why did He do this, why did He do that? Well let me start by saying this. Place your blame on the right source and realize that God can turn any situation, no matter how ugly into something so beautiful and breathtaking. Sometimes your test has to be part of your testimony. You're here to help someone else. Be there for someone else. Guide them so they don't go down the wrong path or make the same mistakes you've made. Show them the love and grace that God has so graciously given you. You're here, you're alive and that means you have a purpose that has yet to be fulfilled. Have faith for that purpose, get connected to the one that holds all the answers to every question you have. Through prayer and through faith, trust that He will listen and that He will answer, because He will. Do you believe that?"

I blinked, allowing the traitor tear to slip down my rounded cheek gracefully while the congregation shouted joyous responses. All feeling rejuvenated from this morning's teaching.

"Well stand to your feet! Let us pray," he said happily as I sniffed and set my Bible beside me, standing with my family.

"Bow your heads," he instructed while I did what I was told, shutting my eyes tight. Jesse eased his hand into mine, gripping his palm against my own, instantly relaxing me for this prayer.

"Father, we come to you today first and foremost repenting for any way that we have sinned against you. We thank you right now for your forgiveness and love. Father, I ask that you ease all of the troubled hearts in this room. I ask that you renew the faith of your people and help those that have trouble believing in you, believing your word. Provide promise, where there is doubt. Provide wholeness where there are shattered pieces. Provide peace in the midst of the storm. I

Tiffany Campbell

may not know what each and every one of them is dealing with God, but you do. You are all knowing, all loving and all powerful. Protect them in the ways I cannot. I declare right now that no evil weapon; person or thing will harm them. Provide understanding where there is confusion and fill them up with so much love that being disconnected from you is no longer an option. Get them connected today father. Keep them connected. In Jesus name we pray. Amen."

"Now I see why you guys are always so happy go lucky after church," I spoke, sitting at the table and watching as my mom unpacked the carryout we picked up on the way home.

"I feel so light ... rejuvenated even. That message really spoke to me," I smiled as Jesse took a seat next to me after returning from the bathroom.

Corey grinned from the head of the table, "It was a great message and definitely one to inspire to keep pressing forward. I'm happy you came with us today baby. It was a joy having you there."

I nodded in response to my step-father, receiving the container with the meal I ordered from my mother. "Was I ... was I supposed to get saved when he did that altar call?"

My mom chuckled before shaking her head, "Honey no. You dedicate your life when you're ready. You don't have to go to the altar just because you heard a good word. Just keep coming, and when the time is right, you'll know."

Corey nodded in agreement, "Yeah, don't ever feel pressured. It's something that will truly speak to your heart when you're ready to make that commitment to the relationship that you desire to build."

"How did ya'll know when you were ready?" I asked, looking at all three of them.

Jesse cleared his throat. "It was like a pull. A tug I felt in my chest. I was just so overwhelmed with emotion that my feet just carried me up there and I broke down. I promised I would never be the same again."

My mother grinned, taking a seat across from us and next to Corey.

"Yeah, I would say it was the same for me too. I was bawling like a baby at the ministry I got saved in. But like Jesse was saying, you really never feel the same. I felt like the weight of the world was thrown off my shoulders, and I was just so hungry to know and understand more. I wanted that feeling I felt at that moment to last me a lifetime."

I watched in awe as she talked about her faith, "And has it, so far?"

She smiled, "Like he was saying today. It has its good days and bad days, but the good certainly outweighs the bad. It always will. But having faith – that is truly the key. Without it, everything means nothing."

I was quiet, satisfied with the answers I received and taking the first bite into my dinner.

"So ... " Jesse started, squeezing my hand tight as we walked hand in hand in the middle of the street on the warm comforting Sunday night.

"How are you feeling about today? That was a big step," he peered down at me, the smirk playing at my lips.

I was waiting for this moment all evening. We had spent most of our time with my parents, just enjoying our day, watching an NBA playoff game. But now it was time just for us; for me to be as raw and candid as possible. I trusted Jesse with my truth more than anyone, and he knew that.

"It was a major step. Just the type of person I've always been, I never thought there would be a day I stepped foot in a church and enjoyed myself. Like that's wild to me," I chuckled.

"Yeah I remember even mentioning God to you, you would look at me like He was the eighth wonder of the world or something. It's beautiful to witness the transformation. What do you think was the inspiration behind it all, to change your mindset?"

I bit the inside of my cheek, searching the words in my brain.

"In all honesty, it was Devon and even Lucy. Like, I know they were bad influences on me but it's like I needed them. I needed them to hurt me, to be the straw that broke the camel's back and break me so low that I had no choice but to change for the better. It's crazy how that works."

Jesse hummed in agreement, "Yeah that's how God works baby. He can take anything that's negative or was meant to destroy you and turn it around for your good. It's hard to see that sometimes when you're dealin, but when you come out? It's all there in plain sight. That's your wisdom and knowledge speaking right now. You're viewing it the right way."

I sighed, "Good, cause I didn't know how to feel about giving that bastard credit for anything but I can say, without him, I don't think I would be here. So if there's anything I can appreciate from that situation, it's that."

I looked up at Jesse's toothy grin, "What?"

He shook his head, running his tongue smoothly over his lips.

"Nothing, just sounds like you forgive him."

I paused, thinking to myself. Saying Devon's name out loud didn't make me feel any particular way. I actually almost felt like I made my peace with the entire ordeal.

"Yeah, maybe I do."

"And maybe one day, you think you can forgive the others?" Jesse dared to ask, as I felt the thud in my heart.

I shook my head quickly, looking down to my feet. "Now that may take a little more time."

———————————

I sat on my bed, staring out of my window as Jesse bounced his basketball, looking curiously at our house. He came over, wanting me to come outside to play. Maw Maw denied his request on my behalf, telling him I wasn't feeling well.

She knew I didn't have it in me to say goodbye, not to Jesse. He just wouldn't understand but I had to leave. Mommy had been talking with the police all night and any time she was home I couldn't stand to look at her, this was her fault. She allowed this to happen to me!

I'll never be the same again – how could I?

"Baby," Maw Maw's voice called sweetly from the doorway. I didn't flinch. My eyes were still fixed on Jesse.

"Are you ready to go?"

I blinked, allowing the tears to fall from my eye, turning my head towards my grandmother. She stood calmly, hands clasped as her purse dangled from her elbow. She saw that I was becoming emotional, as this was a lot to bear for anyone, let alone a child. She was quick to sit by my side.

Tiffany Campbell

She pulled me into a loving embrace, shushing me softly as I began to cry into her chest.

"I hate her for doing this to me," I cried as Maw Maw squeezed me tighter.

"Sweetie, she didn't know. She didn't know –"

"She did!" I snapped.

"She knew and did nothing, she did nothing Maw Maw! I told her and she didn't believe me!" I wailed.

The memories began to haunt me like a bad dream.

She began to sing softly, rocking me as I cried. I felt like my chest would explode.

"It's going to be okay Dominic. I know you're hurting right now but it's going to be okay baby."

She tried her best to soothe me but I knew it wasn't ever going to be okay.

"Dominic."

I lifted my head, looking to find where her voice was coming from.

Mommy stood trembling in the door, face flushed with tears. I had barely seen her since the night everything happened.

Seeing her face made anger coil in my belly so strong, I wanted to throw up.

"I hate you!" I bellowed, tears shooting from my eyes as I stood up to charge for her.

"I hate you Sharon, I wish you were dead!"

Maw Maw snatched me up something fierce before I could reach the woman who failed me as a mother. I cried hysterically as I collapsed to the ground, wrapped in my grandmother's arms.

I wouldn't take my eyes off of Sharon. I couldn't.

"Really, I just wish you were dead!" I cried as my entire being shook.

"Dominic, that's enough!" Maw Maw scolded, gripping me tight.

"Dominic ... " Sharon gasped, barely above a whisper.

"Don't talk to me! Don't ever talk to me again!" I spat, before dropping my head.

I couldn't bear to look at her any longer.

———————————

I woke out of my sleep, drenched in sweat as the memory of the last day I was home floated over my head. Since my talk with Jesse about forgiving people from my past, I hadn't slept well. It was like I was experiencing the trauma all over again and I wasn't sure how to deal with it.

I sighed, realizing my mouth was dry so I went for a glass of water. I changed out of my damp clothes into one of Jesse's oversized shirts that I had stolen from him the week before. Feeling a bit better as the memory faded away, I carried myself down the stairs towards the kitchen.

I nearly jumped out of my skin when I saw my mother sitting under a lamp in the living room, reading a book. She noticed I was startled, smiling softly.

"Hi honey, can't sleep?" she asked, shutting her book. I could feel her watching my every move as I went into the kitchen pour my water. I carried it, while carefully taking a sip and sitting in the chair across from her.

"Had a bad dream," I finally answered, as she nodded in understanding.

"Same. That's why I came down to read, it calms me down until I get sleepy again. The light wakes Corey up."

It was quiet for a moment as I searched for the words to say.

"Mom."

I could feel the emotion begin to creep.

"Yes baby?"

Her voice was soft and tender but it provided the calm that I needed.

"H-how did you forgive Larry?" I stuttered, the tear trickling down my cheek.

This caught her by surprise, I could tell. She swallowed as she sat up upright.

"I didn't for a long time," she confessed.

"I was a mess after you left, Dominic. I was deeply depressed for the first couple of years. Just seeing how much you were hurting the day you left, how much hate you had in your heart for me really hurt to the core and I knew I was to blame. God trusted me with you, he trusted your life in my hands and – I failed. You told me and I didn't believe you, I didn't want to believe you."

Her voice shook with each word she spoke.

She sniffed, wiping at her face with an open palm. "I just didn't know how to handle it, I didn't know how to deal with the weight," she continued.

"I had gotten addicted to Percocet dealing with Larry and I used that to numb the pain I felt from losing you. You were my baby Dominic, my baby, my little girl. No one understood why I had you or wanted to keep you, knowing your father wasn't going to be around but I knew you were special. I felt it, you were supposed to be here."

She was smiling through her tears now.

"There was this night, this night that I was fighting to get myself clean – straight cold turkey. I called your grandmother, trying to speak with you. She normally wouldn't let me talk to you when I was high but she could hear the desperation in my voice. She could tell I was trying to change but you refused me. You rejected me like you'd done before but this time was different. This time I just needed to hear your voice so I could make it another day. You wouldn't come to the phone and Maw Maw never made you talk to me when I called and I didn't understand it at the time, I didn't understand that she saw the damage that was done but I didn't."

She shook her head, more tears falling from her eyes.

"I didn't understand how tormented you must've been, how broken you were on the inside. It wasn't until you came back that it finally clicked because I never witnessed it before then. I just – I just thought that since time had passed, you were okay but I was so wrong Dominic and I am so so so sorry for that baby. I am so sorry that I didn't understand."

I looked away, hiding my own tears from her apology.

She didn't know how bad I needed to hear that.

"Keep going," I urged, not wanting to stray away from her original point.

She nodded, wiping at her face once more.

"That night, after you refused to speak with me I went into a panic searching for my pills. I turned this house upside down looking for those things but knew I was too manic to even search properly then I just collapsed. I was just so tired from everything; of the pain, the torment in my mind so I just called out to God. I cursed him, blamed him, I was so angry. I wanted to deflect the blame anywhere I could."

"And then," she continued with a smirk. "He spoke to me. He met me right where I was and spoke to me."

"What did He say?" I asked.

"He said I had to let go of my pain and hold on tight to Him and he was the only way to peace and refuge. He said I was killing myself and that if I didn't get myself together, I would fail you again. He said you still needed me and I was of no use in my condition."

She sniffed, taking in a breath.

"So shortly after that, I went to rehab. They had a minister there and she helped me in rededicating my life to Christ. When I left the facility, I joined the church but even after I was saved, I didn't forgive for a long time. It was hard for me, very hard."

"So what changed?"

"I did."

"God helped me realize that forgiveness is not for the other person. Forgiveness wasn't for Larry or anyone else who I felt wronged me. While I was wallowing in that dark place, it wasn't hurting nobody but me and my relationship with the Lord. I was tired of feeling separated from Him, bound by my own internal Hell. I didn't forgive Larry because he deserved it, I forgave him because I wanted to release the stronghold that was over me. I couldn't do it without God. And you can't either."

I shook my head, emotion swallowing me whole. "He doesn't deserve it Mom. He doesn't deserve it."

"It's true, he doesn't," she agreed.

"But," she continued. "You do. You deserve peace and joy and love, true love, God's love. You deserve to be free from the pain baby. What he did was wrong and God will deal with him but that's not your concern. Your concern should be healing. I want you to be delivered from this baby, I want you to be delivered from this so bad."

We were both crying now, unable to hide how this conversation was making us feel. I watched as she stood, walking over to me before kneeling down. She took my hands into hers, never taking her eyes off of me.

"Dominic, I love you," she choked. "I love you so much baby girl and I am sorry for not protecting you when it mattered most. I'm sorry that I didn't believe you and I am sorry that I allowed our relationship to be broken this long, never taking your feelings into account. I'm sorry for never making you a priority, ignoring your needs when you came home. You were always so strong and resilient; I thought you could handle it but I was wrong baby. I was so wrong and I pray that you forgive me baby."

I broke down.

"I'm so sorry mommy. I'm so sorry – I want to forgive. God please, help me to forgive," I cried in her chest as she held me close, brushing my hair with her fingers.

"Shhh, you don't need to apologize baby. I'm here – just let it out. Let it go, let God have it. He wants it so you don't have to carry it anymore. He loves you, just surrender. You don't have to be afraid; you don't have to live with this any longer," she soothed, rocking me a bit as I continued to cry, squeezing her as tight as I could.

This was the comfort and love I always needed from her, my mother.

As she continued to hold me, I could hear her whispering softly.

"Lord, I lift up my baby girl to you right now. Come into her heart and heal every wound, every broken piece, and every hurt that has been caused throughout her life. I ask you Father to uproot the damage that the enemy tried to use to take over my baby. Uproot it now God and make her whole! We ask for your healing power, Jesus. Reveal yourself to her in a new way. Create a new thing within her Lord. We come against every lying and tormenting spirit that is trying to take over my child right now. We come against every bit of trauma; we come against it right now and call it out! It will not have power over this child another day in her life God! Not another day not another day not another day!" She prayed through tears of her own as she continued to rock with me in her arms.

"This we ask of you. In Jesus name."

"Amen."

CHAPTER
- ELEVEN -

I adjusted the patterned top to my bikini, while fluffing my hair. My hands and toes were freshly manicured and not an ounce of body hair could be traced. I had to be on point today, more than any other.

Today was my birthday. I was another year older, and felt another year stronger. Thinking about this time last year, I was homeless, living in a shelter just to get out of my past situation and now here I was with two loving parents in a home full of structure and order. I had a warm bed and the greatest friend I could ever ask for in Jesse.

I was blessed. And for the first time I could bask in it without a single lick of worry.

Just as the thought came, my phone was vibrating against the bathroom sink. I noticed Jesse's name appear on the screen and straightened out my appearance as if he could see me.

"Hey," I answered the phone with a smile blushing at my own reflection in the mirror.

I thought the butterflies would simmer down after so many years but I don't think they ever will at this point.

"Happy birthday, beautiful," Jesse chimed softly on the other end as my heart felt like it was about to burst.

"Thank you, Jes."

"You about ready? I'm almost there."

I looked at my reflection once more before nodding, "Yeah, I just have to throw on some shorts. I was going to wait until my parents got back but I have no idea where they are. They've been gone for hours."

I could hear his hummed response, "I'm sure they'll be there when we get back. I wouldn't worry about it too much."

I shrugged, just ready to continue my day with my favorite person. "It's cool, I'll just see you when you get here. I'll be on the porch."

"You geek, aight," he teased before ending the call.

I quickly set my phone on the sink and ran to my room to finish getting ready.

"So we're getting on the freeway just for a little pool trip?" I chuckled in disbelief trying to get more of a hint to where Jesse was taking me.

"What I say about asking questions, girl?" he smirked, getting comfortable in his seat while pressing on the gas.

"You told me not to ask – "

"So why are you?"

"Because I'm nosey Jesse, hell! I wanna know where you're taking me! I thought this was going to be something simple," I pouted, crossing my arms and avoiding his teasing stare.

He chuckled, shaking his head. "Never simple for ya birthday, baby. It's a beautiful day out too. We're about to enjoy this to the fullest."

I grinned, zipping my lips and sitting back in my seat, watching the different cars we swiftly moved past. The sun was high in the sky, not a cloud in sight. It was a perfect day to swim.

"Why did you wanna go swimming so bad anyway?" Jesse finally asked.

"It was my favorite pastime with you. You remember the summers when we would walk like a mile to that pool on the days that our moms wouldn't take us? We would spend all day there just swimming, playing and beating other kids in every game we could think of."

Tiffany Campbell

I caught his smile at the memory. "Yeah, that did used to be fun. I didn't think you thought about stuff like that."

"I used to think about the days I spent in Raleigh constantly. Sometimes it would be all that would get me through. It was all I had to hold on to."

It was quiet for a moment before Jesse's voice sounded through the vehicle.

"I really wish you would've reached out to me Nic. I could've been there for you through whatever you were dealing with."

I shrugged, "No. I think we crossed paths again at the right time. I can't think of a better time than now to be where we are."

I caught his dimple just before it melted back into his cheek.

"You want another one of your gifts?"

My eyes widened, "Another one?! You got me something else?"

He snickered, "The Bible wasn't all I got you, open the glove."

I shook my head, "I don't feel comfortable accepting anything else from you Jes. Being with you is enough – "

He waved his hand, "Rah rah rah. Quit all that. You're my baby, it's your birthday and I got you gifts. Now accept them before you make me mad."

The heat came to my cheeks hearing Jesse's stern yet playful voice.

"Wh-where you say they were again?" I stumbled with the hint of a smile in my tone.

He chuckled, "In the glove, baby. Open it up."

I grinned opening the glove compartment and finding a neatly wrapped rectangular box.

I gently picked it up, feeling its lightness and cut my eyes questionably at Jesse.

"You wrap this?"

He laughed, shaking his head, "Nah, Moms got me on the wrapping tip. When I took it over there with my wrapping skills she called it pitiful and hooked me up."

I smiled at the story, tearing open the paper and finding a case labeled *Kay Jewelers*. My eyes darted in Jesse's direction.

"Don't ask questions, just open it," he said lightly, eager for me to see what was inside.

I snapped the box open and gasped at the gold nameplate resting inside. My fingers traced over the letters of my first name in awe. It was the first necklace I would ever own.

"You got this customized for me?"

He nodded, "Yeah. I wanted you to start wearing your name with pride. Dominic is a beautiful name with a powerful meaning. I figured it would help you embrace it a little better if you saw the beauty in it. It's going to look great hanging from your neck."

I was so happy I couldn't find the words so I reached over, wrapped my arms around his neck and kissed him repeatedly on his neck and the side of his lips as he laughed.

"You're gonna make me crash woman! I'm happy you like it if that's what this means." He said happily as I continued to kiss his cheek and sniff back the emotion.

I finally found the strength to pull away and look at my new favorite possession.

"This is now the second best gift I've ever gotten. I love this Jesse. I love ... " I stopped myself.

I'm getting too carried away with these dang feelings bubbling in my chest.

"I'm glad you like it baby, for real. I'm putting it on you as soon as we get to our destination."

I couldn't hide the smile that refused to leave my face. This was already starting to be the best birthday I've ever had.

I can't even imagine what else he could have in store for me.

"Jes it's been two hours! I'm starting to think this has turned into a kidnapping." I groaned, annoyed that he still wouldn't tell me where we were going.

He tipped a brow in my direction, "And that would be a problem?" he dared me to answer as the heat came back to my cheeks again.

How is he so sexy without even trying?

"Just tell me," I said softly, shrinking under his gaze.

He smiled, focusing back on the road. "We're almost there baby, like 15 minutes. Tops."

I rolled my eyes, placing my elbow on the armrest and my chin in my palm.

Jesse snickered.

"You always been a brat on ya birthday?"

I grinned, shaking my head. "Never had someone spoil me the way you are. So I guess the bratty side is second nature."

"Dang, so Im'a have to get used to this then, huh? That's cool. I don't mind." He said easily, darting his tongue across his bottom lip.

I blushed, finding it hard to believe that I was with this beautiful man inside and out, and all he wanted was my happiness.

It was truly unbelievable.

A peaceful silence had consumed the car as I studied our surroundings. I noticed the large body of water surrounding the expressway we were on.

"The ocean is so beautiful," I said, watching as the waves crashed against the shoreline gracefully.

"You ever been to the beach?" he asked as I shook my head no.

"Never. This right here is probably the closest I've been to a beach."

"Good," Jesse commented, veering right for the exit. "Perfect way to celebrate then."

My mouth dropped as I looked around us excitedly while Jesse pulled into a parking garage.

"Are you … are you serious right now, the beach, Jesse?" I asked, heart thumping in my chest with excitement and surprise.

He nodded, "Yeah. That's not even the best part though."

My eyes widened, "What could be better than this?"

He motioned his head towards the door. "Get out, I'll show you."

Without hesitation I took off my seatbelt and exited the car, looking at all of the families, couples and friends walking out of the garage and towards the pier that led to the beach.

Before I could take it all in, Jesse had taken my hand into his, leading us toward the pier.

"I really can't believe this," I said in awe, looking at the mini shops and food stands lined up on the boardwalk.

As we got closer to the west end of the beach, you could hear loud music blaring. "Someone must be having a party," I commented squinting in the direction the music was coming from.

Jesse didn't utter a word as we got closer to the noise. My brows met at the center of my forehead the closer we got.

"That ... that looks like, mom?" I pondered before watching everyone that was near the music turn around.

"HAPPY BIRTHDAY!" The crowd screamed as I came to a sudden halt in shock.

There were a slew of familiar faces that I recognized, from my parents to my aunts and cousins, to Jamie and a number of people I met at the party a few weeks ago.

They were here for me?!

"Happy Birthday Domo!" Jamie belted, throwing his shirtless arms in the air as the small crowd around him cheered.

I blushed at all of the attention before looking at Jesse who had a sneaky grin plastered on his face.

"Really? A surprise beach party over a bum day at the pool?!"

He chuckled, leaning down to place a gentle kiss on my cheek.

"I told you we were going all out for ya b-day baby. Let's have some fun."

I shook my head in disbelief before going to greet the people who were there to celebrate my day. I've never even been surrounded by so many people on my birthday before so all of this was new and exciting. I just couldn't believe Jesse pulled it all off for me.

"Were you surprised, boo?" my mother asked, standing with her best friend and my God-mother, Gloria.

I nodded, sipping on my water and looking around the beach.

"More than surprised. I can't believe all these people drove two hours just to celebrate me."

Gloria chuckled, "It's you and it's the perfect day for the beach. You're worth it, beautiful so bask in it," she encouraged as I nodded, looking around.

Corey and Gloria's husband were on the grill, cooking burgers and hot dogs. My cousins were in the ocean and Jamie had started a volley ball game with the people he had brought all while music was still creating the party atmosphere.

I searched every face, until I spotted Jesse off by himself and looking curiously at his phone. My brows furrowed a bit before I looked to my mom.

"I'm about to go bother Jesse."

She nodded, taking a sip of her drink and shooing me off. "Okay baby, we're about to go nag the men on when the food will be done."

I chuckled at her locking arms with Gloria while they giggled, walking off. It was always cute seeing her comfortable and with her friends.

I trudged towards my interest, loving the way the sun kissed his caramel skin. He looked up, locking eyes with me and began making his way in my direction with determination in his eyes.

He placed his hands on both sides of my hips, as I rubbed his smooth cheek.

"You okay?" I questioned softly, sensing his mood shift.

He wiped his face clean of any emotion before putting on a happy face. "I'm good, baby. You talk to everybody?"

I nodded, "Yeah. People actually got me gifts!" I squealed as he snorted.

"And you're surprised? It is your birthday, dork."

I shrugged, "People don't ever care. It's really cool to see people that care."

"Aye lovebirds!" We heard Jamie call from a short distance, lightly jogging towards us.

"What's good?" Jesse greeted with a head nod as his friend approached.

"We were checking out the jet ski rentals. Ya'll down?" Jamie asked, tipping a brow as I looked to Jesse with excited eyes.

He grinned, playfully rolling his eyes before nodding, "Let's do it."

Drops of water splashed against my ankles as the wind blew my wild hair every which way, but the smile would not leave.

I was in a race with Jesse and Jamie on either side of me, trying to reach a light pole about 50 yards into the ocean. I was beating them both but I think they were allowing me to.

"I'm coming for that ass, Domo!" Jamie bellowed causing me to laugh before turning to stick my tongue out at him.

Jesse was giggling like a child on the side of me, that wild look in his eyes he got every time he was participating in something exciting.

Seeing that alone was enough to make my entire day.

He was concerned about my happiness but I was overjoyed with his. Jesse does so much for me and for the people that he loves and he does it all with such grace even after everything he's been through. He deserved this day, just as much as I did.

I rounded the pole sloppily, careful to give the boys and myself some space. We were instructed how dangerous these things can be if you get too reckless. Once I was in the clear, I raised my arm in victory receiving displeasing responses from my opponents.

I giggled, continuing my ride with ease and enjoying this moment for all it was worth. I could see my family and friends in the distance, all still dancing and carrying on. Everyone was having a good time.

"What you wanna do next?" Jesse yelled over the loud humming of the jet ski.

"Eat! I'm starving!" I yelled back as he nodded.

"We got about 10 more minutes left on the rental. We'll put these back and eat! I'm hungry too," he said, catching Jamie zoom past us. He smirked before taking off in the direction of his best friend.

I smiled at the two friends, picking up my speed to catch up with them.

"Why are you over there looking goofy, dude?" Jesse questioned, taking a large bite of his hot dog.

By now, everyone had been served food and were sitting in their own little circles, eating, drinking and talking. Jesse and I were a little ways away from everyone else, just wanting to have our own personal moment. Most of our time had been spent enjoying the company of everyone who came out. I enjoyed them, but I enjoyed Jesse more.

"I'm just so happy," I sighed, resting my temple against his shoulder.

He pecked the top of my forehead before resuming his chewing, "I'm happy you're happy. I just really wanted you to feel special today. You deserve it."

"You deserve it too," I said softly, watching as the waves rolled against the shoreline.

"I'm happy baby, believe me. I got the most beautiful girl tucked underneath my arm in a bikini. You can't shake my high right now."

Tiffany Campbell

I giggled, rolling my eyes at his honesty. "Yeah, I've caught your eyes traveling a few times."

He shrugged, "I can't help myself ... it's like ... it's like your body is speaking to me. *Look at me Jesse. Touch me Jesse.*"

I laughed out loud at the voice he was using. He wrapped his arm around my shoulder and pulled me closer.

"I don't ever want to leave," I spoke, enjoying the soft breeze from the ocean.

"We don't have to leave ... today," Jesse said as I shot my eyes up at him.

"What do you mean? Like staying in the city overnight?"

He shrugged before nodding, "I mean yeah, unless you didn't want to. I had your mom put together an overnight bag for you just in case you wanted to spend some extra time. I know how you are with people so I wasn't going to force you to have to share your whole day with everyone if you weren't in the mood."

"No I mean it's cool and I've been having such a good time but ... there were some things I wanted to talk to you about before the day was over."

His brows met at the center, "Like what?"

I shook my head, "Now is not the time, maybe a little later? If we stay?"

He searched my eyes for a moment before he leaned in placing a delicate kiss on my lips.

"We'll stay."

"Thank you for all of your help with the party today, Jamie," I said softly, helping him pack up the beach chairs that were spread out across the beach.

The party was dying down and people were packing up to head back to Raleigh. Corey and Jesse were putting all of the gifts and the grill in the car.

"Man, it's not a problem at all homie, you're good people. I told you this the first night I met you. And everyone that came out to show you love remembered you and wanted to be a part of this just as much as I did. Plus it's the beach, everyone loves a good day at the beach," Jamie replied smoothly, flexing his muscles to pick up two chairs at a time.

I followed him with my one chair as we walked back to the tent that held all of the chairs for the beach workers to pick up once it closed.

"I know, but you really didn't have to –"

"Domo, you're good baby. It was all love. Jesse loves you, so I do too. We got you. You have a friend for life in me," he smiled charmingly as I did the same.

I was hesitant before making my next comment, "Did – did you notice anything off about Jes today?"

Jamie furrowed his brows before quickly shaking his head as we stood a short distance from the tent. "No, not really. He seemed extremely happy today."

I nodded slowly, taking his answer for what it was.

"Okay, so it must've just been me."

Jamie tapped my arm before I made to walk off, "Well what made you say that? Did you notice something off?"

I looked off in the distance before shaking my head, ridding myself of the thought.

"No. I just thought something was bothering him but it was really only for a split second. I could've been reading the whole thing wrong, just worried for nothing."

Jamie looked me in my eyes carefully; searching for the truth I'm sure. He parted his lips to say something before he was being called. He sighed, glancing at the person that called him before looking back to me.

He put a smile back on his face, "Happy birthday again, Domo. I'll see you when you and Jesse get back to city."

He reached in for a tight embrace before letting go.

"Don't do nothing I wouldn't do, girl."

He winked as I rolled my eyes playfully. He laughed at my reaction before jogging off.

I turned around to see Jesse, my mom and Corey all standing not too far away. I dug my bare feet in the sand as I made my way over to my family.

I caught Corey's attention first and he stretched his arm out so I could tuck myself comfortably underneath it. He greeted me with a gentle kiss on my temple.

My mom looked lovingly at the two of us, "You enjoy your birthday, baby?"

I nodded happily, "Best birthday I've ever had."

She smiled, "We're going to have a dinner and cake tomorrow for you when you guys get back, just the four of us."

I grinned, earning one more kiss from Corey before he let go and my mom came to give me a goodbye hug.

"If you need anything just give us a call but I'm sure Jesse will take care of you."

She looked to Jesse sternly, "Right?"

Jesse smirked, hands stuffed in his pockets. "I got her, Ms. Sharon, she's my baby too." He joked, earning a giggle from her.

"Alright, well ya'll be safe and enjoy your night. Let me know when you get on the road tomorrow," she instructed, pointing to us both as her husband grabbed her hand to pull her away.

"Yes Corey, take her away. She's nagging too much," I teased, as her mouth dropped. The three of us laughed as she smacked Corey's arm for laughing at me.

"Bye guys, love you!" I said before I could catch it.

"Love you too baby!" my mom called back sweetly, the smile never leaving her face.

She was probably just as shocked as me that I had said it so ... effortlessly.

Hopefully it can be this easy when I tell Jesse.

"This is ... beautiful," I said in awe, looking above us at the stars.

Jesse and I checked into our room but came back out to the beach to watch the sunset. We'd been out here long after, just lying on beach towels and watching as the flecks of sun dispersed, being replaced by an illuminated night sky. The moon was shining bright, reflecting off the ocean. We could hear the waves crashing gently against the shore.

"It is ... " Jesse said softly, but I could feel his eyes on me.

I turned my head, meeting his gaze, causing me to blush instantly.

"I was talking about the sky," I said, doing my best to hide the smile that just wouldn't go away.

"And I was talking about you. This view is better than stars. The way your skin is shining because of them ... its the real thing."

I snickered, "So corny."

I could hear his grin, "Yeah whatever, you like it," he said cockily, looking back up at the sky.

I smiled, biting my lip as the butterflies flipped in the pit of my stomach. A sigh soon escaped.

It was now or never to speak my mind.

My body lifted up into a sitting position and I lifted my knees, resting my chin on them. I began to run my fingers through the sand, attempting to build the courage.

Jesse sat up too, looking over at me with question, "Something on ya mind?"

I nodded slow, keeping my lips sealed.

"Speak ya heart then, baby. What's up?"

"Remember that talk we had a little while ago? You know, about our feelings for each other? Remember how you said our love is going to be so passionate and strong one day?" I asked, turning my cheek so I could see his face.

He nodded, "Yeah. I remember."

I swallowed, "Well ... that love you were talking about? I feel that for you. I feel it and it grows every single day. It's almost like it's swelling in my soul wanting to burst out. I know you wanted to wait until I loved myself fully, but Jes, I've never loved myself more than I do now.

And I feel like … I love the me that I am when I'm with you and I'm trying to wait and be patient with you but –"

I paused taking in a deep breath, lifting my head. "I just want to experience this in its fullness and entirety. I want to express these feelings I have for you all the time. I want us to grow … together, loving each other and ourselves. I just … I just want this more than I've wanted anything."

"Am I wrong for feeling like this?" I asked almost breathless, my heart wanting to escape out of my chest.

Jesse watched me soulfully, before running his tongue across his lips and shaking his head. "You're not wrong baby."

He bit the inside of his cheek before continuing, "I don't – I don't wanna hurt you Dominic."

Frustration began to grow, "How? How can you hurt me?"

He huffed through his nose, "I just wanna protect you, protect you from things you might not be able to handle. Love, loving somebody as much as I love you –" He stopped.

I froze.

"What?"

He was still silent once he realized.

"You love me?" I asked, trying to keep the joy I felt only inside and not on my face.

He swallowed, nodding confidently.

"That's not evident? I've loved you since I was a kid and I'm in love with you now. I have never felt this before … for anybody and it scares me because I don't know how deep this is going to get or what the future holds."

I could see it. I could see the fear, he couldn't even look me in my eyes.

I placed my hand gently on his cheek, trying to give him the calm he constantly gives me from his touch.

"Look at me, baby," I said softly.

His head immediately turned to my direction.

"Isn't that what comes with love, the risk? The risks of everything completely blowing up in your face but you love that person anyway. If I've learned anything from God, it's that. If I've learned anything from you, it's that"

I shrugged, "It just comes with the territory and I'm scared of hurting you too so don't think I'm not. But you're worth the risk to me. This love is something I can't ignore or downplay anymore. I have to express myself; I have to show you just how much you mean to me Jesse. In every way."

His eyes darted back and forth looking me over before he leaned in and gave me the most passionate kiss I've ever felt. My lips parted, allowing him full access to my heart and soul.

Jesse placed his hand on the back of my neck, pulling me in deeper as both of my arms wrapped around him. I was in pure bliss as the fire ignited within me burned stronger.

This was love – this was it. It's never felt more real, more passionate and I felt so alive. It was dwelling within me and I wanted nothing more than to give it all to Jesse.

He pulled away suddenly, both of us desperately needing our own air to breathe.

Even though sharing with him seemed less suffocating.

The wind had picked up, causing a chill to run up my spine and instinctively I wrapped my arms around myself for warmth.

Jesse frowned, placing both of his hands on my arms and rubbing them to create friction and heat.

"Come on, let's get inside. It's getting late anyway," he suggested as I nodded and stood to my feet.

Ready for my night to simmer down ... or heat up, whichever came first.

I stood in the steamy bathroom, using my palm to wipe the fog from the mirror. I was standing there, in all of my glory, nerves overflowing.

Jesse was on the other side, watching TV from what I could hear. We had been back in the room for a while now, and I waited after him to take my shower, wanting to take him by surprise. I didn't know what was to come of this night, but now that I knew Jesse felt the same way about me that I felt about him, I didn't want to wait any longer.

I took in a deep breath, grabbing the towel from the vanity and wrapping it daintily around my curvaceous dripping wet body. Shaking, I took ahold of the knob, turned it slow before opening the door.

Jesse was lying back on the bed comfortably, with one hand behind his head and the other using the remote to flip channels.

"Aye baby," Jesse started, not looking my way and preparing to turn his head.

"I was thinking we could –"

His brow rose, looking in my direction, only causing my heart rate to increase. Without a second thought, I let go of my grip on the towel, allowing it to fall gracefully at my toes.

I could feel the drops of water easing down my body as Jesse's lips parted in surprise. Slowly, he sat up, flipping his legs over the edge of the bed, his eyes climbing up every inch of me.

"Nic ... what are you doing?" He asked softly, keeping his eyes locked on mine.

I swallowed hard, before looking down at myself and then back to him.

"I want to express myself fully to you ... this way. Words just don't seem like enough."

He ran his tongue over his lips nervously before biting the inside of his cheek, "It doesn't have to be this soon."

"I know I just –I want to express my love to in the way I know how ... if you're ready, of course."

He smiled before bending forward to clutch the towel. He kneeled down and placed a gentle peck on both of my thighs, slowly traveling his way up. He kissed my belly button, and then my collarbone, my cheeks and lastly my lips.

I was quiet as Jesse gently wrapped the towel around my body, staring lovingly into my brown hues.

"I love you, Dominic. I love your spirit, I love your mind and I love you down to the depths of your soul and I know you love me too."

He paused for a moment before continuing. "I don't need you to give me your body to understand that and to feel it. You're beautiful, in every sense of the word. The physical will come, but not like this. You're still healing, baby. Your essence was robbed from you and even though I appreciate you wanting to give me something so precious, I want it in the right way. The way it should've always been done for both of us."

I blinked, allowing the tear of embarrassment to fall. He was quick to dab it away with the pad of his thumb.

"Why are you crying?"

I sniffed, "You don't want me?"

He blew out a breath, resting his forehead against mine. "Baby, I want you. I want every bit of you right now but I can't have you, not like this. You deserve so much more than this."

I put my head down in shame, only to have Jesse take my cheeks in his palms, softly forcing me to look at him.

"I need to show you that, show you what you deserve every day. I don't know what all your past consists of Nic, but I do know that I'm not the men who came before me. I value you and I'm going to take my time with showing you the worth that I know deep down you possess. You just need some help pulling it out, that's all."

I sniffed some more, nodding in understanding. He was right, I didn't need to use my body to show him how much I loved him. I was just ready to make our connection even stronger than it already was.

"Now what I will do," he said, looking me over, "Is give you the best massage you've ever gotten in your life."

I smirked, as Jesse took my hand in his, leading me towards our bed.

"Lay down on your stomach," he instructed. I did as I was told and the heavy emotion I just felt began to leave.

I crossed my arms, resting my cheek against them with my eyes closed as I waited to feel Jesse's hands on me. After a few moments, the towel I had wrapped around me was being pulled down, stopping right at my waistline.

"You sure you know what you're doing?" I teased with a smile, hearing Jesse snort behind me.

"Course I know what I'm doing, girl. These hands are magic," he said, just as he began to rub the lotion onto my back.

I almost moaned in bliss with how good and relaxing it felt.

"This right here, might be better than sex."

"Pft, this is nothing compared to what our love will feel like," he said confidently, continuing to work my back muscles with ease.

"Oh? How do you know?"

"I know things. Plus I already know I'm gonna make you my wife one day."

I hummed happily at the thought, "Yeah? What else you know?"

"That you're going to have my baby," he replied as I chuckled.

"Never pictured myself having kids."

"Well you're gonna have mine and he's going to carry my legacy forever. He'll look like you ... but more like me," he snickered, pressing on my lower back.

"All of that sounds amazing. Life with you sounds amazing."

I sighed happily, appreciating the moment.

A peaceful silence passed over us as Jesse continued to ease every bit of tension I felt in my back. After a short while, I slowly turned over, stopping his massage all together.

I looked up at him, watching as his eyes searched my face.

"Kiss me," I ordered gently.

"All I want you to do right now as my last birthday wish is kiss me."

And without another thought, he obliged. Leaning down, wrapping his arms around my naked body, connecting our souls in another magical kiss. I ran my fingers over his short slick hair, he wrapped his arms around me tighter, dipping his tongue in and out of my mouth.

I couldn't deny the chemistry we shared and it was taking so much restraint not to wrap my legs around him. I've never known what this feeling was like and now that I felt it, it was hard to resist.

Jesse removed his lips from mine as he breathed heavily and stared deep into my eyes.

"Baby, you don't understand how much –" he stopped, pressing his forehead against mine, closing his eyes.

"You don't understand how much I want you right now," he finished, clenching his jaw tight.

God he looked so beautiful.

"I want you too," I breathed, gripping his hair even tighter.

He blew out a short breath, before pecking my lips once more and finding the strength to pull back.

"Clothes? Clothes might be a good idea," he suggested, looking away with a slight nervous chuckle as I smirked, wrapping the towel back around my body.

"Clothes it is … "

CHAPTER
- TWELVE -

Jesse had never been more nervous in his life. He strolled through the entrance of the hospital with his head down, already knowing the direction he needed to go to get to the elevators. He didn't want to lock eyes with anyone, didn't want to speak to anyone. He just wanted answers.

Ever since receiving the message from his doctor's office about needing to come in to talk about his blood work he had taken last week, he knew bad news was to follow. For the past five years since starting his routine checkups, if everything was fine all it took was a phone call. And this ... this was much more than a simple phone call.

He had been doing his best to keep a positive and upbeat attitude around Dominic and his friends but now that the day was finally here, it was getting harder to bear. He spent all night and morning praying, asking God why this had to be his fate. Why he had to be succumbed with sickness, just when pure joy had re-entered his life.

But he knew not to question and not speak things negatively into existence. He served a God that could move mountains with the faith of a mustard seed. A God that heals the sick and delivers the broken hearted. Surely, whatever he was about to be faced with, he could conquer.

He had done it before. He'll do it again.

He reached the 9th floor sooner than he hoped. He sniffed back the emotion before stepping off to approach the nurse's station.

"Hey, I have an appointment with Dr. Morrison at 3," he told the nurse softly as she gave a warm smile in return.

She typed a few things into the computer before nodding, "Yes, Jesse just give us a few moments and we'll call you back. He's finishing up with another patient right now."

He nodded in response before turning to take a seat in the waiting area. He checked his phone, seeing he had another missed call from

Dominic. Probably wanting to tell him about the job interview she had earlier that day. He was happy for her and wanted to hear about it but didn't want to speak to anyone until he knew for sure what was happening with his body.

He rubbed his clammy hands together, attempting to reduce the shaking in his soul. He stared off at nothing in particular, just wishing that none of this was real.

"Jesse?" A nurse called, snapping him out of daze. "Dr. Morrison will see you now."

He huffed, standing tall to his feet and followed the nurse to the office he had hoped to never see again.

The nurse left him at his doctor's door. Jesse peeked in, seeing the elder gray haired gentlemen looking at the contents of a folder. His blue eyes were magnified in his thick-framed glasses, just as he looked to see his young and bright patient standing at the entrance.

"Come on in Jesse," he beckoned gently, watching the young man close the door behind him.

He could see the fear resting in his young brown eyes. The sight alone saddened him even more. This profession had its rewarding moments ... but times like these made it hard.

Jesse released a short breath through his nose, just as he sat in the plush leather chair. He gripped the armrest, refusing to look Dr. Morrison in the eyes as his heart dropped down to the pit of his stomach.

This was more real than he ever wanted it to be.

"How are you today –"

"Just," Jesse was quick to cut him off. "Just please tell me why I'm here. I can't do small talk today doc. I can't."

"I know," Dr. Morrison tried to reason. "I just want to see how you are."

Jesse looked him in his eyes now, "I won't know until you tell me what's going on."

His voice cracked more than he intended.

He sniffed, "Please, just tell me," he begged for the last time, looking back down to the floor.

Dr. Morrison sighed heavily, pulling out the results of Jesse's blood work. "They found traces of the disease in your blood. Not extremely high, but enough to where if we don't do something to control it now, it could get worse. We won't know how serious it is until we run more tests, look for tumors ... "

Jesse began to tune out his words, feeling his entire world crack right down the middle of his chest.

"So you're telling me," he started, sitting up in his seat, "Are you sitting here, telling me I have cancer. Again?"

The doctor frowned; saddened by the news he had to deliver.

"We should start chemotherapy, at least once a month to minimize the cells that are –"

Dr. Morrison was cut off by an emotional Jesse, slamming his palm onto the desk, silencing the doctor completely.

"No."

Jesse started, shaking his head, "No. No! No!"

He brought his fist down to slam on the desk again, but stopped himself, standing to his feet.

"No!" he yelled in the room, pushing the chair over, feeling the doctor's eyes on him. He didn't care. He had to release this anger that he felt burning inside of him somehow.

"This ... " Jesse frowned deeply, feeling the tears pool at the tip of his eyes.

"This isn't supposed to happen to me again. I've been healthy Dr. Morrison. I've been healthy, I swear," his voice shook, pleading.

"I don't drink, I don't smoke. I exercise damn near every day. I run, I take my medicine. I'm – I'm healthy. I'm not sick. I'm not sick."

He pressed his hand against the wall to keep his balance and to keep from passing out right there on the floor. Everything was spinning and all he could think about was Dominic.

He knew something like this could happen. He knew it, and allowed her to love him anyway. He blinked, allowing the tears to stream down his face.

"I'm so sorry, son. I was a bit surprised at the results myself ... "

"Test me again, please." Jesse interrupted him, refusing to accept the news.

"Test me again doc because I'm fine. I'm good, look at me. I've never felt better in my life."

Dr. Morrison sighed, before nodding. "We will test you Jesse. I want to schedule a follow up appointment so we can run some more tests to see if we can find the exact cause before we start your chemotherapy. I wanted to get you in for testing as soon as next Tuesday if you were open."

He nodded quickly, wanting to get more answers before jumping to any conclusions. "Please. I'm open all day."

The doctor stood to his feet, walking slowly to the trembling young man before him. "You're a good man, Jesse, with a strong soul. Whatever this is, I'm confident we can fight it and beat it at the root."

Jesse's glossed over eyes locked with his caregiver's before sticking out his hand.

"And I'm confident it's not even there."

I frowned, staring at my phone for the hundredth time, wondering why Jesse hadn't returned any of my phone calls or texts.

I had been trying to reach him all day since leaving my interview with Costco this morning but for whatever reason he had been ignoring me and I was starting to worry. It wasn't like Jesse to go the whole day and not respond in any way.

I sighed, stuffing my cell phone in my pocket. I decided to leave the comfort of my room to bother my parents. I needed to keep my mind busy until he called.

My feet trudged down the stairs until I reached the bottom step and my eyes nearly popped out of socket when I noticed something out of our front door window.

Jesse's car was parked in his mom's driveway, right across the street.

What the hell was going on?

Without another thought, I opened the front door, squinting my eyes to see if I could see any other signs of him. The house seemed dark like it always did but I was determined to figure out just why I had been ignored all day.

My mind began to fill with memories from our last conversation, trying to decide if I had said anything wrong. Everything had gone back to normal after my birthday. I had just become more focused on finding employment so that I could get my car so nothing was out of the ordinary on my end.

I finally reached his mother's doorstep and took in a deep breath before I rang the bell. I waited patiently for a few moments before I heard feet approaching and held my breath for the moment Jesse would appear.

He didn't. His mother did.

"Hi Dominic baby!" she greeted happily, as I smiled in return. "How are you?"

"I'm fine Ms. Palmer," I replied, trying to slyly peek past her. "Is-is Jesse here? I see his car."

She paused for a moment before shaking her head, "No he's not, sweetie. You can find him at the park though, around the corner."

I smiled with gratitude, getting ready to turn to leave until I stopped myself.

"Do you know if everything is okay with him? I've been trying to reach him all day." I was hopeful that she would give me a truthful response.

She grinned, "It's just one of those days baby. He has them from time to time. As strong and positive as he is, even he has bad days too."

I nodded, giving one last smirk. "Thank you Ms. Palmer. I'm going to go find him."

I waved goodbye as she did the same.

I left off their porch with determination in my step. If Jesse needed me, I wanted to be there.

After a short ten minute walk, I reached our neighborhood park to find Jesse drenched in sweat and dribbling his basketball unmercifully. The streetlight illuminated his light caramel skin beautifully as beads of sweat streamed down the side of his face.

His brows seemed locked in the middle of his forehead as he went to make another shot. He was there to catch the ball the minute it went through the net, grunting as he palmed it against the pavement. He grunted a few more times before turning to throw the ball against the pole; it went flying in the air.

My eyes widened at his sudden outburst, "Jesse!"

His head snapped in my direction, looking on in confusion. I picked up my pace to jog closer to him.

"Jesse, baby what's wrong?" I questioned as I stood a short distance from him.

His hands were planted on his waist, gasping desperately for air.

"Do you have your inhaler? Can you breathe? Are you –"

"I'm fine," he cut me off, looking down, still trying to catch his breath.

"I'm fine baby. What you doing out here?"

My shoulders slouched, looking my love in the face, seeing the pain resting in his eyes. He wasn't even trying to hide it like he normally does.

"I came to check on you. I've been calling all day Jes. What's going on?"

He tucked his lips in before shaking his head, "Just having a bad day. I ain't wanna worry you."

"So ignoring me all day was to get me not to worry? You could've at least told me you were breathing!" I spoke louder than intended, causing his eyes to shut at my last statement.

"It wasn't like that Nic. I just needed some time, that's all."

I stepped closer, only inches away now, "Well talk to me." I pleaded, using my right hand to wipe the drips of sweat from his cheek. I held it there to caress him, only wanting to bring comfort.

"I'm good baby. I don't wanna talk right now. I just- I just want to play basketball."

"I know you're keeping something from me. Why can't you trust me?"

"I'm not keeping nothing from you. Just some days I don't feel one hundred percent. I just need my time to regroup."

He stepped out of my touch, leaving me to go get the ball that had rolled off into the grass.

I turned, watching his retreating back.

"Isn't that what I'm supposed to be here for? To be here for you just as much as you're there for me? You don't have to carry the weight of the world by yourself Jes."

He bent down to pick up the ball before standing straight up, not turning around to face me.

"Just let me in. Don't shut me out when you need me, please," I begged softly, watching his shoulders slump slightly.

He turned around, a calmer expression on his face now only causing me to get annoyed. He wasn't going to tell me what was bothering him. I could see it.

He approached me, tucking the ball underneath his arm, placing a gentle peck against my pouted lips.

"I'm good, baby. I promise. I just need to work out this aggression. After I get to my mom's and shower I'm coming over and we can chill at your place, ok? Talk about how that interview went and all that. Just let me – just let me finish this up."

He needed his time and I wasn't going to force it out of him. I blew out a soft breath before nodding in understanding.

"Come right after, Jesse. I mean it," I said sternly as he bit his lip and nodded, giving me one last sweet kiss.

"Right after, I promise."

I left Jesse with heaviness on my heart that I couldn't ignore. Something was torturing his soul, that much I could tell. But I wouldn't dare force it out of him, as bad as I wanted to know what it was, I couldn't do that.

I decided to talk to the one person that knew Jesse better than anyone.

I decided to pray.

I took in a deep breath, as my feet stepped against the pavement, walking further and further away from the park, building the courage to talk to God for the first time.

How do I start?

"Uh, hey God," I began, shoving my hands deep in the pockets of my jacket. "It's me. It's me Ko- Dominic. I don't know if this is orthodox or not ... or how you pray but ... Jesse always told me it was like having a conversation. I don't know any scriptures by heart to repeat back to you, I don't know anything by heart but I know what's on my heart. I know what's in my heart and that is to pray for Jesse."

I sighed, breathing deep and gathering my thoughts, feeling the emotion prick at the surface. "I don't know what's going on with my friend God but I know he needs you. He's hurting and it's something I can't fix. It's something he can't deal with alone. Can you ... can you help me? Can you help me, help him or just help him period? Fix whatever is broken. Keep him healthy and whole and happy. It's so hard ... it's so hard seeing the light dim in his eyes. It's so hard watching him hurt and

I know it's not good for him to hold it in. I've been there, and he was there for me. So ... please be there for him. Be there for him like never before. I know he talks to you all the time, just please help my friend."

I used my sleeve to wipe at the tear that slipped out, before sniffing.

"Amen."

––––––––––––––––––

"Dang, so you wowed them like that?" I could hear the smile in Jesse's voice.

We were in my room while my parents were gone out for a late night dinner and movie. His back was pressed against my headboard while my arms were wrapped around his waist, my cheek against his chest so I could hear the sound of his calming heartbeat. He came over after his workout like he promised and it was as if our moment on the court never existed. He seemed full of life, full of the positive energy that I had grown to adore.

It seemed genuine and I hoped my prayer had been answered.

"Yeah, they hired me on the spot! $13.23 an hour, I start next Monday," I said proudly, tightening my grip on him.

"That's awesome baby. I'm proud of you. I'm sorry I couldn't take you today. I had too many moves to make," he replied, running his long fingers through my straightened tresses.

"It's okay. I learned the bus route up there. I used to take the bus everywhere back home. It's kind of relaxing."

He snickered, "The bus? How so?"

I shrugged, "I like to watch people. I used to try to guess everyone's story when they would get on. I would make up all kinds of things for people. Some would be funny, some would be sad, some would be wild and impossible. It was fun."

I could feel Jesse's chest hop in amusement, "You are so weird, man."

It was quiet between us as Jesse continued to run his fingers through my hair softly.

"Jes," I started after the quiet had become too hard to bear.

"Yeah baby."

"Are you okay?"

I felt his fingers pause for a moment before he continued.

"I told you girl, I'm fine. I just had to get it out that's all. I didn't want to take it out on anyone."

I nodded, "You know … you know you can trust me right? When I say I love you, I mean it. I just want to be here, in every way possible. I don't want you worried about how I'm going to take something all the time. I just want to help you the same way you helped me."

"You're helping me more than you know right now, just by your company. I don't need much more than this."

I sighed, "Yeah I get that but to talk too. You can't hold back from me and then not want me to hold back from you, it's not fair. We should always be able to come to one another about anything."

"You're right," he agreed softly. "I'm sorry for that. I just need you to know that you have nothing to worry about, I'm fine, everything is fine, okay?"

I nodded slowly.

His lips graced the top of my hair.

"Just trust me, aight."

"Trust me too."

"So when does it start to click?" I asked aloud, over the buzzing of a cars zooming by.

It was a gorgeous Sunday afternoon. Jesse and I had just left church and decided to explore downtown to find a new spot to have lunch.

The last few weeks had been a whirlwind. I started my job and loved the freedom and independence it gave me. Jesse and I had grown closer since the talk we had. He seemed to have been in much better spirits than he was the other day. I had chose to stop pushing the issue and just allowed everything to flow naturally like it had been before.

I couldn't have been happier.

Jesse snorted in response to my random question, turning up his nose, "When does what start to click?"

"Like ... God, church. I don't know. When does it start to feel, I guess like how everyone else feels. People in there be shouting, running, crying. They just feel His presence I guess. Maybe that's the question I'm looking to ask."

Jesse pushed his hands deep in his pants pockets, brows meeting at the center.

"When do you start to feel God?" he questioned for clarity.

I nodded, eager to get a deeper understanding. I was enjoying church, I just didn't understand it all. It seemed like there was much more that I had yet to learn and I wasn't sure if I was patient enough.

"I guess, when you accept Him. When you get saved, that's when I felt Him in my heart."

"But," I frowned. "Why is getting saved so important? I go to church, I pray. I read the Bible more than I ever have. I mean, it's not every day but, it's a lot."

He grinned, "Getting saved means you accept God's word as truth and believe Jesus died for your sins. You're becoming a new creature in Christ. It binds you and Him together eternally."

My shoulders slumped, "That just seems so unfair. If I do everything I'm supposed to do but don't say I believe Jesus died for my sins then I just have to cut my losses? If there's anything I'm learning about God, that just doesn't seem like Him."

He nodded, "And I agree. I'm still working on getting a full understanding of some things myself. We weren't placed here to have all the answers."

"I can see that," I said, walking casually down the street. "I guess I just need to read more."

He smiled, draping his arm across my shoulder. "You're good Nic. You're moving at a smooth pace. You're learning about the faith and just growing in it – a relationship is not something that just forms overnight, it grows over time. The more you get to know the person and trust the person, the deeper the understanding you have of them. Keep reading and keep coming to church. God will reveal to you what He wants you to understand about Him. You're doing perfect."

My heart beamed with reassurance. I thought I was getting more lost because I had more questions, but it's like Jesse explained; the more I get to know God for myself, the better I'll understand Him and maybe the more I'll feel him.

"It's just weird being this person," I stated, with a shake of my head.

"What person is that?"

I shrugged, "Into church, into God. He seemed so nonexistent or more so like I refused to believe He existed. But then, you came back heavy and it seemed like God could be the only explanation as to why you're here and a part of my life. Heaven sent, that's how this feels."

I looked up at Jesse now, noticing the faraway look in his eye before a small spread across his face.

"That's a beautiful thing baby. You are a Heaven sent to me."

He looked down at me, placing a tiny peck on my forehead.

"You're just saying that," I teased, just wanting to hear him tell me more about the way I made him feel.

"I'm not. God made you just for me, just for moments like this where you make everything so much better," he breathed happily, looking down at his feet.

"What's so bad that it has to be better?" I probed, hoping he would let me in, just a little bit more.

"Nothing anymore," he grinned before locking his focus on the building we were approaching.

"We can try this pizza shop! You down?" he asked, changing the subject completely.

I took note, but I wasn't going to ruin the good time we were having.

"Sure."

———————

"You do know lying is a sin, right?" Jameson asked his best friend as they sat in the living room of his house, playing video games.

It was the only thing to distract the two of them from the seriousness and sensitivity of the topic at hand.

Jesse shook his head quickly, "I'm not lying."

"Okay ... deceiving, omitting the truth? Whatever the hell you wanna call it, it's wrong and you know it. You need to tell Dominic what's going on with you man before it gets real."

Jesse waved his controller-free hand, not wanting his friend to continue.

"Stop. Don't talk like that."

Frustrated now, Jamie paused the game, tossing his controller to the side.

"Don't talk like what? Like you don't got Cancer?! Like you don't gotta start chemotherapy next week and the one person you need by ya side to get through this, you refuse to tell what's going on!"

Jesse sank into the couch; hearing his condition out loud was still too hard to bear on his heart.

He had cancer – multiple myeloma to be exact. The cancer had found a way into his bone marrow and he was devastated with the news.

Because he hadn't shown any symptoms, the doctor's had high hopes that if they treat it early, they can attack the disease at the root, diminishing it completely but he had to be careful. Any infection, no matter how minor, could be life threatening.

"I know," Jesse spoke softly, watching the hurt fill Jamie. He was hurting for his friend, more than he wanted to show in this moment.

"If you know then why are you not telling her? Acting like everything is all good like she's not picking up that something is off about you?"

Jesse sighed, running a tired hand down his face and leaving it to rest against his cheek. "I don't want to."

"What?" Jamie yelled in disbelief. "That's seriously the best reason you're giving me right now?"

Jesse bit his lip, feeling his own anger from his situation beginning to creep out of the dark place he had it hidden in.

"Am I not allowed to be selfish?" he questioned louder than intended.

The emotion was getting harder to contain the closer he got to his first chemotherapy appointment.

"I'm always," he breathed, "I'm always fighting for my life man. I'm always fighting to be alive. Am I not allowed to be selfish? Am I not allowed to have one area of my life that is bringing me the most joy and happiness? Do I have to taint it with this disease that's been plaguing my existence?"

He shook his head, clenching his jaw. "I watch everybody around me be selfish and they still get to live. I've been nothing but giving and I still get hit with this man. I still get hit with it."

Jamie was quiet, allowing Jesse to express his truth. He knew his friend knew better but he needed this moment. He needed to vent and share his pain with someone.

"It ain't fair and because it ain't fair to me, I don't wanna be fair man. I thought God don't place nothing on you that you can't bear? I can't bear this, not for a second time. Not again bruh," he choked, sniffing back the cry that desperately wanted to escape.

Jamie frowned, placing a gentle hand on Jesse's shoulder.

"I'm sorry man. I'm truly sorry you gotta go through this shit. You don't know how sick I was in that hospital room when you got the news but don't get swallowed by ya mountain, man. Our God gives us the faith that talks to mountains and tell em to move. This ya mountain, and you gotta tell it to move," he spoke, attempting to lift Jesse's spirits, no matter how cliché the advice was.

"You're going to beat this," he continued. "But you can't keep this from her. I know you wanna be selfish and you don't wanna be fair but she don't deserve that. She deserves the truth. You don't want her finding out the hard way and risk losing her in more ways than one."

Jesse sniffed again, using the back of his hand to wipe at his nose. "I'm already scared of losing her. I'm scared of losing me! I'm just- I'm scared man, period. This doesn't get easier the second time around, I tell you that much."

"I just wanna live, that's all I want. I wanna spend the rest of my life with her, happy and content and yet, it seems like the hardest thing ever to do."

"Well don't sound so defeated. You want that happily ever after then get it, fight this. Beat this but don't give up just as you're getting in the ring," Jamie sighed.

He hated this but he hated hearing Jesse speak as if he were dying.

He wasn't going to die, not on his watch.

"I'll talk to her," Jesse stated after a few moments of silence. "Just … on my time. It's gotta be the right way."

"Ain't no right way to say that," said Jamie with a shake of his head.

"Which is why it's taking me this long. I just need more time; more time to process this for myself before I can allow her to take this on because I know her and I know this is going to break her heart. I gotta be strong for her. I can't do that right now."

Jesse frowned, Dominic's face appearing in his mind.

"Just need more time … "

———————————

"Is everything alright?" Corey asked from the kitchen.

He and my mother were in the middle of making dinner together when I got home from work. I sat sluggishly at the table watching them from the other side of the counter, my mind everywhere but home.

Jesse was imprinted into my brain. Something had been off about him, and I still wasn't able to figure out what. No matter how much I tried to rid myself of the nagging feeling in my gut, it wouldn't go away and I just wasn't sure what to do with it at this point.

"What do you do when you feel like someone you care about isn't telling you the truth about something?" I asked aloud, waiting for either one of my parents to answer.

Corey looked to my mother and her large brown eyes darted back to his in uncertainty. He cleared his throat before glancing back to me.

"Not telling you the truth about what?" he questioned, getting a shrug in response from me.

"I don't know, something that's bothering them, hurting them and they won't tell you, maybe to protect you? I don't know,"

I sighed with a shake of my head, feeling like I was probably wrong about my assumptions.

"Well," he started, leaning his hands against the counter top, "I pray for them. I pray for them every day and hope that one day they'll trust me with the information. Until then, God knows and He knows what that person needs."

I sighed, "I don't feel like God always hears me when I pray."

A confused expression spread across his features, "Of course He hears you when you pray."

"How do you know?" I quipped, genuinely seeking an answer.

"Baby," my mom interjected. "If you believe God is hearing your prayer, then He is. Without a shadow of a doubt, if that's where your faith is."

"Even though I'm not saved?" I asked, earning a smirk from her.

"God is still God and if you're talking to Him, He's listening. He may not answer the prayer the way you think He should, but He will."

I felt better with that newfound information, but it didn't help me feel any better in regard to Jesse.

I just hope that wherever he is and whatever he is doing, he's okay.

"Okay Jesse, you're all set," the nurse said softly, after ensuring his IV was intact to receive his dosage of chemo.

"How are you feeling?" she asked Jesse, noticing the distraught look in his eyes.

Seeing that look never got easier in this business, she discovered. The younger they were, the harder it was.

Jesse forced the best grin he could muster, taking his eye off the tube that would administer the drug, looking up at the nurse. "I'm cool, thanks."

She smiled softly, placing a gentle hand on his shoulder. "Let me know if you need anything hun. I'll be right at the station."

He nodded, watching as she walked off.

It had been years since he had been in this oncology center to receive a treatment. He winced as the machine started to beep and cool liquid began to enter through his veins.

"Poison killing poison," he whispered softly to himself, running a hand over his bed of hair. He only hoped that the follicles on his head would remain throughout the course of his treatments.

He glanced around the room, noticing the other patients and what they did to pass time. Several had visitors with them and in that moment he wished he had Dominic there or even Jamie. Just the first treatment was always the hardest for him. It made what was happening real and he still was in denial about that.

A cough close by broke him away from his thoughts, causing his eyes to seek where the noise was coming from.

It was a younger boy, maybe in his teens that sat one chair away from him. His skin was pale and his eyes were blackened from sickness and exhaustion. He had a beanie to cover his assumingly bald head. He was layered in thick clothing although it was 90 degrees outside. Jesse's heart felt for him and immediately he wanted to engage in conversation.

"Yo, you alright?" Jesse asked, raising a brow, giving the young boy a once over.

The boy gave a sarcastic smirk in return before replying, "Other than the fact that I'm dying? Yeah I'm fine."

He didn't even look his way.

Jesse couldn't help the chuckle that escaped, realizing he was almost looking at a younger version of himself when he was first diagnosed years ago.

This angered his neighbor, causing him to look at Jesse now. "What's funny about that?!"

The smile was still present on his face before he turned his head, "Your attitude. I just asked if you were okay. I'm up here getting the same poison you are. I get it, cancer sucks."

"Ass," the boy finished the sentence, looking back up at the muted TV.

"They don't even let us hear the sound in here. I got cancer, I'm not deaf."

"What's your name bro?" Jesse inquired, taking an interest in him.

"Peter," he answered, turning his head. "You?"

"I'm Jesse."

He reached out his hand to pound fists with Peter, who looked excited to return his gesture, "How old are you?"

"14."

He nodded, "I was a year older than you when I got diagnosed for the first time."

Peter's eyes widened. "The first time? You were in remission before you came back here?"

"Yeah," Jesse sighed. "Thought I was in the clear. Life is funny though, it doesn't always work out how you plan."

"Tell me about it," Peter agreed.

"How did you get through it the first time around? Being my age, I feel like I was supposed to have so much more life to live. This wasn't supposed to happen to me."

Jesse smirked, "At first I was like you, mad at the world, depressed and said I was dying."

Peter listened intently, wanting to obtain as much knowledge as he could from someone who had been where he was.

"But then ... I didn't want to be mad anymore. I didn't want to be sad. I didn't want to die. So, I chose life and I chose a life in God. Through my faith, friends and family, I was able to keep a good attitude and it gave me the willpower I needed to get through."

"I believe in God too. It's just- it's hard when you get dealt with cards like these though. It's hard for me to understand," Peter admitted with heaviness, feeling the guilt wrack his heart.

"I couldn't agree more because I've been there. I'm going through it now but I know regardless, God's got a plan Pete. He's got a plan for us. Just may not be our plan but we're gonna come out victorious no matter what the outcome is. Either way, we're free."

Peter looked to Jesse, his eyes sparking something that hadn't existed since he was diagnosed.

Hope.

Jesse held out his fist, waiting for Peter to match it with his own. He grinned when the teenager obliged, a faint smile on his face.

"Keep fighting," Jesse encouraged, resting his head back against the plush chair.

Jesse understood right then that this battle was bigger than him and his emotions.

I sat on Jesse's kitchen counter, watching him patiently as he moved fluently, preparing our dinner.

He had picked me up tonight as an apology for being distant and wanted to prepare something special to make it up to me.

I was just happy to be in his presence, sharing his space. It seemed like forever since I saw him last.

I studied his tall and slender figure as his long arms reached to the top of his cabinet. My eyes danced from the tip of his head to the bottom of his chin, imprinting his beautiful face in my memory.

He became even more beautiful each and every time I laid eyes on him.

"This better be good," I teased, lightly kicking my feet against the cabinet below.

He rolled his eyes, pouring milk into a measuring cup.

"Anything I make is good, girl."

"Mmm, as I recall you almost burned my house down trying to make ramen noodles."

He busted out into a boyish laughter before shaking his head, "Yo that was different."

I scoffed. "Jes. You cooked the noodles before adding water."

He laughed harder, "Man chill. I was 7."

"And stupid."

He giggled, pouring the milk into a pot, using a spoon to stir what he had mixed so far.

"Well this is gonna be better than that. I was inexperienced then but this is gonna bless ya life though," he said happily, earning a small smile from me.

Whether it was good or not, I was going to act like it was the best thing I'd ever tasted.

I looked on as he placed the chicken breast on a cutting board, steadying the knife to cut. His fingers wouldn't stop shaking.

My brows furrowed, noticing how it would continue each time he attempted to dice the chicken. He was pretending as if it wasn't bothering him but I could see otherwise.

"Babe you need me to cut that?" I asked, leaning forward on my hands.

He quickly shook his head.

"Nah, I got it,"

He took in a deep breath and went to cut again before the knife slid out of his hand, landing unceremoniously on the counter.

He bit down hard, squeezing his fist as I jumped off the counter to be at his side.

"Let me cut it up Jes, its cool," I eased, sensing his mood shift.

"Sorry, I keep having muscle spasms in my hand," he explained, opening his palm and then closing it again. I could still see the shaking.

"Just work on the sauce, I'll take care of this part."

He nodded to my suggestion and walked over to the pot.

I was secretly hoping I didn't leave tonight without some answers.

"You like it?" Jesse asked, his brow climbing his forehead.

I smirked, popping a forkful of noodles into my mouth. "It's delicious, baby. Dream team."

He crossed his eyes, "You diced some chicken. I made the sauce from scratch, cooked the noodles and cooked the meat."

"But!" I added, holding a finger up, "I helped."

His shoulders hopped in humor as he went to take another bite of his meal.

I kept peeking looks at him. He was eating slower than he normally did and kept taking short pauses to clear his throat after every swallow.

Something seemed off about tonight and I wasn't sure what –

Suddenly Jesse jumped up from his seat and ran to the bathroom. I was quick to throw my fork down and follow him in haste.

"Jes!" I called, rushing to the bathroom.

He was face down, gripping the toilet bowl while vomiting profusely inside.

Anxiety filled me I placed my hand on his back, rubbing my hand clockwise as he continued to empty the contents from his stomach into the toilet.

When I was sure he was about done, I finally found it safe to speak.

I pushed my finger onto the lever to drain the toilet. "Baby, are you okay?"

Jesse kept his head down, shaking it softly, instantly breaking my heart.

"Was it the food or something you ate earlier?"

He shook his head no again.

"Well what could be making you sick?" I cooed softly, only wanting to bring him comfort.

"I can run out and get some pepto or someth-"

"Cancer," he said in a voice so small, I could barely recognize it as his own.

"Huh? What are you –"

He pushed himself off the toilet bowl, sitting helplessly on the tile floor, using the back of his hand to wipe at the corner of his mouth.

He sniffed, taking in a deep breath as I watched his reddened face with anticipation.

"Cancer," he spoke again as the air left my lungs. "Cancer is what's making me sick."

My eyes darted back and forth before I shut them tight. Not at all able to process what I was hearing.

"What are you talking about? How could cancer make you sick when you're in remission? That doesn't make sense."

He sniffed again, resting his forearms on his knees and placing his head down in shame.

"I'm not in remission any more, Nic. The doctors found cancer in my bone marrow. Placed me back on chemo and that's what's making me nauseous. I get sick after my first treatment –"

"Whoa." I stepped back in the hallway and paced a bit.

I stopped at the bathroom entrance doorway, feeling myself get hot with anger and sadness all in one.

"Doctors, chemo, are you kidding me? This what's been going on with you?!"

Still refusing to meet my stare, he nodded.

"How long have you known this?!" My voice was shaking. It was hard to contain my hurt at this point.

"Four weeks."

"Four weeks?!" I shouted in utter disbelief. "Four weeks Jesse. Seriously?! And you didn't think to say something to me?! Four weeks you have been holding this in?!"

He looked up now, eyes glossed over.

"I didn't ... I didn't wanna hurt you with this."

My arms flapped in the air, "And this was better?! Telling me a month after you've known?! When I could've been at your appointments, praying for you, being there for you!"

He was silent as my being shook with hurt and rage.

"This is your way of not hurting me?" I yelled, wanting an answer.

"I was trynna protect you."

"Protect me from what, you?! Protect me from your heart?! Not letting me in all the way?! That's not fair Jes. It's not fair you robbed me of being there for you. Going through this with you!"

"You can't go through this with me!" he argued back, voice cracking and breaking my heart even more because I could hear the pain he desperately tried to hide.

"You can't go through this with me, you're not me! This ain't ya sickness! It's nobodies but mine, mine! So forgive me for not wanting to be reminded by the one person I care about the most that there's a possibility I won't always be here for her!" he cried, angry tears dropping from his eyes.

I sank, dropping to my knees in the doorway. I was hurting but not for me anymore, for him.

He sniffed. "I'm sorry. I'm sorry I ain't say nothing but this is heavy, man. This pain is heavy."

He released a shaky breath, before sniffing back. "This hurts, baby. God, this hurts so bad."

The tears fell freely from his eyes as I crawled to him, cradling him in my arms as he released a heart-wrenching sob into my chest. He gripped the material of my shirt for dear life as I dropped a few tears of my own, feeling awful for yelling at him.

"I'm scared," he cried softly. "I don't want to lose you,"

"You're never losing me. I swear on my life, you're never losing me. I'm here, just please Jesse please, trust me with you. Trust me with everything. I don't want to leave your side," I pleaded, hoping he felt me in this moment.

He was quiet, catching his breath and simmering down from his emotional release. He needed it, I could tell.

I kissed the crown of his head repeatedly as we both wrapped our arms around each other.

"You're too good of a soul for God to want you back so soon, baby. Too many people out here need to feel your spirit first. I'm convinced," I encouraged, mustering up my own strength to help him.

"Don't be fearful because there's nothing to fear. You're stronger than this."

"Even the strongest get weary," he spoke with exhaustion.

"That's why we don't rely on our own strength, our strength comes from God. It says that in Phillip."

A small soft chuckle escaped him.

"Philippians, baby. But I know what you mean," he corrected, earning smirk from me.

"I love you and I want to be here. Just trust me Jesse, please. I'm not going to beg for this again. I've been worried sick about you and it's much bigger than anything I've ever imagined. We're in this together. You and I."

He nodded, holding me tighter if at all possible. "You got my word."

CHAPTER
- THIRTEEN -

"Cancer huh? Wow. That's heavy." Dr. Tracy spoke into the room, a look of remorse and sorrow on her face.

It was my first appointment with her since I had found out the news about Jesse and I was just trying to process the emotions and how I felt.

"How are you taking all of this? I'm sure it's hard,"

I sighed, sitting back on the firm leather couch.

"I just, I don't know. There are times where I'm angry, times where I'm sad, times where I just don't understand why this has to happen to him. He doesn't deserve this."

She nodded, "From what you've told me about him it seems like such an unfortunate situation."

"That's an understatement," I huffed, looking anywhere but at her. Even talking about this out loud made me emotional.

"So how have things been between the two of you now that it's out in the open?"

I shrugged, facing my eyes towards my lap. "It's awkward sometimes on my part. I just don't know what to say. It seems like things can never be normal now."

"Mm," she hummed. "This could be the very reason why he didn't want to tell you. Jesse is craving normalcy and peace right now. People with his condition need to be as happy as possible, enjoying every moment filled with laughter and love. You bring that to him."

I looked up now, never considering things from that point of view.

"I want that. I want to be that, I do. I just feel like everything is so small compared to what he's going through."

She nodded, "And I can understand why you're saying that but look at it from his point of view, sweetie. He is literally in a fight for his life. The last thing he wants is to be reminded of the fight every chance he gets and not enjoying what, God forbid, could be his last days. He needs to be reminded why he should be fighting right now."

"So," I started, eyes darting back and forth across the room in thought.

"What should I do?"

"What do you think you should do? What makes Jesse the happiest?"

I paused, thinking for a short moment. "People, being surrounded by people and love."

"So get him around people."

"Maybe," I thought out loud. "Maybe I can talk to his best friend and we could plan something special for him. To take his mind off everything and just celebrate the person he is to us."

She smiled warmly, "That's a wonderful idea Kole."

I stopped mid thought, throwing her a strange look. The name sounded so foreign to me. So strange like it no longer fit the person I was now. Sure it was my name but only a small part of the woman I was evolving into.

Kole had no place in my life now. That darkness I had allowed into my world for such a long time was beaming with light.

"It's Dominic," I corrected.

———————————

Jesse walked into the oncology center, briskly, wanting to make his visit there quick and painless. His doctor advised him that he should start taking medicine to counteract his symptoms from taking the chemo so he was there to pick up the prescription.

Tiffany Campbell

He stuffed his hands in his pockets, keeping his head down low as he made way to the elevators to reach the ninth floor. Once he stepped off, he smiled softly at a few strangers before approaching the nurses' station.

"Hey Pam," he greeted the head nurse as she smiled back at him.

"Doc got a script for me? Jesse Palmer."

She smirked, "You know I know your name Jesse. Let me go check with him and see, be right back."

He nodded, watching her stand from her post and made her way back to the offices. Jesse turned his body, taking in his surroundings before his eyes landed on the chemotherapy administration center. His feet carried him over to the entrance in curiosity just to see who all was in there.

"Jesse!" he heard his name called from a small voice he recognized as Peter's. He smiled at his young friend, walking happily in his direction.

"Pete, my man," Jesse greeted, taking a seat next to him and reaching out his fist.

Peter smiled faintly, tapping fist with his older friend; happy to see his face.

"Thought you were gonna be here this week," Peter said softly, earning a headshake from Jesse.

"Nah. I just get treatment once a month right now. How are you feeling though? You good?" Jesse questioned, noticing the softer tone in Peter's voice today.

He shrugged, "Not feeling too hot to be honest. I've been positive though. You just know how this goes. You have your good days, and then you have your not so good days."

Jesse nodded in understanding, heart hurting for his new friend.

"I know what you mean. That's why I'm here now, I've been sick as hell since last week. I gotta get some meds to help."

Peter scoffed, shaking his head, "Fighting medicine with medicine. It's too much."

"Tell me about it," Jesse sighed, sitting back some more. He pulled out his phone out of habit, checking to see if Dominic had returned his text.

She hadn't.

He sent it two hours ago.

He was beginning to grow fearful of their relationship. He was noticing her distance lately and it didn't sit right with him. He just prayed she wasn't choosing now to back up from him. Not when he needed her the most.

"You got a girlfriend Pete?" Jesse asked, breaking the silence that passed between the two.

Peter blushed before shaking his head bashfully. "No, I mean, I didn't before this. Now that the school is finding out I have cancer, I've been getting a lot of messages on Facebook from all the hot girls in my class. Some juniors too."

Jesse raised his brows in surprise, earning a giggle from his friend. "Well check you out!"

Peter turned his head, grinning in embarrassment.

"Yeah yeah. Let's just hope I lose my virginity before I croak."

Jesse gazed sternly at him, causing Peter to retract his statement. "Okaayy, before the chemo causes me to be limp. Better?"

He laughed, shaking his head. "You're a character, man."

I tapped my fingers impatiently against the table at Panera Bread, not too far from my job. I was on my lunch break, waiting for my guest to arrive, hoping he did within the next few minutes.

My eyes darted towards the door in expectation and I smiled the moment Jameson walked through. He carried himself coolly, searching around the restaurant for me.

I stood to my feet, "Jamie!" I called, catching his attention.

He smiled that gorgeous smile of his once his eyes landed on me and made his way towards the table.

We greeted each other with a quick hug before both of us sat opposite of one another.

"Sup Domo. What was so important that I had to rush down here?" he asked, an amused expression on his face.

I had made it seem like life or death when I made the phone call a few hours ago. That's just because I was excited.

"Jesse," I announced, earning a furrowed brow from him.

He cleared his throat, getting more comfortable in his chair. "What about Jesse?"

I dropped my shoulders, seeing through his cover up.

"It's okay Jamie, I know. He told me over the weekend."

Jamie released a heavy sigh, slightly angling his head down.

"Oh thank God. I thought this was about to be a weird ass conversation. I'm not good at keeping secrets."

I chuckled softly before taking a deep breath. "Well you're going to have to keep this one."

His eyes widened. "Yo, what? What you got cooking?"

"Well, nothing yet. I want to plan something for Jesse. Lift his spirits. Not necessarily a party but something to make him feel special and just … normal."

Jamie's confused look soon turned into a warm grin. He wagged his index finger in my direction.

"Aye, that's a good idea. I've wanted to plan something with bro too. Maybe we can do a road trip?"

My heart warmed. "Really? To where?"

He pondered on it for a short moment before shrugging. "Maybe Atlanta? I know Jesse's never been and it's only like a 6-hour drive. We can take my truck."

I beamed at the thought, "I'm down for that! He'll love that, honestly. You think we should invite his other friends?"

He tossed his lips to the side in thought before shrugging.

"I don't really know. Maybe we should make this a more intimate thing. You and me know what's up, and I doubt his other homies even know. He doesn't like depressing people with it."

I nodded in understanding, "Yeah you're right. I don't want to overwhelm him too much."

"Exactly. So it should just be us, and I can bring this girl I've been hanging with for a little minute. Jesse knows her and you'll like her, she's cool."

"Ok, I'll start looking up some hotels and stuff and try to get a peek at his schedule. I think he's off next weekend, and I am too."

Jamie nodded, "Sounds dope," he paused, smiling softly at me. "You're a great friend Dom. Jesse's really lucky to have somebody like you in his corner."

I sighed softly, "Yeah, just wish he would've told me sooner ya know? Just seeing how broken up he's been about this, I could've been helping him stay focused."

"Yeah," Jamie agreed. "We all make our decisions. He felt he was doing what was best. But we have to stay strong during this. We have to stay strong for him because he's not always going to be."

"It's just hard watching the strongest man I know be shook up. It's so hard and I hurt for him always."

"It's okay to hurt Dom. We just can't stay there. Keep praying and keep having faith. It'll get easier, believe me," he encouraged.

I smiled, crossing my arms over my chest. "Jesse's really lucky to have someone like you too Jameson."

———————

"What's been up with you?" Jesse asked with a risen brow, watching me from the other side of the couch.

We were at his house watching movies. My legs were stretched out over his lap and my mind was on Atlanta.

"Wh-what do you mean?" I asked, nearly giving myself away with my stuttering.

Keep it together Dom.

"You've been weird dude and I don't like it. Is it because of this disease?"

"No!" I said louder than I intended. "Goodness, no."

He frowned, still not satisfied with my answer.

"Then what's up? I practically had to beg you to even come over today. You were tryna stay home."

I sighed, not realizing I had been distant towards him. I definitely didn't want him thinking it was because of what he told me.

"I'm sorry babe. It's unintentional. I've just been picking up these extra hours at the store for some extra cash."

"Why? If you need money for anything, I got you. You know that. Just ask."

"I really don't – "

"How much you need?"

"How much I gotta pay to have my girl around?" he asked sincerely, only causing me to feel like crap.

Next weekend needs to get here fast so he can understand why I've been so secretive.

I sat up, wrapping my arms around his shoulders and pecking his perfectly perched and freckle covered nose.

"You got me, I'm here, I'm sorry. Every hour I'm not on the clock is dedicated to you."

He smirked dryly, not believing me and turning his head to face the TV.

"Yeah whatever."

"Don't make this awkward, Nic. This already sucks, don't make it awkward too."

I was screaming inside, realizing he was being overly emotional and he had good reason. He just didn't fully know my reasoning.

And now what was I supposed to say back that wouldn't sound pathetic?

"I'm not being awkward," I quietly defended myself, not able to hold it in.

"Tell that to the awkward fairy that's in this room," he shot back, only causing me to giggle.

He did his best to hold his angry face looking over at me. "What's funny?"

"The awkward fairy," I cackled, only laughing harder. He kept trying to hold his dry expression until the annoyed smile spread across his face.

He dropped his shoulders in an attempt to push me off him, only causing me to hold on tighter and laugh even more.

"Aww da baby mad? Him mad at me and the fairy," I cooed in a baby voice, pecking his dimpled cheek repeatedly.

"You're so annoying," he chuckled shaking his head, earning another kiss from me.

"No more weirdness I promise. It's not what you think it is. I'm here like I said I would be and I'll ease up on the schedule."

He sighed, "It's not that. I mean make your money if that's what you need to do. Just be considerate you know? If I hit you, hit me back. Sometimes I just be needing to feel you, see your words just to get me through. I need stuff like that."

I nodded, understanding completely.

Pretty soon he'll see that I've had him in mind this whole time.

"Come to me, all you who are weary and burdened, and I will give you rest. Take my yoke upon you and learn from me, for I am gentle and humble in heart, and you will find rest for your souls. For my yoke is easy and my burden is light." (Matthew 11:28-30)

Jesse read over the words from the passage carefully; holding their meaning deep within his spirit.

This was him, weak and burdened. He hated what he allowed the return of his disease to become. He wasn't this person; he was never weak, never frail. He knew God's promises and had faith in better days.

But this ... this had somehow become too much. He found himself worried about things beyond his own control.

He knew better ... and because of that he had to do better.

He closed his Bible shut, setting it down gently on his coffee table, before standing tall to his feet.

He barely made it out of the living room before he was down on bended knees.

He needed God to hear him. He needed God to feel him in this prayer and his body wouldn't allow him to move another step until he obeyed the spirit man within him.

"Lord," he spoke, pressing his hands against his hardwood floor, too ashamed to look up for answers.

"Lord, I come to you right now ... weak, burdened and broken-hearted. I'm ... I ... I can't do this without you. And I'm sorry for trying to this long."

His chest heaved for air as the emotion dwelled within his throat. He squeezed his eyes shut to prevent the tears from falling.

"I was mad at you God. I was mad at you because I couldn't understand why you would allow this to happen to me, what it is you're trying to make of my struggle. I didn't think it was fair and to be honest I still don't," he admitted, knowing he could no longer hide from his truth.

"But in all … BUT in all," he sobbed, "and through it all, I'll trust you. I have faith that I will live and not die. I have faith in my healing and restoration. I have faith in you Father. Please forgive me for my disbelief, please forgive me for my deceit, please forgive me for my doubts. I'm a man and I too fall short."

He clasped his hands together into a fist, resting his forehead against his long arms as he poured his soul to the Lord, needing the comfort only He could provide.

"I lay my burdens down because I can't carry them anymore. And they were never meant for me to carry. I give it to you God. I give it all to you. I just need you to bring some peace into my troubled soul. Provide some normalcy, give my friends the strength to be there for me through this on days when I won't have it in me to be strong for them, days like today."

He sighed, looking to his ceiling now. "Please just send me some peace," he prayed, shutting his eyes before hearing a knock at the door.

He looked behind him questionably before he heard the knock starting again and then gradually turning into a beat.

He smirked, rolling his eyes before sniffing and standing to his feet, having to wipe clean the emotion he just felt for his unexpected guest.

Jesse dusted himself off, strolling to his front door and opened it; finding none other than Jamie and Dominic standing there.

His brows furrowed, looking between the two of their smiling faces.

"What is –"

"Pack a bag," Jamie announced stopping Jesse altogether. "We're kidnapping you for the weekend."

"Now look," Jamie started from the front seat, turning down his music. Charli, his friend, was in the passenger seat smirking at him as Jesse and I were in the back.

He questioned me the entire time he was packing, about where we were going but Jamie and I swore each other to secrecy. I could tell we appeared at the right moment and Jesse's smile hadn't left his face since we showed up.

This was the Jesse I knew. This was the man I was happy to see.

"I know you're not a club man but I think we should really head out tonight bro. It'll be fun!" he urged as I looked amusingly at Jesse for his response.

"Well it would be cool to know where I'm going first," he started to reply but Jamie began to wave his hand to stop him.

"Nah. You're not getting all that out of me. You'll know when we get there. Just know you're taken care of. You don't gotta worry about a thing," Jamie assured, receiving an eye roll from his friend.

"Well fine. It's whatever, I'll go the club," he said, giving in as I squealed with excitement.

It wasn't that I liked taking Jesse out of his comfort zones in a bad way; I just wanted him to experience new things. I hoped I wasn't wrong for that.

"Anyway, how are you Charli? How this fool convince you to join him in any type of get away?" Jesse asked, leaning forward.

Charli was beautiful and a perfect match for Jamie from what I had discovered about her so far. She was mocha chocolate in complexion, had a warm smile and a likeness about her that I enjoyed. She didn't seem to be too down or stressed about anything in life. She seemed to enjoy it actually.

"Hey, I'm always down for a good trip and Jameson is okay company I guess. But once he said you were coming? I couldn't say no," she teased, making a face at Jamie as he crossed his eyes.

"Let em know, Chuck!" Jesse said reaching out his fist to pound with hers. "We go way back!"

Jamie flicked the both of them off as we laughed. I sighed happily, leaning back into my seat while Charli turned the music back up, allowing the conversation to fade out easily.

I was glad, because I wanted to have a few moments to talk to Jesse without everyone being in our conversation.

I scooted closer to him, wrapping my arms around his bicep and nestling my chin on his shoulder, gently pecking his cheek. He smirked down at me.

"Are you okay?" I asked softly, gazing into his honey brown hues.

"More than okay," he answered. "I'm happy right now, happy ya'll did this. I needed this."

I smiled, "I know, you deserve it. You deserve to be taken care of too, Jes. You're always looking out for us, me especially. So I had to make this happen for you."

"So this is what you been up to the past few weeks?"

I grinned, "Guilty. This is why I've been working overtime to have a little extra in my savings for my car just so I could spoil you on this trip."

He smiled softly, before leaning in to peck my lips.

"I love you."

"I love you more," I replied confidently.

"Baby that ain't possible."

"How is it not?" I replied with mock sassiness.

"Because the love I got for you in my heart runs deep. I'm not sure if my heart can beat without it," he said coolly, licking his lips.

I was lost for only a moment before I rolled my eyes. "Always trying to run game. One day, I swear I'm going to get you good with the word play like you get me."

He chuckled boyishly as I tried to back off of him, but he was pulling me closer while kissing my forehead. "No game, girl. It's all love."

"But thank you," he finished as I looked up at him. "Thank you for this. I appreciate it more than you can understand right now."

"Anything for you, Jes. If I could take it all away I would," I returned shyly, never breaking eye contact.

He pecked my lips softly. "You do every day just by being here. That's all I need."

I nodded, kissing him one last time.

"Now let's just focus on the present. I just want to live here," he added, resting his cheek on the top of my hair.

I wanted to live here forever.

_____

"Are we really in Atlanta right now?" Jesse asked, looking out of our hotel window with so much light and happiness in his eyes. It warmed my entire world. Since the moment he realized we were going to Atlanta, he was ecstatic and couldn't stop thanking Jamie and me for pulling this off for him. He didn't have to worry about a thing as long as he had us.

I walked up behind him, wrapping my arms around his slender waist, placing my cheek against his shoulder blade.

"We're really here." I answered softly, closing my eyes in bliss.

I could hear his heartbeat through his back. As long as I could feel it, it brought a peace I couldn't explain.

He was alive. He was here, with me.

"Thank you baby. You don't understand how fast God answer's prayers."

"You're here with me aren't you?" I questioned rhetorically. "I understand."

He placed his hands over my arms. "So, what's the plan for today?"

I shrugged, "Just resting up from the drive then going to Compound tonight."

"I've heard of that club," he said as I peeled my eyes open, bending my neck to look up at him.

"You sure you're okay with going out?"

He scoffed, "I'm good, more than good. All I care about is the music and you being tucked under me. That's all I need."

I smirked before he gently pulled me from behind him so that my back was now pressed against his front. He wrapped his arms lovingly around me, placing light pecks on my neck and cheek.

"I love you so much girl," he whispered in my ear, causing a chill to shoot up my spine in response.

"Nobody has my heart like you got it," he continued, squeezing me tighter and pressing our cheeks together.

"I'm nothing special."

"You're the world to me," he said coolly, kissing my cheek again.

"You gonna be my wife?"

"Of course," I breathed without a second thought, closing my eyes.

"When?" he asked, causing my eyes to flutter open.

"When do you want me to be?"

I could feel his smile, "When you'll have me. I gotta get a ring first though."

My brows furrowed as I chuckled. "Wait, you're serious?"

"I would never play like that. I'm so serious. I wanna marry you."

I turned slowly in his arms as he placed his hands on both of my elbows, looking intently into my eyes.

"You really want to make me your wife or are you saying this because of everything that's going on?"

He smiled, revealing his dimples. "You say it like you don't deserve to be my wife? Like I don't want you to be."

I was quiet, allowing him to continue. "I mean yeah, everything I'm going through has me thinking about the future and some things I wanna rush quicker than others but I want you to be mine Dominic, in the fullest extent. I've known forever that you're supposed to be with me."

The butterflies were swarming in my chest and if I could turn red I would be the brightest shade.

"It isn't gonna happen tomorrow as much as I would like it to but it's gonna happen soon. You gonna be cool with that?" he asked.

He was so serious about this.

"If it could've been yesterday I would've been good. With you, I can conquer the world Jesse, no matter what's against us."

He landed a sweet kiss on my lips.

"All I needed to know baby."

"You have such beautiful skin Dominic. You really don't need too much of this," Charli complimented as she continued to do my make-up for our evening out.

Jamie and I switched rooms. I came over here to get dressed with Charli as he went to my room to get ready with Jesse and just chill while we took forever to get dressed.

His words, not mine.

"Thank you. That means a lot coming from you, you're gorgeous," I complimented.

Charli and I became fast friends over the course of the day. She always made sure to include me in any conversations she had with the group, and her energy was refreshing.

She was much different than Lucy.

"You and Jesse are so adorable, I gotta say. You guys make me wish I was in a relationship, I swear." she giggled, walking back over to her make-up kit to grab some eyeliner.

I smiled at the compliment, "You and Jamie are cute too."

She made a funny face before smirking, "Gotta tell him that. Let that boy tell it, I'm perfect for him, but he's still not ready for the whole commitment aspect of a relationship."

My eyes widened. From what I could see, Jameson was crazy about her.

"Hopefully after this weekend he changes his mind," I encouraged as she grinned, applying the eyeliner to my lids.

"You're optimistic, Dom. I like that."

"You don't think he will?"

She shrugged, "Once upon a time I did, before the fraternity. I mean Jamie is still the amazing man he was before he pledged but with the title comes a lot of attention. Plus, he's attractive so it's harder to want to commit when you get used to the lifestyle. I tell him all the time I get it, because I'm in a sorority too but I don't let that define me. My feelings are real; college will pass on once we graduate."

I nodded, feeling her completely and was saddened that Jamie didn't realize what he had in front of him.

"But he invited you to something so intimate. You don't think that means anything?" I questioned. She gave another shrug.

"Yeah sure and I'm grateful because I'm having such a good time with you all. It just still doesn't feel like enough, you know? I'm a woman, I need more and I deserve it. It's simple as that," she explained. I was in awe of her self-worth.

She seemed so confident and sure of herself and she was absolutely okay if the odds weren't in her favor.

That was something to truly admire.

She stood up fully, showing a toothy grin.

"You look amazing, take a look," she said, stepping off to the side so I could see myself in the full-length mirror in the room.

My eyes widened a bit as I stood up, looking myself over from head to toe.

I ran my manicured fingers over my black dress that hugged my curves to perfection. I was shocked with how well Charli did my makeup. My skin looked radiant with a healthy brown glow and she feathered the layers in my hair to fall gracefully against my shoulders.

I looked beautiful.

"Jesse won't be able to keep his hands to himself tonight, girl." she complimented, smacking my butt before rushing to the bathroom.

I smiled to myself, ready for our night to begin.

"I'm not gonna lie bro," Jamie started, sitting comfortably in the hotel lobby with Jesse, sipping on a drink from the bar.

"You and Domo got me thinking," he finished after swallowing the fused concoction of liquor and soda.

Jesse rolled his eyes at his friend and adjusted the collar of his black crew neck, making sure his chain wasn't snagged. "You and thinking? That's never a good combination."

Jamie's expression was stone, none too pleased with Jesse's jab, only causing him to laugh in response.

"I'm playing bro, what's up? What got you thinking too hard about? Don't want you to hurt yourself," Jesse teased, sitting up in the lounge chair, more alert than before.

"Nah, like about relationships and stuff. Ya'll really look happy and in love and shit," Jamie replied, taking another sip of his drink.

Jesse nodded in response, "We are happy and in love and stuff."

He chuckled as Jamie shook his head.

"But you was always that type of dude though, JP. You was always the relationship type. Always liked to be locked down with somebody."

"Well," he shrugged. "I just enjoy companionship. When I like a girl, I get selfish. I don't want her rocking with nobody else like she rock with me. Sharing never been my thing."

Jamie sat up, stretching his hand out to stop Jesse from continuing.

"Yo chill, I don't share either. Just because I never been in a relationship, doesn't mean I'm out here sharing."

Jesse laughed, shaking his head. "What's this about, Charli?"

"Of course it's about her. You know we've been doing ... whatever it is we're doing, for a minute now. She's special you know? But like I was telling her the other day before this trip, I don't really see myself committing to nobody right now and she was cool with it. But she said we can't do what we've been doing anymore because she deserves more from me."

His face was contorted as he explained his situation.

Jesse looked to him expectedly, "You don't agree? She's right; she deserves more if more is what she wants right now. She was settling for you because she liked you that much."

Jamie pointed at his friend in agreement, "Right! Exactly. And usually, when a girl tells me that, I don't feel any way about it. But with Chuck, that hurt a little. It hurt because I agreed, and because I didn't understand what was stopping me from giving her more. She's worth it and I hate that she doesn't feel like she's worth it to me."

"So is that why you invited her on this trip?"

He nodded, "Yeah, just to show her more but it doesn't mean anything without the commitment. I just don't want to enter something that I don't know if I'm ready for."

He stopped himself before continuing, "But I'm willing to try for her. I'm willing to drop it all for her and I need her to know that."

Jesse smirked, "Then tell her like you telling me. Tell her exactly that. One thing I've never been afraid of is how I feel about any woman. As men, we gotta provide that validation. If that's the woman you want, you can't leave her hanging. If you do, don't be mad when someone else is willing to do everything you wasn't."

Jamie blew out a breath, rubbing his hands uneasily against his jeans. He squinted in Jesse's direction. "You gon – you gon tell her for me?"

Jesse smacked his lips, looking away in annoyance.

Jamie's face turned puzzled, darting his eyes back and forth. "So is that a no or ... "

"This conversation over bro."

———————————

"The boys said they're in the lobby having a drink, waiting on us." Charli said as I nodded and looked myself over in the mirror for the umpteenth time.

"You look beautiful, girl," Charli reassured me, reapplying her lipstick.

"Simple and gorgeous, I wish I had those hips."

I blushed. She looked amazing as well. She had a black dress on like me, but hers was a bit edgier than mine with the slit above her thigh and a low cut top.

"Watch the moment they see us, they'll go from dates to bodyguards," she joked, playfully rolling her eyes as I stuffed my ID, debit card, and lip gloss into my clutch.

"Are you drinking tonight?" she questioned, opening the door and waiting for me to walk out first.

I shook my head. I had already decided I would be sober just because I knew Jesse would be and I wanted to experience this with him without being under the influence. I was trying more and more to see the world through his eyes. He always enjoyed himself regardless, so I was confident I could too.

I followed Charli's lead to the lobby and noticed Jesse and Jamie laughing together from afar. I smiled at the two friends just as they both turned their heads in our direction, hearing the click of our heels.

Both of them froze, only causing Charli and me to giggle as we approached.

"So?" Charli started, placing her hand on her hip. "Worth the wait?"

Jamie stood to his feet quickly, roaming his eyes over Charli.

"Definitely worth the wait. Do we even have to go to the club? I mean we can just all kick it here."

We laughed as Charli playfully rolled her eyes, placing her hand in Jamie's face to blow him off.

Jesse and I stared shyly at each other before he finally rose to his feet to pull me closer to him by my hips.

"You look beautiful baby," he complimented softly before lacing his soft lips with mine.

"Thank you, so do you. Trying to match me?" I asked, noticing his black t-shirt and black snapback.

Tiffany Campbell

He scoffed, "Pft, you was tryna match me. You saw what I was packing, don't play." he joked as I giggled and kissed him once more, feeling eyes on us.

"Aight, enough of all that cute stuff man, let's go!" Jamie teased, grabbing Charli's hand and walking towards the front entrance of the hotel.

Jesse and I chuckled, following their lead hand in hand.

The energy in the club was magnetic to say the least. Everyone's good vibe just bounced, you couldn't help but feel it.

I clutched Jesse's hand as Jamie led the way to a small section he reserved near the DJ booth. It was perfect because you could see the crowd of people all moving to the music. We greeted the group next to us politely as we all got situated.

"Yo it's crazy in here!" Jamie yelled over the music as we all nodded in agreement. He went to fix him and Charli a drink as Jesse draped his arm over my shoulder, bending his lips towards my ear.

"You good baby, you not drinking?" he asked, his sweet breath tickling my earlobe.

"No, I'm good. I'm just gonna vibe tonight," I responded, meeting his eyes as he revealed a toothy grin.

"You sure? You ain't gotta worry about me, I'm good. I just want you to have a good time."

"I don't need it to have a good time. I got you." I assured as he playfully rolled his eyes before placing a sloppy kiss on my cheek. I knew he wanted to call me corny, but he refrained.

"You twerkin some'n?" he questioned, raising a mischievous brow as I giggled.

"You keepin up?" I shot back, his eyebrows rising in pure surprise and amusement.

"Are you keeping up with *me* is the question girl, you know that," he challenged.

"Yeah, we'll see."

Jamie and Charli finished their first drink and I watched as my newfound friend sashayed in my direction.

She laced our hands together, "Let's go dance with the people! You down?" she asked as I nodded before looking to the boys.

"Ya'll coming?"

"We'll catch up!" Jamie answered as Jesse flashed a reassuring smile.

I nodded before allowing Charli to take us to the dance floor.

We were three songs in and having the time of our lives. I had already started busting a sweat, along with Charli as we danced to every single song that played.

"Oh my God I love this song!" Charli said happily as Controlla by Drake began to play, making the entire club go crazy.

It was the perfect song for the mood.

I rocked side to side, enjoying the song myself.

Suddenly, I felt hands placed on my hips and instantly turned my head ready to snap at whoever thought they could grab me up.

My irritation instantly subsided when I realized the hands belonged to Jesse.

I smiled before pressing myself against him and beginning to wind my hips to the song against his pelvis. He fell in motion with me quickly, gripping my hips tighter and matching my rhythm.

Jesse could dance ... well!

He grabbed my hand and turned my body so that I was facing him. He stalked me slowly, devouring me with his eyes, a sneaky grin on his face as he danced towards me, winding and thrusting his hips. He wrapped his arm aggressively around my lower back, pulling me into him causing me to gasp excitedly in surprise.

He chuckled, sneaking a kiss on my lips before we continued to dance to the rest of the song, lost in each other.

The four of us continued the next few songs like that before heading back to our section. We invited the group next to us to join, making the energy even better.

I was sipping on orange juice rocking to the current song when Jamie approached.

"Aye you wanna go the bar with me real quick? I want to cop another bottle," he asked over the music as I nodded, following him towards the bar.

"You having a good time?" I asked, noticing the haze in his eyes from his alcohol consumption. He had taken a few shots with some of the guys that joined us.

"Yeah man, but what's even better is that Jesse is enjoying himself."

That same smile hadn't left Jesse's face since we got there. He loved to dance and everyone that met him adored him and wanted his company.

I didn't mind sharing, for now.

"You did a good thing Domo, you a real one," he complimented as I nodded my thanks, taking another sip of my juice.

"I didn't do this alone," I said, watching as Jamie tried to get the attention of the bartender.

"I wanna ask you something though," he said, looking down at me quickly before attempting to flag the bartender down once she noticed him.

"What's up?"

"You think I would make a good boyfriend?"

Even though he was yelling over the noise, I could tell he was serious and wanted my opinion.

My eyes lit up, "You're gonna make it official with Charli?"

He nodded, with a smile. "Yeah, tonight!"

My brows rose just as the bartender approached us, taking Jamie's order. When he finished, he looked down at me.

"What you think? Yeah?"

"Hell yeah!" I said happily, earning laughter from him.

"Dang. Was she dogging me while ya'll was alone or something?"

I grinned shaking my head, "Not at all but she deserves more from you Jamie and you deserve her too! You're a good guy, and it's never a bad thing to settle down with someone you really care about."

"Exactly. Seeing you and JP really got me realizing I'm truly missing out on someone amazing because I wanna be selfish but now I just wanna be selfish with her," he said honestly, causing my insides to tingle with happiness.

Now that I understood love, I loved to see it. Especially with two people as great as Jamie and Charli. They were perfect together.

"You should do it – not here but after, if you're not too drunk."

"Now I can't promise that! But if I am gone, I'll ask her tomorrow. We're not leaving Atlanta without her being mine, believe that!" he said confidently just as the bartender approached us with the lit bottle in her hand.

The trip was off to a great start. It could only get better from there.

"No, Jamie throwing up, hanging out the door of the car on the highway was the funniest and scariest thing ever!" I shrieked in laughter as Jesse joined me.

We were back from the club, laying in our hotel bed in comfortable clothes and laughing as we recapped the rest of our night.

Jamie definitely couldn't promise his sobriety. He drank like a fish when we returned back to our section, getting hyped up by the other guys.

"Man, that Uber driver looked like he wanted to cut our heads off! He was so pissed." Jesse snickered as I shook my head.

"Poor Charli. She has to take care of him. He could barely get out of the car alone."

"It was still a dope time though." Jesse smiled.

"It was," I agreed. "Charli said you and Jamie had some kind of agenda tomorrow?"

He nodded, "Yeah we were gonna let ya'll get the car for a few hours while we made a run. Ya'll can go the mall or something."

I raised a brow, "What are ya'll doing that we can't go to?"

"None-ya-business. Just know we'll link up again before dinner." he answered, dismissing me all together.

I rolled my eyes. No longer caring.

"I love you Nic. I tell you that today? It feels like I didn't tell you enough," he answered, picking at a hangnail.

I swooned, loving the way it rolled so effortless off his lips.

"I love you too."

"You're not afraid to marry me are you, even with everything going on? I don't want you thinking I'm setting you up for failure or something." he admitted as I frowned.

"I would never think that. What's happening to you right now is beyond your control. I would never punish you for it. I want to be with you forever, just as much as you want to be with me."

He nodded slowly, craning his neck up to look at me. "Even if forever might be shortened?"

I sighed, "Don't talk like that baby, please."

"I'm not thinking negative, just being real about it. You down for the ride?"

"I'm not going anywhere, regardless. I'm here," I assured for what seemed like the millionth time.

I would assure for a million more just to make sure he knew how serious I was.

"Okay."

"What are the guys up to, do you know?" I questioned Charli as we both sat comfortably in the hotel's hot tub.

Neither one of us was in the mood to go out to the mall to shop after our morning of tourist activities. We just wanted to relax and unwind while the guys took the car to God knows where.

She took a sip of her glass of wine, shaking her head. "No clue, Jameson wouldn't tell me a word."

Jamie stuck true to his word. He and Charli were an official item, and already you could see the difference with how they interacted with each other. It was much more obvious that they were in love and crazy about one another. I was so happy.

I sighed, smacking my lips. "Jesse's been acting weird all morning. He's been in his head and now he won't even return my text messages."

Charli snickered at my impatience, "Girl just relax. I'm sure whatever they're doing can't be anything bad. It's probably something really sweet."

"Yeah I know," I sulked. "I just really want to know what he's up to. He wouldn't give me a hint or anything."

She shrugged, "It'll be fine, I'm sure of it. Do you know where you guys are going to dinner?"

I shook my head, "Nope. I really don't understand how I surprise him with this trip, and already he has secret plans for the two of us?"

Charli giggled, "Damn. Could he be any more perfect? You got a good one Dom, a great one actually. Jamie better take notes."

I smirked, "Jamie is amazing too but Jesse is truly one of a kind. He's the best thing that's ever happened to me."

"Cherish him girl for forever if you can."

I sunk in the tub, allowing the bubbles to run across my shoulders. "I plan on it."

———————

"Where are we going?"

"You'll see."

"Where did you go?"

"Don't worry about it."

"Why won't you tell me?"

"Man, Nic!" Jesse giggled, looking up at me from tying his shoes. He looked really nice in his black and dark gray plaid shirt and black jeans.

I smiled, honing in on his dimple.

"Why won't you tell me anything?" I asked, flapping my arms in the air in frustration.

"I'll tell you what you need to know. You're just upset I'm not telling you on your time. Patience is a virtue, you know that?" he asked with a teasing grin, only causing me to roll my eyes.

I turned to collapse on the bed in surrender, only causing him to laugh.

"Man I got you spoiled. I don't know if this is a good thing. You're a brat sometimes." He leaned on his hand to look over my face.

I opened my eyes, happy to see my caramel drop looking down at me.

"I'm happy you know where to place blame," I smirked.

"You ready?" he asked, eyes roaming my stretched out body.

The dress I wore was another body shaper but this time it was red and Charli pinned my hair up into an elegant bun, letting my bangs fall gracefully over my right eye. The red complimented my brown skin so well.

I nodded, watching Jesse stand tall from the bed and reached his hand down to help me up.

I was going to grab my clutch that sat on the nightstand before Jesse stopped me. "You don't need that."

Tiffany Campbell

"I don't? I was going to pay for the cab fair."

He shook his head, grabbing my hand. "No need, come on." he instructed, leading us out of our room.

When we passed the elevator heading for the stairs, I had to speak up.

"Baby, I don't wanna walk down the stairs in these heels. That's like six flights!" I complained as we reached the staircase entrance.

He turned, swooping me up in his arms in one motion before carrying me through the door.

"There, now you don't gotta worry about ya feet. And we're not going downstairs," he said, as if carrying my weight meant nothing.

"We're not?" I asked puzzled, wrapping my arms around his neck as he carried me up the stairs.

There was only one more floor after ours, then the roof.

"Nope." he answered smoothly, passing the door that took us to the 7th floor.

"We're going to the roof? What's up there?" I asked, truly confused about where this night was taking us.

We reached the top, and Jesse skillfully opened the door with me still in his arms.

I looked at him before turning my head and gasped at the sight.

On the roof was a romantically lit pool and table for two. Soft music was playing and a waiter stood patiently by our table, waiting for our arrival.

I covered my mouth in shock as Jesse carefully placed my feet to the ground.

I felt like they would give out, causing me to collapse at any moment.

Jesse walked up behind me, bending his lips towards my ear.

"Surprise, you like it?" he asked softly as I nodded completely speechless.

He laced his fingers with mine, pulling me from my frozenness. "Right this way beautiful, your dinner awaits."

"So how do you manage to plan something for me on a trip that is supposed to be all about you?" I asked, taking a bite of my steak. Jesse had our hotel cook a beautiful dinner for us.

"You know I can't help myself when it comes to you. I had to show you my appreciation for you taking the time out to do all of this for me and taking me out of the funk I was in. You don't understand how much faith this sparked in my heart. God hears me and I needed to know that."

I looked up, swiping my bang out of my eye. "God speaks to you through me?"

He smirked, swallowing his water. "All of the time. You don't think He uses you?"

I shrugged, "I guess, I don't know how to tell."

"It's nothing that you can tell, really. I just know He confirms things for me through you in many ways, whether it's in your words or your actions."

I smiled, "I know He speaks to me through you. He has to. When I see you, I see God and I see who He is supposed to be to me." I explained, shocked at my own answer.

Where did that come from?

The expression on Jesse's face was unreadable. It's like he was searching for something within my eyes. I just wasn't sure what.

"Dominic." Jesse spoke, my name rolling effortlessly from his lips, so smooth and crisp.

"Yes?"

"You know why I love you? Why I'm drawn to you so much?" He asked, running his tongue quickly over his lips.

I shook my head no.

"Something about you, something buried deep within you calls to me. It's like soul shifting, magnetic even. Every part of me knows that you're supposed to be a part of my life forever – back then, I didn't understand it. I didn't understand what it was about you Nic. I thought it was just a crush ... something that would pass."

He slowly stood to his feet as I looked to him in wonder; already emotional off of the way his heart spoke to mine.

"Baby, we have a connection so strong and a purpose so great within each other that the enemy has tried to destroy it by destroying you. By crushing your spirit, robbing you of your youth and placing you in a space where you felt death was the only release. He didn't want us to prosper so much, that he threw everything he could in our path to separate us."

He stepped closer, only causing my heart to flutter even harder.

"But God ... God had other plans for us. He had other plans for our story and through our love? We found Him, we found the peace, love and joy that we have been searching for our whole lives."

Jesse bent down on one knee, causing me to lose my breath all together.

Is he – no ... no he can't be! This isn't really happening right now.

"And I know," he grinned, taking my trembling hand in his. "I know that His will is for us to be together baby. Whether our forever is five minutes or 60 more years. You and I, we're it. We're love expressed in its purest form and if you'll have me … "

He dug in his pocket pulling out a jewelry box as I placed my free hand to my lips, the tear slipping from my eye. He opened the box, revealing the most beautiful ring I've ever seen.

"If you will have me," he choked a bit, sniffing back his own emotion. "I promise I'll take care of you to the best of my ability and with all of the strength I have left. As long as I'm breathing, Dominic Kole Sommers, I'll never let you slip through the cracks. I'll never let you fall. I know this is soon, but love is timeless baby. When you know, you know and I've known since the day you re-entered my life."

I sucked in air, trying to keep my heart from bursting with the intensity I felt in the moment. He slipped the ring onto my finger, making this all the more real.

"Will you marry me, please?" he asked shyly, chuckling at the end with a tear of his own falling gracefully down his cheek.

I covered my mouth once more, emotion deep in my throat as I nodded my answer.

"Yeah?"

"Yes! Yes baby, yes! I'll marry you. You know I will!" I cried, pulling him from his knees and into my arms.

I squeezed him tight before cuffing his cheeks with my hands and pulling him closer to meet his lips with mine.

I heard whistling in the distance and quickly removed my lips from his to look to my left, seeing Charli and Jamie smiling brightly.

CHAPTER
- FOURTEEN -

"So how did my parents react when you asked them, they weren't freaked?" I asked, blowing on the broccoli and cheese soup I made for Jesse as I walked into his bedroom. He looked peaceful laying there, his eyes closed and head perched upon his pillows.

Our trip had been cut short, due to him not feeling well not long after his proposal. His body was aching him and nausea had hit him hard. We checked out of the hotel early this morning and I've been watching after him carefully ever since we got home.

In true Jesse fashion, he was doing his best to be light hearted and outgoing, but I could see in his eyes how much pain he was in. It was hurting my heart to see him like this.

I set the soup down on his nightstand while planting myself next to his body. I ran my fingers over his hair, before feeling his forehead and taking his cheek in my palm.

"Still warm." I frowned as he smirked.

"Your touch feels good though," he spoke, his eyes fluttering open to look me in mine.

My heart skipped a beat.

He cleared his throat before adjusting himself to sit up in the bed, "But what you say baby? I missed it."

I smiled, "Doesn't matter."

He shook his head, "It does, I wanna talk to you. I ain't talked to you all day cause I been tired. What you say?"

I smiled, admiring his strength. He was mustering everything he could to have this conversation with me.

"I asked what my parent's reaction was when you asked for my hand in marriage."

He rested his head back against his headboard, shutting his eyes, a wide toothy grin on his face. "They were excited for real. They know I got you. I mean we're young, but they get it you know? Ms. Sharon said she always knew since we were kids. She was really happy for us."

I chuckled, "We're really getting married."

He nodded, "Yeah, we are. When you wanna?"

I shrugged, "Doesn't matter. I was never the little girl that dreamed of a crazy wedding. All I care about is that you're there. That's it."

He nodded, "Let's do it around my birthday then, that's my wish."

My eyes widened, "That's the end of October! Like a month and a half from now!"

He opened one eye, "That too soon?"

I shook my head quickly, "No, not at all. Seems kind of too far honestly."

"Aight, let's plan for that. That's what I want," he sighed peacefully before a cough rumbled in his chest.

He sat up, coughing uncontrollably as I rubbed his back, saddened all over again.

I hated seeing him going through this.

"I'm sorry baby." he apologized after catching his breath and getting comfortable again.

"You don't have to apologize Jes, it's not your fault."

He blew out a breath before shaking his head, "Crazy how I was perfectly fine before taking the meds. Now it's like I'm more prone to sickness."

I kissed his cheek before crawling into bed with him, wrapping my arms around his small waist, resting my head against his chest.

His heartbeat. It was there and beating strong.

"I want your dress to be beautiful," he spoke into the quiet. I could hear the smile in his voice.

"Like," he continued, "I want it to look royal with a crazy long train and your hair to be pinned up so I can see your face. You're going to be so beautiful, man. I see it in my dreams all the time."

I craned my neck to look up at him, pecking the hairs on his chin. He blushed.

"That's gonna be the happiest day of my life Nic, I swear."

I smirked at the thought, praying for many more days and nights like this.

My brain was fried, flipping through my Bible one late Wednesday evening for the right scripture.

I just got back from bible study with my mom and the entire service was about praying and being there for others in need. It went hand in hand, because Jesse invited me to attend his chemotherapy appointment tomorrow. I was honored he wanted to share something so intimate with me, but I was fearful at the same time.

How could I offer the most support? How could I be of use?

The Bible seemed to be the book with all of the answers, and I was searching desperately for answers.

I just had no idea where to look.

"It's getting dark out here baby girl," I heard Corey's strong yet nasally voice boom behind me.

I deflated, looking over my shoulder at my father as he stood tall, shutting the screen door behind him. His feet carried him to me, his warm blue eyes peering inquisitively down into mine.

"Whatcha doing?" he asked curiously, resting his broad shoulder against the tall white post that connected our porch to the roof.

I sighed, turning my eyes back to the holy book, flipping another page. "Looking for a scripture."

"Why do you seem so frustrated?" he chuckled, noticing the attitude in my actions.

"Because! I can't find it and as much as I've been going to church lately, I still feel like an infant in this whole thing! Like why can't I find what I need when I need it! Why is it this hard?" I groaned, running my fingers through my mess of hair.

I was frustrated.

"Calm down baby girl, breathe."

I stopped, taking his advice and took in a deep breath, counting down from ten in my head until my heart rate slowed.

"This isn't anything you should be worked up over."

"I know," I sighed. "It's just when it comes to Jesse, I take it so serious. I just want to be the best I can be to him."

I looked up, noticing his puzzled face. "What does finding a scripture have to do with Jesse?"

I shrugged, "He's been going through a lot with his health and ... I don't know. I just thought finding a scripture would help me help him"

He gave a quick nod of understanding, stuffing his hands in his pockets.

"Ah I see now. Well you're in the right place, your heart is. But don't let this stress you," he continued. "His burden is not yours to carry either. Just focus on your part and ways you can help him, like what you're doing now. Scriptures are good because it contains God's promises and His truth to His people. There are plenty of scriptures in regard to healing that will help you pray for Jesse."

My eyebrows rose with excitement, "Can you tell me one? Your favorite?"

His face lit up with a smile as he motioned for me to scoot over. He stretched out his long legs, perching himself right next to me on the concrete porch.

"You know Jesus was known to be a healer of many sicknesses and diseases in the Bible," he began to explain to me, his elbows resting against his knees and large hands clasped together.

"That was part of his purpose while he was here on earth. He traveled all throughout the city of Galilee, healing and delivering the sick. He even raised a man from the dead."

My eyes widened in shock, "He did?"

He nodded firm, "Yep and a lot of the time when he healed people, he didn't even touch them. You know what healed them?"

I shook my head no, giving Corey permission to answer the question. "Their faith."

He took in a light breath, "Their faith would make them whole. It's because they believed, without a shadow of a doubt that this man was sent from God and had the power to heal them and it actually did. They would be freed from their suffering almost instantaneously."

I deflated, "It sounds like a good story and I'm not saying I don't believe it to be true Corey but Jesse is different. Jesse has faith and he's still sick."

"If your faith is in that kind of state baby girl, maybe Jesse's sickness shouldn't be your focus, maybe your faith should be."

I huffed, "I'm trying! I'm seriously trying but it's been a battle for me, honestly. It's so hard to trust in God when He's allowing Jesse to go through this pain all over again! It's not fair to him and he doesn't deserve it!"

"And I'm not saying he does either," Corey interjected softly, understanding the sensitivity of the topic.

This was going to be my husband. His suffering is my suffering and I was never going to be okay with him having to suffer at all, ever.

"There's a scripture, Isaiah 57 verse 17 that says no weapon formed against you shall prosper. You know what that scripture tells me?"

I shook my head no.

"It tells me that either way it goes, the weapons will form but it doesn't mean they will prosper. As believers though, our response can't be how the world will respond. That's how the devil wants us to view things. The devil wants us to crack, wants us to fold under pressure, wants us to give up the moment the weapons form, wants us to turn against God but God placed everything we need down on the inside of us to fight every battle that we are to ever face. We're in the world, but we're not of it. We do not have to feed into the lies."

"I'm not saying," he continued, "that Jesse deserves to be sick. I'm not saying that at all. But I do have faith that he will beat this and he will be healed and I need you to be strong with him, baby. Don't fold when it doesn't make sense to you. Some things never will. Just understand that these are the cards you all are dealt and you have to get your faith up. It's the only way you're going to survive."

He draped his arm around my shoulder, pulling me into his side and kissing me against my temple.

"Take a look at Matthew 8:13, Jeremiah 17:14 and Matthew 9:22. Those are good places to start for healing. If you need more just come in and find me. Don't be out here too much longer, it's getting too dark," he warned lovingly, standing to his feet.

I watched the ground, taking in everything he had said, hearing his footsteps become more faint the closer he got to the door.

"Corey," I called, stopping him in his tracks. "Why did God create us?"

I turned my head, watching the thoughtful grin on his face. "Many reasons but the main one was for relationship."

He opened the screen door, "A relationship with God is the most important relationship you can have."

––––––––––

My eyes watched the nurse carefully as she set Jesse up to the machine that was going to administer the drug. I studied her every movement and watched the way Jesse fell into routine, answering every question before she even had a chance to ask.

As she was finishing up, my eyes danced around the room, bouncing from patient to patient. Some were young, some were old, and some were middle aged. Everyone looked worn, disgruntled and pale.

Jesse seemed to be the only patient that contained even a little bit of light and life.

I'm sure his faith was to thank for that.

I looked back to Jesse, noticing his furrowed brows, as he seemed to be searching the room for something or someone.

"Okay, I'll be at the nurse's station if you need anything Jesse."

She looked to me with a smile. "It was nice meeting you Dominic. Happy to have you join us."

I grinned back, "Thank you, nice meeting you too," I said, watching as she left our company.

I took in a deep breath, looking over at Jesse as he eyed the IV in his hand before sitting back comfortably, turning his cheek to stare at me.

"You comfortable baby? You want me to tell the nurse to get you a better chair?" he asked, worried about me like always.

I chuckled, rocking side to side in the office chair.

"No this one's fine. I'm good, are you good?"

He nodded, "Just glad you're here. I usually have my friend Pete but I don't see him today. I really wanted you to meet him."

He had been telling me about the young teen he had been mentoring since starting his chemotherapy. I was saddened to not have a face to match the name.

"Maybe his appointment was moved to later. He'll be here, don't worry," I encouraged, scratching the back of his head, relaxing him.

"I'm not, I got you here," he said, closing his eyes at my touch before opening them again. "Thank you for coming."

"You know I wouldn't miss it."

I was the only visitor here so far.

"Do people typically come here alone?" I asked, looking back to Jesse for an answer, retreating my hand from his scalp.

He shrugged, "Depends. Sometimes people just wanna be alone. Sometimes they want company."

I nodded, trying not to stare too hard. I cleared my throat and looked back to Jesse, talking softer. "Everyone just looks so drained."

"They are baby. Cancer takes a lot out of you not only physically but emotionally too. Everybody is dealing differently."

I nodded my head, understanding. "How are you today?"

He smiled. "I'm here, in the moment, enjoying your company," he reached his hand, grabbing my left so that he could graze my ring finger with his thumb.

"I keep thinking about the wedding," he started, but I cut him off.

"Babe, you don't gotta focus on that. We have bigger things to worry about."

His brows furrowed, eyes trained on my ring. He ran his tongue smoothly over his plump lips, shaking his head.

"Nah. It keeps me going, gives me something to look forward to. I gotta marry you, I gotta make you my wife."

I grinned, my emotions were beginning to peak.

"I got something to live for and I can't quit. No matter how hard it gets sometimes." He breathed, lifting my hand and kissing it.

I always loved the feel of his lips against my skin.

"I know we don't got the time to really plan our honeymoon and stuff right now but I still wanna make our wedding night special. We can have a reception, the whole nine." he said, resting his head back, looking over at me.

All of the love he had for me resting in his brown hues.

"Lots of dancing?" I asked, entertaining the idea because I knew that's what he needed right now.

He nodded.

"Lots of dancing, lots of music, lots of food. My mom wants to cater the whole thing. You know she loves to cook and got her culinary thing going," he explained as I hummed in remembrance.

His mother was an excellent cook. She always had been.

"And we're going to get married at the church?" I asked, earning a head nod from him.

"Yeah. I'm gonna be standing there looking all good in my white tux."

My eyes widened, "White?"

He nodded. "Yeah, all white looking Godly," he joked, earning a laugh from me.

"Best man?" I questioned with a risen brow, already knowing who would rightfully have the title.

He shook his head, "I don't think we should do all that baby. I kind of just want it to be us up there. Just us and the pastor, that's it; everyone else can just watch."

My eyes widened at the revelation, "Wow, really?"

He nodded. "Yeah. That's how I always envisioned it, just us and me waiting patiently for you to meet me at the altar, our favorite love song playing."

"What is our favorite love song?" I questioned, as he chuckled with a shrug.

"I don't know, what's your favorite?" he asked, the smile permanent on his face now. "One that reminds you of me?"

I giggled, covering my face bashfully with my knuckles. "I don't know Jes!"

He snickered, rolling his eyes playfully. "It'll find us before the time comes. I'm sure of it, something classic."

I grinned, moving my chair next to his and I leaned my temple to rest against his shoulder. I laced my hand with his, careful not to touch his IV. I used my freehand to rub his tattooed covered arm.

"I love talking about our wedding with you. It's such a beautiful thought," I said quietly, getting comfortable up against him.

He rested his cheek against the top of my hair, squeezing my hand tighter. "Soon to be reality."

"Man, I declare war really is the longest game in life!" Jesse groaned, throwing down another card just as I did.

Mine was higher. I smiled, adding the two cards to my pile.

"You're saying this because you have three cards left in your hand or?" I teased with a risen brow.

"So we're just gonna forget about the time where I was beating you and you were down to two cards?" he asked, throwing down his next card.

Mine was higher, again.

"Yeah and you see how Jesus had other plans? I'm the God of I declare war!" I bragged, taking the two cards and throwing down my ace of spades with confidence, knowing Jesse didn't have any cards left to beat me.

He smacked his lips, throwing down his two of clubs and becoming even more annoyed. I couldn't help but laugh.

"Now we already know I got a 3 of hearts left in my deck. We already know I lost. Why you waiting for me to throw it down like we don't already know the answers?" he asked, frustrated with an irritated smile on his face.

I cackled, allowing my hair to brush past my cheeks.

"You don't know! I could have a two next!"

He poked his lips to the side, "We know it ain't gonna be no two, Nic! Why you playing with me man? Take your winnings with pride; don't drag me down in the process," he sulked as I laughed even harder.

He threw his three down with an attitude as I flipped over my card.

Four of hearts –

He grumbled, pushing all of the cards off the table childishly as I laughed.

"Oh my God, you are the biggest sore loser I've ever met!" I laughed as he chuckled too, bending over to pick up the scattered cards.

I helped him until all of the cards were back on the table.

We were nearing the end of his appointment.

Jesse began to scoot the table up to the best of his ability because the IV had him hooked to the machine. I helped him, picking up the small table and placing it back where I had retrieved it near the nurse's station.

I strolled back over near Jesse, meeting his eyes as he watched me the entire way.

He reached his hand out to me the closer I got, and I looked at it curiously.

I placed my hand in his calloused and warm hand. He pulled in his direction.

"Comeer." he commanded gently with a tip of his head and quick lick of his lips.

I rose a brow, "Where Im'a go?"

"In my lap," he smirked, patting the empty spot.

I blushed, looking around us nervously. "Is that permitted?"

He chuckled, pulling me. "Girl if you don't come here!"

I obeyed, carefully molding my body into his, already engulfed with his scent.

This was my favorite place in the world, right in his arms.

"I just wanna cuddle with you till they come unhook me. Is that okay?" he asked softly, rubbing his pointed nose around my ear, sending chills throughout my being.

I nodded, mesmerized by his effect on my soul.

"Yes," my voice was nearly inaudible, leaving me completely.

"Can I have a kiss?" he asked against my lobe, leaving several provoking pecks.

I tucked my lips in, feeling bashful as Jesse lifted his free hand, brushing some hair from my face.

"Hmm?" he asked again, gripping my chin with his index finger and thumb, turning my face to meet his.

"I don't care about whose watching, do you?" he asked, voice heavy with seduction.

He stared intently into my eyes before beginning to lean in until our lips were pressed lovingly against one another. He started slow and sensual, before leaning in more, hungry and eager for full access. I answered his need, placing my hands on his cheeks, deepening our lip lock earning a grunt from him as his arms wrapped tightly around my small frame.

I could feel him growing underneath me and he pulled away, pressing his forehead against mine, regaining the breath he lost in our kiss.

"You awakening me girl," he breathed, eyes shut tight and jaw clenched. I rubbed my fingers along his strong jaw line, wanting him more than ever before in this moment.

I had to remember we were in a damn hospital.

"I luh you, you know that?" he asked, opening his eyes into low thin slits.

"Y-yes." I stuttered, nearly intoxicated in his beauty. "I love you too."

He squeezed me tighter, shutting his eyes once again.

"Just sit with me and hold me till it's time to go?" he requested softly, voice drenched with vulnerability.

I nodded feverishly, tucking my arms around his thinning waist, resting my head against his chest, feeling his rapidly beating heart against my cheek.

"And they lived happily ever after … the end," Jesse finished, closing the classic storybook of Cinderella. He looked down at the sleeping beauty, a seven-year-old girl named Amaya, as she slept peacefully tucked underneath his arm.

She had been sleeping just a few pages into the story but Jesse finished anyway, unaware of her deep slumber.

He closed the book carefully, just as her mother walked into the hospital room, a warm tired smile graced upon her brown cheeks.

"She really loves when you come and read to her. It makes her Thursday nights," she smirked, watching as Jesse climbed out of the bed.

"It's really not a problem at all Ms. Carpenter. I love the energy that the kids bring. It helps keep my own spirits up," he grinned, handing her the children's storybook.

She took it gratefully and walked to the side of her daughter's bed, running her hands over her bald head, kissing her cheeks softly. Jesse frowned a bit at the sight, seeing the pain in her shaky fingers as she pulled the blanket over her child.

"Tell Amaya I'll be back to see her next Thursday. I'm going to go up and visit with a friend of mine in chemo," he informed Ms. Carpenter as she nodded her response, never taking her eyes off her child.

"Jesse," she called just before he could exit completely.

He looked over his shoulder in curiosity.

"Thank you."

Jesse's brows furrowed as he searched the room for Peter's face. There was no sign of him.

Tonight was his night, he was always here after Jesse would read to the kids.

A tinge of worry pricked his heart as he ran his hand over his bed of hair, looking for the nurse.

Nurse Kelly was on duty and she making her way back to her station when Jesse spotted her. She noticed the look of distraught on his face. She then instantly became concerned.

"Hey Kelly," he started. "Did Pete get moved? He wasn't here at my appointment last week and he's not here today. You know where he is? I wanna see him."

At the mention of Peter's name her face instantly fell, along with her head.

Jesse didn't know.

He watched her expression in fear, bending his head so he could meet her eyes.

"Kelly, what's going on? What happened with Pete?"

She drew in a breath before lifting her head high, "He … "

She couldn't find the words the moment she started.

He grew impatient, "Tell me Kelly, please."

She sighed, "We lost him Jesse, last week.."

The breath left his body at the news. He struggled to regain air, finding it hard to process.

"Wh-what?" His voice was faint and barely audible.

"I'm so sorry – "

"Why didn't ya'll tell me? Why ain't no one tell me?!" Jesse's voice boomed in the hospital hallway, startling Kelly a bit.

But she understood. She dealt with reactions like this almost every week in her profession.

"I don't- I don't know, Jesse. We all knew how special you were to him. His family just needed their time and privacy. I'm sorry," she apologized, watching the solemn look she received back.

Jesse tucked his lips in, resting his hands on his waist, unsure of how to deal with this blow to his heart.

It hurt. It hurt because he was always encouraging Peter to stay strong and to keep fighting. They talked of his future, graduating and full life after cancer. They talked God and faith.

They talked survival.

He couldn't accept that Peter hadn't.

"If you want, I can take you down to the counselor to talk –" Kelly's advice went unheard as Jesse quickly turned, heading towards the exit staircase.

"Jesse," she called after him. "Jesse, wait!"

But before she knew it, he was out of her sight. Unsure of where he was headed.

Jesse burst through the hospital doors, desperately searching for the air he couldn't seem to find.

He was having a panic attack.

The tears pricked the surface of his eyes as he doubled over, thankful he was in the back of the hospital where he couldn't be seen.

He rested his hands on his knees, gasping for air before looking up to the moonlit sky.

"Why you have to take Peter man? I don't- I don't.." he huffed, breathing heavily through his nose.

"This ain't fair!" he shouted, standing tall and placing his hands on the back of his head.

He felt as if he just finished a marathon.

"This ain't … this ain't fair God. What you tryna say to me, huh?" he asked, raising a brow and looking to the sky for answers unknown.

"You could've at least let me say goodbye," he choked and the tears began to flow.

"I could've at least told him how much he inspired me, how much he meant to me. He was too young. 14? That's too young."

He shook his head, beginning to pace in the dark alley.

"Am I next?!" he called out, feeling nearly depleted of his energy.

"Let me know now. I don't wanna drag this out, I don't wanna hurt nobody man. I don't wanna … I don't wanna die. I got too much to live for … just let me make it, please."

He drew in as much air as his lung would allow, "Just let me make it."

"How do you expect me to help if you won't talk to me?" I pleaded with Jesse from his bedroom doorway.

He sat on his bed, still as a rock, elbows on his knees and eyes pressed forward.

He wasn't looking at anything in particular, he was just in another world it seemed like.

He's been like this since the moment he came home from the hospital.

"What happened? Did you see your doctor or something?" he gave a shake of his head.

Finally – some type of reaction.

"Then what happened baby, please talk to me. Say something." I begged, just wanting to provide some type of comfort.

I couldn't even fathom what had gotten his spirit so low.

I've seen Jesse in his down and sad states, but this, this was different. He was hurting and I could tell it was for something other than himself.

Daringly, I walked towards him, slow in my steps until I was standing in front of his perched body.

He had barely even blinked.

"Baby," I whispered, placing my fingers in his hair and beginning to scratch softly.

In an instant, he wrapped his arms around my waist, resting his forehead against my abdomen and broke, right then and there.

My heart sank, as I searched the top of his head frantically while he gripped the material of my tank top.

"Jesse ... wh-what is it?"

"It's Pete baby, Pete," he whimpered softly into my shirt, rubbing his forehead against the cotton material.

"What about Pete, did you see him today?"

This only made him cry harder as he violently shook his head.

"Jesse!" I pleaded.

"He's gone baby. I didn't," he sobbed. "I aint get to say bye to him man. I ain't get to tell him to be strong and that everything was going to be okay."

My heart tugged, hearing his brokenness and I wanted nothing but to patch up the pieces but he needed to grieve.

If there was one thing I understood, it was loss.

"Baby he knows, you told him every time you saw him. He knew."

"But he was so young though."

I nodded. "We were only promised life Jes, not to live forever. Not everyone that lives is going to die old. That's just how it is sometimes."

"What about me though? What does that mean for me?"

I frowned deeply, realizing what was hurting him so bad.

He was afraid and this was where my faith had to step in.

I bent down to his level, grabbing his dampened cheeks in my hands, forcing him to look me in my face.

"You need to hear me, okay? Hear me."

He sniffed, nodding feverishly.

He needed me so bad in this moment.

"You need to have faith baby! You can't take what happened to Peter so personal. He's free; he's not suffering anymore. God had different plans for him."

I took in a deep breath. "Be thankful that you knew him, be thankful that he lived and that he fought as long as he could. He needed to go home. The why is not for us to understand."

He sniffed again, allowing his head to drop before I was quick to lift it back up.

"As for you baby, I need you to hear me!" I pleaded, voice cracking and the emotion deep in my throat.

"You will LIVE and NOT die!" I declared, voice strong and thick.

His lips parted, as his eyes glossed over, listening to my every word.

"You hear me? You will LIVE and NOT die! Say that with me – please say it with me! Speak it and *believe* it. I need you to!"

"You will live! You will live! And not die!" I said again, as his lip trembled with emotion.

He dropped his head again.

"Pick up your head baby. Pick up your strength," I encouraged, releasing my hands from his face.

Jesse needed to fight for himself just as hard as I was in this moment.

"Pick it up baby, you can do it."

He coughed another sob before using the back of his hand to wipe at his nose.

"Please." I prayed out loud, needing God now more than ever.

I didn't know who else to lean on for support because this was draining me too.

"You will live!" I placed my hands on my knees, attempting to look Jesse in his bloodshot eyes.

"You will live Jesse! And not die! You will live! And not die!" I cried, begging for him to believe me. I needed him to.

He nodded, lifting his head slowly, meeting my eyes lazily.

"It's hard," he confessed.

I blinked, the tears falling unceremoniously to the carpet floor.

"Say it."

My voice sounded so small in the room but I knew he heard me loud and clear.

He took in a deep breath, nodding again. "I'll ... I'm going to live."

I wiped at my cheek, never taking my eyes off of him. "And what?"

"And not die," he finally spoke as I cried and wrapped my arms lovingly around him in an earth-shattering embrace.

"I'm ... I'm so sorry Nic. I ... " he stuttered as I shushed him.

"Shhh, it's going to be okay, I'm here."

"I'm so sorry."

CHAPTER
- FIFTEEN -

" Smile girl. This is supposed to be a good day!" Charli encouraged, taking a sip of her wine.

We were in a local bridal shop, looking for my wedding dress. She and my mother had accompanied me for the occasion.

I turned my head, catching a concerned look from them both, and put on the best smile I could muster.

"I'm fine, really. I just didn't think choosing a dress would be this difficult," I lied, praying that I sounded believable.

In all actuality, I was a nervous wreck.

It had been a month since Peter had passed away and Jesse still wasn't coping with the loss as well as I thought he would.

He was trying. I could see it in his eyes every day that he was trying to stay positive and stay in faith, but it was hurting him to do so. I couldn't understand it, and it was getting harder on me to accept.

I didn't know what to do, I didn't know how to help and because of his lack of faith, I was starting to lose mine as well. I felt so weak and helpless.

The only thing that lightened his mood was this wedding. He wrapped himself into the planning of it and I allowed him to because I knew it was therapeutic for him.

His love for me seemed to be all that was getting him through each day. And though I was flattered, I knew he needed more. His strength had to come from something deeper than us, and I had no idea how to pull it out of him.

"Well I saw this beautiful one over by the door, you want me to go get it?" My mother offered, her big brown eyes pleading for a way to help my mood.

I nodded and smiled, "Sure, go get it."

Jesse straightened out his dress shirt, looking over himself in the large mirror in the dressing area of the tuxedo shop.

He and Jamie were trying on suits for the wedding.

"So where you say ya pops was gonna be at again?" Jamie asked, fixing the collar of his shirt and looking back at his friend.

His brows pulled together while taking a glance at him.

Jesse cleared his throat, attempting to keep down the cough that so desperately wanted to escape. He woke up feeling terrible but didn't want to cancel and didn't want people to worry.

He was tired of people worrying about him.

He was tired ... period.

His muscles ached, his chest burned and he would feel chills passing up his spine off and on.

He knew he was sick, but he had to stay strong. He had to fight through this.

He had a wedding to attend soon.

"He uh, he had to work. He said he would come up here tomorrow on his off day."

Jamie eyed Jesse carefully, noting the lazy look in his eye, as he looked himself over.

"Yeah, you aight? That's not bothering you?" He asked, keeping the conversation up but refusing to look away.

Afraid something might happen if he did.

Jesse shook his head, dabbing at his nose while reaching for his suit jacket.

"Ain't nothing new. There's always something more important to him than me. I've learned to just accept it."

He began to cough, feeling the nagging ache in his chest burn harder than ever.

Jamie was quick to be at his side, resting his hand carefully on his back.

He could feel the heat from Jesse's skin through his shirt.

"Dawg, you're burning up! You sure you're good, man?" Jamie asked, watching Jesse recover from his coughing fit.

"Yeah, yeah. I'm good man. I'm good, I swear," Jesse lied just as well as Jamie saw through it.

———————————

"Ma can you zip me up?" I called from the dressing room as I felt a drop in my heart.

What was that?

"Sure baby, here I come," my mother said cheerfully, as I looked myself over in the mirror.

I looked … amazing – the dress was gorgeous.

This was the one, the one Jesse had described to me. It was perfect.

My mom moved the curtain and stopped in her tracks at the sight of me.

She had been on the verge of tears all day.

"Nicky you look … you look beautiful, baby." she stammered, using her nickname for me.

"Like absolutely beautiful," she choked, placing her hand to her lip as I chuckled nervously.

"Ma, don't cry."

She took in a deep breath, trying to fan away her tears.

"Jesus, Charli gonna have to come in here and do dis," she cried, walking away as I shook my head at her dramatics.

I smiled though. It was nice to see her so choked up over me.

I was growing up, I was becoming a woman and I was marrying the man of my dreams.

"Mm." I huffed, feeling the pang return to my heart again.

What was going on?

———————————

Jesse's heart was beating rapidly as he struggled to put on his suit jacket.

His muscles ached. He could feel the pulsating of his veins and it became harder and harder to breathe.

He had to fight through; he couldn't succumb to this sickness, not this soon.

Everything just hurt so badly.

"We should probably wrap up here soon," Jamie started, turning his head to peek at Jesse. Everything stilled within him when he saw Jesse's reflection in the mirror.

He had become pale and his eyes crossed while his body began to give out.

"JP!" Jamie yelled, sprinting to Jesse's side and catching him before his frail body could hit the ground.

"JP! Jesse!" Jamie yelled, cradling Jesse in his arms, watching his eyes roll to the back of his skull.

"Jesus, HELP! Somebody call 911!!" he shouted.

———————

"Mmph!" I clutched my chest as my knees buckled beneath me.

Something was wrong. Something was terribly wrong.

Charli and my mom looked at me with worry filled eyes as they were quick to join me by my side.

"Baby what's wrong?"

I stopped, feeling worry beginning to consume me.

I knew there was only one thing that could cause me to feel this way.

"It's Jesse."

———————

"Pneumonia?" Jesse's mother repeated back to the doctor as he nodded sadly.

"Well what," she stuttered as all of us stood around, listening to the devastating news, "what does this mean, will he be okay?"

He sighed, "I can't say. Pneumonia along with Multiple Myeloma is a deadly combination, considering this particular strain of cancer of already weakens the immune system. I'm sure that's how he was able to catch the infection so easily. We need to keep him on antibiotics and on close watch until he is able to get better. I can't provide how long that will be. It all depends on how well he responds to the treatment. In the meantime we'll be on the search for donor's for a bone marrow transplant to remove the disease completely."

I was numb. *Deadly combination?*

"He's not going to die." I blurted, as all eyes fell on me. "Deadly combination? Why would you say that?"

"I'm sorry sweetheart but I'm just stating what we're up against. He's resting now and he is able to have two visitors at a time during visiting hours. I'll provide more information after we get some of his other lab work back." he informed, ending the uncomfortable conversation and dismissing himself.

I looked to his parents, both of them a wreck. I nodded my head towards his room. "You guys should go on in. I already asked if I could stay overnight."

They looked to me with grateful eyes.

Mrs. Palmer walked up, lightly grabbing my cheeks and kissing my temple softly. "I'm so sorry baby. He'll make it through this. He's a fighter," she encouraged before her husband took her hand and led them towards Jesse's room.

He was a man of few words.

I turned, meeting the solemn stares of Jamie, Charli, and my parents, all of whom were there to provide support and comfort.

"Are you okay baby?" my mom asked nearly in a whisper.

She was broken for Jesse – for me, for us.

"I just," I started, feeling the emotion wracked in my chest.

"I just need a moment."

"He looks so weak," Marilyn, Jesse's mother, studied him as she rubbed his sunken cheeks.

They were always so full, and the sickness was starting to thin out her baby boy.

It was hard to witness this for a second time.

"I'm going to make sure I cook him dinner and bring it up here every night. He won't eat their food here. I already know," she sighed, looking up at her husband who stared out of the window aimlessly.

She could feel the anger developing in her gut, the resentment.

"Say something Jack," she begged, needing some type of support from him.

This was their son.

"What you want me to say? I'm hurting just like you," he huffed quietly, still not taking his eyes off the city lights.

He couldn't look at Jesse again. Not right now, not like that.

"You sure do have a funny way of showing emotion. Our son is lying in the hospital, fighting to stay alive and you won't look at him. You won't even speak.

"You should know me by now. Twenty-seven years together and you know nothing about me." he hissed, cutting her off, looking at her through the windows reflection.

"Same goes for you. You don't know me or Jesse. You've always acted like we don't exist. Like we don't matter. Like –"

"Gone wit all dat."

A quiet faint voice rang out, hushing the two of them completely.

Jack was quick to turn around to be at his son's bedside, grateful to have heard his voice.

"Y'all gone be ... " Jesse began, voice weak. "Y'all gone be arguing and what not then just go home. I'ont need that energy wit me right now."

Marilyn sighed, guilt wrecking her heart. "I'm sorry baby. We're worried about you is all."

He licked his dry lips, never attempting to open his eyes.

"Yeah? Well be worried in the hallway. Y'all are waking me up wit all that nonsense. Don't make this about you. It ain't about you right now."

Marilyn blinked, the tear gliding down her cheek before looking to her husband.

"We're sorry, son," Jack finally spoke, resting a hand on Jesse's shoulder.

"How you feeling champ?" he asked, studying every feature, attempting to remain strong for his family.

Jesse cleared his scratchy throat, causing Marilyn to stand up to get him some water.

"I'm tired," was all he could say, having used the last of his energy to scold them.

"Thirsty too?" Jack asked as Marilyn handed him the cup of water with a straw.

Jesse nodded. "Yeah."

"Okay, open up," His father instructed, carefully placing the straw to Jesse lips.

He watched his son slowly take a few sips and swallow before Jesse refused more.

"I'm good. It hurts to do that right now."

He frowned before placing the cup on the tray near his bed.

"Where's my baby, she good?" Jesse asked, earning a smile from his mother.

She knew the question was coming.

"She's holding up, being strong. She's staying with you all night," she answered, rubbing Jesse's clammy forehead with her fingers.

He nodded short in response. "Good. Let 'em know she's the only visitor I want after this. Too tired."

Another tear fell from her eye as she nodded to her son's request.

"I'll let them know."

I sat uncomfortably in the leather chair in Jesse's room, watching as he slept seemingly peaceful.

He had tubes of oxygen running through his nose and two IV's on his hands as the machine beeped steadily, letting us all know that he was still here with us.

I sent my parents home shortly after Jesse's parents informed us that he didn't want any more visitors. I knew it had to do with him being exhausted but also because he didn't want anyone to worry. It was too late for that though; we were all worried.

Jesse only has one lung, making this situation even more detrimental.

The tear escaped and I was quick to dab at it. Not wanting to crack in this moment.

"God please," I begged quietly, unable to formulate what I wanted to say.

I wasn't even sure if God could hear me at this point. It seemed like all my prayers were falling on deaf ears.

Not if he's lying in this hospital like this. How can my prayers have been heard?

"Baby, you in here?" Jesse croaked out.

I was quick to sit up; he had been asleep since I arrived in his room.

"Yeah Jes, I'm here."

I smiled, so thankful to hear him speak.

"Grab my hand," he instructed as I scooted the chair even closer, taking his frail but warm hand into my own.

He relaxed in his pillow even more, turning his cheek slightly to face me. His eyes were closed, and I could feel my heart racing as they fluttered open.

The smile slowly spread across his face as his eyes looked into the depths of my soul.

"Hey you," he breathed lovingly as the emotion split me in half.

I couldn't stop the tears at this point.

"Hey hey," he cooed, still holding his soft smile as I sniffed attempting to contain my pain.

"Don't cry. I'm here, with you," he said, in his attempt to comfort me.

"I'm- I'm so sorry this is happening to you baby. I just wanna take the pain away." I choked, finding it harder and harder to speak through my tears.

"You're already taking it away. This is the best I've felt all day, looking at you, feeling your touch," he assured, nestling his head into his pillow and looking at me through thin slits.

He was exhausted.

"How ... how are you trying to make me feel better when you look and feel like you do?" I questioned, wiping my eyes with my free hand.

He smirked. "You tryna say I don't look good?" he teased, causing me to chuckle.

"You always look good. You're beautiful even now," I complimented, causing his smile to grow.

"You know how to make a man feel good with pneumonia, girl. Flirting wit me and stuff."

I laughed, even as the tears fell from my eyes. I leaned in to kiss his forehead. He closed his eyes as my lips connected to his soft skin.

"Mm. Thank you baby, I needed that," he said as I removed my lips, his eyes still closed.

He'll be asleep soon.

"I'm able to do it cause I love you. I don't want you hurting over me," he finally answered softly, my heart cracking at his words.

"That's impossible Jesse. I'm always going to feel this with you," I answered, my eyes dancing all over his face.

He cleared his throat, resting into the pillow. "I don't want you to. I'm gonna be good no matter what. I need you to be too."

I frowned, leaning in to place several more pecks on his forehead. "Get some sleep baby. We'll talk more tomorrow."

I carried the home cooked lunch I made for Jesse in my hands while walking down the now familiar hospital hallways.

We had been here for a nearly a week and there was no sign of improvement in his pneumonia and it was actually making the cancer in his body worse. They were talking bone marrow transplants, medical induced comas, the whole nine.

And still somehow, Jesse found a way to smile for me every day. He wasn't worried for some reason, but I on the other hand? I was a wreck on the inside.

I took in a deep breath, entering his room to find him sleeping peacefully. He was wrapped up in blankets and his mouth was parted slightly, allowing the air to fill his lung.

My sweet baby.

I smirked, keeping my steps quiet as I set his lunch down on the couch and began to open the blinds to allow the sun into the room.

He loved waking up to sunshine.

I sighed, looking out at the streets below me, resting my hands against my waist trying not to let the tears fall.

This was usual for me, the crying. I only tried to do it while he was asleep now. He hated to see me cry.

It just seemed so hard not to.

"God," I whispered quietly into the room, careful not to wake my fiancé.

"God ... I'm trying to trust you with this. I'm trying to pray and remain full of faith but this is hard. How could you allow this to happen to him? Why Jesse?"

I let out a slow shallow breath as I continued to release my thoughts. "It's like I want to cross that line, cross the line and get saved and really walk out this life with you but how can I do that without him? How am I gonna be able to do any of this without him? Am I missing something? There's something that's not connecting here for me and I feel it. I feel it when I pray I just –"

I frowned, the tear dropping freely from my eye. "Just help me so I can be of some type of help. Please heal him. Allow his faith to heal him, please."

"Amen." His voice rang out, nearly causing me to jump out of my skin.

"Jesus Jes, you scared me!" I said, clutching my chest, attempting to slow my racing heart.

His eyes were still closed but the smile was evident on his face.

I playfully rolled my eyes before strolling towards his bed with my arms crossed.

"How long have you been up?"

He licked his lips, blinking his eyes open before looking to me, the smile still present on his face. "Since before you walked in. I was faking."

I smacked my lips, shoving him lightly in his arm as he laughed. "You creep! You heard me?"

He coughed a little from his laughter and cleared his throat. "I ain't know you was about to do all that. I was waiting for you to sit by me so I could scare you."

I huffed, "You don't think you're scaring me enough already?!"

He frowned mockingly at me before looking to the chair next to his bed.

"Sit down, I gotta explain something to you."

I sighed, running my fingers through my hair before having a seat. He had energy today and I was noticing that I had to appreciate these moments because they were far and few between.

Jesse eyed me soulfully, seemingly studying every feature on my face. He honed in on certain spots more than others causing me to blush.

"Tell me how you're feeling." He requested, catching me off guard. "Honestly."

I froze. "Honestly?"

He nodded. "Yeah. I need to know, talk to me."

I chewed on my bottom lip, searching for how to even start.

"I don't want to discourage you –"

"Baby, I'm asking because I want to know so tell me, please."

"I'm – I don't know Jes. I'm scared. I'm scared for you, and I'm trying to have faith but it's hard. It's hard without you. It's hard trying to be strong in my faith without you."

"Nic.. You understand why you love me so hard? What drew you to me when you first got back?"

I had my reasons, but I knew he was about to reveal to me something I haven't heard before.

I needed some good old Jesse wisdom in this moment.

"Tell me."

He smiled, licking his lips once more. "It was the God in me. The God in me was calling you, baby, because He had no other way to reach you. He knew the only way to reach you was through me."

My brows furrowed, trying to understand. And when I was quiet, it gave him room to continue.

"So yeah, you fell for me, I fell for you too because that's just how it was supposed to work. But you're missing the real love story Nic, you're missing the real one."

He took in a breath, "The greatest love that has ever existed is the one that God has for His people, the love that He shares with us and for us. Why do you think the Bible is the greatest selling book of all time? It's a love story. It's what makes all of this make sense. What makes all of us connected. It's the most important piece of our lives and baby if you don't have that for yourself without me? It's never gonna click. It's never gonna get easier. You need Him more than me. You need Him more than anything and He's been tryna show you that. You just gotta commit yourself to the relationship with Him. It's the only thing that will set you free from it all."

My chest was tingling at his words. Deep down, I knew he was right.

"I'm going to help you as much as I can when I get better, I promise but you have to go after it yourself. As bad as you fight for our love, you gotta fight for that relationship with Him. He's worth it. He'll always be worth it."

I tucked my lips in, containing the emotion lodged in my throat. "It's scary to trust that Jesse with everything I've been through. It's scary to fully trust that … "

He nodded, "I know and I get it. You see what I'm going through right now? You think it's easy to trust through this, like it's easy for all of this to make sense? I'll tell you what I got that I wouldn't have without Him – that's peace. Peace in knowing everything will be okay because His word tells me so and it's rooted so deep in my heart I can't even help it at this point. I want that for you. I need that for you. I pray about it all the time … "

"But it's why you're feeling like your prayers are going unheard, because your faith isn't there. You haven't fully committed yourself to Him and the relationship y'all building because you're so focused on ours. Don't get lost in us baby. We're gonna thrive, but don't get lost in it. A relationship with God is the most important relationship you can have."

His words rang true; reminding me of the words Corey spoke just a few weeks before. It was all confirmation that he was right.

"That's all Im'a speak on it right now. The rest will make sense in due time. You'll know for yourself. I just had to make some things clear because I can't have you hurting anymore. Not cause of me and not cause of the disconnect in your faith."

I smiled, wondering if it were possible for me to fall more in love with him than I was in this moment.

"I've never known someone to love me as much as you do."

He smirked shaking his head, "I know someone that loves you more than me baby. He died for you on the cross."

––––––––––––––––

Today was ... weird.

I felt weird. I was saddened by it a little.

Today was my wedding day; well it was supposed to be.

Jesse has been making a little progress in the hospital in regard to the pneumonia but it was causing his cancer to become more aggressive.

He was currently on the list for a bone marrow transplant. It was his only hope at this point.

It all had me nervous and him not really being able to walk this last week was making it worse on my heart.

He couldn't stop talking about the wedding though, no matter how many times I tried to say we weren't having it.

He's not even able to leave the hospital, how were we going to have a wedding?

Tiffany Campbell

After several attempts to explain we were no longer having it, I allowed him to speak on it. Talk as if it were happening. It was the only thing keeping his spirits up.

Who was I to take that from him?

He even begged me to sleep at home last night, regardless of how much I told him I was staying with him. He said he could tell I was exhausted and he knew my back and shoulders were in pain from sleeping on the hard couch, but I didn't care.

Knowing he was okay and next to me every night was all I needed to keep my sanity.

He refused to allow me to stay though, against my pleading and to my surprise I did feel well rested this morning.

I took in a breath, regaining my composure before approaching Jesse's room.

"Morning baby," I greeted, walking in before I froze.

He wasn't in here. The room was empty.

My heart dropped to the pit of my stomach as I dropped everything in my hands to the ground and ran out into the hall.

"Nurse!" I shouted, rushing to the station, receiving looks from strangers.

The blonde nurse eyed me as I approached her in a panic.

"Hi, the patient in room 502, Jesse Palmer. He's not in there. Has he been moved or something?! I'm his fiancé and no one called me!" I rushed out, looking wildly back and forth between her and his door.

She furrowed her brows for a moment before a look of realization spread across her features.

"Oh! You're Dominic right?"

I was confused. "Yes ... what is going on?"

She pointed to his room. "You didn't see what was in there for you?"

My face contorted, "What, in the room? No. I just saw that he wasn't in it. Can you tell me if he was moved or something, I don't understand."

She smiled, standing to her feet. "Follow me."

I followed her curiously back to Jesse's room. I didn't want to go back in there. He wasn't in there.

"Listen I don't care to be in here, he's not in here." I said, watching as she walked to the closet, opening the door.

I waited impatiently at the entrance, looking around to see if I saw any sign of him.

There was none.

"He left this for you," she announced, as my eyes snapped to her.

They were about to pop out of my skull.

There, lying across her arms was my wedding dress. The dress I tried on but never purchased from the store. How was it here?

"Wh-what's going on?"

Her smile grew, "You're getting married today Dominic."

The breath had left me.

"Wh- but how? He's not allowed to leave. He's too – he's too weak. He couldn't even walk yesterday."

She grinned.

"Where is he?" I asked, the tears pricking the surface.

I couldn't wrap my head around all of this.

"He'll be waiting for you at the altar. We need to take you to get your hair and makeup done for the ceremony," she rushed, handing me my dress and ushering me out of the room.

"Hair and makeup? Who's going to do that?" I asked, looking to her as we stepped into the hallway.

"We are." I snapped my head at the sound of my mother's voice and was surprised to see her and Charli standing there. The two of them were beaming with smiles on their faces.

I was about to pass out.

"Baby it's going to be impossible for me to do your makeup if you keep crying like this." My mother chuckled, on the verge of tears herself.

I sniffed, unable to even hide the emotion as Charli attempted to pin up my hair behind me. We were in a large office that the hospital was letting us use near the chapel.

I was so overwhelmed.

"I just," I choked. "I just can't believe this man loves me this much Ma. A man loves me this much, that he is fighting through his pain just to keep his promise to me? Like ... " I had to inhale, and fan my face.

My mother blinked, the tear slipped from her eye.

Happy tears.

"It's a blessing. It's a blessing that you've met somebody with that type of love for you Dominic. He's going to love you forever, if not longer. You deserve him, and he deserves you," she encouraged, wiping at my tears.

"Ma, I've been so broken and so damaged, what if I don't measure up? What if I can't fulfill him as his wife?"

She smirked, bending down to grab my dampened cheeks in her warm palms.

"Jesse is going to love you through it all."

"What if we don't have much time –"

She shushed me. "You stop it. Stop thinking like that right now and focus on this moment. Focus on today. There is a man, a beautiful man that loves you even beyond comprehension and you love him just as much. You marry that man today. Marry him," she said before kissing me on my forehead.

"Now 'nuff with all that crying. We have a bride to beautify," she chuckled again, wiping her own face.

I sniffed again, nodding and trying to pull myself together.

Nothing but thoughts of Jesse filling my brain.

Jesse sat in his wheelchair in the small hospital chapel, taking deep breaths trying to gain all of his energy.

Truth was, he had little to none but the thoughts of seeing Dominic's face in her wedding dress was keeping him going. He had arranged with her mother a week prior to purchase the dress Dominic wanted and to bring it to the hospital on this day.

Nothing was going to stop him from making her his wife on the date they set, nothing was going to prevent their dream of becoming reality, not even the frailty he felt in his limbs.

He sat upon the altar, watching as small groups of their close loved ones filled the room, all flashing him looks of pity and sympathy, not wanting to hold eye contact too long.

He understood, sickness was uncomfortable but this wasn't his fate. He had faith that this disease wasn't going to take him, not without a fight.

"Hey man," he felt two strong hands cover his shoulders. "You good? Feeling okay?" Jamie asked his best friend, nervous about him sitting in the wheelchair just moments before the ceremony was due to start.

Jesse nodded, "Yeah. Just trying to make sure I'm good before everything."

"Aight. You rolling into matrimony or what?" Jamie teased, earning a small laugh.

"I'm not trying to. I really wanna stand up for her but it's hard, man. My legs shake every time I put too much pressure on em."

"I feel it. Don't stress it too much. If you can, you can. Domo is gonna marry you regardless."

"Yeah I know," he agreed. "I'm just really trying to make this special for her even under the circumstances."

"You already have, I'm sure of it," Jamie said, taking a look around the chapel. "It doesn't look half bad in here for everything to be so last minute. They did a nice job."

Jesse hummed a response, waving at his parents who had just walked in.

"Yo ... Doc said you good to kiss or nah?" Jamie asked quietly, earning another laugh from Jesse.

"He cleared me to kiss her. I'm solid." Jamie held out his fist as Jesse dapped him up.

"Cool. Let's have us a wedding!"

"You look beautiful," A nurse told me in passing as I stood in my dress before the closed chapel doors.

I smiled, nodding my thanks.

My heart was swelling with so many different emotions it was hard to catch just one.

I couldn't believe this was really about to happen. I was about to marry the greatest person I've ever known.

It all seemed surreal. My life in the past seven months all seemed surreal.

I had found my home. I had found my family. I had found love.

I had found myself. And now I was about to share that with one person for the rest of my life. And honestly, I couldn't have been happier about that.

"You ready baby girl?" Corey approached, looking cleanly shaven and dapper in his tuxedo.

His blue eyes twinkled with a wink before he reached his arm out for me.

"More than ready ... just nervous. Have you seen him?" I asked, hearing the music beginning to play in the chapel, queuing my expected entrance.

Heaven by Jamie Foxx.

I loved this song.

"Don't worry. He's ready for you," he assured, straightening himself and looking straight ahead as we waited for the doors to open.

This was it.

I bent my head down, allowing the veil to shield my eyes completely. I could hear the doors open and people standing to their feet.

Corey took the first step, startling me as I looked up. The breath leaving my body as my eyes trained on Jesse.

He was in his wheelchair, next to the minister. His mouth dropped, looking at me as his brown hues lit up with love.

I smirked, feeling the tears already wanting to reveal themselves.

I watched Jesse as he tucked his lips in, gripping the handles of the chair strongly. His head fell forward as he mustered up everything in him to lift his body up.

My heart stopped in my chest, worried he was going to fall. Jamie felt the same. He stepped to him, but Jesse held up his hand, stopping him completely, refusing any help.

In a moment, his eyes fell back on me. He smirked confidently, as he slowly rose tall to his feet. He never took his eyes off mine as he stepped forward, straightening himself to stand at the altar, waiting for my arrival.

I sucked in a breath as the tear fell graciously down my cheek, my hand quickly rising to my lips to stop the sob that wanted to escape.

He was standing, just for me, just for this day, no matter how bad he could be hurting in this moment.

He looked beautiful in his all white suit, hair freshly cut and cheeks full of life. You could never tell he was sick. He had a healthy glow about him.

Nothing but love could make this possible.

His smile became brighter the closer Corey and I stepped. I wanted to run to that altar just to hug him, I couldn't wait to be his wife.

I locked eyes with my mother, her cheeks already wet from her own emotion. She mouthed 'I Love You', blowing me a kiss as Corey and I finally reached the altar just as the song was lowered to fade out.

I caught Jesse's hard soulful stare, the faint smirk resting on his lips. He stepped forward reaching his hand out for me and taking mine into his own.

The minister looked down to me with a grin before he looked out to our audience.

"You may all be seated," he instructed warmly as everyone sat down behind us.

"We're gathered here today," his strong voice boomed, "to celebrate the relationship of Jesse and Dominic and to be witnesses and supporters of the commitment they share with one another before God."

I smirked, locking eyes with Jesse, earning a silly kissy face from him.

I snickered, enthralled to see him in good spirits.

"Who here gives Dominic away in marriage to this man?"

Corey cleared his throat, "Her Mother and I do," he answered, his deep voice providing me comfort.

He turned to face me, smiling as he lifted my veil, revealing my face to the room.

He placed a gentle kiss on my temple, "I love you baby girl," he whispered, pulling me into a warm hug.

I wanted to break in two right there, but I held it together, accepting all the love he had grown for me in our embrace.

He pulled back, wiping his eye quickly before shaking Jesse's hand.

"Take care of her man," he said to him, earning a strong nod from my soon to be husband.

Corey took his rightful side by my mother who was dabbing her eyes with a tissue.

I smiled at my parents before feeling Jesse grip my hand tight, escorting me up the two altar steps.

He intertwined our fingers as we stood before the minister, awaiting the next part of the ceremony.

I shook with nerves, feeling another gentle squeeze from him.

I could barely hear what the minister was saying as he gave his speech to everyone else, discussing the purpose of marriage and the journey we're about to embark on together.

"It's okay baby. I got you," Jesse said for my ears only, instantly relaxing me.

He sounded so strong.

"The couple has chosen to conduct their own vows," the minister announced, pulling me back into his words.

Vows? I hadn't even thought of any.

"Dominic, would you like to go first?" he questioned sweetly as I looked nervously between him and Jesse.

After a short pause, I nodded. Ready to express myself to the man I love.

I took in a breath, before turning my feet, coming face to face with Jesse. He looked down at me, the loving smirk resting on his lips, ready to hear what I had to say.

"Jesse," I spoke, instantly smiling at his name rolling off my lips.

"Your name alone means God exists and I couldn't have thought of a better definition for you baby. When I see you, when anyone sees you, they see God. They see the power He has on your life. It was one of the first things that captivated me when it came to you. Your soul had me locked in because it is so genuine and so pure."

I began to get choked up, so I had to take a moment to breathe.

"Your soul is so pure ... and you're so strong that you're here, standing before me, professing your love and devotion to me and this relationship before our family, before God, during one of the hardest times of your life. I am in awe of you baby – in awe of all that you do and all that you are. You're perfect and I am honored that I was chosen to share the rest of your journey with you, the rest of our journey together."

I watched the tear slip from his eye, but his smile never left.

"I love you Jesse, more today than I did yesterday. And tomorrow, I'll love you even more than that."

He grinned bashfully, capturing his bottom lip with his top row of teeth, squeezing my hands tight.

The minister smiled, looking to Jesse. He nodded, taking his cue.

"What can I say after that? That was beautiful," he smiled, earning a few chuckles from the crowd. I looked nervously at them, watching as some were dabbing their eyes with tissue.

"Baby," he began, shifting on his feet to stand even straighter. "The love I have for you is what is inspiring my strength to stand before you right now. Sometimes ... sometimes I don't even know how I'm going to make it through the day and then I ask God for strength, and I ask Him for peace and I see your face. You're the answer to my prayers baby, and I know I'm the answer to yours."

He released a shaky breath, his hands trembling in mine.

"I know how we're entering into our marriage is not how either one of us imagined, but I can say one thing, I'm so glad you're here. I'm so thankful you didn't step down and leave my side but instead, you stepped up. Not only to be there for me but in your faith as well and I'm proud, so proud of the woman you're becoming. You're so amazing and your growth is truly one to admire. I'm in awe of you Dominic. I've been in awe since the first day I met you. Every day God blesses me to lay eyes on you is a good day, and it's a day that I am thankful for. I'm so ready to experience the rest of my life with you, no matter how long that is because I know it will be nothing short of Heaven sent. I love you, more than you can ever understand, and I promise that as long as I'm breathing I'll never give up. I'll never stop fighting. I'll never stop being there for you," he ended, smiling through his tears as I smiled through mine.

My heart swelled at his words that only Jesse knew how to capture me with. I had never heard anything so beautiful in my life.

The minister smiled, looking down at the two of us before he looked out into the audience, "The rings," he requested.

Charli came up and handed me mine, as Jamie handed Jesse his. We took them graciously before looking at each other, waiting for our next instructions.

"Dominic if you would, place the ring on Jesse's finger."

The silver band slid on so easily.

"Do you, Dominic Kole Sommers, take this man to be your lawfully wedded husband? To have and to hold from this day forward, for better, for worse, for richer, for poorer, in sickness and in health, to love and to cherish, till death do you part?" The minister asked, as I never took my eyes off of Jesse.

"I do." Jesse winked, causing me to giggle.

"And do you, Jesse Aaron Palmer, take this woman to be your lawfully wedded wife. To have and to hold from this day forward, for better, for worse, for richer, for poorer, in sickness and in health, to love and to cherish, till death do you part?"

"You know I do,"

He slid the ring onto my hand with ease, before caressing it with his thumb.

I smiled bashfully, unable to contain it anymore.

I was marrying my best friend.

"By the power vested in me, I now pronounce you Mr. and Mrs. Jesse Palmer!

You may now kiss your bride!"

The crowd erupted as *You Are My Lady* by Freddie Jackson began to play. Jesse took my cheeks into his warm palms, glancing over my every feature before embracing my lips with his.

I hadn't kissed him in so long it seemed like.

His full lips tugged at my bottom one before he pecked them again and pulled away.

"We did it," he said, rubbing his pointed nose against mine, his eyes closed in bliss. "I kept my promise to you. I made you my wife."

"You did," I cooed with a giddiness I just couldn't hide. "I love you."

"I love you too, girl."

His eyes opened, pressing his forehead against mine. "Forever."

CHAPTER
- SIXTEEN -

"I wanted our honeymoon to be so much better than this," Jesse spoke against my temple as I smiled softly.

We were curled up in his hospital bed, my arms wrapped around his torso and his cheek against my forehead. The hospital had given him a bigger room with a bigger bed, just so we could cuddle and have privacy, even if it were just for one night only.

Our wedding day had been beautiful; full of love and support from family to strangers alike. We were able to take a few photos, dance a little and cherished our guests before Jesse had to be taken back.

Neither one of us were ready to be taken back into reality yet.

"You're here with me, so this is perfect," I said softly, his heart beating strongly against my eardrum.

The only gift I needed today.

"Yeah, but if I had it my way, we would've been out of the country, seeing the world. Not cooped up in a hospital room and me being on meds. I didn't want this for us, but I couldn't just not marry you either. It was tough for me Nic. Trying to decide what was best."

I sighed, bending my neck up to peck his chin.

"Me and you is what's best. This didn't have to be a storybook wedding. This is us right now. This is love and it's all that matters. I got your back for the rest of our lives no matter what."

He cracked a grin, his dimple revealing itself before melting back into his cheek. "I love you."

"I know," I smirked, he wrapped me in his arms tighter.

"I'm going to get better. I promise," he said, causing my heart to drop at the thought.

"Jes – "

"No, hear me out," he pleaded. "I'm going to get better soon. I'm not leaving you yet. Not like this. You just gotta have faith baby."

I nodded, "I'm trying … I do. Let's just please focus on right now. This moment is bringing me all the comfort I ever needed."

He released a breath, holding me closer if at all possible, and rested his cheek on the top of my head.

"Faith is what's going to bring me home Nic. Nothing but that."

———————————

The thumping, I could hear it subconsciously in my sleep. The melodic thumping of a heartbeat – *Thump. Thump. Thump. Thump.*

It was soothing and had its own rhythm. Everything seemed in place with the sound as I stood in a large field of green, dressed in a long white summer gown. The sun was shining, birds were chirping. I twirled on my toes as they dug into the earth below me, feeling the sun's rays beaming against my skin, kissing it with its warmth.

All was right with the continuous melodic thumping.

Thump. Thump. Thump. Thump.

I stopped mid twirl, looking at the sight in the distance. It was a man and a small child; both dressed loosely in white linen outfits. The child ran through the grass amongst the wild flowers, laughter filling the space we were in.

I smiled at the sight, allowing my feet to carry me over, wanting to share in the happiness.

Thump. Thump. Thump. Thump.

The man turned his head the moment my feet led their way, nearly halting me all together.

"Jesse."

Tiffany Campbell

My smile spread wider when he turned completely, awaiting my arrival as the child continued to play not too far away from him.

"My husband," I cooed lovingly the moment he was in near reach. "Wh-what are you doing here?" I asked softly, trying to glance past him at the boy, but my eyes failed me.

I could no longer see beyond Jesse's tall stature.

I looked up at him then, seeing his glowing and smiling face. But his eyes ... his eyes were sad. My brows furrowed at the sight, reaching up to place my palm softly against his warm cheek.

"What's wrong baby?"

His smile faltered, as he placed his hand gently against mine, squeezing.

"I left you with a gift last night that I need you to take care of for me?" he requested as he looked with concern and uncertainty.

Thump. Thump. Thump. Thump.

"A gift? You already gave me a gift last night, you gave me you." I smirked at the memory.

Jesse and I made love. We consummated our marriage by giving ourselves to each other to the best of our abilities. It was beautiful, officially becoming one, given the circumstances we were under.

He sighed softly, removing my hand from his face and placing it over my belly.

Thump. Thump. Thump. Thump.

"My gift is in here, take care of him. Take care of him and love him. Share our love with him, always. Make sure he always knows who I am," he wouldn't remove his eyes from my stomach and I wouldn't remove mine off of him.

"Wh-why are you talking like you won't be here to see this through? Why are you talking like this?" I asked, voice trembling.

This was turning from a beautiful dream to my worst nightmare.

Thump. Thump. Thump. Thump.

He grinned, looking at me now before leaning to place a loving kiss against my forehead.

"I don't know what's to come when you wake up baby. I don't know if your faith is strong enough or mine or if my purpose is complete. I can't- I can't see it. I don't know if I'm coming home," he spoke shakily after removing his lips from my skin.

"What? What do you mean your purpose? What do you mean?" I questioned, tears swelling my eyes as he stepped back.

"I love you, Dominic."

"Jesse," I called the further he stepped away.

He turned his head, the small boy coming back into view. "David, take care of Mommy."

"Jesse! Jesse you can't leave me here! Wait!" I called again, carrying my feet towards him but it was becoming harder. I felt the resistance.

"You'll be okay, baby. I promise. You'll be okay. I'll always be with you, no matter what." he tried to assure; the further he left from my clouded vision.

The thumping. It could still be heard. As long as I could hear it this world still existed. I wasn't going to leave.

Thump. Thump. Thump. Thump.

"Jesse!"

And then ... it stopped. The melodic thumping was replaced with a bellowed pitch.

Beeeeeeeeeeeeeppppppp.

I jumped suddenly out of my slumber. Realizing the beeping was coming from the machine in the hospital room and the thumping I could no longer hear was ...

Jesse's heart.

Everything within me went still in a panic as I searched my love's face. He seemed peaceful, yet eerily still. The sight alone shook me to my core.

"Mrs. Palmer you have to get up!" a nurse called, trying to pull me from my husband's body.

I wouldn't move. The room had filled with doctors and nurses in an instant and I couldn't move.

"Wh-what's going on? Jesse!" I called to him, attempting to grab his arm before two strong hands pulled my body forcefully off of his.

"He went into cardiac arrest! We have to get him into surgery stat!" A doctor yelled over me as I was being dragged out of the room against my will.

"Wait, Noo! Nooo! Let me stay with my husband! Let me stay with my husband!!" I shrieked inconsolably, tears staining my cheeks.

One nurse looked at me sympathetically before looking to the man that was carrying me out, kicking and screaming.

"Get her out of here now!"

"Noo! Not my husband! Baby! Baby wake up! Wake up!! Please!" I called onto deaf ears before the door closed in my face.

I was stalk still in the waiting area. Numb and void of any emotion. The doctors weren't telling me what was going on with Jesse and said he would be in surgery for the next few hours.

All they were telling me right now is that machines were keeping him alive while they operated on his heart. No one could tell me why this happened. No one could tell me why the one thing that was giving me peace of mind stopped beating.

No one.

And it was killing me on the inside.

"Dominic baby," Jesse's mother called to me, placing a hand on my shoulder.

"Why don't you go get cleaned up? You look like you need to rejuvenate yourself," she suggested softly, as I just sat there unresponsive.

I can't rejuvenate myself until I know he's okay.

She sighed, realizing she wasn't going to get much out of me. She sat back in her seat, next to her husband, not uttering another word.

How can I go home knowing that they're operating on him? How can I just walk away like that?

I just want to save him. I want him to be okay. But I didn't have the answers and I was running out of patience, right along with faith.

Wait.

Faith?

Jesse told me faith was what was going to bring him home. Faith was always the key. Love was the key. God was the key.

God was who I needed. God was who I needed more than anything right now.

Tiffany Campbell

It's Sunday.

I shot up to my feet, startling everyone sitting around us.

"Dom?" Jamie called but I ignored him, my feet willing me towards the exit.

"Dom!" Jamie called again, but my feet had started to move faster into a run.

And before anyone could process, I was gone.

My feet slowed, along with my racing heart as I stood outside of the sanctuary doors, hearing the music beginning to play. I stuffed Jesse's car keys in my pocket, before I sniffed and wiped at my nose.

I had come to church. Somewhere I knew God would be waiting for me at the doors.

I needed to do this, not only for Jesse ... but for me. I needed to get connected. I needed to connect to the one who has always had the answers. The one that kept a smile on Jesse's precious face while he was being faced with the hardest battle of his life.

God was the root. God was the root to freedom, the root to healing, the root to life.

I could only find refuge in Him.

Give me you ...

That song. *Give Me You* by Shana Wilson. It was Jesse's favorite.

I took in a breath, pushing the doors open as I saw the sanctuary filled with people all standing in worship.

I tuned them out; the altar the only thing on my radar. I had to get there. I had to get there to tell God how much I needed Him. How much I can't go another day without surrendering myself to His will. I was tired of fighting what I knew was right. Tired of fighting this relationship that He wanted so desperately with me.

I was tired of being disconnected.

Lord, give me you ...

I took a step forward, ignoring the ushers trying to take me to a seat. My feet quickened as they carried me to the altar while the lead vocalist continued to belt out the lyrics to the song.

I hope I'm not too late ...

The moment I approached my intended destination, my legs gave out in pure exhaustion. I was knelt down, my hands resting on the carpeted floor as my head dropped in agony.

And I cried. I cried out to anyone that was listening. Just praying that it was God.

It's me oh Lord ... I'm on my knees ...

"I-I need you! I need you so much. I'm- I'm so sorry God. I'm so sorry." I bawled to the floor, shaking with emotion.

Thoughts of my childhood raced through my brain. Images of rape, images of fear, images of pain, years of mental torment, years of trouble, losing my grandmother, being homeless, selling my body, fighting to stay alive. All of it was racing through my mind and bursting out in tears as the song carried on even louder around me.

Everything else can wait!

"Give me you!" I cried with the song, looking up at the brightened lights, feeling people beginning to surround me as I yelled out for God.

I needed Him. I only wanted Him. This was the love I needed all along. This is what Jesse meant by the true love story.

The love God has for me. The love He has for Jesse. The love He has for His people.

This was the greatest love ever known, the Bible containing the greatest love story ever told.

I needed to get connected because I had been disconnected for so long. Disconnected from the root of life.

Don't disconnect Dominic ...

_____

"We're losing him!" the doctor called out.

"We have to revive his heart! We have to stop the blockage around his heart!" A frantic nurse called out, handing him the next tool he needed to save the young man.

"I'm trying! I swear I need a miracle!"

_____

"Dominic baby!" The voice sounded like my mother's, but I was too engulfed in the energy surrounding me to care or to hear any voice but God's.

I lifted my hands. Just wanting to feel his presence a little closer. I felt I was being locked in a comforting hug, blanketing with peace.

I hope I'm not too late!

"Dominic, is it?" A sweet, yet deep, voice said, approaching me from the front. I looked up, seeing it was the Pastor of the church. I recognized him from all of the Sunday's I had visited before.

I nodded feverishly, wiping my eyes.

Humbly, he knelt before me, never taking his eyes off mine.

"Sweetheart, are you saved?"

———————

"Save him! Please! Save him!"

"Come on Jesse, don't give up on me now! Almost there buddy! Almost there!"

———————

I shook my head no, sniffing back more tears.

Lord give me you!

"Would you like to be? Would you like God to give you all He has to offer you through his spirit, by accepting Jesus as your Lord and Savior? Would you like to enter this new relationship with Him?"

I coughed a sob as more tears streamed down my cheeks. I nodded.

"Ye-yes. Yes I do."

He smiled warmly, grabbing my shaking hands.

"Okay, repeat after me."

Lord give me you!

———————

"His blood pressure is dropping! He's flat lining! Doctor he's flat lining!" the nurse panicked, watching Jesse's vitals plummet.

Beeeeeeeeeeeeeeeeeppppppppppppp

———————

"Father God, you are the Christ," He began, gripping my clammy hands tight.

I could hear my mother's voice praying behind me.

"Father God you are the Christ."

"Son of the Living God."

"Son of the Living God ... " I could barely recognize my voice as my own but I know I felt better as I confessed along with him.

"I believe with all my heart."

"I believe with all my heart."

"That you died for my sins."

"That you died for my sins."

"And God raised you from the dead."

"And God raised you from the dead."

"I invite you into my heart Lord Jesus."

"I invite you into my heart Lord Jesus."

"And make me a new creature in your image."

"And make me a new creature in your image."

"I'm saved now."

"I'm saved now!"

"I'm born again now!"

"I'm born again now!"

"In Jesus name!" he shouted as everything within me burst with new life.

"AMEN!"

Give me you ...

Beeeeeeeeeeeeeeeeeeeeeeeeeeeeeeeeeeeeeeppppppp ...

The sound of the flat line was the only thing that could be heard in the room as everyone stilled.

The doctor deflated, visibly defeated as he set down with instrument in his hand, looking at the young man lying on the operating table.

"Doctor?" a nurse uttered, watching their leader quickly pick up the tool he had just set down, careful in his next moves in the extensive heart surgery. A move he wasn't sure to make, but he had to take the chance. He had to try.

Right ... there.

The young patient's body twitched suddenly, startling the room.

Beeeeeeeeeeeeeeeeeppppppppp ... beeeeep ... beeep ... beep ... beep ...

I tapped my foot against the floor, impatiently waiting for the elevator doors to open. Once they did I rushed out searching frantically around for a familiar face, anyone that could tell me the current status of Jesse's condition.

My eyes landed on Jamie as he stood with his hands on his waist, talking to someone that seemed like a doctor with Jesse's parents on either side of him. He turned his head, feeling my eyes and instantly flashed a look of relief at the sight of me.

"Dom!" he called, waving me over as I quickly hurried myself over to the group.

"Hey hey, what's going on?" I asked looking to the doctor, running a hand through my wild tresses.

Tiffany Campbell

He glanced at me with slight question before looking to Jesse's mother.

"It's okay, she's his wife," she explained as he nodded, feeling comfortable to share the information he had.

"His heart had stopped beating on the operating table and we were able to revive him. He's stabilized now, and we will be performing a bone marrow transplant in a few hours as we received a donor that matched his blood type." We all released a sigh at the news.

"The transplant will completely remove the cancer from his body," he added as I placed a hand on my chest.

"Thank you God," I breathed as Jesse's mother clasped my hand in hers.

Finally, a breakthrough.

"When will we be able to see him?" I couldn't help but ask; just wanting to see my husband and make sure he was okay.

"His body is very fragile right now. We have to see how he responds to the transplant. I cannot promise an answer of when it will be safe for him to have visitors in his room. If he responds well – maybe tonight or first thing tomorrow morning. He was placed on a medically induced coma after we revived him, so after his surgery we will start the process of weaning him off the medication so that he can wake up on his own."

I took in a breath as I blinked, allowing the tear to slip from my eye.

I just wanted to see him.

"He'll be okay baby. It'll be okay," His mother encouraged as she wrapped her arm around me to pull my shaking body close.

Please God just bring him home.

Jesse sat perched on a large rock, kicking his legs absently as his hands rested against the cool granite. He didn't know how long he had been there, or when he would leave, but he found solace in it. The area was much like the one he had shown Dominic when she first got out of the hospital. It was his place of refuge when he wanted to shut out the world.

He looked down to the body of water in front of him. In it, he could see his loved ones all worried for him. He could hear every prayer and feel every bit of pain that rested in their souls.

It hurt him to see them like that. A part of him wanted to go back, just to assure all of them that he was okay.

But then there was a part of him that enjoyed where he was. He felt peace. A peace he hadn't felt since the day he found out he had been stricken with cancer again.

Why did this have to happen to him?

"Jesse," he heard a young familiar voice call out from behind. His brows squinted at the sound, believing he was hearing things.

"Jesse!"

They called again, causing Jesse to turn his head slowly to look behind him.

Everything within him stilled – "Peter?"

"Why won't he wake up? The transplant was over last night and they said he could wake up at any moment. It's been 24 hours, why won't he wake up?" I cried, wiping at my face as my mother frowned at the sight of me.

We were outside of Jesse's hospital room. I had been at his side since the moment they cleared him to have visitors. It was hard watching him so still, no life in his face.

"You just have to keep praying baby. Have faith."

I blew out a shaky breath, sniffing my nose.

"I do have faith mom I do but does he?" I questioned, looking through the glass at my husband.

I could feel him slipping away from me.

"Does he?" I whispered to myself again, tearing my eyes away from the sight.

"You can't stay here forever you know," Peter spoke at Jesse's side, breaking the silence that had passed between them.

The two had been sitting on the boulder, looking at the scene unfolding below them. Jesse had torn his eyes away, unable to witness the breaking of Dominic's heart.

He had done enough of that.

"I don't get it," Peter added after Jesse left his comment unanswered.

"Don't get what?" Jesse finally returned, curious.

"You were the strongest guy I knew. You had so much faith and hope and yet, you're healed and still here. Why won't you go back?" Peter asked him, watching his hero crumble at the seams.

He couldn't understand the conflict in Jesse's mind right now.

"Answer me Jesse, please! Why are you here?"

Jesse clenched his jaw tight, the tear trickling down his face.

"I'm- I'm scared."

I used the cool rag in my hand to run across Jesse's forehead gently. He would get beads of sweat on his nose, and twitched in his deep sleep.

That's how I had to keep looking at this. That he was resting after all he had been through the past few months.

He would wake up soon and everything would be okay. It had been two days, but I was hopeful that today would be the day. He just needed some more sleep.

"What are you dreaming about baby?" I asked softly, picking apart every feature.

He was beautiful, even still.

"You have to come back to me Jes. It's not time for you to leave yet, not now." I said shakily as I grabbed his limp hand into my own. I lifted it up, placing my lips against his knuckles.

"Not now."

"Scared of what? It's okay now. It's over –"

"Is it?" Jesse returned, cutting off his young counterpart standing to his feet. "Is it over? Is it ever over?! This was the second time, Pete. The second time I had to be faced with this! Who's to say it won't happen again? Who's to say the next time won't take me out?"

"Who's to say you can control it if it does? Regardless of what happens it's out of your hands Jesse! You can't take what happened to me and believe you'll have the same fate the same way! Either way you'll end up here. No matter when it happens! Or how!"

Peter's words stung. The reality hit him once more that Peter was no longer present on earth. He died from the same disease Jesse had been fighting for nearly half his life.

"But –" Jesse choked, swallowing the sob. "But why did it have to happen to you? You think I was giving you hope, but you gave it to me, Pete. You gave me hope when I saw none because – because I wanted to be strong for you."

"It was my time Jesse. You may not have viewed it as a long time, but it was my time. I lived the life I was supposed to live in the time I was supposed to live it. We weren't meant to be down there forever. No one could control it and because of you, before I died, I got saved. You saved me. Now I'm in paradise where there's no pain. There's no pain here –"

"Then why can't I stay?"

Peter frowned, looking down to the water seeing the reflection of Dominic crying at Jesse's bedside. Hearing her prayers ringing in his ears.

"Do you hear her?" Peter asked him, watching Jesse's eyes flutter closed.

"Do you hear her, praying for you?"

Jesse squeezed his eyes tight, "I hear everything."

My hands were clasped together as I rested my forehead against my fist, eyes shut. It was going on day three and I could feel myself breaking. I could feel Jesse slipping away from me, more and more as the hours carried on.

But I was determined not to give up. I wasn't sure why Jesse's faith was failing him, but I wasn't going to allow that to fail mine. I believed that God was going to restore him to total health and bring him back.

"Father," I sniffed, shaking my head and squeezing my eyes shut tighter. "It says in your word that our faith will make us whole."

I released a shaky breath before opening my eyes and standing to my feet, placing a hand on Jesse's forehead.

"I call healing to this body, Lord. Healing from the tip of his head down to the soles of his feet. I believe it is your will for Jesse to be healed, but I know that he has to extend his faith along with mine. Bring faith back to this vessel. Allow him to hold on to your promises Lord. I cast out fear from his mind because fear is not something that you have given us. Fear and faith cannot dwell in the same space ... "

"You hear that?" Peter asked, referring to Dominic's prayer.

Her prayers were getting louder and Jesse knew Heaven was reacting to the words she spoke with such power.

It sparked the faith he needed within him. She had never been more beautiful in his eyes.

"Yeah," he replied softly. "I heard it."

"You can't allow the fear of what you can't control to rule you any longer Jesse. Your fear is what made you sick. Nothing else, but that. You were confident before this and had faith so strong, nothing could shake it. The moment you lost sight of that was the moment you allowed sickness to return to your body," Peter explained as the tear trickled down Jesse's cheek.

" ... I was so afraid of losing and hurting Dominic, I couldn't see anything else but that."

Peter nodded, "And now you have a woman, a wife by your side whose faith is blossoming before our eyes. There's nothing to fear. God is with you. There's nothing –"

Tiffany Campbell

"To fear," Jesse finished for him, standing tall. He swallowed before looking down at his young friend.

Peter looked healthy. His olive skin glowed with life and his brunette head was full with a slick bed of hair. He knew his young inspiration was at peace. He understood death now, why it happens was something the human mind could not fully comprehend. He had to let the grief he felt from Peter's death go, and realize that it was only the death of his body and not his spirit.

His spirit was something Jesse would remember forever.

His eyes left Peter as they traveled back to the stilled waters, Dominic's appearance becoming more blurry to his vision.

He squeezed his lids tight, allowing the tear to escape his eye, preparing for the journey back to his rightful place, at her side.

I jolted out of my sleep and looked around in panic. I deflated the moment I saw that I was still in Jesse's room and he was still sleeping, looking so sweet in his bed. I blew out a breath running a hand over my face then turning my wrist to look at my watch.

It was 11:43 p.m.

The third day of Jesse's slumber was coming to a close. I hadn't even realized I had fallen asleep. The last thing I could remember was praying, like I had been doing for the past three days. I smiled small looking at Jesse's face; happy to see his color was returning.

I stood up and headed to the bathroom to freshen up from my unplanned nap. I looked in the mirror and scoffed at my appearance. My hair was all over the place, eyes baggy and skin looked dreadful. I shook my head at the sight before taking the time gather myself. Once I appeared human again I laughed, shaking my head once more before heading out of the restroom.

"Baby, I'm kinda glad you're sleeping right now. You would have thought I looked crazy."

I lightly giggled knowing Jesse would get the joke, walking around the room to straighten up the mess that had become of it over the past few days.

When Jesse did finally wake up, I didn't want him to come to an unclean place.

Once the room had become decent again I walked over to the large windows, crossing my arms over my chest and gazing at the star lit sky.

"I wonder if you can see the stars where you are," I spoke into the quiet, hoping Jesse could hear me.

"The sky is just so beautiful tonight. I wish we could spend a day at the beach and gaze at them again." I finished, reminiscing.

My birthday was such an amazing day. I was praying Jesse would be here to join me for another one.

"I really miss hearing your voice Jes. I just want to hear it again."

I sighed, quickly wiping at the tear that had formed at the thought.

I missed my best friend more than ever right now.

I sniffed causing a slight tickle in my nostril. I felt the sneeze coming before I could catch it.

"Achoo!" I sneezed, sniffing again and dabbing at my nose.

"Bless you."

"Ah, thank you baby," I spoke with second nature catching my breath again before everything in me stopped.

That tone. That rasp kissed tone I had grown to love more and more over the past seven months. It seemed like it had been an entire lifetime since I heard it last.

I turned my head in shock, looking at his bed. He was still and I truly thought I had just been hearing things until he started squirming, wincing his face in pain.

"J-Jesse?" I asked cautiously, turning my body fully to face the hospital bed.

He squinted hard again before giving a quick nod, "Yeah."

I lost it, everything within me.

My eyes searched all over his face.

He was in pain, which was evident. But he was awake. He was here.

He had come back from his three-day journey to oblivion.

I reached my shaky hand out, running it down the side of his temple. He squinted his eyes tight before relaxing into my touch.

The tears were streaming down my face at this point. I was in awe of this moment. I sniffed before looking to the ceiling, envisioning God looking down on us.

"Thank you." I spoke to Him, barely above a whisper before looking my love in the face.

"Thank you thank you thank you." I sobbed, before gently placing Jesse's face in my hands and kissing him repeatedly on the cheek before resting my forehead there.

"It's ok b-baby. I'm here, I'm not leaving you," He voiced as best he could as I nodded through tears, kissing his cheek once more.

"Let me get you some water baby and tell everyone you're awake," I said to him, finally removing my dampened face from his. I wiped at my cheeks with the back of my hand standing up straight and preparing to leave the room to spread the good news.

My heart felt like it was preparing to explode out of my chest.

"Faith brought me home," he spoke so soft yet so clear just as I reached the door.

I sighed with happiness at his words, tapping the doorpost.

" ... me too."

AUTHOR'S NOTE

"I am the true grapevine, and my Father is the gardener. He cuts off every branch of mine that doesn't produce fruit, and he prunes the branches that do bear fruit so they will produce even more. You have already been pruned and purified by the message I have given you. Remain in me, and I will remain in you. For a branch cannot produce fruit if it is severed from the vine, and you cannot be fruitful unless you remain in me."
                                   – John 15: 1-4 New Living Translation

Although Jesse and Dominic had a beautiful love story, Don't Disconnect was not centered around their love. This was about a love story that we all might have shared in, but just maybe with a slightly different ending. This was a love story between God and the people He created to love Him in return. This was a novel that showed imagery of the love He has for each and every one of us, and how He never gives up until the very end.

Most of the main characters represented in this story had a very distinct function:

Kole was a representation of who we are before Christ. She was the person that had disbelief, little faith and little knowledge of the word of God. While we're in this state, we're full of sin, brokenness, carnal mindsets and worldly belief systems. We're too stuck in our sorrow to believe that God could be watching over us, and we reject His love at every turn.

Lucy represented the angel Lucifer, who was very jealous and spiteful, but was not always that way. Lucifer was favored by God, but eventually wanted his position, and fell because of it.

Devon represented the Devil in our lives that manipulates, lies and does everything he can to pull us away from our love for God. He hates it and envies it, and will do everything in his power to make us think that we are not loved and favored by the King to keep us away from growing in our knowledge of Him and who we are in Him.

Jesse represented Jesus and the love and fight He has for us. I made sure to give Jesse a lot of the same characteristics that Jesus also possessed. His kindness, his acceptance of where we are, his unconditional love for us that He has even when we reject Him time and time again. His wanting and desire to see us whole and well. His wisdom, His knowledge, His closeness to the Father. Jesse knew early on that he was going to be what led Dominic to Christ. He knew his purpose and knew that even if that meant death, his purpose had to be fulfilled. In the same token, Jesse was still human, so I had to show his weakness in his faith just to show that even the most resilient of believers, still have their challenges to face and overcome. Not one single person is perfect, but we are being perfected in our striving to resemble Christ.

Dominic was the new creature that we become after we get saved. Being saved and accepting Jesus as our Lord and Savior is simply only the beginning. We're going to have questions, we're going to fall, we're going to have our times where it doesn't make sense. That is why it is important to get connected in a local church where you can connect with others who are seeking the same thing. This will help you to grow in your beliefs and to get a solid understanding of the faith.

This book was only meant to be an introduction and to let you know you are not alone. My only hope is that by you making it to the end, you not only enjoyed the story but you learned a few things and are inspired to live life with a new purpose! God's love for us is much stronger than the love identified in this book and I pray that you are compelled to learn more about that love and to create a love story of your very own.

With Love,
  Tiff.

Tiffany Campbell